SYLVIA AND MICHAEL

Sylvia and Michael

Compton Mackenzie

NEW ENGLISH LIBRARY
TIMES MIRROR

TO FAITH

First published in 1919
First published with *Sylvia and Philip* and *Sylvia and Arthur* as
a Complete Edition by Macdonald and Co. Ltd in 1950

✿

FIRST NEL PAPERBACK EDITION JULY 1971

✿

NEL Books are published by
New English Library Limited from Barnard's Inn, Holborn, London, E.C.1.
Made and printed in Great Britain by Hunt Barnard Printing Ltd., Aylesbury, Bucks.

45000767 7

Chapter I

BY THE time that Sylvia reached Paris she no longer blamed anybody but herself for what had happened. Everything had come about through her own greed in trying simultaneously to snatch from life artistic success and domestic bliss: she had never made a serious attempt to choose between them, and now she had lost both; for she could not expect to run away like this and succeed elsewhere to the same degree or even in the same way as in London. No doubt all her friends would deplore the step she had taken and think it madness to ruin her career; but after so much advertisement of her marriage, after the way she had revealed her most intimate thoughts to Olive, after the confidence she had shown in Arthur's devotion, there was nothing else but to run away. Yet now that the engagement had been definitely broken she felt no bitterness towards Arthur: the surprising factor was that he should have waited so long. Moreover, behind all her outraged pride, behind her regret for losing so much, deep in her mind burned a flickering intuition that she had really lost very little, and that out of this new adventure would spring a new self worthier to demand success, and more finely tempered to withstand life's onset. Even when she was sitting beneath the mulberry-tree in the first turmoil of the shock, she had felt a faint gladness that she was not going to live in Mulberry Cottage with Arthur. Already on this May morning of Paris with the chestnuts in their flowery prime she could fling behind her all the sneers and all the pity for her jilting; and though she had scarcely any money she was almost glad of her poverty, glad to be plunged once again into the vortex of existence with all the strength and all the buoyancy that time had given her. She thought of the months after she left Philip. This was a different Sylvia now, and not even yet come to what Sylvia might be. It was splendid to hear already the noise of waters round her, from which she should emerge stronger and more buoyant than she had ever imagined herself before.

Immediately upon her arrival – for with the little money she had there was not a day to be lost – Sylvia went in this mood to visit her old agent; like all parasites he seemed to know in advance that there was little blood to suck. She told him briefly what she had been doing, let him suppose that there was a man in the case, and asked what work he could find for her.

The agent shook his head : without money it was difficult, nay, impossible to attempt in Paris anything like she had been doing in London. No doubt she had made a great success, but a success in London was no guarantee of a success in Paris, indeed rather the contrary. It was a pity she had not listened to him when she had the money to spend on a proper *réclame*.

'*Bref, ill n'y a rien à faire, chère madame.*'

There was surely the chance of an engagement for cabaret work? The agent looked at Sylvia; and she could have struck him for the way he was so evidently pondering her age and measuring it against her looks. In the end he decided that she was still attractive enough, and he examined his books. She still sang of course and no doubt still enjoyed dancing? Well, they wanted French girls in Petersburg at the Trocadero cabaret. It would work out at four hundred and fifty francs a month, to which of course the commission on champagne would add considerably. She would have to remain on duty till three a.m., and the management reserved the right to dispense with her services if she was not a success.

'*Comme artiste ou comme grue?*' Sylvia demanded.

The agent laughed and shrugged his shoulders: he was afraid that there was nothing else remotely suitable. Sylvia signed the contract, and so little money was left in her purse that from Paris to Petersburg she travelled third class, an unpleasant experience.

The change from the Pierian Hall to the place where she was now singing could scarcely have been greater. For an audience individual, quiet, attentive, was substituted a noisy gathering of people that was not an audience at all. It had been difficult enough in old days to sing to parties drinking round a number of tables; but here to the noise of drinking was added the noise of eating, the clatter of plates, and the shouting of waiters. In a way Sylvia was glad, because she did not want anybody to listen to the songs she was singing: she preferred to come on the small stage as impersonally as an instrument in the music of the restaurant orchestra, and retire to give way to another singer without the least attention being paid either to her exit or to her successor's entrance.

Sylvia wished that the rest of the evening could have passed

6

away as impersonally; she found it terribly hard to endure again after so long the sensation of being for sale, of being pulled into a seat beside drunken officers, of being ogled by elderly German Jews, of being treated as an equal by waiters, of feeling upon her the eyes of the manager as he reckoned her net value in champagne. There were moments when she despaired of her ability to hold out and when she was on the verge of cabling to England for money to come home. But pride kept her back and sustained her; luckily she had to do nothing at present except talk in order to induce her patrons to buy champagne by the dozen. She knew that it could not last, that sooner or later she should acquire the general reputation of being no good for anything except to sit and chatter at a table and make a man spend money on wine for nothing, and that then she should have to go because nobody would invite her to his table. She was grateful that it was Russia and not America or France or England, where a quicker return for money spent would have been expected.

When Sylvia first arrived at Petersburg, she had stayed in solitary misery at a small German hotel that lacked even the merit of being clean. After she had been performing a week, one of her fellow-artistes recommended her to a pension kept by an Englishwoman, the widow of a *chancelier* at the French Embassy: it was a long way from the cabaret, beyond the race-course, but there was the tram, and one would always find somebody to pay for the drozhky home.

Sylvia visited the pension, which was a tumble-down house in a very large garden of the rankest vegetation, a queer embrangled place; but the first impression of the guests appealed to her, and she moved into it the same afternoon. Mère Gontran, the owner, was one of those expatriated women that lose their own nationality and acquire instead a new nationality compounded of their own, their husband's, and the country they inhabit. She was about fifty-five years old, nearly six feet in height, excessively lean, with a neck like a turkey's, a weather-beaten veinous complexion, very square shoulders, and thin colourless hair done up in a kind of starfish at the back. Her eyes were very bright of an intense blue, and she had a habit of wearing odd stockings, which like her hair were always coming down, chiefly because she used her garters to keep her sleeves above her elbows. One of the twin passions of her life was animals; but she also had three sons, loutish young men who ate or smoked cigarettes all day and could hardly speak a word of English or French. Their mother on the contrary, though she had come to Petersburg as a

7

governess thirty-five years ago and had lived there ever since, could speak hardly any Russian and only very bad French. Mère Gontran's animals were really more accomplished linguists than she, if it was true, as she asserted, that a collie she possessed could say *'Good-bye'*, *'adieu'*, and *'proschai'*. Sylvia suggested that the Russian salute had really been a sneeze, but Mère Gontran defied her to explain away the English or the French, and was angry at any doubts being cast on what she had heard with her own ears. In addition to Samuel the talking collie there was a senile bulldog called James who on a pillow of his own slept beside Mère. Gontran in her bed, which was in a hut two hundred yards away from the house, at the other end of the garden. High up round the walls were hung boxes for nine cats: into these they ascended by ladders, and none of them ever attempted to sleep anywhere but in his own box, an example to the rest of the pension. There were numerous other animals about the place, the most conspicuous of which were a pony and a goat that spent most of their time in the kitchen with the only servant, a stunted Tartar who went muttering about the house and slept in a cupboard under the stairs. Mère Gontran's other great passion was spiritualism; but Sylvia did not have much opportunity to test her truthfulness in this direction, because at first she was more interested in the guests at the pension, accepting Mère Gontran as one accepts a queer fact for future investigation at the right moment.

The outstanding boarder in Sylvia's eyes was a French aviator called Carrier, who had come to give lessons and exhibitions of his skill in Petersburg. He was a great bluff creature with a loud voice and what at first seemed a boastful manner, until one realised that his brag was a kind of game which he was playing with fate. Underneath it all there lay a deep melancholy and a sense of always being very near to death; but since he would have considered the least hint of this a disgraceful display of cowardice, he was careful to cover what he might do with what he had done, which was, even allowing for brag, a great deal. It was only when Sylvia took the trouble to make friends with him that he revealed to her his fierce ambition to finish with flying as soon as possible and with the money he had made to buy a little farm in the country.

'Tu sais, la terre vaut mieux que le ciel,' he told her.

He was superstitious, and boasted loudly of his materialism: venturing upon what was still largely an unknown element he relied upon mascots, while preserving a profound contempt for God.

'I've not ever seen him yet,' he used to say, 'though I've flown higher than anybody.'

His chest of drawers was covered with small talismans, some the pledges of fortune given him by ladies, others picked up in significant surroundings or conditions of mind. He wore half-a-dozen rings, not one of which was worth fifty francs, but all of which were endowed with protective qualities. By the scapulars and medals he carried round his neck he should have been the most pietistic of men, but however sacred their inscriptions they counted with him as merely more portable guarantees than the hideous little monkeys and mandarins that littered his room.

'When I've finished,' he told Sylvia, 'I shall throw all this away. When I'm digging in the good earth, my mascot will be my spade, nothing else, *je t'assure*.'

Sylvia asked him why he had ever taken up flying.

'When I was small I adored my *bécane:* afterwards I adored my *automobile. On arrive comme ça.* Ah, if the fools hadn't invented biplanes, how happy I should be.'

Then perhaps a few moments later he would find himself in the presence of an audience, and one heard him at his boasting:

'*Bigre!* I am sorry for the man who cannot fly. One has not lived if one has not flown. The clouds! One would say a featherbed beneath. To-morrow I shall loop the loop at five thousand *mètres*. One might say that all Petersburg will be regarding me.'

There were two young acrobatic jugglers staying at the pension, who performed some extremely dangerous acts, but who performed them with such ease that they seemed like nothing, especially as the acrobats themselves were ladylike to a ludicrous degree.

'Oh, Bobbie, say, wouldn't it be fine to fly? Would you be terribly frightened? I should. Oh, I should be frightened.'

'Don't you ever feel s-sick?' Bobbie asked the aviator.

For these two young men Carrier reserved his most hairraising tales, which always ended in Willie's saying to Bobbie:

'Oh, Bobbie, I s-s-simply can't listen to any more. So now! Oh, it does make me feel so funny. Doesn't it you, Bobbie?'

Then arm-in-arm, giggling like two girls, they used to trip out of hearing, and Carrier would spit in bewilderment. Once he invited Bobbie to accompany him on a flight, at which Willie screamed, flung his arms round Bobbie's neck, and created a scene. Yet that same evening they both balanced themselves with lamps on a high ladder, until the audience actually stopped

9

eating for a moment and held its breath.

Sylvia found the long hours of the cabaret very fatiguing: even in old days she had never thought the life anything but the most cruel exaction made by the rich man for his pleasure. She was determined to survive the strain that was being put upon her, but she had moments of depression during which she saw herself going under with the female slaves round her. Her fatigue was increased by having to take the long tram-ride down to the cabaret, when the smell of her fellow-passengers was a torture: she could not afford, however, to pay the fare of a drozhky twice in one day, and she did not always find somebody to pay for her drive home. The contract with the management stipulated that she should be released from her nightly task at three o'clock; but she was very often kept until five o'clock when the champagne was flowing and when it would have been criminal in the eyes of the management to break up a profitable party. She found that the four hundred and fifty francs a month was not enough to keep her in Petersburg; it had sounded a reasonably large salary in Paris, but it barely paid the board at Mère Gontran's: she was therefore dependent for everything above this on the commission of about five francs she received on each bottle of champagne opened under her patronage. Fortunately it seemed to give pleasure to the wild frequenters of this cabaret when a bottle was knocked over on the floor; yet with every device it was not always possible to escape drinking too much.

One day at the beginning of July Sylvia discussed the future with Carrier, and he advised her to surrender and return to England; he even offered to lend her the money for the fare. It was a hot day, and she had a bad headache; she called it a headache, but it was less local than that: her whole body ached beneath a weight of despair. Sylvia had taken Carrier into her confidence about her broken marriage and explained why it was impossible to return to England yet awhile; he contested all her arguments, and in the mood that she was in she gave way to him. They spoke in French, and arguments always seemed more incontestable in a language that refused to allow anything in the nature of a vague explanation: besides, her own body was responding against her will to the logic of surrender.

'Pride is all very well,' said Carrier. 'I am proud of being the greatest aviator of the moment, but if I fall and smash myself to pulp, what becomes of my pride? It's impossible for you to lead the life you are leading now without debasing yourself,

10

and then where will your pride be? Listen to me. You have been at the cabaret very little over a month, and already it is telling upon you. It is very good that you are able even for so long to keep men at a distance, but are you keeping them at a distance? For me it is the same thing logically if you drink with men or – ' he shrugged his shoulders. 'You sell your freedom in either case. *N'est-ce pas que j'ai raison, ma petite Sylvie?* For me it would be a greater pride to return to England and walk with my head in the air and laugh at the world. Besides, you have a *je ne sais quoi* that will prevent the world from laughing, but if you continue you will have nothing. When I fall and smash myself to pulp, I shan't care about the world's laughter. Nor will you.'

Indeed he was right, Sylvia thought: that first impulse of defiance seemed already like a piece of petulance, the gesture of a spoilt child.

'And you will let me as a good *copain* lend you the money for your fare back?'

'No,' Sylvia said. 'I think I can just manage to earn it by going once more to-night to the cabaret. I've arranged to meet some count with an unpronounceable name, who will probably open at least twenty-four bottles. I get my week's salary to-night also. I shall have with what I have saved enough to travel back as I came, third-class. It has been a thoroughly third-class adventure, *mon vieux*. A thousand thanks for your kindness, but I must pay my pride the little solace of earning enough to get me home again.'

Carrier shrugged his shoulders.

'It must be as you feel. That I understand. But it gives me much pleasure that you are going to be wise. I wish you *de la veine* tonight.'

He pressed upon her a mascot to charm fortune into attendance: it was a little red devil with his tongue sticking out.

Sylvia went down to the cabaret that evening with the firm intention of its being the last occasion; her headache had grown worse all the afternoon and the gloom upon her spirit was deepening. What a fool she had been to run away with so much assurance of having the courage to endure this life, what a fool she had been! For the first time the thought of suicide presented itself to her as a practical solution of everything. In her present state she could perceive not one valid argument against it. Who had attacked existence with less caution than she, and who had deserved more from it in consequence? Had she once flinched? Had she once taken the easier path? Yes, there had

11

been Arthur: that was the first time she had given way to inde-cision, and how swiftly the punishment had followed. Was it really worth while to seek now to repair that mistake? Was anything worth while? Except to go suddenly out of it all, passing as abruptly from life to death as she had passed from one society to another, one tour to another, one country to another. She would abide by to-night's decision: if fortune put it into the head of the count with the unpronounceable name to buy enough bottles of champagne to make up what was still wanting to her fare, she would return to England, devote her-self to her work, turn again to books, watch over her godchildren, and live at Mulberry Cottage. If on the other hand the fare should not be made up on this night, why then she should kill herself. To-night should be a night of hell. How her body was burning: how vile the people smelt in this tram: how weari-some was this garish sunset. She took from her velvet bag the red devil that Carrier had given her: in this feverish atmos-phere it had a certain fitness, a portentousness even: one could almost believe it really was a tribute to fate.

The cabaret was crowded that evening; never before had there been such a hurly-burly of greed and thirst. Sylvia by good luck was feeling thirsty; for the dust from the tram had parched her mouth, and her tongue was like cork: so much the better, because if she was going to win that champagne she must be able herself to drink. The tintamarre of plates, knives, and forks; the chickerchack as of multitudinous apes; the blare and glare would have prevented the loudest soprano in the world from sounding more than the squeak of a slate-pencil; and Sylvia sang with gestures alone, forming with her lips mute words. 'I'm paid for my body not for my voice; so let my body play the antic,' she muttered angrily.

When her turn was over, Sylvia came down and joined the two young Russians, who were waiting for her with another girl at a table on which already the bottles of champagne were standing like giant pawns.

'*Ils ont la cuite,*' the girl whispered to Sylvia. '*Alors, il faut briffer, chérie; autrement ils seront trop soûlés.*'

This seemed good advice, because of their hosts were too drunk too soon they might get tired of the entertainment; and Sylvia proposed an adjournment to eat, though she had little enough appetite. As a matter of fact the men wanted to drink vodka when supper was proposed, and not merely to drink it themselves, but to make Sylvia and the other girl keep them company glass by glass. In Sylvia's condition to drink vodka would have been to drink liquid fire, and she managed to plead thirst with such effect that the count benevolently ordered twenty-four bottles of champagne to be brought immediately for her to quench it. The other girl was full of admiration for Sylvia's strategy: if the worse came to the worst they would have earned seventy-five francs each, and could boast of a successful evening. Sylvia, however, wanted a hundred and fifty francs for herself, and invoking the little red devil she showed a way of breaking a bottle in half by filling it with hot water, saturating a string in methylated spirits, tying the string round the bottle, setting light to it, and afterwards tapping the bottle gently with a knife until it broke. The Count was delighted with this trick, but thought, as Sylvia hoped he would think, that the trick would be much better if practised on an unopened bottle of champagne. In this way twenty-six bottles were broken in childish rage by the Count, because the trick only worked with the help of hot water. He was by now in a state of drunken obstinacy, and being determined to show the superiority of the human mind over matter he ordered twenty-four more bottles of champagne, as a Roman Emperor might have ordered two dozen slaves to test an empirical method of execution. By a fluke he managed to succeed with the twenty-fourth bottle, and having by now gathered round him an audience, he challenged the onlookers to repeat the trick. Other women were anxious for their hosts to excel, particularly with such profit to themselves; soon at every table in the cabaret champagne-bottles were being cracked like eggs. The Count was afraid that there might not be enough wine left to carry them through the evening and ordered another two dozen bottles to be held in reserve for his table.

Sylvia, though she was feeling horribly ill by now, was nevertheless at peace, for she had earned her fare back to England. Unluckily she could not quit the table and go home, because unless she waited until three she would not be paid her commission on the chanpagne. She felt herself receding from the noise of breaking glass all round her, and thought she was going to faint, but with an effort she gathered the noise round her again and tried to believe that the room still existed. She seemed to be catching hold of the great chandelier that hung from the middle of the ceiling, and fancied that it was only her will and courage to maintain her hold that was keeping the cabaret and everybody in it from destruction.

'*Tu es malade, chérie?*' the other girl was asking.

'*Rien, rien,*' she was whispering. '*La chaleur.*'

'*Oui, il fait très chaud.*'

The laughter and shouts of triumph rose higher: the noise of breaking glass was like the waves upon a beach of shingle.

'*Pourquoi il te regarde?*' she found herself asking.

'*Personne ne me regarde, chérie,*' the other girl replied.

But somebody was looking at her, somebody seated in one of the boxes for private supper-parties that were fixed all round the hall, somebody tall with short fair hair sticking up like a brush, somebody in uniform. He was beckoning to her now and inviting her to join him in the box. He had slanting eyes, cruel eyes that glittered and glittered.

'*Il te regarde. Il te regarde,*' said Sylvia hopelessly. '*Il te veut. Oh, mon dieu, il te veut. Quoi faire? Il n'y a rien à faire. Il n'y a rien à faire. Il t'aura. Tu seras perdue. Perdue!*' she moaned.

'*Dis, Sylvie, dis, qu'est-ce que tu as? Tu me fais peur. T'es yeux son comme les yeux d'une folle. Est-ce que tu as pris l'éther ce soir?*'

It seemed to Sylvia that her companion was being dragged to damnation before her eyes, and she implored her to flee while there was still time.

Somebody stood up on a table and shouted at the top of his voice:

'*Il n'y a plus de champagne!*'

The Count was much excited by this and demanded immediately how they were going to spend the money they had brought with them. If there was no more champagne, they should have to drink vodka, but first they must play skittles with the empty bottles that were not already broken to pieces. He picked a circular cheese from the table and bowled it across the room.

'*Encore du fromage! Encore du fromage!*' everybody was shouting, and soon everywhere crimson cheeses were rolling along the floor.

'The cheeses belong to me,' the Count cried. 'Nobody else is to order cheeses. *Garçon! garçon!* bring me all the cheeses you have. The cheeses are mine. Mine! Mine!'

His voice rose to a scream.

'*Mon dieu, il vont se battre à cause du fromage,*' cried the other girl, holding her hand to her eyes and cowering in her chair.

By this time the management thought it would soon lose

14

what it had made that evening and ordered the cabaret to be closed. The girls, who were anxious to escape, ran to be paid for their champagne. Sylvia swayed and nearly fell in the rush; her companion kept her head and exacted from the management every kopeck. Then she dragged Sylvia with her to a drozhky, put her in, and said good-night.

'*Tu ne viens pas avec moi?*' Sylvia cried.

'*Non, non, il faut que j'aille avec lui.*'

'*Avec l'homme qui te regardait de la loge?*'

'*Non, non, avec mon ami.*'

She gave the address of the pension to the driver and vanished in the confusion. Sylvia fancied that this girl was lost for ever, and wept to herself all the way home, but without shedding a single tear: her body was like fire. There was nobody about in the pension when she arrived back; she dragged herself up to her room and lay down on the bed fully dressed. It seemed that all reality was collapsing fast, and she clutched the notes stuffed into her corsage as the only solid fact left to her, the only link between herself and home. Once or twice she vaguely wondered if she were really ill, but her mental state was so much worse than the physical pain that she struggled feebly to quieten her nerves and kept on trying to assure herself that her own unnatural excitement was nothing except the result of the unnatural excitement at the cabaret. She found herself wondering if she were going mad, and trying to piece together the links of the chain that would lead her to the explanation of this madness.

'What could have made me go mad suddenly like this?' she kept moaning.

It seemed that if she could only discover the cause of her madness she should be able to cure it. All her attention was soon taken up in watching little round red devils that kept rising out of the floor beside the bed, little round red devils that swelled and ripened like tomatoes, burst, and vanished. Her faculties concentrated upon discovering a reasonable explanation for such a queer occurrence; many explanations presented themselves, hovered upon the outskirts of her brain, and escaped before they could be stated. There was no doubt in Syliva's mind that a reasonable explanation existed, and it was tantalising never to be able to catch it, because it was quite certain that such an explanation would have been very interesting; at any rate it was a relief to know that there was an explanation and that these devils were not figments of the imagination. As soon as she had settled that they had an objective existence, it became rather amusing to watch them: there was a new variety now that floated about the floor like bulbbles before they burst.

Suddenly Sylvia sat up on the bed and listened: the stairs were creaking under the footsteps of some heavy person who was ascending. It must be Carrier. She should go out and call to him: she should like him to see those devils. She went out into the passage dove-grey with the dawn, and called. Ah, it was not Carrier: it was that man who had stared from the box at her friend! She closed the door hurriedly and bolted it; every sensation of being ill had departed from her; she could feel nothing but an unspeakable fear. She put her hand to her forehead: it was dripping wet, and she shivered. The devils were nowhere to be seen; dawn was creeping about the room in a grey mist. The door opened, and the bolt fell with a clatter upon the floor: she shrank back upon the bed, burying her face in the pillow. The intruder clanked up and down the room with his sword, but never spoke a word; at last Sylvia, finding that it was impossible to shut him out by closing her eyes and ears to his presence, sat up and asked him in French what he wanted and why he had broken into her room like this. All her unnatural mental excitement had died away before this drunken giant who was staring at her from glazed eyes and leaning unsteadily with both hands upon his sword; she felt nothing but an intense physical weariness and a savage desire to sleep.

'Why didn't you wait for me at the cabaret?' the giant demanded in a thick voice.

Sylvia estimated the distance between herself and the door, and wondered if her aching legs would carry her there quickly enough to escape those huge freckled hands that were silky with golden hairs. Her heart was beating so loudly that she was afraid he would hear it and be angry.

'You didn't ask me to wait,' she said. 'It was my friend whom you wanted. She's still there. You've made a mistake. Why don't you go back and look for her?'

He banged his sword upon the floor angrily.

'A trick! A trick to get rid of me,' he muttered. Then he unbuckled his sword, flung it against a chair, and began to unbutton his tunic.

'But you can't stay here,' Sylvia cried. 'Don't you understand that you've made a mistake? You don't want *me*. Go away from here.'

'Money?' the giant muttered. 'Take it.'

He put his hand in his pocket, pulled out a bundle of notes

16

and threw them on the bed, after which he took off his tunic.

'You're drunk or mad,' Sylvia cried, now more exasperated than frightened. 'Go out of my room before I wake up the house.'

The giant paid not the least attention, and seating himself on a chair bent over to pull off his boots. Sylvia again tried to muster enough strength to rise, but her limbs were growing weaker every moment.

'And if you're not the girl I wanted,' said the giant looking up from his boots, 'You're a *girl*, aren't you? I've paid you, haven't I? A splendid state the world's coming to when a cocotte takes it into her head to argue with a Russian officer who pays her the honour of his intentions. The world's turning upside-down. The people must have a lesson. Come, get off that bed and help me undo these boots.'

'Do you know that I'm English?' Sylvia said. 'You'll find that even Russian officers cannot insult English women.'

'A cocotte has no nationality,' the giant contradicted solemnly. 'She is common property. Come, if you had wished to talk, you should have joined my table earlier in the evening. One does not wish to talk when one is sleepy.'

The English acrobats slept next door to Sylvia, and she hammered on the partition.

'Are you killing bugs?' the giant asked. 'You need not bother. They never disturb me.'

Sylvia went on hammering: her arms were getting weaker, and unless help came soon she would faint. There was a tap on the door.

'Come in,' she cried. 'Come in at once – at once!'

Willie entered in purple silk pyjamas, rubbing his eyes.

'Whatever is it, Sylvia?'

'Take this drunken brute out of my room.'

'Bobbie! Bobbie!' he called. 'Come here, Bobbie! Bobbie! Will you come. You are mean. Oh, there's such a nasty man in Sylvia's room. Oh, he's something dreadful to look at.'

The drunken officer stared at Willie in amazement, trying to make up his mind if he were an alcoholic vision: his judgement was still further shaken by the appearance of Bobbie in pyjamas of emerald green silk.

'Oh, Willie, he's got a sword,' said Bobbie. 'Oh, doesn't he look fierce. Oh, he does look fierce. Most alarming, I'm sure.'

The intruder staggered to his feet.

'*Foutez-moi camp*,' he bellowed, making a grab for his sword.

'For heaven's sake get rid of the brute,' Sylvia moaned. 'I'm too weak to move.'

The two young men pirouetted into the middle of the room, as they were wont to pirouette upon the stage, with arms stretched out in a curve from the shoulder and fingers raised mincingly above an imaginary teacup held between the first finger and thumb. When they reached the giant, they stopped short to sustain the preliminary pose of a female acrobat: then turning round they ran back a few steps, turned round again and with a scream flung themselves upon their adversary; he went down with a crash, and they danced upon his prostrate form like two butterflies over a cabbage.

The noise had wakened the other inhabitants of the pension, who came crowding into Sylvia's room; with the rest was Carrier and they managed to extract from her a vague account of what had happened. The aviator in a rage demanded an explanation of his conduct from the officer, who called him a *maquereau*. Carrier was strong; with help from the acrobats he had pushed the officer half-way through the window when Mère Gontran, who notwithstanding her bedroom being two hundred yards away from the pension had an uncanny faculty for divining when anything had gone wrong, appeared on the scene. Thirty-five years in Russia had made her very fearful of offending the military, and she implored Carrier and the acrobats to think what they were doing: in her red dressing-gown she looked like an insane cardinal.

'They'll confiscate my property. They'll send me to Siberia. Treat his excellency more gently, I beg. Sylvia, tell them to stop. Sylvia, he's going – he's going – he's gone!'

He was gone indeed, head first into a clump of lilacs underneath the window, whither his tunic and sword followed him.

The adventure with the drunken officer had exhausted the last forces of Sylvia; she lay back on the bed in a semi-trance soothed by the unending bibble-babble all round. She was faintly aware of somebody's taking her hand and feeling her pulse, of somebody's saying that her eyes were like a dead woman's, of somebody's throwing a coverlet over her. Then the bibble-babble became much louder; there was a sound of crackling and a smell of smoke, and she heard shouts of 'fire!' 'fire!' 'he has set fire to the outhouse!' There was a noise of splashing water, a rushing sound of water, a roar of a thousand torrents in her head; the people in the room became animated surfaces, cardboard figures without substance and without reality; the devils began once more to sprout from the floor; she felt that she was dying, and in the throes of dissolution she struggled to explain that she must travel back to England, that she must not be buried in Russia. It seemed to her in a new access of semi-consciousness that Carrier and the two acrobats were kneeling by her bed and trying to comfort her, that they were patting her hands kindly and gently. She tried to warn them that they would blister themselves if they touched her, but her tongue seemed to have separated itself from her body. She tried to tell them that her tongue was already dead, and the effort to explain racked her whole body. Then suddenly, dark and gigantic figures came marching into the room: they must be demons, as it was true about hell. She tried to scream her belief in immortality and to beg a merciful God to show mercy and save her from the Fiend. The sombre forms drew near her bed. From an unimaginably distant past she saw framed in fire the picture of The Impenitent Sinner's Deathbed that used to hang in the kitchen at Lille, and again from the past came suddenly back the text of a sermon preached by Dorward at Green Lanes. *Though your sins be as scarlet, they shall be as white as snow.* It seemed to her that if only she could explain to God that her name was really Snow and that Scarlett was only the name assumed for her by her father, all might even now be well. The sombre forms had seized her, and she beat against them with unavailing hands; they snatched her from the bed and wrapped her round and round with something that stifled her cries; with her last breath she tried to shriek a warning to Carrier of the existence of hell, to beg him to put away his little red devils lest he when he should ultimately fall from the sky should fall as deep as hell.

Sylvia came out of her delirium to find herself in the ward of a hospital kept by French nuns; she asked what had been the matter with her, and smiling compassionately they said it was a bad fever. She lay for a fortnight in a state of utter lassitude, watching the nuns going about their work as she would have watched birds in the cool deeps of a forest. The lassitude was not unpleasant; it was a fatigue so intense that her spirit seemed able to leave her tired body and float about among the shadows of this long room. She knew that there were other patients in the ward, but she had no inclination to know who they were or what they looked like; she had no desire to communicate with the outside world, nor any anxiety about the future. She could not imagine that she should ever wish to do anything except lie here watching the nuns at their work like birds in the cool deeps of a forest. When the doctor visited her and spoke cheerfully, she wondered vaguely how he managed to keep his very long black beard so frizzy, but she was not sufficiently interested to ask him. To his questions about her bodily welfare, she let her tired body answer automatically, and often, when the doctor was bending over to listen to her heart or lungs, her spirit would have mounted up to float upon the shadows of sunlight rippling over the ceiling, that he and her body might commune without disturbing herself. At last there came a morning when the body grew impatient of being left behind and when it trembled with a faint desire to follow the spirit. Sylvia raised herself up on her elbow, and asked a nun to bring her a looking-glass.

'But all my hair has been cut,' she exclaimed. She looked at her eyes: there was not much life in them, yet they were larger than she had ever seen them, and she liked them better than before, because they were now very kind eyes: this new Sylvia appealed to her.

She put the glass down and asked if she had been very ill.

'Very ill indeed,' said the nun.

Sylvia longed to tell the nun that she must not believe all she had said when she was delirious: and then she wondered what she had said.

'Was I very violent in my delirium?' she asked.

The nun smiled.

'I thought I was in hell,' said Sylvia seriously. 'When are my friends coming to see me?'

The nun looked grave.

'Your friends have all gone away,' she said at last. 'They used to come every day to enquire after you, but they went away when war was declared.'

'War?' Sylvia repeated. 'Did you say war?'

The nun nodded.

'War?' she went on. 'This isn't part of my delirium? You're not teasing me? War between whom?'

'Russia, France, and England are at war with Germany and Austria.'

'Then Carrier has left Petersburg?'

'Hush,' said the nun. 'It's no longer Petersburg. It's Petrograd now.'

'But I don't understand. Do you mean to tell me that everybody has changed his name? I've changed my name back to my real name. My name is Sylvia Snow now. I changed it when I was delirious, but I shall always be Sylvia Snow. I've been thinking about it all these days while I've been lying so quiet. Did Carrier leave any message for me? He was the aviator, you know.'

'He has gone back to fight for France,' the nun said, crossing herself. 'He was very sorry about your being so ill. You must pray for him.'

'Yes, I will pray for him,' Sylvia said. 'And there is nobody left? Those two funny little English acrobats with fair curly hair. Have they gone?'

'They've gone too,' said the nun. 'They came every day to enquire for you, and they brought you flowers, which were put beside your bed, but you were unconscious.'

'I think I smelt a sweetness in the air sometimes,' Sylvia said.

'They were always put outside the window at night,' the nun explained.

The faintest flicker of an inclination to be amused at the nun's point of view about flowers came over Sylvia; but it scarcely endured for an instant, because it was so obviously the right point of view in this hospital where even flowers not to seem out of place must acquire orderly habits. The nun asked her if she wanted anything and passed on down the ward when she shook her head.

Sylvia lay back to consider her situation and to pick up the threads of normal existence, which seemed so inextricably tangled at present that she felt like a princess in a fairy tale who has been set an impossible task by an envious witch.

In the first place, putting on one side all the extravagance of delirium, Sylvia was conscious of a change in her personality so profound and so violent, that now with the return of reason and with the impulse to renewed activity she was convinced of her rightness in deciding to go back to her real name of Sylvia Snow. The anxiety that she had experienced during her delirium to make the change positively remained from that condition as something of value that bore no relation to the grosser terrors of hell she had experienced. The sense of regeneration that she was feeling at this moment could not entirely be explained by her mind's reaction to the peace of the hospital, to the absence of pain, and to her bodily well-being. She was able to set in its proportion each of these factors, and when she had done so there still remained this emotion that was indefinable unless she accepted for it the definition of regeneration.

'The fact is I've eaten roseleaves and I'm no longer a golden ass,' she murmured. 'But what I want to arrive at is when exactly I was turned into an ass and when I ate the roseleaves.'

21

For a time her mind unused since her fever to concentrated thinking wandered off into the tale of Apuleius. She wished vaguely that she had the volume so inscribed by Michael Fane with her in Petersburg, but she had left it behind at Mulberry Cottage. It was some time before she brought herself back to the realisation that the details of the Roman story had not the least bearing upon her meditation and that the symbolism of the enchanted transformation and the recovery of human shape by eating roseleaves had been an essentially modern and romantic gloss upon the old author. This gloss, however, had served extraordinarily well to symbolise her state of mind before she had been ill, and she was not going to abandon it now.

'I must have had an experience once that fitted in with the idea, or it would not recur to me like this with such an imputation of significance.'

Sylvia thought hard for a while; the nun on day duty was pecking away at a medicine-bottle, and the busy little noise competed with her thoughts so that she was determined before the nun could achieve her purpose with the medicine-bottle to discover when she became a golden ass. Suddenly the answer flashed across her mind; at the same moment the nun triumphed over her bottle, and the ward was absolutely still again.

'I became a golden ass when I married Philip and I ate the rose-leaves when Arthur refused to marry me.'

This solution of the problem, though she knew that it was not radically more satisfying than the defeat of a toy puzzle, was nevertheless wonderfully comforting, so comforting that she fell asleep and woke up late in the afternoon refreshingly alert and eager to resume her unravelling of the tangled skein.

'I became a golden ass when I married Philip,' she repeated to herself.

For a while she tried to reconstruct the motives that fourteen years ago had induced her toward that step. If she had really begun her life all over again, it should be easy to do this. But the more she pondered herself at the age of seventeen, the more impossibly remote that Sylvia seemed. Certain results, however, could even at this distance of time be ascribed to that unfortunate marriage: amongst others the three months after she left Philip. When Sylvia came to survey all her life since, she saw how those three months had lurked at the back of everything, how really they had spoilt everything.

'Have I fallen a prey to remorse?' she asked herself. 'Must I for ever be haunted by the memory of what was after all a

22

necessary incident to my assumption of assishness? Did I not pay for them that day at Mulberry Cottage when I could not be myself to Michael, but could only bray at him the unrealities of my outward shape?'

Lying here in the cool hospital Sylvia began to conjure against her will the incidents of those three fatal months, and so weak was she still from the typhus that she could not shake off their obsession. Her mind clutched at other memories; but no sooner did she think that she was safely wrapped up in their protecting fragrance than like Furies those three months drove her mind forth from its sanctuary, and scourged it with cruel images.

'This is the sort of madness that makes a woman kill her seducer,' said Sylvia, 'this insurgent rage at feeling that the men who crossed my path during those three months still live without remorse for what they did.'

Gradually, however, her rage died down before the pleadings of reasonableness; she recalled that somewhere she had read how the human body changes entirely every seven years: this reflection consoled her, and though she admitted that it was a trivial and superficial consolation, since remorse was conceived with the spirit rather than with the body, nevertheless the thought that not one corpuscle of her present blood existed fourteen years ago restored her sense of proportion and enabled her to shake off the obsession of these three months, at any rate so far as to allow her to proceed with her contemplation of the new Sylvia lying here in this hospital.

'Then of course there was Lily,' she said to herself. 'How can I possibly excuse my treatment of Lily, or not so much my treatment of her as my attitude towards her? I suppose all this introspection is morbid, but having been brought up sharp like this and having been planked down on this bed of interminable sickness, who wouldn't be morbid? It's better to have it out with myself now, lest when I emerge from here – for incredible as it seems just at present I certainly shall emerge one fine morning – I start being introspective instead of getting down to the hard facts of earning a living and finding my way back to England. Lily!' she went on. 'I believe really when I look back at it that I took a cruel delight in watching Lily's fading. It seemed jolly and cynical to predestine her to maculation, to regard her as a flower, an almost inanimate thing that could only be displayed by somebody else and was incapable of developing herself. Yet in the end she did develop herself. I was very ill then; but when I was in the clinic at Rio I had none of the sensations that I have now.

23

What sensations did I have then? Mostly I believe, they were worried about Lily, because she did not come to see me. Strange that something so essentially insignificant as Lily could have created such a catastrophe for Michael, and that I, when she went her own way, let her drop as easily as a piece of paper from a carriage. The fact was that having smirched myself and survived the smirching I was unable to fret myself very much over Lily's smirching. And yet I did fret myself in a queer irrational way. But what use to continue? I behaved badly to Lily, but I can't excuse my attitude towards her by saying that I behaved badly to myself also.'

The longer Sylvia went on with the reconstruction of the past, the more deeply did she feel that she was to blame for everything in it.

'And yet I had the impudence to resent Arthur's treatment of me,' she cried.

The nun hastened to her bedside and asked her what she wanted.

'I'm so sorry, sister, I was talking to myself. I think I must really be very much better today.'

The nun shook her forefinger at Sylvia and retired again to her table at the end of the ward.

'Why, I deserved a much worse humiliation,' Sylvia went on. 'And I got it too. The fact was that when I ate those roseleaves and became a woman again I was so elated really that I thought everything I had done in the shape of an ass had been obliterated by the disenchantment. Ah, how much, how tremendously I deserve the humiliation which that Russian officer inflicted. And then mercifully came this fever on top of it, and I have got to rise from this bed and confront life from an entirely different point of view. I'm going to start from where I was that afternoon in Brompton Cemetery, when I was speculating about the human soul. Obviously, now I look back at it, I was just then beginning to apprehend that I might after all possess a soul with obligations to something more permanent than the body it inhabited. What a fool Philip was! If he'd only nurtured my soul instead of my body. If he'd only not bit by bit dried it up to something so small that it became powerless to compete with the arrogant body that held it. I wonder if he's still alive. But of course he's still alive. He's only forty-six now. Really I'd like to write and explain what happened. However, he'd only laugh – he was always so very contemptuous of souls. Anyway, nothing will ever induce me to believe that my soul hasn't grown in the most extraordinary way during this fever. What a triumph she has had over her poor body. Where's that looking-glass?'

She called to the nun and begged her to bring her the looking-glass again. The nun brought it and tried to console Sylvia for the loss of her hair.

'But I'm rejoicing in it,' Sylvia declared. 'I'm rejoicing in the sight I present to the world. Look here, can't you sit down beside me and tell me something about your religion? I'm absolutely bursting for a revelation. You fast, don't you, and spend long nights and days in prayer? Well, I am in the sort of condition in which you find yourself at the end of a long bout of fasting and prayer. I'm as light as a feather. I could achieve levitation with very little difficulty.'

The nun regarded Sylvia in perplexity.

'Have you thanked Almighty God for your recovery?' she asked.

'No, of course I haven't. I can't thank somebody I know nothing about,' said Sylvia impatiently. 'Besides, it's no good thanking God for my recovery unless I am sure I ought to be grateful. Mere living for the sake of living seems to me as sensual as any other appetite. Sister, can't you give me the key to life?'

The nun sheltered herself beneath an array of pious phrases; she was like a person who has been surprised naked and hurriedly flings on all the clothes in reach.

'All that you're saying means nothing to me,' said Sylvia sadly. 'And the reason of it is that you've never lived. You've only looked at evil from the outside; you've only heard of unbelief.'

'I'll make a Novena for you,' said the nun hopelessly. She said it in the same way as she would have offered to knit a woollen vest. 'To-day is the Assumption.' It was if she justified the woollen vest by a change in the weather.

Sylvia thanked her for the Novena just as she would have thanked her for the woollen vest.

'Or perhaps you'd like a priest?' the nun suggested.

Sylvia shook her head.

'I don't feel I require professional treatment yet,' she said. 'Don't look so sad, little sister, I expect your Novena will help me to what I'm trying to find – if I'm trying to find anything,' she added pausively. 'I think really I'm waiting to be found.'

The nun retired disconsolate, the next day Sylvia's spiritual problems vanished before the problem of getting up for the first time, of wavering across the ward and collapsing into a wicker chair among three other convalescent patients who were talking and sewing in the sunlight.

The uniformity of their grey shawls and grey dressing-gowns made Sylvia pay more attention to the faces of her fellow sufferers than she might otherwise have done; she sat in silence for a while, exhausted by her progress across the ward, and listened to their conversation which was carried on in French, though as far as she could make out none of them was of French nationality. Presently a young woman with a complexion like a slightly shrivelled apple turned to Sylvia and asked in her own language if she were not English.

Sylvia nodded.

'I'm English too. It's pleasant to meet a fellow-countrywoman here. What are you going to do about the war?'

'I don't suppose much action on my part will make any difference,' said Sylvia with a laugh. 'I don't suppose I could stop it, however hard I tried.'

The Englishwoman laughed because she evidently wanted to be polite; but it was mirthless laughter like an actor's at rehearsal, a mere sound that was required to fill in a gap in the dialogue.

'Of course not,' she agreed. 'I was wondering if you would go back to England as soon as you got out of hospital.'

'I shall if I can rake together the money for my fare,' Sylvia said.

'Oh, won't your family pay your fare back? Didn't you get that in the agreement?'

'I don't possess a family,' Sylvia said.

'Oh, aren't you a governess? How funny.'

'It would be very much funnier if I was,' said Sylvia.

'My name is Eva Savage. What's yours?'

Sylvia hesitated a moment and then plunged.

'Sylvia Snow.'

Immediately afterwards with an excess of timidity she supplemented this by explaining that on the stage she called herself Sylvia Scarlett.

'On the stage,' repeated the little governess. 'Are you on the stage? You are lucky.'

Sylvia looked at her in surprise, and realised how much younger she was than a first glance at her led one to suppose.

'I came out to Russia when I was nineteen,' Miss Savage went on. 'And of course that's better than staying in England to teach, though I hate teaching.'

Sylvia asked how old she was now, and when she heard that she was only twenty-four she decided that illness must be the cause of that shrivelled rosy skin that made her look like an old maid of fifty.

They talked for a while of their illness and compared notes, but it seemed that Miss Savage must have had a mild attack, for she had been brought into the hospital some time after Sylvia and had already been up a week.

'I'm going to ask the sister-in-charge to let me sleep in the bed next to yours,' said Miss Savage. 'After all, we're the only two English girls here.'

Sylvia did not feel at all sure that she liked this plan, but she did not want to hurt her companion's feelings and agreed without enthusiasm. Presently she asked if the other two women spoke English, and Miss Savage told her that one was a German-Swiss, the wife of a pastry cook called Benzer, and that the other was a Swedish masseuse; she did not think that either of them spoke English, but added in a low voice that they were both very common.

'Interesting?'

'No, common, awfully common,' Miss Savage insisted.

Sylvia made a gesture of impatience: her countrywomen always summed up humanity with such complacent facility. At this moment a little girl of about thirteen habited like the rest in a grey shawl came tripping down the ward, clapping her hands with glee.

'How lovely war is,' she cried in French. 'I am longing to be out of hospital. I've been in the other ward, and through the window I saw thousands and thousands of soldiers marching past. *Maman* cried yesterday when I asked her why *papa* hated soldiers. He hates them. Whenever he sees them marching past he shakes his fist and spits. But I love them.'

This child had endeared herself to the invalids of the hospital; she was a token of returning health, the boon of which she seemed to pledge to everyone in the company. Even the grim Swedish masseuse smiled and spoke gently to her in barbaric French. Moreover, here in this quiet hospital the war had not yet penetrated, it was like a far distant thunderstorm, which had driven a number of people who were out of doors to take shelter at home; as Miss Savage said to Sylvia: —

'I expect everybody got excited and afraid; yet it all seems very quiet really, and I shall stay here with my family. There's

27

no point in *making* oneself uncomfortable.'

Sylvia agreed with Miss Savage and decided not to worry about her fare back to England, but rather to stay on for a while in Russia and get up her strength after leaving the hospital; then when she had spent her money she should work again, and when this was was over she should return to Mulberry Cottage with one or two Improvisations added to her repertory. Now that she was out of bed life seemed already simple again, and perhaps she had exaggerated the change in herself; she wished she had not spoken to the nun so intimately; one of the disadvantages of being ill was this begetting of an intimacy between the nurse and the patient, which grows out of bodily dependence into mental servitude: it was easy to understand why men so often married their nurses.

'I am not sure,' said Sylvia to herself, 'that the right attitude is not the contempt of the healthy animal for one of its kind who is sick. There's a sort of sterile sensuality about nursing and being nursed.'

Sylvia's feelings about the war were confirmed by the views of the doctor who attended her. He had felt a little nervous until England had taken her place beside Russia and France, but once she had done so, the war would be over at the latest by the middle of October.

'It's easy to see how frightened the Germans are by the way they are behaving in Belgium.'

'Why, what are they doing?' Sylvia asked.

'They've overrun it like a pack of wolves.'

'I have a sister in Brussels,' she said suddenly.

The doctor shook his head compassionately.

'But of course nothing will happen to her,' she added.

The doctor hastened to support this theory: Sylvia was still very weak, and he did not want a relapse brought on by anxiety. He changed the conversation by calling to Claudinette, the little girl who thought war was so lovely.

'Seen any more soldiers to-day?' he asked jovially.

'Thousands,' Claudinette declared. 'Oh, *monsieur,* when shall I be able to leave the hospital? It's terrible to be missing everything. Besides, I want to make *papa* understand how lovely it is to march along with everybody thinking how fine and brave it is to be a soldier. Fancy, *maman* told me he has been invited to go back to France and that he has actually refused the invitation.'

The doctor raised his eyebrows and flashed a glance at Sylvia from his bright brown eyes to express his pity for the child's innocence.

At this point Madame Benzer intervened.

'The only thing that worries me about this war is the food: it's bound to upset custom. People don't order so many tarts when they're thinking of something else. And the price of everything will go up. Luckily I've told my husband to lay in stores of flour and sugar. It's a comfort to be a neutral.'

The Swedish masseuse echoed Madame Benzer's self-congratulation:

'Of course one doesn't want to seem an egoist,' she said, 'but I can't help knowing that I shall benefit. As a neutral I shan't be able to go and nurse at the front, but I shall be useful in Petersburg.'

'Petrograd,' the doctor corrected her with marked irritation.

'I shall never get used to the change,' said the massseuse. 'When do you think I shall be strong enough to begin my work again?'

The doctor shrugged his shoulders.

'November perhaps.'

'Why, the war will be over by then,' said the masseuse indignantly.

'They're calling for volunteers in England,' Miss Savage observed to Sylvia. 'I'm sure my two brothers have gone. They've always been mad about soldiering. They're like you, Claudinette.'

'If only I could be a *vivandière*,' cried the child. She was unable to contain her romantic exultation at the idea, and snatching the doctor's stethoscope, she marched up and down the ward pursing her lips to a shrill Marseillaise.

'Children are children,' said Madame Benzer fatly.

'It's true,' sighed the doctor.

'*She*'s quite well again,' said the masseuse enviously.

'I love children,' Sylvia exclaimed.

'Do you?' said Miss Savage. 'Wait till you've had to teach them. You'll hate them then!'

Claudinette's march was interrupted by the nun on duty, who was horrified at the ward's being used so noisily: though there were no fresh patients, the rule of stillness could not be broken like this. Claudinette having been deprived of her bugle, went and drummed out her martial soul upon a window-pane; the doctor, who felt a little guilty, stroked his beard and passed on.

The governess carried out her intention of having her bed

moved next to Sylvia; on the first night of the change she whispered across to her in the darkness, which seemed the more intense round their beds, because at the far end of the ward a lamp burned before the image of the Virgin and enclosed by two screens the nun on night-duty sat in a dim golden mist.

'Are you awake?'

Sylvia answered in a low voice in order not to disturb the other patients; she could not bring herself to answer in a whisper, because it would have made this conversation seem surreptitious.

'Hush! Don't talk so loud. Are you a Catholic?'

'I'm nothing,' said Sylvia.

'Do tell me about your life.'

'We can talk about that in the morning.'

'Oh no, one can't talk secrets in the morning. I want to ask you something. Do you think that everybody in Russia will go and fight? You see Prince Paul isn't a soldier. You remember I told you that Prince George and Prince Paul, the two elder sons of the family, were both very handsome? Well, Prince George is in the army, but Prince Paul isn't. They both made love to me,' she added with a stifled giggle.

Sylvia lay silent.

'Are you shocked?'

'Neither shocked nor surprised,' said Sylvia coldly. 'The nobility of Russia seems to think of nothing else but making love.'

'Paul gave me a book once. I've got it here with me in my box. It's called the *Memories of a German Singer*. Would you like to read it?'

'That book,' Sylvia exclaimed scornfully. 'Why, it's the filthiest book I ever read.'

'You are shocked then,' the governess whispered. 'I thought you'd be more broad-minded. I shan't tell you now about Prince Paul. He makes love divinely. He said it was so thrilling to make love to somebody like me who looked so proper. I'm dreadfully afraid that when I get back I shall find he's gone to fight. It's awful to think how dull it will be without either George or Paul. Haven't you had any interesting love-affairs?'

'Good god,' exclaimed Sylvia angrily. 'Do you think there's anything to be proud of in having love-affairs like yours? Do you think there's anything fine in letting yourself be treated like a servant by a lascivious boy? You make me feel sick. How dare you assume that I should be interested in your – oh, I have no word to call it that can be even spoken in a whisper.'

'You *are* proper,' the governess murmured resentfully. 'I thought girls on the stage were more broad-minded.'

'Is this muttering going to continue all night?' an angry voice demanded. Further along the ward could be heard the sound of a bed rattling with indignation.

The nun pushed back her screen, and the candlelight illumined Madame Benzer sitting up on her ample haunches.

'One must not talk,' said the nun reproachfully. 'One disturbs the patients. Besides, it is against the rules to talk after the lights are put out.'

'Well, please move me away from here,' Sylvia asked, 'because if Mademoiselle stays here I shall have to talk.'

'I'm sure I'd much rather not stay in this bed,' declared Miss Savage in an injured voice. 'And *I* was only whispering. There was no noise until Mademoiselle began to talk quite loudly.'

'Is this discussion worth while?' Sylvia asked wearily.

'Am I ever to be allowed to get to sleep?' Madame Benzer demanded.

'I should like to sleep too,' protested the masseuse. 'If I'm to get strong enough to resume work in November, I need all the sleep I can get. I'm not like a child that can sleep through anything.'

'*I'm* not asleep,' cried Claudinette shrilly. 'And I'm very content that I'm not asleep. I adore to hear people talking in the night.'

The nun begged for general silence, and the ward was stilled. Sylvia lay awake in a rage, listening to Madame Benzer and the masseuse while they turned over and over with sighs and groans and much creaking of their beds. At last, however, all except herself fell asleep; their united breathing seemed like the breathing of a large and placid beast. Behind the screens in that dim golden mist the pages of the nun's breviary whispered now instead of Miss Savage; the lamp before the image of the Virgin sometimes flickered and cast upon the insipid face subtle shadows that gave humanity to what by daylight looked like a large pale blue fondant.

'Or should I say "divinity"?' Sylvia asked herself.

She lay on her side staring at the image, which was the conventional representation of Our Lady of Lourdes with eyes upraised and hands clasped to heaven. Contemplated thus the tawdry figure really acquired a supplicatory grace, and in the night the imagination dwelling upon this form began to identify itself with the attitude and to follow those upraised eyes towards an unearthly quest. Sylvia turned over on her other side with a perfectly conscious will not to be influenced externally by what she felt was an unworthy appeal. But when she had turned over she could not stay averted from the image; a restless curiosity to know if it was still upon its bracket seized her, and she turned back to her contemplation.

'How ridiculous all those stories are of supernatural winkings and blinkings,' she thought. 'Why I could very easily imagine the most acrobatic behaviour by that pathetic little blue figure. And yet it has expressed the aspirations of millions of wounded hearts.'

The thought was overwhelming: the imagination of what this figure reduplicated innumerably all over the earth had stood for descended upon Sylvia from the heart of the darkness about her, and she shuddered with awe.

'If I scoff at that,' she thought, 'I scoff at human tears. And why shouldn't I scoff at human tears? Because I should be scoffing at my own tears. And why not at my own?'

'You dare not,' the darkness sighed.

Sylvia crept out of bed and bending over the governesss waked her with soft reassurances, as one wakes a child.

'Forgive me,' she whispered, 'for the way I spoke. But oh, do believe me when I tell you that love like that is terrible. I understand the dullness of your profession, and if you like I will take you with me on my gipsy life when we leave the hospital. You can amuse yourself with seeing the world; but if you want love, you must demand it with your head high. Every little governess who behaves like you creates another harlot.'

'Did you wake me up to insult me?' demanded Miss Savage.

'No, my dear, you don't understand me. I'm not thinking of what you make yourself. *You* will pay for that. I'm thinking of some baby now at its mother's breast, for whose damnation you will be responsible by giving another proof to man of woman's weakness, by having kindled in him another lust.'

'I think you'd do better to bother about your own soul instead of mine,' said Miss Savage. 'Please let me go to sleep again. When I wanted to talk, you pretended to be shocked. I asked you if you were a Catholic, and you told me you were nothing. I particularly avoided hurting your susceptibilities. The least you can do is to be polite in return.'

Sylvia went back to bed, and thinking over what the governess

32

had said decided that after all she was right: she ought to bother with her own soul first.

Three weeks later Sylvia was told that she was now fit to leave the hospital. The nuns charged her very little for their care; but when she walked out of the door she had only about eighty roubles in the world. With rather a heavy heart she drove to Mère Gontran's pension.

Chapter II

THE PENSION was strangely silent when Sylvia returned to it; the panic of war had stripped it bare of guests. Although she had known that Carrier and the English acrobats were gone and had more or less made up her mind that most of the girls would also be gone this complete abandonment was tristful. Mère Gontran's influence had always pervaded the pension; even before her illness Sylvia had been affected by that odd personality and had often been haunted by the unusualness of the whole place; but the disconcerting atmosphere had always been quickly and easily neutralised by the jolly mountebanks and Bohemians with whose point of view and jokes and noise she had been familiar all her life. Sylvia and the other guests had so often laughed together at Mère Gontran's eccentricity, at the tumbledown house, at the tangled garden, at the muttering handmaid, and at the animals in the kitchen, that through this careless merriment the pension had come to be no more than one of the incidents of the career they followed, something to talk of when they swirled on and lodged in another corner of the earth's surface. There would be no city in Europe at which in some cabaret one would not find a *copain* with whom to laugh over the remembrance of Mère Gontran's talking collie. But how many of these gay mountebanks dispersed by the panic of war would not have been affected by the Pension Gontran, had they returned to it like this, alone?

The garden with its rank autumnal growth was more like a jungle than ever; the unpopulous house reasserted its very self, and there was not a crack in the stucco nor a broken tile nor a

warped plank that did not now maintain a haunting significance. The Tarter servant with her unintelligible mutterings, her
head and face muffled in a stained green scarf, her bent form,
her feet in pattens clapping like hoofs, the animals that sniffed
at her heels, and her sleeping cupboard beneath the stairs heaped
with faded rags, seemed an incarnation of the house's reality.
For a moment when Sylvia was making signs to her that she
should fetch her mistress from where buried in docks and
nettles she was performing one of her queer solitary operations
of horticulture, she was inclined to turn round and search anywhere else in Petrograd for a lodging rather than expose herself
to the night-time here. But the consciousness of her uncertain
position soon scattered such fancies, and she decided that the
worst of them would not be so unpleasant as to find herself
at the mercy of the material horrors of a fourth-rate hotel while
she was waiting for vigour to resume work; at any rate Mère
Gontran was kind-hearted and English. As Sylvia reached this
conclusion, the mistress of the pension followed by two cats,
a hen, two pigeons, a goat, and a dog came to greet her; putting
the table-fork with which she had been gardening into the pocket
of her overall, she warmly embraced Sylvia, which was like being
flicked on the cheek by a bramble when driving.

'Why, Sylvia, I *am* glad to see you again. Everybody's gone.
Everything's closed. No more vodka allowed to be sold in public,
though of course it can always be got. The war's upon us, and
I'm sowing turnips under Jupiter in case we starve. All your
things are quite safe. Your room hasn't been touched since you
left it. I'll tell Anna to make your bed.'

Anna was not the maid-servant's real name; but one of Mère
Gontran's peculiarities was, that though she could provide an
individual name for every bird or beast in the place without
using the same one twice, all her servants had to be called Anna
in memory of her first cook of thirty years ago – a repetition
that could hardly have been due to sentiment, because the first
Anna, when she ran away to be married, took with her as much
of her mistress's plate as she could carry.

'Hasn't my bed been made all these weeks?' Sylvia asked with
a smile.

'Why should it have been made?' Mère Gontran replied.
'There hasn't been a single newcomer since you were taken off
in the ambulance.'

Sylvia asked if the drunken officer had done much damage.
'Oh no, it was quite easy to extinguish the fire. He burned

34

half the tool-shed and frightened the guinea-pigs; that was all. I was quite relieved when war was declared, because otherwise the police would probably have taken away my licence; but there again, if they had taken it away, it wouldn't have mattered much for I haven't had any lodgers since; but there again I've been able to use Carrier's room for the owls, and they're much happier in a nice room than they were nailed up to the side of the house in a packing-case. If you hear them hooting in the night, don't be frightened: you must remember that owls being night birds can't be expected to keep quiet in the night, and when they hoot it shows they're feeling at home.'

'There's nothing in the acrobats' room?' Sylvia asked anxiously; the partition between her and them had been thin.

'Such a reek of scent,' Mère Gontran exclaimed. 'Phewff! Benjamin went in after they'd gone, and he regularly shuddered. Cats are very sensitive to perfumes, as no doubt you've observed.'

'Mère Gontran,' Sylvia began. 'I want to explain my position.'

'Don't do that,' she interrupted. 'Wait till the evening and you shall throw the cards. What's the good of anticipating trouble? If the cards are unfavourable to any immediate enterprise, settle down and help me with the garden until they're favourable again. When favourable, make the journey.'

Sylvia, however, insisted on anticipating the opinion of the cards, and explained to Mère Gontran that it would be impossible for her to attempt any work for at least another six weeks on account of her weakness, and also because of her short hair which, though it was growing rapidly with close chestnut curls, was still remarkably short.

Mère Gontran asked what day it had been cut, and Sylvia said she did not know, because it had been cut when she was unconscious.

'Depend upon it they cut it when the moon was waning.'

'I hope not,' said Sylvia.

'I hope not too. I sincerely hope not,' said Mère Gontran fervently.

'It would be serious?' Sylvia suggested.

'Anything might happen. Anything!'

Mère Gontran's vivid blue eyes fixed a far horizon lowering with misfortune, and Sylvia took the opportunity of her temporary abstraction to go on with the tale of present woes.

'Money?' Mère Gontran exclaimed. 'Put it in your pocket. You were overcharged all the weeks you were with me when you were well. Deducting overcharges, I can give you six weeks' board and lodging now.'

Sylvia protested, but she would take no denial.

'At any rate,' said Sylvia finally, 'I'll avail myself of your goodness until I can communicate with people in England and get some money sent out to me.'

'Useless to communicate with anybody anywhere,' said Mère Gontran. 'No posts. No telegraphs. Everything stopped by the war. And that's where modern inventions have brought us. If you want to communicate with your friends in England, you'll have to communicate through the spirits.'

'Isn't that rather an uncertain method too?' Sylvia asked.

'Everything's uncertain,' Mère Gontran proclaimed triumphantly. 'Life's uncertain. Death's uncertain. But never mind, we'll talk to Gontran about it tonight. I was talking to him last night, and I told him to be ready for another communication tonight. Now it's time to eat.'

In the old days at the Pension Gontran the meals had always been irregular, though a dozen clamorous and hungry boarders had by the force of their united wills evoked the semblance of a set repast. With the departure of her guests Mère Gontran had copied her animals in eating whenever inclination and opportunity coincided. One method of satisfying herself was to sit down at the kitchen-table and rattle an empty plate at the servant, who would either grunt and shake her head (in which case Mère Gontran would produce biscuits from the pocket of her apron) or would empty some of the contents of a saucepan into the empty plate. On this occasion when they visited the kitchen there was something to eat, a fact which was appreciated not only by the dogs and cats, but also by Mère Gontran's three sons, who lounged in and sat down in a corner, talking to each other in Russian.

'They don't know what to do,' said their mother. 'It hasn't been decided yet whether they're French or Russian. They went to the Embassy to see about going to France, but they were told that they were Russian; and when they went to the military authorities here, they were told that they were French. The work they were doing has stopped, and they've nothing to do except smoke cigarettes and borrow money from me for their trams. I spoke to their father about it again last night, but his answer was very irrelevant, very irrelevant indeed.'

'What did he say?'

'Well, he was talking about one of his fellow-spirits called Dick at the time and he kept on saying *"Dick's picked a daisy,"* till I got so annoyed that I threw the planchette board across the room. He was just the same about his sons when he was alive. If ever I asked him a question about their education or anything, he'd slip out of it by talking about his work at the Embassy. He was one of the most irrelevant men I ever knew. Well, I shall have to ask him again to-night, that's all, because I can't have them hanging about here doing nothing for ever. It isn't as if I could understand them or they me. Bless my soul, it's not surprising that I come to rely more and more on so-called dumb animals. Yesterday they smoked one hundred and forty-six cigarettes between them. I shall have to go and see the Ambassador myself about their nationality. He knows it's not my fault that Gontran muddled it up. In my opinion they're Russian. Anyway they can't say "bo" to a goose in any other language, and it's not much good their fighting the Germans in what French *they* know.'

The three young men ate solidly throughout this monologue, oblivious of its bearing upon their future, indifferent to anything but the food before them.

After the neatness and regularity of the hospital the contrast of living at the Pension Gontran made an exceptionally strong impression of disorder on Sylvia. It vaguely recalled her life at Lillie Road with Mrs Meares, as if she had dreamt that life over again in a nightmare: there was not even wanting to complete the comparison her short hair. Yet with all the grubbiness and discomfort of it she was glad to be with Mère Gontran, whose mind long attuned to communion with animals had gained thereby a simplicity and sincerity that communion with mankind could never have given her. Like the body after long fasting, the mind after a long illness was peculiarly receptive, and Sylvia rejoiced at the opportunity to pause for a while before re-entering ordinary existence in order to contemplate the life of another lonely soul.

The evening meal at the Pension Gontran was positively formal in comparison with the haphazard midday meal; Mère Gontran's three sons rarely put in an appearance, and the maid used to come in with set dishes and lay them on the table in such a close imitation of civilised behaviour that Sylvia used to watch her movements with a fascinated admiration, as she might have watched the performance of an animal trained to wait at table. The table itself was never entirely covered with a white cloth, but that even half of it should be covered seemed miraculous after the kitchen-table. The black and red chequered cloth that covered the dining-room table for the rest of the day was pushed back to form an undulating range of foothills, beyond which the relics of Mère Gontran's incomplete undertakings piled themselves in a mountainous disarray: stockings that ought to be mended, seedlings that ought to be planted out, garden-tools that ought to be put away, packs of cards, almanacs, balls of wool, knitting-needles, flower-pots, photograph-frames, everything that had been momentarily picked up by Mère Gontran in the course of her restless day had taken refuge here. The dining-room itself was long, low, and dark with a smell of birdcages and withering geraniums; sometimes when Mère Gontran had managed to concentrate her mind long enough upon the trimming of a lamp, there would be a lamp with a shade like a draggled petticoat; more frequently the evening meal (dinner was too stringent a definition) was lighted by two candles, the wicks of which every five minutes assumed the form of large fiery flies' heads and danced up and down with delight like children who have dressed themselves up, until Mère Gontran attacked them with a weapon that was used indifferently as a nutcracker and a snuffer, but which had been designed by its maker to extract nails. Under these repeated assaults the candles themselves deliquesced and formed stalagmites and stalactites of grease, which she used to break off, roll up into balls, and drop on the floor, where they perplexed the greed of the various cats, whose tails upright with an expectation of food could dimly be seen waving in the shadows like seaweed.

On the first night of Sylvia's arrival she had been too tired to sit up with Mère Gontran and attend the conversation with her deceased husband, nor did the widow over-persuade her because it was important to settle the future of her three sons by threatening Gontran with a visit to the Embassy, a threat that might disturb even his astral liberty. Sylvia gathered from Mère Gontran's account of the interview next morning that it led to words, if the phrase might be used of communication by raps, and it seemed that the spirit had retired to sulk in some celestial nook as yet unvexed by earthly communications; his behaviour as narrated by his wife reminded Sylvia of an irritated telephone subscriber.

'But he'll be sorry for it by now,' said Mère Gontran. 'I'm expecting him to come and say so every moment.'

Gontran, however, must have spent the day walking off his

wife's ill-temper in a paradisal excursion with a kindred spirit, for nothing was heard of him, and she was left to her solitary gardening, as maybe often in life she had been left.

'I hope nothing's happened to Gontran,' she said gravely, when Sylvia and she sat down to the evening meal.

'Isn't the liability to accident rather reduced by getting rid of matter?' Sylvia suggested.

'Oh, I'm not worrying about a broken leg or anything like that,' Mère Gontran explained. 'But supposing he's reached another plane?'

'Ah, I hadn't thought of that.'

'The communications get more difficult every year since he died,' the widow complained. 'The first few months after his death, hardly five minutes used to pass without a word from him, and all night long he used to rap on the head of my bed, until James used to get quite fidgety.' James was the bulldog who slept with Mère Gontran.

'And now he raps no longer?'

'Oh, yes, he still raps,' Mère Gontran replied, 'but much more faintly. But there again, he's already moved to three different planes since his death. Hush! what's that?'

She stared into the darkest corner of the dining-room.

'Is that you, Gontran?'

'I think it was one of the birds,' Sylvia said.

Mère Gontran waved her hand for silence.

'Gontran! Is that you? Where have you been all day? This is a friend of mine who's staying here. You'll like her very much when you know her. Gontran! I want to talk to you after dinner. Now mind, don't forget. I'm glad you've got back. I want you to make some enquiries in England tomorrow.'

Sylvia was distinctly aware of a deep-seated amusement all the time at Mère Gontran's matter of fact way of dealing with her husband's spirit, and she could never make up her mind how with her sense of amusement could exist simultaneously a credulity that led her to hear at the conclusion of Mère Gontran's last speech three loud raps upon the air of the room.

'He's got over last night,' said Mère Gontran in a satisfied voice. 'But there again, he always had a kind nature at bottom. Three nice cheerful raps like that always mean he's going to give up his evening to me.'

Sylvia's first instinct was to find in what way Mère Gontran had tricked her into hearing those three raps; something in the seer's true gaze forbade the notion of trickery, and a shiver roused by the inexplicable, the shiver that makes a dog run away from an open umbrella blown across a lawn, slipped through her being.

Although Mère Gontran was puffing at her soup as if nothing had happened, the house had changed, or rather it had not changed so much as revealed itself in a brief instant. All that there was of queerness in this tumbledown pension became endowed with deliberate meaning, and it was no longer possible to ascribe the atmosphere to the effect of weakened nerves upon a weakened body. Sylvia began to wonder if the form her delirium had taken had not been directly due to this atmosphere; more than ever she was inclined to attach a profound significance to her delirium and perceive in it the diabolic revelation with which it had originally been fraught.

When after dinner Mère Gontran took a pack of cards and began to tell her fortune, Sylvia had a new impulse to dread; but she shook it off almost irritably and listened to the tale.

'A long journey by land. A long journey by sea. A dark man. A fair woman. A fair man. A dark woman. A letter.'

The familiar rigmarole of a hundred such tellings droned its course accompanied by the flip-flap, flip-flap of the cards. The information was general enough for any human being on earth to have extracted from it something applicable to himself; yet against her will, and as it were bewitched by the teller's solemnity, Sylvia began to endow the cards with the personalities that might affect her life. The King of Hearts lost his rubicund complacency and took on the lineaments of Arthur: the King of Clubs parted with his fierceness and assumed the graceful severity of Michael Fane: with a kind of impassioned egotism Sylvia watched the journeyings of the Queen of Hearts, noting the contacts and biting her lips when she found her prototype associated with unfavourable cards.

'Come, I don't think the outlook's so bad,' said Mère Gontran at the end of the final disposition. 'If your bed's a bit doubtful, your street and your house are both very good, and your road lies south. But there again, this blessed war upsets everything, and even the cards must be read with half an eye on the war.'

When the cards had been put away, Mère Gontran produced the *planchette* and set it upon a small table covered in red baize round the binding of which hung numerous little woollen pompons.

'Now we shall find out something about your friends in England,' she announced cheerfully.

Sylvia had not the heart to disappoint Mère Gontran, and she placed her hands upon the heart-shaped board, which trembled so much under Mère Gontran's eager touch that the pencil affixed made small squiggles upon the paper beneath. The *planchette* went on fidgeting more and more under their four hands like a restless animal trying to escape, and from time to time it would skate right across the paper leaving a long pencilled trail in its path, which Mère Gontran would examine with great intentness.

'It looks a little bit like a Y,' she would say.

'A very little bit,' Sylvia would think.

'Or it may be an A. Never mind. It always begins rather doubtfully. I *won't* lose my temper with it tonight.'

The *planchette* might have been a tenderly loved child learning to write for the first time by the way Mère Gontran encouraged it and tried to award a shape and purpose to its most amorphous tracks. When it had covered the sheet of paper with an impossibly complicated river-system, Mère Gontran fetched a clean sheet and told Sylvia severely that she must try not to urge the *planchette*. Any attempt at urging had a very bad effect on its willingness.

'I didn't think I was urging it,' Sylvia said humbly.

'Try and sit more still, dear. If you like, I'll put my feet on your toes and then you won't be so tempted to jig. We may have to sit all night, if we aren't careful.'

Sylvia strained every nerve to sit as still as possible in order to avoid having her toes imprisoned all night by Mère Gontran's feet, which were particularly large even for so tall a woman. She concentrated upon preventing her hands from leading the *planchette* to trace the course of any more rivers toward the sea of baize, and after sitting for twenty minutes like this she felt that all the rest of her body had gone into her hands. She had never thought that her hands were small, but she had certainly never realised that they were as large and as ugly as they were; as for Mère Gontran's, they had for some time lost any likeness to hands and lay upon the *planchette* like two uncooked chops. At last when Sylvia had reached the state of feeling like a large pincushion that was being rapidly pricked by thousands of pins, Mère Gontran murmured:

'It's going to start.'

Immediately afterwards the *planchette* careered across the paper and wrote a sentence.

'*Dicks picked a daisy*,' Mère Gontran read out. 'Drat the

41

thing! Never mind, we'll have one more try.'

Again a sentence was written and again it repeated that Dick had picked a daisy.

Suddenly Samuel the collie made an odd noise.

'He's going to speak through Samuel,' Mère Gontran declared. 'What is it, dear? Tell me what it is?'

The dog, who had probably been stung by a gnat, got up and putting his head upon his mistress's knee gazed forth ineffable sorrows.

'You heard him trying to talk?' she asked.

'He certainly made a noise,' Sylvia admitted.

There was a loud rap on the air – an unmistakable rap, for the five cats which had remained in the room all twitched their ears toward the sound.

'Gone for the night,' said Mère Gontran. 'And he's very angry about something. I suppose this daisy that Dick picked means something important to him, though we can't understand. Perhaps he'll come back later on when I've gone to bed and tell me more about it.'

'Mère Gontran,' said Sylvia earnestly. 'Do you really believe in spirits? Do you really think we can talk with the dead?'

'Of course I do. Listen! they're all round us. If you want to feel the dead, walk up the garden with me now. You'll feel the spirits whizzing round you like moths.'

'Oh, I wonder, I wonder if it's true,' Sylvia cried. 'I can't believe it, and yet . . .'

'Listen to me,' said Mère Gontran solemnly. 'Thirty-five years ago I left England to come to Petersburg. I was twenty years old and very beautiful. You can imagine how I was run after by men. You've seen something of the way men run after women here. Well, one summer I went with my family to Finland, and I foolishly arranged to meet Prince Paul in the forest after supper. He was a fine handsome young man as bold and as wicked as the devil himself. But there again, I haven't got to give details. Anyway he said to me, "What are you afraid of? Your parents?" I can hear his laugh now after all these years, and I remember the bough of a tree was just waving very slightly, and the moonlight kept glinting in and out of his eyes. I thought of my parents in England when he said this, and I remember challenging them in a sort of defiant way to interfere. You see I'd never got on well at home. I was a very wayward girl and they were exceptionally old-fashioned. And when Prince Paul held me in his arms I reproached them. It's difficult to explain, but

42

I was trying to conjure them up before me to see if the thought of home would have any effect. And then Prince Paul laughed and said "Or another lover?" Now with the exception of flirting with Prince Paul and Prince George, the two eldest sons, I'd never thought much about lovers. Even in those days I was more interested in animals really, and of course I was very fond of children. But when Prince Paul said "Or your lover?" I saw Gontran leaning against a tree in the forest. He was looking at me, and I pushed Prince Paul away and ran back towards the house.

'Now when this happened I'd never seen my husband. He was working at the Embassy even in those days, and never went to Finland in his life. The next day the family was called back to Petersburg on account of the death of the grandmother, and I met Gontran at some friends'! We were married about six months afterwards.

'So there again, if I could see Gontran when he was alive before I'd ever met him, you don't suppose I'm not going to believe that I've seen him any number of times since he was dead? Until quite recently when he reached this new plane, we talked together as comfortably as when he was still alive and sitting in that chair.'

Sylvia looked at the chair uneasily.

'It's only since he's met this Dick that the communications are so unsatisfactory. Why, of course I know what's happened,' cried Mère Gontran in a rapture of discovery. 'Why didn't I think of it sooner? It's the war!'

'The war?' Sylvia echoed.

'Aren't there thousands of spirits being set free every day? Just as all the communications on earth have broken down, in the same way they must have broken down with the spirits. Fancy my not having understood that before! Well, aren't I dense?'

Five raps of surpassing loudness signalled upon the air.

'Gontran's delighted,' she exclaimed. 'He was always delighted when I found out something for myself.'

Soon after this Mère Gontran, having gathered up from the crowded table a variety of implements that could not possibly serve any purpose that night, wandered out into the garden, followed by Samuel and the five cats; Sylvia thought of her haunted passage through the dark autumnal growth of leaves toward that strange room she occupied, and went upstairs to bed rather tremulously. Yet on the whole she was glad that Mère Gontran left her like this every night at the pension with the Tartar servant in her cupboard under the stairs, and with the three ungainly sons, who used to sleep in a barrack at the end of the long passage on the ground floor. Sylvia had peeped into this room when the young men were out and had been surprised by its want of resemblance to a sleeping-chamber. There were to be sure three beds, but they had the appearance of beds that had been long stowed away in a remote part of a warehouse for disused furniture: the whole room was like that, with nothing human appertaining to it save the smell of stale tobacco-smoke. Yet really now that the migratory guests had gone on their way it would have been even more surprising to find in the pension signs of humanity, so much had its permanent inhabitants, both animals and human beings, approximated to one another. The animals were a little more like human beings; the human beings were a little more like animals: the margin between men and animals was narrow enough in the most distinguishing circumstances, and at the pension these circumstances were lacking.

Before Sylvia undressed, she opened the window of her bedroom and looked down into the moonlit garden. Mère Gontran's light was already lit, but she was still wandering about outside with her cats. Eccentric though she was, Sylvia thought, she was nevertheless typical. Looking back at the people who had crossed her path, she could remember several adumbrations of Mère Gontran – superstitious women with a love of animals. Of such a kind had been Mrs Meares; and attached to every cabaret and theatre there had always been an elderly woman who had served as commission agent to the careless artistes, whether it was a question of selling themselves to a new lover or buying somebody else's old dress. These elderly women had invariably had the knack of telling fortunes with the cards, had been able to interpret dreams and omens, and had always been the slaves of dogs and birds. The superficial ascription of their passion for animals would have been to a stifled or sterile maternity; but as with Mère Gontran and her three sons Sylvia could recall that many of these elderly women had been the prey of their children. If one went back beyond one's actual experience of this type, it was significant that the witches of olden times were always credited with the possession of familiar spirits in the shape of animals; she could recollect no history of a witch that did not include her black cat. Was that too a stifled maternal instinct, or would it not be truer to find in the magic arts they

44

practised nothing but a descent from human methods of intelligence to those of animals, a descent (if indeed it could be called a descent) from reason to instinct?

Here was Mère Gontran fulfilling in every particular the old conventional idea of a witch, and might not all this communion with spirits be nothing but the communion of an animal with scents and sounds imperceptible to civilised man? It could be a kind of atavism really, a return to disused senses, so long obsolete that their revival had a supernatural effect. Sylvia thought of the unusual success that Mère Gontran always had with her gardening; no matter where she sowed in the great dark jungle she gathered better vegetables than a gardener, who would have wasted his energy in wrestling with the weeds that seemed to forbid any growth but their own. Mère Gontran always paid greater attention to the aspects of the moon and the planets than to the laws of horticulture, and her gardening gave the impression of being nothing but a meaningless ritual: yet it was fruitful. Might there not be some laws of attraction of which in the course of dependence upon his own inventions man had lost sight, some laws of which animals were cognisant and by which many of the marvels of instinct might be explained? Beyond witches and their familiar spirits were fauns and centaurs, more primitive manifestations of the communion between men and animals, with whom even the outward shape was still a hybrid. Had scientists in pursuing the antics of molecules and atoms beneath the microscope become blind to the application of their theories? Might not astronomy have displaced astrology unjustly? Sylvia wished she had read more widely and more deeply that she might know if her speculations were after all nothing but the commonplaces of attraction, not least of all the mystery of love and the inscrutable caprices of fortune.

Behold Mère Gontran out there in the garden bobbing to the moon. Were all these gestures meaningless like an idiot's mutterings? And was even an idiot's muttering really meaningless? Behold Mère Gontran in the moonlit garden with cats: it would be hard to say that her behaviour was more futile than theirs; they were certainly enjoying themselves.

Sylvia was conscious of trying to arrive at an explanation of Mère Gontran that, while it allowed her behaviour a certain amount of reasonableness, would prevent herself from accepting Mère Gontran's own explanation of it. There was something distasteful, something cheap and vulgar, in the conception

45

of Gontran's spiritual existence as an infinite prolongation of his life upon earth; there was something radically fatuous in the imagination of him at the end of a ghostly telephone-wire still at the beck and call of human curiosity. If indeed in some mysterious way the essential Gontran was communicating with his wife, the translation of his will to communicate must be a subjective creation of hers; it was somehow ludicrous and even unpleasant to accept Dick's gathering of a daisy as a demonstration of the activity of mankind in another world, it was too much a finite conception altogether. Without hesitation Sylvia rejected spiritualism as a useful adventure for human intelligence. It was impossible to accept its more elaborate manifestations with bells and tambourines and materialising mediums, when one knew the universal instinct of mankind to lie; and in its simpler manifestations, as with Mère Gontran, where conscious or deliberate deceit was out of the question, it was merely a waste of time, being bound by the limitations of an individual soul that would always be abnormal and probably in most cases idiotic.

Sylvia pulled down the blind and, leaving Mère Gontran to her nocturnal contemplation, went to bed.

Notwithstanding her abrupt rejection of spiritualism, Sylvia found when she was in bed that the incidents of the evening and the accessories of the house were affecting her to sleeplessness. That succession of raps declined to come within the natural explanation that she had attempted. Were they due to some action of overcharged atmosphere, a kind of miniature thunderclap from the meeting of two so-called electrical currents generated by herself and Mère Gontran? Were they merely coincidental creakings of furniture in response to the warmth of the stove? Or had Mère Gontran mesmerised her into hearing raps that were never made? The cats had also heard them; but Mère Gontran's intimacy with her animals might well have established such a mental domination, even over them.

Naturally with so much of her attention fixed upon the raps downstairs Sylvia began to fancy renewed rappings all round her in the darkness, and not merely rappings but all sorts of nocturnal shufflings and scrapings and whisperings and scratchings, until she had to relight her candle. The noises became less, but optical delusions were substituted for tricks of hearing, and there was not a piece of furniture in the room that did not project from its outward form the sense of its

46

independent reality. The wardrobe for instance seemed to challenge her with the thought that it was no longer the receptacle of her skirts and petticoats: it seemed to be asserting its essential 'wardrobeishness' for being the receptacle for anything it liked. Sylvia set aside as too obviously and particularly silly the fancy that someone might be hidden in the wardrobe, but she could not get rid of the fancy that the piece of furniture had an existence outside her own consciousness. It was a mere Hans Andersen kind of fancy, but it took her back to remote childish apprehensions of inanimate objects, and after her meditation upon instinct she began to wonder whether after all the child was not quite right to be afraid of everything, which grown-ups called being afraid of nothing; and whether that escape from childish terrors which was called knowledge was nothing but a drug that blunted the perceptions and impeded the capacity for esteeming whatever approximated to truth. Yet why should a child be afraid of a wardrobe? Why should a child be afraid of everything? Because in everything there was evil. Sylvia recalled – and in this room is was impossible to rid herself of that diabolic obsession – that the Devil was known as the Father of Lies. Was not all evil anti-truth, and did not man with his preference for anti-truth create the material evil that was used as an argument against the Divine ordering of matter? Paradoxical as it might seem, the worse ordered the world appeared, the more did such an appearance of pessimism involve the existence of God. Whither led all this theosophistry? Toward the only perfect revelation of God in man: toward Jesus Christ.

How foolish it was to prefer to such divine speech the stammering of spiritualists. For the first time in her life Sylvia prayed deliberately that what she saw as in a glass darkly might be revealed to her more clearly; and while she prayed, there recurred from the hospital that whispered confession of the little English governess. It was impossible not to compare it with the story of Mère Gontran: the coincidence of the names and the similarity of the situation were too remarkable. Then why had Mère Gontran been granted what if her story were accepted was a supernatural intervention to save her soul? By her own admission she had practically surrendered to Prince Paul when she had the vision of her future husband. It seemed very unjust that Miss Savage should have been utterly corrupted and that Mère Gontran should have escaped corruption. Sylvia went back in her thoughts to the time when she left Philip and abandoned herself to evil. Yet she had never really abandoned

47

herself to evil, for she had never had any will to sin; the impulse had been to save her soul, not to lose it. It had been an humiliation of her body like pain, and a degradation of her personality like death. Pride which had cast her out had been her undoing. Looking back now she could see that everything evil in her life had come from her pride: pride by the way was another attribute of the Devil.

Sylvia had a longing to go back to England and talk to the Vicar of Green Lanes. From the past kept recurring isolated fragments of his sermons, texts mostly, which had lain all this while dormant within her consciousness, until the first one had sprung up to flower amid her delirium. In all her reading she had never paid proper attention to the doctrines of Christianity, and she longed to know if some of these dim facts after which she was now groping were not there set forth with transparent brightness and undeniable clarity. Good or evil must present themselves to every soul in a different way, and it was surely improbable that the accumulated experience of the human mind gathered together in Christian writings would not contain a parallel by which she might be led toward the truth, or at least be granted the vision of another lonely soul seeking for itself salvation.

The sense of her loneliness, physical, spiritual, and intellectual overwhelmed Sylvia's aspirations. How could truth or faith or hope or love concern her until she could escape from this isolation? She had always been lonely, even before she came to Russia; yet it had always been possible up to a point to cheat herself with the illusion of company, because the loneliness had been spiritual and intellectual, a loneliness that would be immanent in any woman whose life was ordered on her lines and who had failed to find what was vulgarly called the 'right man.' Now there was added to this the positive physical loneliness of her present position. It would have been bad enough to recover from an illness and wake in a familiar world; but to wake like this in a world transformed by war was indeed like waking in Hell. The remembrance of England, of people like Jack and Olive, was scarcely more distinct now than the remembrance of Lille; everything in her past had receded to the same immeasurable distance. News of England in any familiar form now reached Russia by such devious ways that in a period of violent daily events the papers had, when they did arrive, the air of some ancient, bloody, and fantastic chronicle. No letters came, because nobody could know where she was; her friends must think that she was dead, and must have accepted her death as the death of a sparrow amid the slaughter that was now proceeding. Tomorrow she should send a cablegram, which might some day arrive, to say that she was alive and well. And then she had a revulsion from such a piece of egotism in the midst of a world's catastrophe. Who could wish to be reminded of Sylvia Scarlett at such a moment? Besides, if this determination of hers to begin her life over again was to be made effective, Sylvia Scarlett must preserve this isolation and accept it as the grace of God. How what had once been phrases were now endowed with life! Any communication between her and the people she had known would be like communication between Gontran and his wife; it would be the stammering of spiritualism comparable with that absurd Dick gathering his daisies in the Elysian fields. Unless all these 'soul-spasms,' as once she would have called them, were the weakness of a woman who had been sick unto death, meaningless babblings without significance, her way would be indicated. Whatever the logicians might say, it was useless to expect faith, hope, or love unless one went to meet them: the will to receive them must outweigh the suspicion of receiving. Faith like any other gift-horse must not be looked in the mouth; pride had robbed her long enough, and for a change she would try humility.

When she made this decision, it seemed to Sylvia that what had formerly been evil and terrifying in the inanimate objects of her candle-lit room now lost their menacing aspect and wished her well. Suddenly she accused herself of the most outrageous pride in having all this time thought of nothing but herself, whose misery amid the universal havoc was indeed only the twittering of a sparrow. An apocalypse of the world's despair blazed upon her. This was not the time to lament her position, but rather to be glad very humbly that at the moment when she had been given this revelation of her pride, this return of herself, she was given also the moment to put the restored self to the test of action.

When Sylvia woke in the morning, her ideas that during the night had stated themselves with such convincing logic seemed less convincing; the first elation had been succeeded by the discouragement of the artist at seeing how ill his execution supports his intention. Riddles had solved themselves one after another with such ease in the darkness, that when she had fallen asleep she had been musing with astonishment at the failure of human nature to appreciate the simplicity of life's intention;

now all those darkling raptures burned like a sickly fire in the sunlight. Yet it was consoling to remember that the sun did not really put out the fire, and therefore that the fire kindled within herself last night might burn not less brightly and warmly for all its appearance of being extinguished by the sun of action.

These fiery metaphors were ill-suited to the new day, which was wet enough to make Sylvia wonder if there had ever been so completely wet a day. The view from her window included a large piece of sky which lacked even thunder-clouds or wind to break its leaden monotony. The vegetation of the garden had assumed a universal hue of dull green, the depressing effect of which was intensified by the absence of any large trees to mark autumnal decay with their more precocious dissolution. Weather did not seem to affect Mère Gontran, whose clothes even upon the finest days had the appearance of a bundle of drenched rags; and if the dogs and cats preferred to remain indoors, she was able to paddle about the garden with her ducks and devote to their triumphant quacking a sympathetic attention.

'I'm going to see the Ambassador this morning,' she called up to Sylvia. 'Something must be decided about the boys' nationality and it's bound to be decided more quickly if they see me dripping all over the marble entrance of the Embassy.'

Not even the sight of that elderly Naiad haunting the desks of overworked *chanceliers* could secure a determination to which country her sons' military service was owed; it seemed as if they would remain unclassified to the end of the war, borrowing money for tram-tickets and smoking cigarettes while husbands were torn from the arms of wives, while lovers and parents mourned eternal partings.

Autumn drew on, and here in Russia hard upon its heels was winter; already early in October there was talk at the pension of the snow's coming soon, and Sylvia did not feel inclined to stay here in the solitude that snow would create. Moreover, she was anxious not to let Mère Gontran wish for her going on account of the expense, and she would not have stayed as long as she had, if her hostess had not been so obviously distressed at the idea of her leaving before she could be accounted perfectly well again. In order to repay her hospitality, Sylvia assisted gravely – and one might say reverently – at all her follies of magic. Nor under the influence of Mère Gontran's earnestness was it always possible to be sure about the foolish side. There were often moments when Sylvia was frightened in these fast-closing daylights and long wintry eves by the unending provocation of the dead that was as near as Mère Gontran got to evocation; although she claimed to be always seeing apparitions, of which Sylvia fortunately for her nerves was never granted a vision.

The climax was reached on the night of the first snowfall soon after the middle of October, when Mère Gontran came to Sylvia's bedroom, her crimson dressing-gown dusted with dry flakes of snow, and begged her to come out in the garden to hear Gontran communicating with her from a lilac-bush. It was in vain that Sylvia protested against being dragged out of bed on such a cold night; Mère Gontran candle in hand towered up above her with such a dominating excitement that Sylvia let herself be overpersuaded and followed her out into the garden. From what had formerly been Carrier's room the owls hooted at the moon; Samuel the talking collie was baying dolefully; the snowfall, too light to give the nocturnal landscape a pure and crystalline beauty, was enough to destroy the familiar aspect of the scene and to infect it with a withered papery look, turning house and garden to the colour of dry bones.

'He's in the lilac-bush by the outhouse,' Mère Gontran whispered. 'When I went past, one of the boughs caught hold of my hand, and he spoke in a queer crackling voice, as of course somebody would speak if he were speaking through a bush.'

Sylvia could not bear it any longer; she suddenly turned back and ran up to her bedroom, vowing that tomorrow she would make a serious effort to leave Petrograd.

'However short my hair,' she laughed, 'there's no reason why it should be made to stand on end like that.'

She supposed that Petrograd had not sufficiently recovered from the shock of war to make an engagement there pleasant or profitable; besides, after her experience at the cabaret she was disinclined to face another humiliation of the same kind. The Jewish agent whom she consulted suggested Kieff, Odessa, and Constantinople as a good tour; from Constantinople, she would be able to return home more easily and comfortably if she wished to return. He held up his hands at the idea of travelling to England by Archangel at this season. She could sing for a week at Kieff just to break the journey, take two months at Odessa, and be almost sure of at least four months at Constantinople: it was a great nuisance this war, but he was expecting every day to hear that the English fleet had blown Pola to pieces, and perhaps after Christmas there would be an opportunity of an engagement at Vienna. With so many troops in the city such an engagement would be highly remunerative; and he winked at Sylvia. She was surprised to find that it was so easy to secure an engagement in war-time and still more surprised to learn that she would be better paid than before the war. Indeed if she had been willing to remain in Petrograd, she could have earned as much as a thousand francs a month for singing, so many of the French girls had fled to France and so rare now were foreign artistes. As it was, she would be paid eight hundred francs a month at Kieff and Odessa. For the amount of her salary in Constantinople the agent would not answer, because on second thoughts he might observe that there was just a chance of war between Russia and Turkey, a very small chance; but in the circumstances it would be impossible to arrange a contract.

Sylvia returned to the pension to announce her success.

'Well, if you get ill,' said Mère Gontran, 'mind you come back here at once. You're *not* a good medium; in fact I believe you're a deterrent; but I like to see you about the place, and of course I *do* talk English, but there again, when shall I ever see England?'

When Sylvia had heard Mère Gontran speak of her native country formerly, it had always been as the place where an unhappy childhood had been spent, and she had seemed to glory in her expatriation. Mère Gontran answered her unspoken astonishment:

'I think it's the war,' she explained. 'It's seeing so much about England in the newspapers; I've got a feeling I'd like to go back, and I will go back after the war,' she proclaimed. 'Some kind of nationality my three sons shall have, if it's only their mother's. Which reminds me. Poor Carrier has been killed.'

'Killed,' Sylvia repeated. 'Already?'

In the clutch of apprehension she knew that other and dearer friends than he might already be dead.

'I thought we could celebrate your last night by trying to get into communication with him,' said Mère Gontran.

It was as if she had replied to Sylvia's unvoiced fear.

'No, no,' she cried. 'If they are dead, I don't want to know.'

So Carrier with all his mascots had fallen at last, and he would never cultivate that little farm in the Lyonnais; she remembered how he had boasted of the view across the valley of the Saône to the long line of the Alps: far wider now was his view, and his room at the pension was the abode of owls. She read the paragraph in the French paper: he had been killed early in September very gloriously. If Paradise might be the eternal present of a well-beloved dream, he would have found his farm; if human wishes were not vanity, he was at peace.

The brief snow had melted, and through a drenching afternoon of rain Sylvia packed up; it was pleasant to think that at any rate she should travel southward, for the pension was unbearable on these winter days and long nights filled with a sound of shadows. Again Sylvia was minded to brave the journey north and return to England, but again an overmastering impulse forbade her. Her destiny was written otherwise, and if she fought against the impulse not to go back, she felt that she should be cast up and rejected by the sea of life.

Mère Gontran having caught a slight chill went to bed immediately after dinner, and invited Sylvia to come and talk to her on her last evening. It was an odd place, this bedroom that she had chosen; and very odd she looked lying in the old four-poster, her head tied up in a bandana scarf and beside her with his wrinkled head on the pillow, James the bulldog. The four-poster seemed out of place against the matchboarding with which the room was lined, and the rest of the furniture gave one the impression of having been ransacked by burglars in a great hurry. On the wall opposite the bed was a portrait of Gontran, which by sheer bad painting possessed a sinister power like that of some black Byzantine Virgin; on either side of him were hung the cats' boxes from which they surveyed their mistress with the same fixed stare as her painted husband.

'Of course I should go mad if I slept in this room all by myself, and two hundred yards away from any habitation,' Sylvia exclaimed.

'Oh, I'm very fond of my room,' said Mère Gontran. 'But there again, I like to be alone with one foot in the grave.'

'I want to thank you for all your kindness,' Sylvia began.

'If you start thanking me, you'll make me fidget; and if I fidget, it worries James.'

'Still even at the risk of upsetting James, I must tell you that I don't know what I should have done without you these six weeks. Perhaps one day when the war is over you'll come to England and then you'll have to stay with me in my cottage.'

'Ah, I shall never be able to leave the cats, not to mention the pony. I just happened to have a fancy for England today, but it's too late; I'm established here; I'm known. People in England might stare, and I should dislike that very much.'

Sylvia wanted rather to talk again about spiritualism in order
to find out if Mère Gontran's speculations coincided at any
point with her own; but a discussion of spiritual experience
with her was like a discussion of the liver; she was almost
grossly insistent upon the organic machinery, almost brutal in
her zest for the practical, one might almost say the technical
details. The mysteries of human conduct on earth left her
utterly uninterested except when she could obtain a commentary upon them from the spirits for a practical purpose;
the spirits took the place for her of the solicitor and the doctor
rather than of the priest. Systems of philosophy and religion had
no meaning for Mère Gontran; her spiritual advice never concerned itself with them; and the ultimate intention of immortality was as well concealed from her as the justification of
life on earth. It was this very absence of the high-falutin'
which impressed Sylvia with the genuineness of the manifestations that she procured, but which at the time discouraged her
with the sense that death merely substituted one irrational
form of being for another.

'What's it all for?' Sylvia had once asked.

'For?' Mère Gontran had repeated in perplexity: she had
never considered the utility of this question hitherto.

'Yes, why for instance did you marry Gontran? Did you love
him? Are your children destined to fulfil any part in the world?
And *their* children after them?'

'Why do you want to worry your head with such questions?'
Mère Gontran had asked compassionately.

'But you deny me the consolation of oblivion. You accept
this endless existence after death with its apparently meaningless prolongation of human vapidity and pettiness, and you're
surprised that I resent it.'

But it was impossible to carry on the discussion with somebody who was as contented with what is as an animal and whose
only prayer was *Give us this day our daily bread*. It was a dis-
appointing contribution to the problem of life from one who
had spent so long on the borderland of the grave. Yet it was
Mère Gontran's devotion to this aspiration that had made her
lodge Sylvia all these weeks.

'How can you who are so kind, want to see your sons go to
the war not for any motives of honour or patriotism, but apparently just to keep them away from cigarettes and idleness?
What does their nationality really matter?'

'They must do something for themselves,' Mère Gontran replied. 'Just at the moment the war offers a good opening.'

'But suppose they are killed?'

'I hope they will be. I shall be on much better terms with them than I am now. Gontran talks to me in English nowadays; so would they, and we might get to know one another. Cats don't worry about their kittens, after they're grown up; in fact they're anxious to get rid of them. And kingfishers chase their young ones away, or so I was informed by an English ventriloquist who was interested in natural history.'

'Well, I always congratulated myself on being free from sentimentality,' Sylvia said. 'But beside you I'm like a keepsake-album.'

'If you'd get out of the habit of thinking that death is of any more importance than going to sleep, you wouldn't bother about anything,' Mère Gontran declared.

'Oh, it isn't death that worries me,' Sylvia answered. 'It's life.'

Very early in the twilight of a wet dawn Sylvia started for Kieff. All day she watched the raindrops trickling down the windows of the railway carriage and wondered if her impulse to travel south was inspired by any profounder reason.

Chapter III

On the day after she reached Kieff, Sylvia went for a walk by herself. Since she was going to stay only a week in this city and since she still felt somewhat remote from the world after her long seclusion, she had not bothered to make friends with any of her fellow artistes. Presently she grew tired to walking alone and, looking about her, she saw on the other side of the road a cinema theatre, where she decided to spend the rest of a dreary afternoon. She was surprised to find that the lowest charge for entrance was two roubles; but when she went inside and saw the film, she understood the reason. The theatre was full of men, and she could hear them whispering to one another their astonishment at seeing a woman enter the place; she was thankful that the dim red light concealed her blushes, and she escaped as quickly as possible, quenching the impulse to abuse the door-keeper for not warning her what kind of an entertainment was taking place inside.

This abrupt and violent reminder of human beastliness shocked Sylvia very deeply at a moment when she was trying to induce in herself an attitude of humility; it was impossible not to feel angrily superior to those swine grovelling in their mess. Ordinarily she might have obliterated the incident with disdain, or at any rate have seen its proportion to the whole of human life. But now with war closing upon the world, and with all the will she had to idealise the abnegation of the individual that was begotten from the monstrous crime of the mass, it was terrible to be brought up sharply like this by the unending and apparently unassailable rampart of human vileness. It seemed to her that the shame she had felt on finding herself inside that place must even now be marked upon her countenance, and there was not a passer-by whose criticism and curiosity she could keep from fancying intently directed towards herself. Anxious to elude the sensation of this commentary upon her action, she turned aside from the pavement to stare into the first shop-window that presented itself, until her blushes had burnt themselves out. The shop she chose happened to be a jeweller's, and Sylvia who never cared much for precious stones was now less than ever moved by any interest in the barbaric display that winked and glittered under the artificial stimulus of shaded electric lamps. She tried to see if she could somehow catch the reflection of her cheeks and ascertain if indeed they were flaming as high as she sup-posed. Presently a voice addressed her from behind, and looking round she saw a slim young soldier well over six feet tall with slanting almond eyes and wide nostrils. He pointed to a row of golden handbags set with various arrangements of precious stones and asked her in very bad French if she admired them. Sylvia's first impulse, when her attention was drawn to these bags for the first time, was to say that she thought them hideous; but a sympathetic intuition that the soldier admired them very much and would be hurt by her disapproval tempted her to agree with him in praising their beauty. He asked her which of them all she liked the best; and in order not to spoil this childish game of standing outside a shop-window and making imaginary purchases, she considered the row for a while and at last fixed upon one that was set with emeralds, the gold of which had a greenish tint. The soldier said that he preferred the one in the middle that was set with rubies, sapphires, diamonds and emeralds, which was obviously the most expensive and certainly the most barbaric of the whole collection. Was Sylvia sure that she had chosen the one she liked the best? She assured him that her choice was unalterable, and the soldier taking her arm bade her enter the shop with him.

'I can't afford to buy a bag,' Sylvia protested.

'I can,' he replied. 'I want to buy you the bag you want.'

'But it's impossible,' Sylvia argued. 'Even if I could give you anything in return, it would still be impossible. That bag would cost two thousand roubles at least.'

'I have three thousand roubles,' said the soldier. 'Of what use are they to me? Tonight I go to the front. You like the bag. I like to give it to you. Come. Do not let us argue in the street like this. We will buy the bag, and afterwards we will have tea together, and then I shall go my way and you will go your way. It is better that I spend two thousand roubles on buying you a bag that you want than to gamble them away. You are French. It is necessary that I do something for you.'

'I'm English,' Sylvia corrected. 'Half English – half French.'

'So much the better,' the soldier said. 'I have never met an Englishwoman. None of the soldiers in my company have met an Englishwoman. When I tell them that in Kieff I met an Englishwoman and gave her a golden bag, they will envy me my good fortune. Are we not suffering all of us together? And is that not a reason why I should give you something that you very much want?'

'Why do you think I am suffering?' she asked.

'There is sorrow in your eyes,' the soldier answered gravely.

The simplicity of the man overcame her scruples; she felt that her acceptance of his gift would give him a profound pleasure of which for a motive of petty pride she had no right to rob him. As for herself the meeting with this young soldier had washed away like purest water every stain with which Russia had marked her – from the brutality of the drunken officer to the vileness of that cinema theatre. Sylvia hesitated no longer; she accompanied him into the shop and came out again with the golden bag upon her wrist. Then they went into a confectioner's shop and ate cakes together; outside in the darkness sleet was falling, but in her mood of elation Sylvia thought that everything was beautiful.

'It is time for me to go back to the barracks,' the soldier announced at last.

While they were having tea, Sylvia had told him of many

events in her life, and he had listened most seriously, though she doubted if he were able to understand half of what she told him. He in his turn had not told her much; but he was still very young, only twenty-one, and he explained that in his village not much could have happened to him. Soon after war was declared his father had died, and having no brothers or sisters or mother, he had sold all he had and quitted his village with 35000 roubles in his pocket. Five hundred roubles he had spent riotously and without satisfaction; and he still rejoiced in the money he had spent on the bag and was even anxious to give Sylvia the thousand roubles that were left, but she begged him to keep them.

'And so you must really go?' she said.

She walked with him through the darkness and sleet towards the barracks; soon there was a sound of bugles, and he exclaimed that he must hurry.

'Good-bye,' Sylvia said. 'I shall never forget this meeting.'

She stood on tiptoe, and putting her arm round his neck pulled him towards her and kissed him.

'Good-bye. May you be fortunate and happy,' she repeated.

'It rests with God,' said the soldier; and he vanished into the noise of bugles and the confusion of a regimental muster.

The memory of this casual encounter rested in Sylvia's heart with all the warmth it had originally kindled; nay rather it rested there with a warmth that increased as time went on, and the golden bag came to be regarded with that most essential and sacred affection which may be bestowed upon a relic of childhood, an affection that is not sentimental or comparable in any way to the emotions aroused by the souvenirs of an old love. The bag possessed indeed the recreative quality of art; it was emotion remembered in tranquillity, and as such fiercely cherished by its owner. It was a true mascot, a monstrance of human love; for Sylvia it had a sacramental, almost a Divine significance.

From Kieff much heartened by the omen of fortune's favour Sylvia travelled gladly towards Odessa through leagues of monotonous country shrouded in mist and rain, which seen thus by an unfamiliar visitant was of such surpassing gloom that the notion of war acquired in contrast an adventurous cheerfulness. Often at railway stations that appeared to exist along the track without any human reason for existence Sylvia used to alight with the rest of the passengers and drink glasses of tea sweetened by spoonfuls of rasperry jam; in a luxury of despair she would imagine herself left behind by the train and be sometimes half tempted to make the experiment in order to see how life would adapt itself to such eccentricity. The only diversion upon this endless journey was when the train stopped before crossing a bridge to let soldiers with fixed bayonets mount it and stand in the corridors that they might prevent any traveller from leaving his seat or even from looking out of the window. These precautions against outrages with dynamite affected her at first with a sense of great events happening beyond these mournful steppes; but when she saw that the bayonets were so long that in any scuffle they would have been unmanageable, she had a revulsion from romantic fancies and told herself a little scornfully what children men were and how much playing at war went on behind the bloody scenes of action.

Sylvia reached Odessa on October 28, and the long front looking towards a leaden sea held a thought of England in its salt rain. The cabaret at which she was going to work was like all other cabarets, but being situated in some gardens that opened on the sea it had now a sad and wintry appearance of disuse. A few draggled shrubs, a few chairs not worth the trouble of putting into shelter, a deserted bandstand and open-air theatre served to forbid rather than invite gaiety. However, since the cabaret itself could be reached from a street behind the sea-front and visitors were not compelled to pass through the ghosts of a dead summer, this melancholy atmosphere was obviated. The *pension d'artistes* at which Sylvia stayed was kept by a certain Madame Eliane, a woman of personality and charm with a clear-cut rosy face and snow-white hair who limped slightly and supported herself upon two ebony canes. Madame Eliane objected to being called Mère, which would have been the usual prefix of ironical affection awarded to the owner of such a pension; although she must have been nearly sixty, she had an intense hatred of age and a remarkable faculty for remaining young without losing her dignity. For all the girls under her roof she felt a genuine affection that demanded nothing in return except the acceptance of herself as a contemporary, the first token of which was to call her Eliane; from the men she always exacted Madame. Her nationality was believed to have originally been Austrian, but she had become naturalised as a Russian many years before the war, when she was the mistress of an official who had endowed her with the *pension* before he departed to a remote Baltic province and the respectability of marriage. Sylvia found that Eliane was regarded by all the girls as an illustration of the most perfect success to which anyone of their profession might aspire.

'She's lucky,' said a small cockney called Ruby Arnold, who sang in English popular songs of four years ago that when Sylvia first heard them shocked her with their violent resuscitation of the past. 'Yes, I reckon she's lucky,' Ruby went on. 'There isn't no one that doesn't respect her as you might say. Isn't she cunning too to let her hair go white instead of keeping it gold like what it was once? Anybody can't help talking to anybody with white hair. I reckon with white hair and a house of my own I'd chuck up this life tomorrow, *I* would. *N'est-ce pas que j'ai raison?*' she added in French with a more brutal disregard of pronunciation than Sylvia had ever heard.

'*Oui, petite, tu as raison,*' agreed Odette, a vast French blonde with brilliant prominent eyes, those bulging myopic eyes that are generally the mirrors of vanity and hysteria. 'I have a friend here,' she continued in French, '*une femme du monde avec des idées très larges,* who assured me that if she did not know what Eliane was, she might easily have mistaken her for a *femme du monde* like herself.'

'She and her lady friends,' Ruby muttered contemptuously to Sylvia. 'If you ask me, these French girls don't know a lady when they see one. She had the nerve to bring her in here to tea one day, an old crow with a bonnet that looked as if a dog had worried it. She's bound to ask you to meet her. She can't talk of anything else since she met her in a tram.'

'Well, how's the war getting on? What do they say about it now?' asked a dancer called Flora, flashing a malicious glance at her partner, a young Belgian of about twenty-five with a pale and unpleasantly debauched face, who glared angrily in response. 'Armand cannot suffer us to talk about the war,' she explained to Sylvia.

'She hates him,' Ruby whispered. 'And whenever she can, she gets in a dig because he hasn't tried to fight for his country. Funny thing for two people to live together for three years and hate each other like they do.'

Sylvia said that she had no more information about the war than they had in Odessa, and there followed groans from all the artistes gathered together over coffee for the havoc which the war had brought in their profession.

'I was always *anti-militariste,*' Armand proclaimed, 'even before the war. Why, once in France I was arrested for singing a song that made fun of the army. It's a fine thing to talk about valour and glory and *la patrie* when you're *du premier grade,* but when you're not – ' he shook his fist at a world of generals.

'*Enfin,* Belgium no longer exists. And who first thought of stopping the Germans? The king! Does he have to dance for a living? *Ah, non alors!* She is always talking about the war,' he went on looking at Flora. 'But if I applied for a passport to go back, she'd be the first to make a row.'

'*Menteur!*' Flora snapped. '*Je m'en fiche.*'

'*Alors, ce soir je n'irai pas au cabaret.*'

'*Tant mieux! Qu'est-ce que ça peut me ficher? Bon dieu!*'

'*Alors, nous verrons, ma gosse.*'

'*Insoumis!*' she spat forth. '*comme t'es lâche.*'

'They always carry on like that,' Ruby whispered. 'But they'll be dancing together tonight just the same as usual.'

When Sylvia came down from the dressing-room for her turn she found that Ruby had prophesied truly. Armand and Flora were dancing together on the stage, but though their lips were smiling the eyes of both were sullen and hateful. The performance at the Cabaret de l'Aube could not be said to differ in any particular from that of any other cabaret. Sylvia when she was brought face to face with such evidences of international bad taste wondered how the world had ever gone to war. All over Europe people slept in the same kind of wagon-lits (though here in Russia with a broad gauge they slept more comfortably), ate the same kind of food in the same kind of hotel, clapped the same mediocre artistes, and drank the same sweet champagne: yet they could talk about the individuality of nations. How remote war seemed here in Odessa: it was perhaps wrong of her to escape from it like this, and she pondered the detached point of view of Armand. Had she the right to despise his point of view? Did she not herself merit equal contempt?

'I'm too comfortable,' she decided, 'while there is so much misery in the distance.'

However comfortable Sylvia felt when at a quarter-past three she let herself into the Pension Eliane, she felt extremely uncomfortable about an hour later, when the sound of an explosion and the crash of falling glass made those inmates of the pension who were still gossiping downstairs in the dining-room drop their cigarettes and stare at one another in astonishment.

'Whatever's that?' Ruby cried.

'It must be the gas,' said Armand, who could not turn paler than he was, but whose lips trembled.

Another crash followed; outside in the street rose a moan of frightened voices and the clatter of frightened feet.

Two more explosions still nearer drove everybody that was in the pension out of doors, and when it became certain that war-ships were bombarding Odessa there was a rush to join the inhabitants who were fleeing to what they supposed was greater safety in the heart of the town. In vain Sylvia protested that if the town was really being bombarded, they were just as safe in a pension near the sea-front as anywhere else; the mere idea of propinquity to the sea set everybody running faster than ever away from it. She could hear now the shells whinnying like nervous horses, and with every crash she kept saying to herself in a foolish way:

'Well, at any rate there's no more danger from that one.'

At first in the rush of panic she had not observed any particular incident; but now as shell after shell exploded without any visible sign of damage she began to look with interest at non-combatant humanity in the presence of danger. She did not know whether to be glad or sorry that on the whole the men behaved worse than the women; she put this observation on one side to be argued out later with Armand, who had certainly run faster than anyone else in the pension. The number of the shells was already getting less; yet there were no signs of the populace's recovery. Fear was begetting fear with such rapidity that to stand still and listen to the moans and groans of the uninjured was awe-inspiring. In one doorway a distraught man with nothing on but a shirt and slippers was dancing about with a lighted candle, evidently in a quandary of terror whether to join the onflowing mob or to stay where he was. An explosion quite close made up his mind, and he dived down the steps into the street where the candle was immediately extinguished; nevertheless he continued to hold it as if it were still alight while he ran with the crowd. In another doorway stood a woman confronted with a triple problem. Wearing nothing but a wrapper and carrying in her arms a pet dog, she was trying at the same time to keep her wrapper fastened, to avoid letting the dog drop, and to shut the door behind her. The problem was a nice one: she could either keep her wrapper fastened, maintain the dog, and leave the door open, in which case she would lose her silver; or she could keep her wrapper close, shut the door, and drop the dog, in which case she would lose the dog; or she could keep the dog, shut the door, and let go of her wrapper, in which case she would lose her modesty. Sylvia's anxiety to see how she would solve the problem made her forget all about the shells; and it was only when the perplexed lady in a last desperate attempt slammed the door, so that her wrapper came flying open and the dog went

62

bolting down the street that Sylvia realised the bombardment was over. She turned back toward the pension with a last look over her shoulder at the lady, who was vanishing into the darkness, gathering the wrapper round her nakedness as she ran and calling wildly to her pet.

Next day the military and civil population set out to find who could possibly have told the Turkish destroyers that such a place as Odessa existed. Armand, the Belgian dancer, was particularly loud on the subject of spies; Sylvia suspected it was he who had suggested to the police that Madame Eliane as a reputed Austrian should be severely examined with a view to finding out if the signals of which all were talking could be traced to her windows. If he did inform the police, his meanness recoiled upon his own head, for the examination of Madame Eliane was succeeded by an examination of all her guests, in the course of which Armand's passport was found to be slightly irregular, and he was nearly expelled to Roumania in consequence. The authorities made up their minds that no Turkish destroyer should ever again discover the whereabouts of their town, and the most stringent ordinances against showing lights were promulgated; but a more important result of the declaration of war by Turkey than the lighting of Odessa was its interference with the future plans of the mountebanks at the Cabaret de l'Aube. There was not one of them who had not intended to proceed from here to Constantinople, a much more profitable winter engagement than this Black Sea port.

'C'est assommant,' Armand declared. 'Zut! On ne peut pas rester ici tout l'hiver. On crèvera.'

'But at any rate one should be thankful that one was not hit by an obus,' said Odette. 'I nearly died of fright.'

'It wasn't the fault of the Turks that we weren't hit,' Armand grumbled. 'They did their best.'

'Luckily the shells didn't travel so fast as you,' Sylvia put in.

Flora laughed at this; but when everybody began to tease Armand about his cowardice she got angry, and invited any girl present to produce a man that would have behaved differently.

At last the flotsam that had been stirred up by the alarm of the bombardment drifted together again and stayed idly in what was after all still a backwater to the general European unrest. The manager of the cabaret was glad enough to keep his company together for as long as they would stay. It was getting more difficult all the time to import new attractions; and since as much money was being made out of human misery in

63

Odessa as everywhere else, the champagne flowed not much less freely because since the Imperial edict some bribery of the police was required in order to procure it. Sylvia was puzzled to find what was fate's intention in thus keeping her from moving farther south: it seemed a tame end to all her expectation to be stranded here, lost to everything except the petty life of her fellow players. However, she sang her songs every night; somehow her personality attracted the frequenters of the cabaret, and when after a month she informed the manager that she must leave and go north again, he begged her to stay at any rate for another two months – after that he would arrange for her to travel north and sing at Kieff, Warsaw, and Petrograd, whence she could make her way back to England.

'Or you might go to Siberia,' he suggested.

'Siberia?' she echoed.

That anyone should propose a tour in Siberia seemed a joke at first; when Sylvia found the suggestion was serious, she plunged back with a shiver into the warmer backwater of Odessa. Deciding that with a comfortable pension, a friendly management, and an appreciative audience, it would be foolish to risk her health by moving about too much, she settled down to read Russian novels and study the characters of her associates.

'You are a funny girl,' Ruby said. 'Don't you care about fellows?'

'Why should I?' Sylvia countered.

'Oh, I don't know. It seems more natural somehow. I left home over a fellow and went with a musical comedy to Paris. That's how I started touring the continong. Funny you and I should meet like this in Odessa.'

'Why?'

'Well, I don't know. We're both English. Talk about the World's End, Chelsea! I wonder what they'd call this? Do you know, Sylvia, I sometimes say to myself – supposing if I was to go back to England and find it didn't really exist any more? I'm a funny girl. I think a lot when I'm by myself, which isn't often, thank god, or I should get the willies worse than what I do. I don't know: when I look round and see that I'm in Odessa, I can't somehow believe that there's such a place as London. Do you know, sometimes I'd go mad to hear a bus-driver call out to a cabbie, "You bloody – , where the – hell do you think you're shoving yerself!" Well, after seven years without seeing England, anyone does get funny fancies.'

'There aren't any cab-drivers now,' Sylvia said.

'I suppose that's a fact. Taxis were only just beginning to bob up when I went away. Oh well, I reckon the language is still just as choice. But I would love to hear it. Of course I might hear you swear in the dressing-room over your corsets or anything, but it's the tone of voice I hanker after. Oh well, it'll all come out in the wash, and I don't suppose they notice the war much in England. Still I hope the squareheads won't blow London to pieces. I once did a tour in Germany, and a fellow with a moustache like a flying trapeze wanted to sleep with me for ten marks. They've got nerve enough for anything. What's this word "boche"? I suppose it's French for rubbish.' She began to sing softly:

> 'Take me back to London Town,
> London town, London town!
> That's where I want to be,
> Where the folks are kind to me.
> Trafalgar Square, oh, ain't it grand?
> Oxford Street, the dear old Strand!
> Anywhere, anywhere, I don't care . . .'

Oh god, it gives anyone the hump to think about it. Fancy England at war. Wonders will never cease. I reckon my brother Alf's well in it. He was never happy without he was fighting somebody.'

It was curious, thought Sylvia that evening, as she watched Ruby Arnold singing her four-year-old songs, how even to that cynical rat-faced little Cockney in her red velvet baby's frock the thought of England at war should bring such a violent longing for home. She tried to become intimate with Ruby; but after that single unfolding of secret aspirations and regrets, she drew away from Sylvia, who asked the reason of her sudden reserve.

'It's not that I don't like you,' Ruby explained. 'I reckon no girl could want a better pal than you if she was your sort. Only I'm not. I like fellows. You don't. Besides, you're different. I won't say you're a lady, because when all's said and done we're both of us working girls. But I don't know. Perhaps it's because you're older than me, only somehow you make me feel fidgety. That's flat, as the cook said to the pancake; but you asked me why I was a bit stand-offish and I've got to speak the truth to girls. I should go barmy otherwise with all the lies I tell to men. I reckon you'd get on better with Odette and her fam dee mond.'

Sylvia was vexed by her inability to bridge the gulf between herself and Ruby; it never occurred to her that the fault lay with anyone but herself, and she felt humiliated by this failure that was so crushing to her will to love; it seemed absurd that in a few minutes she should have been able to get so much nearer the heart of that Russian soldier who accosted her in Kieff than to one of her own countrywomen.

'Perhaps I've learnt how to receive good will,' she told herself, 'but not yet how to offer it.'

It was merely to amuse herself that Sylvia approached Odette for an introduction to her famous *femme du monde*. The suggestion, while it gratified Odette's sense of importance, caused her nevertheless several qualms about Sylvia's fitness for presentation to Madame Corvelis.

'*Elle a des idées très larges, tu sais, mais –* ' Odette paused. She could not bring herself to believe that Madame Corvelis' broad-mindedness was broad enough to include Sylvia. '*Pourtant,* I will ask her quite frankly. I will say to her, "*Madame,* there is an artiste who wishes to meet a *femme du monde.*" *Ses idées sont tellement larges que peut-être elle sera enchantée de faire to connaissance.* She has been so charming to me that if I make a *gaffe* she must forgive me. *Enfin,* she came to take tea with me *chez Eliane,* and though of course I was careful not to introduce anybody else to her, she assured me afterwards that she had enjoyed herself. *Alors, nous verrons.*'

Madame Corvelis was a little French Levantine who had married a Greek of Constantinople. Odette had made her acquaintance one afternoon by helping to unhitch her petticoats, which had managed to get caught up while she was alighting from a tram. Her gratitude to Odette for rescuing her from such a blushful situation was profuse and had culminated in an invitation to take tea with her 'in the wretched little house she and her husband temporarily occupied in Odessa,' owing to their flight from Constantinople at the rumour of war.

'What was M. Corvelis?' Sylvia asked, when she and Odette were making their way to visit madame.

'Oh, he was a man of business. I believe he was secretary to some large company. You must not judge them by the house they live in here; they left everything behind in Constantinople. But don't be frightened of M. Corvelis. I assure you that for a man in his position he is very simple.'

'I'll try not to be very frightened,' Sylvia promised.

'And madame is charming. She has the perfect manners of a woman of forty accustomed to the best society. When I think that eight years ago – don't tell anybody else this – but eight

66

years ago, *chérie,*' Odette exclaimed dramatically, '*je faisis le miché autour des boulevards extérieurs! Ma chérie,* when I think of my *mauvais début,* I can hardly believe that I am on my way to take tea with a *femme du monde. Enfin, on arrive!*'

Odette flung proud glances all round her; Sylvia marvelled at her satisfied achievement of a life's ambition, nor did she marvel less when she was presented to Madame Corvelis, surely the most insignificant piece of respectability that had ever adorned a cocotte's dream. It was pathetic to see the way in which the great flaunting creature worshipped this plump *bourgeoise* with her metallic Levantine accent: anxious lest Odette's deference should seem too effusive Sylvia found herself affecting an equally exaggerated demeanour to keep her friend in countenance, though when she looked at their hostess she nearly laughed aloud, so much did she resemble a little squat idol receiving the complimentary adoration of some splendid savage.

'I am really ashamed to receive you in this miserable little house,' Madame Corvelis protested. '*Mais que voulez-vous?* Everything is in Constantinople. Carpets, mirrors, china, silver. We came away like beggars. *Mais que voulez-vous?* My husband is so nervous. He feared the worst. But of course he's nervous. *Que voulez-vous?* The manager of one of the largest companies in the East! Well, I say manager, but of course when a company is as large as his, one ought to say secretary. "Let us go to Odessa, Alceste," he begged. My name is Alceste, but I've no Greek blood myself. Oh no, my father and mother were both Parisian. *Enfin,* my father came under the glamour of the East and called me Alceste. *Que voulez-vous?*'

All the time that Madame Corvelis was talking, Odette was asking Sylvia in an unbroken whisper if she did not think that madame was *charmante, aimable, gentille,* and every other gracious thing she could be.

'Have you ever been to Constantinople? Have you ever seen the Bosphorus?' Madame Corvelis went on, turning to Sylvia. 'What, you've never seen the most enchanting city in the world? Oh, but you must! Not now, of course. The war! It robs us all of something. Don't, please don't think that Odessa resembles Constantinople.'

Sylvia promised she would not.

'*Mais non,* Odessa is nothing. Look at this house! Ah, when I think of what we've left behind in Constantinople. But M. Corvelis insisted, and he was right. At any rate we've brought a few clothes with us, though of course when we came to this dreadful place we never thought that we shouldn't be back home in a month. It was merely a precaution. But he was right to be nervous, you see: the Turks have declared war. When I think of the poor Ambassador. You never saw the Ambassador?'

Sylvia shook her head.

'I remember he trod on my toe – by accident, of course, oh yes, it was entirely an accident. But he was so apologetic. What manners! But then I always say, if you want to see good manners you must frequent good society. What a pity you never saw the Ambassador!'

'*N'est-ce pas que c'est merveilleux?*' Odette demanded.

'*Merveilleux,*' Sylvia agreed fervently.

'*Encore, madame!*' Odette begged. '*Vos histoires sont telle-ment intéressantes.*'

'Ah well, one can't live all one's life in Constantinople without picking up a few stories.'

'Adhesive as burrs,' Sylvia thought.

'But really the best story of all,' Madame Corvelis went on, 'is to find myself here in this miserable little house. That's a pretty bag you have,' she added to Sylvia. 'A very pretty bag. Ah, *mon dieu,* when I think of the jewellery I've left behind!'

At this moment M. Corvelis came in with the cunningly detached expression of a husband who has been hustled out of the room by his wife at the sound of a bell in order to convey an impression, when he has had time to change his clothes, that he habitually dresses *en grande tenue.* It was thus that Odette described her own preparatory toilet, and she was ravished by M. Corvelis' reciprocity, whispering to Sylvia her sense of the compliment to his humble visitors.

'*Homme chic! homme du monde! homme elégant! Mais ça se voit. Dis, t'es contente?*'

Sylvia smiled and nodded.

The mould of form who had drawn such an ecstasy of self-congratulatory admiration from Odette treated the two actresses as politely as his wife had done, and asked Sylvia the same questions. When his reduplication of the first catechism was practically complete, Odette gave the signal for departure, and in a cyclone of farewells and compliments they left.

'*Elle est vraiment une femme du monde?*' Odette demanded.

'*De pied en cap,*' Sylvia replied.

'*Ton sac en or lui plaissait beaucoup,*' said Odette a little enviously. 'Ah, when I think of myself eight years ago, she went on, 'it seems *incroyable*. I should like to invite them both to tea again *chez Eliane*. If only the other girls were like you! And last time I put too much sugar in her tea! *Non, je n'ose pas!* One sees the opportunity to raise oneself, but one does not dare grasp it. *C'est la vie,*' she sighed.

Moved by the vision of herself thwarted from advancing any higher Odette poured out to Sylvia the story of her life, a sad squalid story lit up here and there by the flashes of melodramatic events and culminating in the revelation of this paradise that was denied her.

'What would you have done if you had been invited to her house in Constantinople where the carpets and the mirrors are?'

'She would never have invited me there,' Odette sighed. 'Here she is not known. However broad her ideas, she could not defy public opinion at home. *À la guerre comme à la guerre! Enfin, je suis fille du peuple, mais on me regarde: c'est déjà quelque chose.*'

The *pension* that to Odette appeared so mean after the glories of Madame Corvelis' little house had never been so welcome to Sylvia, and it was strange to think that anyone could be more impressed by that pretentious little *bourgeoise* with her figure like apples in a string bag than by Madame Eliane who resembled a mysterious lady in the background of a picture by Watteau.

It was in meditation upon such queer contrasts that Sylvia passed away her time in Odessa, thus and in pondering the more terrifying profundities of the human soul in the novels of Dostoievsky and Tolstoy. She was not sorry, however, when the time came to leave; she could never exclude from her imagination the hope of some amazing event immemorially predestinate that should decide the course of the years still to come. It would have been difficult for her to explain or justify her conviction, but it would have been impossible to reject it, and it was with an oddly superstitious misgiving that she found herself travelling north again, so strong had been her original impulse to go south. If anything had been wanting to confirm this belief, her arrival in Warsaw at the beginning of February would have been enough.

Sylvia left Kieff on the return visit without any new revelation of human vileness or human virtue, and reached Warsaw to find a mad populace streaming forth at the sound of the German guns. She had positively the sensation of meeting a great dark wave that drove her back, and her interview with the distracted Jew who managed the cabaret for which she had been engaged was like one of those scenes played in a front set of a provincial drama to the sounds of feverish preparation behind the cloth.

'Don't talk to me about songs,' the manager cried. 'Get out! Can't you hear the guns? Everything's closed. Oh, my God, my God, where have I put it? I had it in my hands a moment ago. Get out, I say.'

'Where to?' Sylvia demanded.

'Anywhere. Listen, don't you think they sound a little nearer even in these few minutes? Oh, the Germans! They're too strong. What are you waiting for? Can't you understand me when I say that everything's closed?'

He wiped the perspiration from his big nose with a duster that left long black streaks in its wake.

'But where shall I go?' Sylvia persisted.

'Why don't you go to Bucharest? Why in the devil's name does anyone want to be anywhere but in a neutral country in these times? Go to the Roumanian consul and get your passport *visé* for Bucharest and for the love of God leave me in peace. Can't you see I'm busy this evening?'

Sylvia accepted the manager's suggestion and set out to find the consul: by this time it was too late to obtain a visa that night, and she was forced to sleep in Warsaw – a grim experience that remained as a memory of distant guns booming through a penetrating reek of onions. In the morning the guns were quieter, and there was a rumour that for the third time the German thrust for Warsaw had been definitely foiled. Sylvia, however, could not get over the impression of the evening before, and what the manager had suggested to rid himself of an importunate woman she accepted as a clear indication of the direction she ought to follow.

In the waiting-room of the Roumanian Consulate there was an excessively fat girl who told Sylvia that she was an accompanist anxious like herself to get to Bucharest. Sylvia took the occasion to ask her if she thought there was a certainty of being engaged in Bucharest, and the fat girl was fairly encouraging. She told Sylvia that she was a Bohemian from Prague who had been warned by the Russian police that she would do well to seek another country.

'And will you get an engagement?' Sylvia asked.

'Oh well, if I don't, I may as well starve in Bucharest as in Warsaw,' she replied.

There seemed something ludicrous in the notion of anyone

so fat as this starving; the accompanist seemed to divine Sylvia's thoughts, for she laughed bitterly.

'I daresay you think I'm pretending, but ever since I was warned, I've been scraping together the money to reach Bucharest somehow; I haven't eaten a proper meal for a month. But the less I eat, the fatter I seem to get.'

Sylvia was vexed that the poor girl should have guessed what she was thinking, and she went out of her way to ask her advice on the smallest details of the proposed journey; she knew that there was nothing that restored a person's self-respect like a request for advice. The fat girl whose name inappropriately for a Bohemian appeared to be Lottie, cheered up, as Sylvia had anticipated, and brimmed over with recommendations about work in Bucharest.

'You'd better go to the management of the Petit Maxim. You're a singer, aren't you? Of course Bucharest is very gay and terribly expensive. You're English, aren't you? You are lucky. But fancy leaving England now! Still, if you don't get any work you'll be able to go to your consul and he'll send you home. I'll be able to get home too from Bucharest, but I don't know if I want to. All my friends used to be French and English girls. I never cared much for Austrians and Germans. But now I get called *sale boche* if I open my mouth. How do you explain this war? It seems very unnecessary, doesn't it?'

'I don't want to be inquisitive,' said Sylvia. 'But I wish you'd tell me why you're called Lottie.'

'Ah, lots of people ask that.' It was evident by the way she spoke that the ability of her name to arouse the curiosity of strangers was one of the chief pleasures life had brought to this fat girl. 'Well, I had an *amant de cœur* once, who was English. At least his mother was English: his father was from Hamburg, in fact I think he was more Jewish than anything. He didn't treat me very well and he threw me over for an English dancer called Lottie who died of consumption. It seems a funny thing to tell you, but the only way I could be revenged was to take her name when she died. You'd have been surprised to see how much my taking her name seemed to annoy him. He threatened me with a pistol once, but I stuck to the name, and then I got fond of it, because I found it created *beaucoup de réclame*. You see, I travelled all over Europe, and people remember me as the fat girl Lottie; so I've never gone back to my own name. It's just as well, because nobody can pronounce Bohemian names.'

The long formalities at the consulate were finished at last, and as they came out Sylvia suggested to the fat girl that they should travel together. She looked at Sylvia in astonishment.

'But I'm an Austrian.'

'Yes, I know. I daresay it's very reprehensible, but unfortunately I can't feel at war with you.'

'Thank you for your kindness,' said Lottie, 'which I'm not going to repay by travelling with you. After we get out of Russia, yes. But till we're over the frontier, I shan't know you for your own sake. You'd only have trouble with the police.'

'Even police could surely not be so stupid as that?' Sylvia argued.

'*À la guerre comme à la guerre*,' the fat girl laughed. '*Au revoir, petite chose.*'

Sylvia left Warsaw that night. Having only just enough money to pay her fare second-class she found the journey down through Russia almost unendurable, especially the first part when the train was swarmed with fugitives from Warsaw, notwithstanding the news of the German failure to pierce the line of the Bzura, which was now confirmed. Yet with all the discomfort she was sustained by an exultant relief at turning south again; and her faculties were positively strained to attention for the disclosure of her fate. She was squeeezed so tightly into her seat, and the atmosphere of the compartment was so heavy with the smell of disturbed humanity that it was lucky she had this inner assurance over which she could brood hour after hour. She was without sleep for two nights, and when toward dusk of a dreary February afternoon the frontier station of Ungheny was reached and she alighted from the third train in which she had travelled during this journey, she felt dazed for a moment with the disappointment of somebody who arrives at a journey's end without being met.

However, there was now the frontier examination by the Russian authorities of passengers leaving the country to occupy Sylvia's mind, and she passed with an agitated herd towards a tin-roofed shed in the middle of which a very large stove was burning. She had noticed Lottie several times in the course of the journey, and now finding herself next to her in the crowd she greeted her cheerfully; but the fat girl frowned and whispered:

'I'm not going to speak to you for your own sake. Can't you understand?'

Sylvia wondered if she were a spy, who from some motive of charity wished to avoid compromising her; but there was no time to think about such problems, because an official was taking her passport and waving her across to the stacked up heaps of luggage. There was something redolent of old sensational novels in this frontier examination, something theatrically sinister about the attitude of the officials when they commanded everybody to turn everything out of the trunks and bags. The shed took on the appearance of a vast rag-heap and the accumulated agitation of the travellers was pitiable in its subservience to these machines of the State; it seemed incredible that human beings should consent to be treated thus. Presently it became evident that the object of this relentless search was paper; every scrap of paper, whether it was loose or used for wrapping and packing, was taken away and dropped into the stove. The sense of human ignominy became overwhelming when Sylvia saw men going down on their knees and weeping for permission to keep important documents; yet no appeal moved the officials, and the stove burned fiercely with the mixed records of money, love, and business; with contracts and receipts and title deeds; even with toilet-paper and old greasy journals. Sylvia fought hard for the right to keep her music, and proclaimed her English nationality so insistently that for a minute or two the officials hesitated and went out to consult the authorities who had taken charge of her passport; but when it was found that she was entered there as a music-hall artiste, the music was flung into the stove at once. Confronted with the proofs of her right to carry music, this filthy spawn of man's will to be enslaved took from her the only tools of her craft; orang-outangs would have been more logical. And all over the world the human mind was being debauched like this by war, or would it be truer to say that war was turning ordinary stupidity into criminal stupidity? Oh, what did it matter? Sylvia clasped her golden bag to reassure herself that nobility still endured in spite of war. Now they were throwing books into the stove! Sylvia sat down and laughed so loudly that two soldiers came across and took her arms to lead her outside: they evidently thought she was going to have hysterics, which would doubtless have been unlawful in the shed. She waved aside their attentions and went across to pick up her luggage.

When Sylvia had finished and was passing out to find the office where she had to receive back her passport inscribed with illegible permits to leave Russia, she saw Lottie being led through a curtained door on the far side of the shed. The sight made her feel sick: it brought back with horrible vividness her emotion when years ago she had seen on the French frontier the woman with the lace being led away for smuggling contraband. What were they going to do? She paused, expecting to hear a scream issue from that curtained doorway. She could not bring herself to go away, and with an excuse of having left something behind in the shed she went back. The curtain was pulled aside a moment for someone within to call the assistance of someone without, and Sylvia had a brief vision of the fat girl half undressed, with her arms held high above her head while two police officers prodded her like a sheep in a fair.

'Oh, God!' Sylvia murmured. 'God! God! Grant these people their revenge some day!'

The passengers were at last free to mount another train and Sylvia saw with relief that Lottie was taking her place with the rest. She avoided speaking to her, because she was suffering herself from the humiliation inflicted upon the fat girl and felt awed at the idea of any intrusion upon her shame. The train steamed out of the station, crossed a long bridge and pulled up in Roumanian Ungheny, where everybody had to alight again for the Roumanian officials to look for the old-fashioned contraband of the days before the war. They did this as perfunctorily as in those happy days; and the quiet of the neutral railway-station was like the sudden lull that sheltering land gives to the stormiest seas. If she only had not lost all her music, if only she had not seen the fat girl behind that curtain, Sylvia could have clapped her hands for pleasure at this unimpressive little station, which merely because it belonged to a country at peace had a kind of innocence and jollity that gave it real beauty.

'Well, aren't you glad I wouldn't have anything to do with you?' said Lottie, coming up to her with a smile. 'You'd have had to go through the same probably. The Russian police are brutes.'

'All policemen are brutes,' Sylvia declared.

'I suppose they have their orders, but I think they might have a woman searcher.'

'Oh don't talk about it,' Sylvia cried. 'Such things crucify the soul.'

'You're very *exagerée* for an English girl,' said Lottie. 'Aou yes! Aou yes! I never met an English girl who talked like you.'

The train arrived at Jassy about nine o'clock; here they had to change again, and since the train for Bucharest did not leave till about eleven and she was feeling hungry, Sylvia invited Lottie to have dinner with her. While they were walking along the platform toward the restaurant there was a sound of hurried footsteps behind them, and a moment later a breathless voice called out in English:

'Excuse me, please! Excuse me, please! They told me there was being an English artiste on the train.'

That voice reproduced so many times by Sylvia at the Pierian Hall was the voice of Concetta and turning round she saw her.

'Concetta!'

The girl drew in her breath sharply.

'How was you knowing me? My name is Queenie Walters. How was you calling me Concetta? Ah, the English girl! Oh, my dear, I am so content to see you.'

Sylvia took her in her arms and kissed her.

'Oh, Sylvia! You see I remember your name. I can't get away from Jassy. I was being expelled from Moscow, and I had no money to come more than here, and the man I am with here I hate. I want to go to Bucharest, but he isn't wanting to let me go and gives to me only furs, no money.'

'You're not still with Zozo?'

'*Ach,* no! He – how do you say – he shooted me in the leg three years from now and afterwards we were no more friends. The man I am with here was of Jassy. I had no money. What else must I do?'

Sylvia had not much money either; but she had just enough to pay Concetta's fare to Bucharest, whither at midnight they set out.

'And let no one ever tell me again that presentiments don't exist,' murmured Sylvia, falling asleep for the first time in forty-eight hours.

Chapter IV

CONCETTA'S HISTORY – or rather Queenie's, for it was by this name that she begged Sylvia to call her now – had been a mixture of splendour, misery, and violence during the six years that almost to a day had elapsed since they met for the first time at Granada. She told it in the creeping light of a wet dawn while the train was passing through a flat colourless country and while in a corner of the compartment Lottie's snores rose above the noise, told it in the breathless disjointed style that was so poignantly familiar to the one who listened. There was something ghostly for Sylvia in this experience; it was as if she sat opposite a Galatea of her own creation, a double-ganger from her own brain, a dream prolonged into the cold reality of the morning. All the time that she was listening she had a sensation of being told about events that she ought to know already, as if in a trance she herself had lived this history through before; and so vivid was the sensation that when there were unexplained gaps in Queenie's narrative she found herself puzzling her own brain to fill them in from experience of her own, the recollection of which had been clouded by some accident.

When Queenie told how she was carried away by Zozo from Mrs Gainsborough at the railway-station of Granada, she gave the impression of having yielded to a magical and irresistible influence, and it was evident that for a long while the personality of the juggler had swayed her destiny by an hypnotic power that was only broken when he wounded her with the pistol-shot. Even now after three years of freedom his influence, when she began to talk of him, seemed to regather its volume and to be about to pour itself once more over her mind. Sylvia perceived this danger, and forbade her to talk any more about Zozo. This injunction was evidently a relief to the child – she must be twenty-one by now, though seemed still a child – but it was tantalising to Sylvia who could not penetrate beyond her own impression of the juggler as an incredible figure, incredible because only drawn with a kind of immature or tired fancy. He passed into the category of the Svengalis, and became one of a long line of romantic impossibilities with whom their creators had failed to do much more than can be done by a practical joker with a turnip, a sheet, and some phosphorus. Zozo had always been the weakest part of Sylvia's improvisation of Concetta, a melodramatic climax that for her had spoilt the more simple horror of the childhood; she determined that later on she would try to extract from Queenie bit by bit enough to complete her performance.

Although Queenie had managed to break away from the man himself, she had paid in full for his direction of her life, and Sylvia rebelled against the whim of destiny which at the critical moment in this child's career had snatched her from herself and handed her over to the possession of Zozo. What could have been the intention of fate in pointing a way to safety and then

76

immediately afterward barring it against her progress? The old argument of free will could not apply in her case, because it was the lack of that, and of that alone, which had caused her ruin. What but a savage and undiscerning fate could be held accountable for this tale that had for fit background the profitable and ugly fields through which on this tristful Roumanian day the train was sweeping? Queenie seemed to have had no lovers apart from the purchasers of youth, and to be able to look back with pride and pleasure at nothing except furs and dresses and jewellery with which she had been purchased. In the rage that Sylvia felt for this wanton corruption of a soul, she suddenly remembered how long ago she had watched with a hopeless equanimity and a cynical tolerance the progress of Lily along the same road as Queenie; and this memory of herself as she once was and felt revived the torments of self-reproach that had haunted her delirium in Petrograd. Then, as Queenie's tale went on, there gradually emerged from all the purposeless confusion of it one clear ambition in the girl's mind, which was a passion to be English – a passion feverish, intense, absorbing.

When in France Sylvia had first encountered continental music-hall artistes, she had found amongst them universal prejudice against English girls; later on, when she met in cabarets the expatriated and cosmopolitan mountebanks that were the slaves rather than the servants of the public, she had often been envied for her English nationality: Lottie sleeping over there in the corner was an instance in point. But she had never found this fleeting envy crystallised to such a passionate ambition as it was become for Queenie. The circumstances of her birth in Germany from an Italian father of a Flemish mother, her flight from a cruel stepmother, her life with the juggler whose nationality seemed as indeterminate as her own, her speech compounded of English, French, German, and Italian each spoken with a foreign accent, her absence of any kind of papers, her lack of any sort of home, had all combined to give her a positive belief that she was without nationality, which she coveted as some Undine might covet a soul.

'But why do you want to be English so particularly?' Sylvia asked.

'Don't you know? Why, yes, of course you know. It was you was first making me to want. You were so sweet, the sweetest person I was ever meeting, and when I lost you I was always wanting to be English.'

So after all, her own swift passage through Queenie's life had

77

not been without consequence.

'People were always saying that I looked like an English girl,' Queenie went on. 'And I was always talking English. I will never speak other languages again. I will not know other languages. Until this war came it was easy; but when they asked me for my passport I had only a *billet de séjour* given to me by the Russian police, and after six months I was expelled. When I was coming to Roumania, there was a merchant on the train who was kind to me, but he made me promise that if he helped me I was never to leave him until he was wanting. He was very kind. He gave me these furs. They are nice, yes? But I was always going to the station at Jassy to see if some English girl would be my sister. There was once in Constantinople an English girl who would be my sister – but Zozo was jealous. If I was becoming her sister, I would be having a passport now, and England is so sweet!'

'But you've never been in England,' Sylvia observed.

'Oh yes, I was going there with another English girl, and we lived there three months. I was dancing into a club – a nice club, all the men were wearing smokings – but she was ill and I wanted to be giving her money, so I was going to Russia, and then came the war. And now you must be my sister, because that other sister will be perhaps dead, so ill she was. *Ach* yes, so ill, so very ill! When I will have my English passport we will go to England together and never come away again. Then for the first time I shall be happy.'

Sylvia promised that she would do all she could to achieve Queenie's purpose.

'Tell me, why did you call yourself Queenie Walters?' she asked.

'Because the girl who was my sister in England had once a real little baby sister who was called Queenie. Oh, dead long ago, long ago! Her mother who I was calling *my* mother told me about this baby Queenie. So I was Queenie Walters and my sister was Elsie Walters.'

'And your real brother, Francesco?' Sylvia asked. 'Did you ever see him again?'

That dreamlike and inexplicable meeting between the brother and the sister in the streets of Milan had always remained in Sylvia's memory.

'No, never yet again. But I am so sure he is being in England that when we go there we will find him. And if he is English too, what fun we will have.'

Sylvia looked at these two companions who had both assumed English names. Not even the cold and merciless grey light of the Roumanian morning could destroy Queenie's unearthly charm, and the longer she looked at her, the more like an Undine she thought her. Her eyes were ageless, limpid as a child's; and that her experience of evil should have left no sign of its habitation Sylvia was tempted to ascribe to the absence of a soul for evil to mar. The only indication that she was six years older than when they met in Granada was her added gracefulness of movement, the impulsive gracefulness of a gazelle rather than that serene gracefulness of a cat which had been Lily's beauty. Her hair of a natural pale gold had not been dimmed by the fumes of cabarets, and even now all tangled after a night in the train it had a look of hovering in this railway-carriage like a wintry sunbeam. In the other corner sat Lottie snoring with wide-open mouth, whose body relaxed in sleep seemed fatter than ever. She too had suffered, perhaps more deeply than Queenie, certainly more markedly; and now in dreams what fierce Bohemian passions were aroused in the vast airs of sleep, what dark revenges of the spirit for the insults that grotesque body must always endure?

At this point in Sylvia's contemplation Lottie woke up and prepared for the arrival of the train at Bucharest by making her toilet.

'Where's the best place to stay?' Sylvia enquired.

'Well, the best place to stay is in some hotel,' Lottie replied. 'But the hotels are so horribly expensive. Of course, there are plenty of *pensions d'artistes,* and – ' she broke off and looked at Sylvia curiously, who asked her why she did so.

'I was thinking that it's a pity you can't share a room together,' she said after a momentary hesitation.

'So we can,' Sylvia answered sharply.

'Well, in that case I should go to a small hotel,' Lottie advised. 'Because all the *pensions* here are run by old thieves. There's Mère Valérie – she's French and almost the worst of the lot – and there's one kept by a Greek who's not so bad, but they say most of her bedrooms have bugs.'

'We'll go to an hotel,' Sylvia decided. 'Where are you going yourself?'

'Oh, I shall find myself a room somewhere. I don't stand a chance of being engaged at any first-rate cabaret, and I shan't have much money to spend on rooms. *Entre nous, je ne dis plus*

79

rien aux hommes. Je suis trop grasse. A quoi sert une jolie chambre?'

Sylvia had a feeling that she ought to ask Lottie to share a room with Queenie and herself, and after a struggle against the notion of this fat girl's ungainly presence she keyed herself to the pitch of inviting her.

'No, no' said Lottie. 'It wouldn't do for two English girls to live with an Austrian.'

Sylvia could not help being relieved at her refusal; perhaps she showed it, for Lottie smiled cynically.

'I think you'll feel a little less charitable to everybody,' she said, 'before much longer. You've kept out of this war so far, but you won't be able to keep out of it for ever. I've often noticed about English girls that they begin by thinking such a lot of themselves that they have quite a store of pity for the poor people who aren't like them; and then all of a sudden they turn round and become very unpleasant; because they discover that other people think themselves as good as they are. Mind you, I'm not saying you'll do that, but I don't want to find myself *de trop* after being with you a week. Let's part as friends.'

Sylvia in the flurry of arrival did not pay much attention to Lottie's prophecies, and she was glad to be alone again with Queenie. They discovered a small hotel kept by Italians, which seemed clean and, if they obtained a reasonable salary at the Petit Maxim, not too expensive. When they had dressed themselves up to impress the manager of the cabaret and were starting out to seek an engagement, the wife of the proprietor called Sylvia aside.

'You mustn't bring gentlemen back to the hotel except in the afternoon.'

'We don't want to bring anybody back at any time,' said Sylvia indignantly.

The woman shrugged her shoulders and muttered a sceptical apology.

The interview with the manager of the cabaret was rather humiliating for Sylvia, though she laughed at it when it was all over. He was quite ready to engage Queenie both to dance *en scène* and afterwards, but he declared he had nothing to offer Sylvia; she proposed to sing him one of her songs, but he scarcely listened to her and when she had finished repeated that he had nothing to offer. Whereupon Queenie announced that unless her sister was engaged the Petit Maxim would have to forgo her own performance. The manager argued for a time, but he was evidently much impressed by Queenie's attraction as a typical English girl and finally rather than lose her he agreed to engage Sylvia as well.

'It's a pity you look so unlike an English girl,' he said to Sylvia in an aggrieved voice. 'The public will be disappointed. They expect an English girl to look English. You'll have to sing at the beginning of the evening, and I can't pay you more than three hundred *lei* – three hundred francs that is.'

'I was getting eight hundred in Russia,' Sylvia objected.

'I daresay you were, but girls are scarcer there. We've got thousands of them in Bucharest.'

Sylvia was furious at being offered so little, but Queenie promptly asked nine hundred and when the manager objected suggested that he might engage them both for twelve hundred: it was strange to find Queenie so sharp at business. In the end Sylvia was offered three hundred and fifty *lei* and Queenie seven hundred and fifty, which they accepted.

'You can have a band rehearsal tomorrow,' he said, 'and open on Monday week.'

Sylvia explained about the loss of her music; and the manager began to curse, demanding how she expected an orchestra to accompany her without band parts.

'I'll accompany myself,' she answered.

'Oh well,' he agreed, 'being the first item on the programme, it doesn't really matter what you do.'

It was impossible for the moment not to feel the sting of this when Sylvia remembered herself a year ago, fresh from her success at the Pierian and inclined to wonder if she were not dimming her effulgence as a moderately large star by appearing at English music-halls. Now here she was being engaged for the sake of another girl and allowed on sufferance to entertain the meagre listless audience at the beginning of a cabaret performance – for the sake of another girl who owed to her the fare to Bucharest and whom all the way in the train she had been pitying while she made plans to rescue her from a degrading existence. There was a brief moment of bitterness and jealousy; but it passed almost at once and she began to laugh at herself.

'There's no doubt you'll have to establish your English nationality,' she told Queenie, as they left the manager's office. 'I really believe he thought it was I who was pretending.'

'It's what I was saying you,' Queenie answered. 'They was all thinking that I was English.'

'Well, now we must decide about our relationship. Of course, you don't look the least like my sister, but I think the best way will be for you to pass as my sister. My name isn't really Sylvia Scarlett, but Sylvia Snow; so what I suggest is that you shall go on calling yourself Queenie Walters on the stage, though when we try to get our passport you must be Queenie Snow. Trust me to get round the English authorities here, if it's necessary. We can always go back to England through Bulgaria and Greece, but we must save up enough money, and it'll take us a good many weeks to do that in Bucharest.'

Sylvia did not tell Queenie that she could always write to England and borrow the money to go back, because the child would not have understood her disinclination to be helped home. Indeed, she never confided anything about herself to Queenie, one of whose charms was a complete lack of curiosity about other people, a quality which she shared with Lily, and which looking back on their life together Sylvia decided must have been Lily's great charm for her. This absence of curiosity about other people gave Queenie a kind of unworldliness – apart from the bargain she knew how to drive with the manager – and made her accept with the philosophy of an animal anything that did not positively hurt her. She wanted Sylvia to think for her, and the way in which she yielded up her will with an affectionate surrender brought home vividly the danger of exposing her to any external influence. After they had lived together for a while, Sylvia began to realise that no great hypnotic power had been required by the juggler to make Queenie his slave; she seemed to have a natural propensity toward slavery, and Sylvia often had to check herself from assuming too much of Queenie's character upon herself, partly because she was trying hard to create in Queenie a conception of egoism. The girl's absence of nationality seemed to have deprived her of this to such an extent that often when she talked about herself she gave the impression of talking about a third person; it was extraordinary, but Queenie's conception of her own individuality was hardly as strong as Sylvia's conception of herself as Queenie in the days when she used to give the Improvisations. Indeed Sylvia could easily have claimed that she was more of Queenie than Queenie herself, and this assumption of another person's being made her fear anything that might befall her more acutely than she would have feared for herself.

'Which must she be given first?' Sylvia asked herself. 'A soul or a nationality? The ultimate reason of nationality is civilisation, and the object of civilisation is the progress and safety of the

State. The more progressive and secure is the State, the more utterly is the individual soul destroyed, because the State compels the individual to commit crimes for which as an individual he would be execrated. Hence the crime of war, to which the individual is lured by a virtue created by appealing to mankind's sense of property, a virtue called patriotism that somehow or other I'm perfectly sure must be anti-divine, though it's a virtue for which I have a great respect. *What shall it profit a man if he shall gain the whole world and lose his own soul?* That's surely the answer to civilisation, which after all has no object except the physical comfort of humanity. I suppose one might call the civilisation that is of the spirit and not of the flesh 'salvation'. I wonder what the Germans mean by Kultur – really I suppose the aggregate soul of the German people. I think Kultur in their sense must be a hybrid virtue like patriotism. I think it's their own ascription of a divine origin to a civilisation which has been as rapid and as poisonous and as ugly as a toad-stool. We other civilised nations revile the Germans as barbarians, particularly we English, because in England, thank heaven, we've always had an uncomfortable feeling that man is a greater thing than men, and we perceive in war a sacrifice of the individual that no State has the right to demand. I wonder why the Russians went to war. I can't understand a country that has produced Tolstoy and Dostoievsky going to war. If I had not met that soldier in Kieff I might have been sceptical about Russian idealism after my adventures in Petrograd, after that filthy cinema, and the scene in the station at Ungheny; but having met him I know that Tolstoy and Dostoievsky *are* Russia.

'All of which has taken me a long way from Queenie who is neither ready for civilisation nor for salvation. It's a most extraordinary thing, but I've suddenly got an idea that she has never been baptised. If she has not, I shall persuade her to be batised. Baptism – the key to salvation! A passport – the key to civilisation! The antithesis is not so ludicrous nor so extravagant as it sounds at first. Without a passport Queenie has no nationality and does not possess elementary civic rights. She is liable to be expelled from any country at any moment, and there is no certainty that any other country will receive her. In that case she will spend the rest of her life on earth in a kind of Limbo comparable to the Limbo which I believe is reserved for the souls of those unbaptised through no fault of their own. I shall be able to procure her a passport and introduce her to the glories of nationality by perjuring myself, but I can't give her a soul and by perjuring myself, and I've got so strongly this intuition that she was never baptised that I shall dig out a priest and talk to him about it. And yet why am I bothering whether she was baptised or not? What have I to do with churches and their ceremonies? No doubt I was baptised, confirmed, and made my communion; yet for more than twenty years I have never entered a church except as an onlooker. Is this anxiety about Queenie's soul only another way of expressing an anxiety about my own soul? Yes, I believe it is. I believe that by a process of sheer intellectual exhaustion I am being driven into Christianity. Oh, I wish I could talk it all out! It's a damned dishonest way of satisfying my own conscience, to go to a priest and ask questions about Queenie. Why can't I go and ask him straight out about myself? But she is just as important as I am. I think that was brought home to me rather well, when the manager engaged me because he wanted her. There was I in a condition of odious pride because I had been given the chance of helping her by paying the beggarly fare to Bucharest, and boomph! as dear Gainsborough used to say, there was she given the chance of paying me back a hundred-fold within twenty-four hours.'

Queenie was out, and Sylvia was lying down with a headache which was not improved by the procession of these vagrant speculations round and round her brain. She got up presently to look for some aspirin, and, opening the drawer of the table between the two beds, she found a bundle of pictures – little coloured lithographs of old masters. She was turning them over idly, when Queenie came back.

'*Ach,* you was looking at my pictures. They are so nice, yes? See, this is the one I love the best.'

It was the Primavera, and Sylvia was astonished for a moment that Queenie's childlike and undeveloped taste should care for something so remote from the crudities that usually appealed to such a mind. Then she remembered that Botticelli as a painter must have appealed to contemporaries who by modern standards were equally childlike and undeveloped; and also that Queenie, whose nationality by the standards of civilisation did not exist, had an Italian father, the inheritor perhaps of Botticelli's blood. Queenie sat on the bed and looked at her pictures with the rapt expression of a child poring over her simple treasures. From time to time she would hold up one for Sylvia's admiration.

'See how sweet,' she would say, kissing the grave little Madonna or diminished landscape that was drawing her out of

Bucharest into another world.

'I've got a book somewhere about pictures,' Sylvia said. 'You must read it.'

Queenie hid her face in her arms; when she looked up again she was crimson as a carnation.

'I can't read,' she whispered.

'Not read?' Sylvia echoed.

'I can't read or write,' she went on. 'Ach? Now you hate me, yes? Because I was being so stupid.'

'But when you went to the school in Dantzig, didn't they teach you anything?'

'They taught me ballet dancing and acrobatic dancing and step dancing. Now I must go to have my hair washed, yes?'

Queenie got off the bed and hurried away, leaving Sylvia in a state of bewilderment before the magnitude of the responsibility that she represented.

'It's like giving birth to a grown-up baby,' she said to herself; on a sudden irresistible impulse, she knelt down upon the floor and began to pray, with that most intense prayer of which a human being is capable, that prayer which transcends all words, all space, all time, all thought, that prayer which substitutes itself for the poor creature who makes it. The moment of prayer passed, and Sylvia, rising from her knees, dressed herself and went in search of a priest.

When she reached the door of the little Catholic mission church to which the proprietor of the hotel had directed her, she paused upon the inner threshold before a baize door and asked herself if she were not acting in a dream. She had not been long enough in Bucharest for the city to be reassuringly familiar; by letting her fancy play around the unreality of her present state of mind she was easily able to transform Bucharest to a city dimly apprehended in a tranced voyage of the spirit and to imagine all the passers-by as the fantastic denizens of another world. She stood upon the threshold and yielded a moment to what seemed like a fainting of reason, while all natural existence swayed round her mind and while the baize door stuck thick with pious notices, funereal objurgations, and the petty gossip as it were of a new habitation at which she was looking with strange eyes, seemed to attend her next step with a conscious expectancy. She pushed it open and entered the church; a bearded priest, escaping the importunities of an aged parishioner with a voluble grievance, was coming towards her; perceiving that Sylvia was looking round in bewilderment, he took the

85

occasion to get rid of the old woman by asking in French if he could do anything to help.

'I want to see a priest,' she replied.

Although she knew that he was a priest, in an attempt to cheat the force that was impelling her she snatched at his lack of resemblance to the conventional priestly figure of her memory and deluded herself with vain hesitations.

'Did you want to make your confession?' he asked.

Sylvia nodded, and looked over her shoulder in affright; it seemed that the voice of a wraith had whispered 'yes'. The priest pointed to the confessional, and Sylvia with a final effort to postpone her surrender asked with a glance at the old woman if he were not too busy now. He shook his head quickly and spoke sharply in Italian to the parishioner who retired grumbling; Sylvia smiled to see with what an ostentation of injured dignity she took the holy water and crossed herself before passing out through the baize door. The old woman's challenging humanity restored to Sylvia her sense of reality; emotion died away like a falling gale at eve, and she walked to the confessional imbued with an intention as practical as if she had been walking upstairs to tidy her hair. The priest composed himself into a non-committal attitude and waited for Sylvia, who now that she was kneeling felt as if she were going to play an unrehearsed part.

'I ought to say before I begin that, though I was brought up a Catholic, I've not been inside a church for any religious duties since I was nine years old. I'm now thirty-one. I know that there is some set form of words, but I've forgotten it.'

Sylvia half expected that he would tell her to go away and come back when she had learnt how to behave in the confessional; now that she was here, she felt that this would be a pity, and she was relieved when he began the *Confiteor* in an impersonal voice, waiting for her to repeat every sentence after him. His patience seemed to her almost miraculous in the way it smoothed her difficulties.

'I shall have to give you a short history of my life,' Sylvia began. 'I can't just say baldly that I've done this or not done that, because nearly all the sins I've committed weren't committed in their usual classification.'

As she said this, she had a moment of acute self-consciousness and wondered if the priest were smiling, but he merely said in that far-away impersonal voice:

'I am listening, my daughter.'

'I was brought up a Catholic. I was baptised and confirmed and I made my first communion. It was the only communion I ever made, because somehow or other at home there was always work to be done in the house instead of going to mass. My mother was French and she married an Englishman much younger than herself. Of this marriage I was the only child. My mother had six other daughters, two by a lover who died and four by her first husband who was a Frenchman. My mother was illegitimate; her father was also an Englishman. I only knew this after she died. The man who married my grandmother always acknowledged her as his own daughter. My mother was very strict and, though she was not at all religious, she was really good: I don't want to give the idea that she was responsible for anything I did. The only thing is, perhaps, that being passionately in love with my father she was very demonstrative in front of me, which made the idea of passion shocking to me when I was still young. Therefore for whatever sins of the flesh I have committed I cannot plead a natural propensity. I don't know whether this would be considered to make them worse or not. My father was a weak man; when my mother died, he robbed his employers and had to leave France, taking me with him. I was twelve at the time. I suppose if I wanted to justify myself, I could say that no child could have spent a more demoralising childhood from that moment. But though when I look back at it now and realise some of the horrible actions that my father and a friend of his who lived with us committed, I can't think that at the time they influenced me towards evil. I suppose that any kind of moral callousness *is* a bad example, and certainly I had no conception that swindling people out of money was anything but a perfectly right and normal procedure for anybody who was without money. My mother was angry with me once because by accident I spent some money of hers, but she was angry with me because it was a serious loss to the household accounts: there was no suggestion of my having spent money that did not belong to me. Other things that my father and his friend did I never understood at the time, and so I can't pretend that they set me a bad example. My father took a woman to live with him, and I was angry because it upset what had hitherto seemed a comfortable existence, but the revelation of the passionate side of it disgusted me still more with the flesh. I was a mixture of precocity and innocence. Looking back at myself as a child I am amazed at the amount I knew and the little I understood – the amount I understood and the little I

87

knew. I read all sorts of books and accepted everything I read as the truth: I read dozens of novels, for instance, before I understood the meaning of fiction. I should say that no child was ever exposed so naturally to the full tide of human existence, and why or how I managed to escape degradation and damnation I've never been able to explain until now. As a matter of fact it's not true really to say that I did escape degradation, but I will come to that presently.

'Well, my father killed himself on account of this woman, and I was left with his friend when I was fifteen. Once I happened to be left altogether alone when this man was away turning a dishonest penny somewhere, and I suppose I fell mildly in love with a youth two years older than myself. This made my father's friend jealous, and one night he tried to make love to me. I was as much disgusted by this as if I had really been the innocent child I might have been. I ran away with the youth, and nothing happened. I ran away from him and lived with a young Jew, but nothing happened. I met the woman who had lived with my father, and – which shows how utterly unmoral I was – I made great friends with her and even went to live with her. She used to have all sorts of men, and I just accepted her behaviour as a personal taste of her own which I could neither understand nor share. Then I met a gentleman, a man fifteen years older than myself who was attracted by my unusualness and sent me to school with the idea of marrying me. Well, I married him, and I think that was the first sin I committed. I was seventeen at the time. I think if my husband had understood how stunted my emotional development was in proportion to my mental acquisitiveness he would have behaved differently. But he was fascinated by my capacity for cynicism and encouraged me to think as I liked with himself for audience; at the same time he tried to make me for outsiders' eyes a conventional young miss whom he had rather apologetically married. He demanded from me the emotional wisdom to sustain this part, and of course I could see nothing in his solicitude but a sort of snobbish egotism. He was delighted by my complete indifference to any kind of religion, supernatural or natural, and when I made friends with an English priest – not a Catholic – but half a Catholic – it's impossible to explain to a foreigner – I don't think anybody would understand the Church of England out of England, and very few people can there – he was afraid of my turning religious. I don't know – perhaps I might have done; but somebody sent an anonymous letter to my husband, suggesting that this priest and I were having a love affair, and my husband forbade me to see him again. So I ran away. I suppose my running away was the direct result of my bringing up, because whenever I had been brought face to face with a difficult situation I ran away. However, this time I was determined from some perverted pride to make myself more utterly myself than I had ever done. It's hard to explain how my mind worked. You must remember I was only nineteen, and already at thirty-one I am as far from understanding all my motives then as if I were trying to understand somebody who was not myself at all. Anyhow, I simply went on the streets. For three months I mortified my flesh by being a harlot. Can you understand that? Can you possibly understand the deliberate infliction of such a discipline, not to humiliate one's pride but to exalt it? Can you understand that I emerged from that three months of incredible horror with a complete personality? I was defiled: I was degraded: I was embittered: I hated mankind: I vowed to revenge myself on the world: I scoffed at love: and yet now, when I feel that I have at last brushed from myself the last speck of mud that was still clinging to me, I feel that somehow all that mud has preserved me against a more destructive corruption. This does not mean that I do not repent of what I did, but can you understand how without a pride that could lead me to such depths I could not have come through humility to a sight of God?'

Sylvia did not wait for the priest to answer this question, partly because she did not want to be disillusioned by finding so soon that he had not comprehended anything of her emotions or actions, partly because there seemed more important revelations of herself still to be made.

'I stayed a common harlot until I was offered by chance an opportunity to rescue myself by going on the stage. Then I sent my husband as much money as I had saved and the evidences of my infidelity, so that he might divorce me, which he did. Now comes an important event in my life. I met a girl – a very beautiful girl doomed from the creation of the universe to be a plaything of man.'

The priest held up his hand to protest.

'Ah, I know you'll say that no one can possibly be so foredoomed, and indeed I know the same myself now, or rather I'm trying hard to believe it, because predestination without free will seems to me a doctrine of devils. At the time, however, I could see nothing that would save this girl, and with a perverted idealism I determined that she should step gracefully downhill. I think the hardest thing to do is to go downhill gracefully. We can climb uphill, and a certain awkwardness is immaterial, because the visible effort lends a dignity to our progress, and the air of success blows freshly at the summit. We can walk along the level road of mediocrity with an acquired gracefulness that is taught us by our masters of the golden mean – particularly in England, where it's particularly easy to walk gracefully along the flat. Very well, instead of using my influence to prevent this girl descending at all, I was entirely occupied with the aesthetic aspects of her descent. I'm not going to pretend that I could have stopped her – a better person than I tried and failed – but that doesn't excuse my attitude. And there's worse to my account. When this other person wanted to marry her, I did all I could to stop the marriage at first, and it was not until the engagement between them was broken off that I discovered that my true reasons for hating it sprang entirely from my own jealousy. I felt that if this man had loved me, I could have regained myself, the self that was myself before those three months of prostitution. I should say here that I had nothing to do directly with the destruction of the other marriage, but I hold myself to blame ultimately, because, if from the beginning I had bent my whole will to its being carried through, it *would* have been carried through. Looking back at the business now, I am convinced that what happened happened for the best, and that such a marriage would have been fatal to the happiness of the man and useless to the girl, but that does not excuse my own share in the smash.

'Well, the man left this girl in my charge, and finally she threw me over and married a foreigner, since when I have never heard that she even still lives. I had the good fortune to be given enough money by somebody to enable me to be independent, and for two or three years I looked at life from the outside. I had nothing to do with men, and as a result I began to be afraid that youth would pass without my ever knowing what it was to love. Friends of mine married and were happy. Only I seemed fated to be always alone.

'I wonder sometimes if when we judge the behaviour of others we pay enough attention to this loneliness that haunts the lives of so many men and women. You will say that no one can be lonely with God; unfortunately thousands of lonely souls are destitute of the sense of God from birth to death, and these lonely souls are far more exposed to temptation than the rest.

Faith they have not: hope has died in their hearts: love slowly withers. All the vices of self-destruction surround their path. Pride flourishes in such soil, and jealousy and envy. I believe their only compensation is the fact that lies and self-deception find small nourishment in such spiritual wastes. I'm sure that, if the pride of such people could be pierced, there would gush forth a cry of despair that ascribed everything in this life to a feeling of loneliness. In my own case in addition to the inevitable loneliness fostered by such a childhood as mine – the natural loneliness caused by living with two men who were perpetually on the verge of imprisonment – there was the loneliness of my own temperament. I know that every human being claims for himself the right to be misunderstood and unappreciated; it's not that kind of loneliness of which I speak. Mine was the loneliness of someone who is so masculine and so feminine simultaneously that reason is sapped by emotion and emotion is sterilised by reason. The only chance for such a temperament is self-expression either in love, art, or religion. I tried vaguely to express myself in art, but without success at first; and I was too proud and not vain enough to persevere. I then fell back on love. I let myself get into a condition of wanting to be in love, and at this moment of emotional collapse I met by accident the youth – now a man of thirty – with whom I had effected one of my childish elopements. With this man I lived for a year. I can't pretend that I did not take pleasure in the passionate relationship, though I always felt it was a temporary surrender to the most feminine side of me that I despised. I think I can best explain my emotions by saying that all the time I was with him I was like a person under the influence of a sedative drug.

'Now there are people who pass from drug to drug with increase of pleasure; but there are others to whom the notion of being drugged becomes suddenly obnoxious and in whom the reaction creates an abnormal activity. Quite suddenly I abandoned my pleasure and became ambitious to express myself in art. I succeeded. I was for one who begins so late in life exceptionally successful, and then behold, my very success took on the aspect of yielding to another sedative drug. It never seemed anything but a temporary expedient to defeat the claims of existence. Just as love had seemed a surrender to the exclusively feminine side of me, so art seemed a surrender to the exclusively masculine side. There was always an unsatisfied unexpressed part of me that girded at the satisfied part. As a result of

91

this, I made up my mind that a happy marriage with children and a household to look after was a better thing than artistic success. Here was obviously another experiment for the benefit of the feminine side. I knew perfectly well that if I had carried out my intention I should not have remained content when the sedative action of the new drug began to cease, and I am grateful now that circumstances interfered. I was jilted by the man who was going to marry me, and the fact that I had already lived with him and refused to marry him dozens of times made the injury to my pride intolerable. In a fit of rage I flung behind me everything – success, love, marriage, friends – and left England to take up again at the age of thirty-one a life I had forsaken for several years. And now I found that even the mere externals of such a life were horrible. I could not bear the idea of being for sale; while I had no intention of ever giving myself to a man again, I had to drink for my living and dance with drunkards for my cab fare, which though it may not be a technical prostitution differs only in degree from the complete sale of the body.

'Scarcely a month had passed when I became seriously ill, and in the dreadful delirium of my fever I imagined that I was damned. I do not think that anybody has the right to accept seriously the mental revelations that are made to a mind beside itself; I think indeed it would be a blasphemy to accuse God of taking such a method to rouse a soul to a sense of its being, its duties, and its dangers; and I dread to claim for myself any supernatural intervention at such a time, partly because my reason shies at such a thought and partly because I think it is presumptious to suppose that God should interest Himself so peculiarly in an individual. It seems to me almost vulgarly anthropomorphic.'

'Are not five sparrows sold for two farthings, and not one of them is forgotten before God?' the priest murmured.

'Yes, yes,' Sylvia agreed. 'I have expressed myself badly, and of course when I think of it I have been driven ever since the delirium really to accept just that. You can understand, can't you, the dread of presumption in my revolt against pride?'

'But by insisting upon what seemed to happen in my delirium I am giving you a wrong impression. It was when I came to myself again in the hospital that I felt changed. I longed then for knowledge of God, but I was afraid that my feeling was simply the natural result of weakness after a severe illness. I almost rejected God in my fear of supposing myself hysterical and egotistical. However, I did try hard to put myself into a state of

92

resignation, and when I came out of the hospital I felt curiously awake to the sense of God and simultaneously an utter indifference to anything in my old life that might interrupt my quest by restoring me to what I was before this illness. While I was ill war had broken out, and I found myself utterly alone. Ordinarily I am sure that such a discovery would have terrified me; now I rejoiced in such loneliness. I deliberately turned my back on England and waited for something from my new life to fill this loneliness. I felt like someone who has swept and garnished a room that he may receive guests. My chief emotion was a tremendous love of the whole world and an illimitable desire to make up for all my cynicism in the past by the depth of this love. I went back to the pension where I had lived before I was ill, and it seemed to me a coincidence that the woman who kept it should be a spiritualist and that for two months my mind should be continuously occupied by what I might call the magic side of things. The result was that, though I was often puzzled by inexplicable happenings, I conceived a distaste for all this meddling with the unknowable, this kind of keyhole peeping at infinity: it seemed to me vulgar and unpleasant. Nevertheless I was driven back all the time in my meditations on the only satisfactory revelation of God, the only rational manifestation, which was Jesus Christ. Every other explanation crumbled away in my brain except that one fact. Then, although I believe it was only some fortune-telling with cards that first put the notion into my head, I was obsessed with the idea that I must go south. On my way I met a soldier at Kieff who bought me a golden bag for no other reason than because it seemed to him that to give pleasure to somebody else was a better way of spending his money than in gambling or self-indulgence. In the state of mind I was in I accepted this as a sign that I was right to go south. So you see that I had really arrived at the point of view of accepting the theory of a Divine intervention in my favour.

'After three months at Odessa – where I read Tolstoy and Dostoievsky and found in them, ah, such profundities of the human soul lighted up – against my instinct I went north again; the Germans were advancing upon Warsaw, and circumstances brought me here. On the way, at Jassy, an extraordinary thing happened. I met a girl whom I had tried to adopt six years ago at Granada, but who was taken from me by a blackguard and who since then was what people call sunk very low. It seemed to me that in finding this child again, for she is still really a child, I was being given an opportunity of doing what I had failed to do

93

for that first girl of whom I told you. Then suddenly I conceived the idea that she had never been baptised; when I began to think about her soul, I was driven by an unknown force to this church. When I came in I did not know what to do, and when you asked me if I wanted to make my confession the force seemed to say "yes".'

Sylvia was silent, and the priest finished the *Confiteor* which she repeated after him.

'My daughter,' he said, 'it is the grace of God. I do not feel that in this solemn moment – a moment that fills me as a priest with humility at being allowed to regard such a wonderful manifestation of God's infinite mercy – any poor words of mine can add anything. It is the grace of God: let that suffice. But wonderful as has been God's mercy to a soul that was deaf so long to His voice, do not forget that your greatest danger, your greatest temptation, may be to rely too much upon yourself. Do not forget at this solemn moment that you can only enjoy this Divine grace through the Sacraments. Do not forget that only in the Church can you preserve the new sense of security that you now feel. One who has been granted such mercy must expect harder struggles than less fortunate souls. Do not by falling back into indifference and neglect of your religious duties succumb to the sin of pride. By the height of your uplifting will be measured the depth of your fall, if in your pride you think to stand alone.'

When the priest had given her absolution, Sylvia asked him about Queenie; and when he seemed a little doubtful of Queenie's willingness to be a catechumen, she wondered if he were deliberately trying to discourage her in order to mortify that pride he had seemed to fear so much.

'But if she wants to be baptised?' Sylvia persisted.

'Of course I will baptise her.'

'You think that I'm too much occupied with her when I have still so much to learn myself?' she challenged.

They were walking down the church toward the door, and Sylvia felt rather like the importunate parishioner whom she had interrupted by her entrance.

'No, no, I think you are quite right. But I fear that you will expect miracles of God's grace all round you,' said the priest. 'What has happened to you may not happen to her.'

'But it must,' Sylvia declared. 'It shall.'

The priest shook his head, and there was a smile at the back of his eyes.

'If you fail?'

'I shan't fail.'

'Is God already put on one side?'

'I shall pray,' said Sylvia.

'Yes, I think that is almost better than relying too much upon the human will.'

Two things struck Sylvia when she had left the church and was walking back to the hotel: the first was that the priest had really said very little in response to that long outpouring of her history, and the second was that here in this street it did not seem nearly as easy to solve the problem of Queenie's soul as it had seemed in the church. Yet when she came to think over the priest's words she could not imagine how he could have spoken differently.

'I suppose I expected to be congratulated as one is congratulated upon a successful performance,' she said to herself. 'That's the worst of a histrionic career like mine: one can't get rid of the footlights even in the confessional. As a matter of fact I ought to be grateful that he accepted the spirit of my confession without haggling over the form, as from his point of view he might have done most justifiably. Perhaps he was tired and didn't want to start an argument. And yet no, I don't think it was that. He came down like a hammer on the main objection to me – my pride. He was really wonderfully unecclesiastical. It's a funny thing, but I seem to be much less spiritually exalted than I ought to be after such a reconciliation. I seem to have lost for the moment that first fine careless rapture of conversion. Does that mean that the whole business was an emotional blunder and that I'm feeling disappointed? No, I don't feel disappointed: I feel practical. I suppose my friend the priest wouldn't accept the comparison, but it reminds me of how I felt when after I had first conceived the idea of my Improvisations I had to set about doing them. Everything has its drudgery: love produces household cares, art endless work, religion religious duties. The moment of attraction, the moment of inspiration, the moment of conversion, if they could only endure! Perhaps Heaven is the infinite prolongation of such moments.

'And then there's Queenie. It's not much use my leading her to the font as one leads a horse to water, because though I should regard it as Infant Baptism, the priest would not. Yet I don't see why he shouldn't instruct her like a child. Poor priest! He could hardly have expected such problems as myself and Queenie when he was so anxious to get rid of that old woman who was pestering

95

him. I think I won't bother about Queenie for a bit, until I have practised a little subordination of myself first. She's got to acquire a soul of her own; it's no use my presenting her with a piece of mine.'

Queenie had been back from the hairdresser's for a long time when Sylvia reached the hotel and was wondering what had become of her friend.

'You've been out alone,' she said reproachfully. 'Your headache is better, I think. Yes?'

'My headache?' Sylvia repeated. 'Yes, it's much better. I've been indulging in spiritual aspirin.'

'I'm glad it's better, because it is our first night at the Petit Maxim tonight. I wonder if I will be having much applause.'

'So it is,' Sylvia said. 'I'd forgotten my approaching triumph with the waiters; it's not likely that there'll be any audience when I appear. At 9 p.m. sharp the programme of the Petit Maxim opened with Miss Sylvia Scarlett's three songs. The gifted young lady – I've reached the age when it's a greater compliment to be called young than beautiful – played and sang with much *verve*. several waiters ceased from dusting the empty tables to listen and at the close her exit was hailed by a loud flourish of *serviettes*. The solitary visitor who clapped his hands explained afterwards that he was trying to secure some attention to himself, and that thirst not enthusiasm had dictated his action.'

'How you were always going on, Sylvia,' said Queenie. 'Nobody was ever going to understand you when you talk so quick as that.'

'Miss Sylvia Scarlett's first song was an old English ballad set to the music of Handel's Dead March.'

'If we were ever going to have any dinner, we must go and eat now,' Queenie interrupted.

'Yes, I don't want to miss the sunset with my last song.'

'But what does it matter if you are paid to sing, if you sing first or last?'

'The brightest star, my dear, cannot shine by daylight.'

'But you are stupid, Sylvia, It is no more daylight at nine o'clock.'

'Yes, I am very stupid,' Sylvia agreed and, catching hold of Queenie's arms, she looked deep into her eyes. 'Believe me, you little fairy thing, that I should be much more angry if you were put first on a programme than because I am.'

The cabaret Petit Maxim aimed at expressing in miniature the essence of all the best cabarets in Paris, just as Bucharest aimed at expressing in miniature the essence of Paris. The result, though pleasant and comfortable enough, was in either case as little like Paris as a scene from one of its own light operas is like Vienna. What Bucharest and the petit Maxim did both manage to effect, however, was an excellent resemblance to one of those light operas. Sylvia in the course of her wanderings had once classified the capitals she had visited as metropolitan, cosmopolitan, and neapolitan. Bucharest belonged very definitely to the last group; it stood up like a substantially built Exhibition in the middle of a ring of industrial suburbs which by their real squalor heightened the illusion of its unreality. The cupolas of shining bronze and the tiled domes shimmering in the sun like peacocks' tails dazzled the onlooker with an illusion of barbaric splendour; but the city never escaped from the self-consciousness of an Exhibition, which was heightened by the pale blue and silver uniforms of the officers, the splendid equipages for hire, and the policemen dressed in chocolate like commissionaires, and accentuated by the inhabitants' pride in the expensiveness and 'naughtiness' of their side-shows, of which not the least expensive and 'naughty' were the hotels. One might conceive the promoter of the Exhibition taking one aside and asking if one did not think he had been successful in giving Paris to the Balkans, and one might conceive his disappointment on being told that magnificent though it all looked it was no more Paris than Offenbach was Molière.

At the time when Sylvia visited Bucharest the sense of being one of the chorus in a light opera was intensified by the dramatic plot that was provided by the European war. Factions always grew more picturesque with every mile away from England, the mother of Parliaments, where they ceased to be picturesque three hundred years ago when the chief punchinello's head tumbled into the basket at Whitehall. The comedy of kingship had been prolonged for another century and a half in France, and in France they were a century and a half nearer to the picturesque and already two or three hundred miles away from England. In Italy the picturesqueness grew still more striking with such anachronisms as the Camorra and the Mafia. But it was not until the Balkans that factions could be said to be vital in the good old way. Serbia had shown not so long ago what could still be done with a thoroughly theatrical regal murder; and now here was Roumania jigging to the manipulation of the French faction and the German faction with just enough possibility of all the plots and counter-plots ending seriously by plunging the country into war on one side or the other to give a background or real drama to the operatic form.

At the Petit Maxim the Montagues and Capulets came to blows nightly. Everything here was either Ententophile or German-ophile: there were pro-German waiters, pro-German tables, pro-German tunes, for the benefit of the Germans and pro-Germans who occupied one half of the cabaret and applauded the Austrian performers. Equally there was the Ententist complement. If the first violin was pro-French and played sharp for an Austrian singer, the cornet was pro-German ready to break time to disconcert a French dancer. On the whole, as was natural in what is called 'a centre of amusement,' the pro-French element predominated, and though it was possible to sing the *Marseillaise* at the cost of a few broken glasses, the solitary occasion when *Deutschland Über Alles* was attempted ended in several broken heads, a smashed chandelier, and six weeks in bed for an Austrian contralto whose face was scratched with a comb by a French artiste under the influence of ether and patriotism.

Nor was this atmosphere of plot and faction confined to general demonstrations of friendliness or hostility. Bucharest was too small a city to allow deep ramifications to either party; the gossip of the Court on the day before became the gossip of the cabaret on the evening after; scarcely one successful conveyance of war material from Germany to Turkey but was openly discussed at the Petit Maxim. Intrigues and flirtations with the great powers increased the self-esteem of Roumania, who took on the air of a coquettish schoolgirl that finds herself surrounded by the admiration of half a dozen elderly rakes. Her dowry and good looks seemed both so secure that any little looseness of behaviour would always be overlooked by the man she chose to marry in the end.

Sylvia could not help teasing some of the young officers that frequented the Petit Maxim. They changed their exquisite operatic uniforms so many times in the day: they accepted with such sublime effrontery the salute of the goose step from a squad of magnificent peasants dressed up as soldiers; they painted and powdered their faces, wore pink velvet bands round their *képis* under nodding *panaches;* and not one but could display upon his breast the ribbon of the bloodless campaign against Bulgaria of two years before. When they came jangling into the cabaret, one felt that the destinies of Europe were attached to their sword-belts, as comfort hangs upon the tinkling of a housekeeper's *châtelaine.*

'If Italy declares war, we shall declare war; for we are more Roman than they are. If Italy remains neutral we shall remain neutral; because the Latin races must hold together,' the patrons of the Entente avowed.

'Italy will not declare war; and we shall have to fight the Russians. We won Plevna for them and lost Bessarabia as a reward. As soon as Austria understands that she must give us Transylvania we shall declare war,' said the patrons of the Central Powers.

'We shall remain neutral. Our neutrality is precious to both sides,' murmured a third set.

And after all, Sylvia thought, the last was probably the wisest view, for it would be a shame to spoil the pretty uniforms of the officers and a crime to maim the bodies of the nobler peasants they commanded.

In such an atmosphere Sylvia had to postpone any solution of the spiritual side of Queenie's problem and concentrate upon keeping her out of immediate mischief. The manager of the Petit Maxim had judged the tastes of his clients accurately, and Queenie had not been dancing at the cabaret for a fortnight when one read on the programme: QUEENIE, LA JEUNE DANSEUSE ANGLAISE ET L'ENFANT GATEE DE BUCURESTI. Chocolates and flowers were showered upon her, and her faintest smile would uncork a bottle of champagne. But every morning at three o'clock when the cabaret closed, Sylvia snatched her away from all the suitors and took her home as quickly as possible to their hotel. She used to dread nightly the arrival of the moment when Queenie would refuse to go with her, but the moment did not come; and the child never once grumbled at Sylvia's sigh of relief to find themselves back in their own bedroom. In order as much as possible to distract her from the importunities of hopeful lovers Sylvia would always aim at surrounding herself and Queenie with the political schemers, so that the evening might pass away in speculation upon the future of the war and the imminence of Roumanian intervention. She impressed upon Queenie the necessity of seeming interested in the fate of the country of which he was supposed to be a native. They were the only English girls in the cabaret, in fact the only English actresses apparently anywhere in Bucharest; Sylvia finding that man is much more of a political animal in the Balkans than elsewhere took advantage of the general curiosity about England's personality to get as many bottles of champagne opened for information from her own lips as out of admiration and desire for Queenie's.

From general political discussions it was a short way to the more intimate discussions of faction's intrigue; and Sylvia became an expert on the ways and means of the swarm of German agents who corrupted Bucharest as bluebottles taint fresh meat. She sometimes wondered if she ought not to convey some of the knowledge thus acquired to the British Legation; but she supposed on second thoughts that she was unlikely to know anything that the authorities therein did not already know much better, and being averse from seeming to put herself forward for personal advantage, she did not move in the matter.

One of the chief frequenters of their company was a young lieutenant of the cavalry called Philidor with whom Sylvia made friends. He was an enthusiast for the cause of the Entente, and she learnt from him a great deal about the point of view of a Balkan state, so that when she had known him for a time she was able to judge both Roumania as a whole and the individual extravagances and vanities of Roumanians more generously.

'I don't think you quite understand,' he once said to her, 'the fearful responsibility that will rest upon the Balkan statesman who decides the policy of his country in this crisis. Whatever happens, England will remain England, France will remain France, Germany will remain Germany; but in Roumania, although our sympathies are with you, our geographical position makes us the natural allies of the Germans. Suppose we march with you and something goes wrong. Nothing can prevent us from being Germanised for the rest of our history. You mustn't pay too much attention to the talk you hear about the great power of Roumania and the influence we shall have upon the course of the war. Such talk springs from a half-expressed nervousness at the position in which we find ourselves. We are trying to bolster ourselves up with the sense of our own importance in the hope that we shall have the wisdom to direct our policy rightly. We are not a great power; we are a little power; and our only chance of becoming a great power would be that Austria should break up, that Russia should crumble away, and that the whole vile country of Bulgaria should be obliterated from the surface of the earth. It is certain that Bulgaria will march with Germany; nothing can stop that except the defeat of Germany this year. Possibly Italy may come in on your side this spring, but tied as we are to her by blood, we are separated from her by miles of alien populations, and Italy cannot help us. Greece is in the same plight as we are – not quite perhaps, because she can depend for succour upon the sea: we can't. Ah,

if you could only open the Dardanelles! If you only had a statesman to see that there lies the key to certain victory in this war.
But statesmen no longer exist among you great powers. You've
become too big for statesmen and can only produce politicians.
The only statesmen in Europe nowadays are to be found in the
Balkans, because since every man here is a politician it requires a
statesman to rise above the ruck. Paradox though it may seem,
statesmen create states; they are not created by them. We have all
our history before us in the Balkans, if we can only survive being
swallowed up in this cataclysm; but I doubt if we can. To you
this country of mine is like a comic opera, but to me, one of the
players, it is as tragic as *Pagliacci*.

'You are right in a way to mock at our aristocracy, though
much of that aristocracy is not truly Roumanian, but bastard
Greek; yet we have such a wonderful peasantry, and an idealist
like myself dreads the effect of this war. All our plans of
emancipation, all our schemes for destroying the power of the
great landowners,' and in a whisper he added, 'all our hopes of
a republic are doomed to failure. I tell you, my dear, it's tragic
opera, not comic opera.'

'But if you are a republican, why do you wear the uniform of
a crack cavalry regiment?' Sylvia asked.

'Oh, I've thought that out,' Philidor replied. 'I belong to a
good family. If I proclaimed my opinions openly, I should
merely be put on one side. Aristocratic rule is more powerful in
Roumania than anywhere in Europe except Prussia. The aristo-
crats have literally all the capital of the country in their hands;
our peasants are serfs. As an avowed republican I could do
nothing to spread the opinions that I believe to be the salvation
of my country and the preservation of her true independence;
we are a young state – not a state at all in fact, but a limited
liability company with a director imported from the chief
European firm of king-exporters – and we have still to realise
our soul as by fire.'

'The soul of a country,' Sylvia murmured. 'It's only the
aggregate of the human souls that make it, but each soul could
be the microcosm of the universe.'

'True, true,' Philidor agreed. 'And the soul of Roumania is
the soul of a girl who's just out, or of a boy in his first year at
college. Hence all the prettiness and all the complacent naughtiness and all the imitation of older and more worldly people and
all the tyranny and contempt for the rights of the poor, the
want of consideration for servants really. Though I must be

young like the rest and dress myself up and lead the life of my friends, I am always hoping to influence them gradually, very gradually. Perhaps if I were truly a great soul I should fling over all this pretence; but I know my own limitations, and all I pray is that when the man arises who is worthy to lead Roumania toward liberty and justice I shall have the wit to recognise him and the courage to follow his lead.'

'But you said just now,' Sylvia reminded him, 'that all the European statesmen were to be found in the Balkans.'

'I still say that, but our statesmen – we have only two – dare not in the presence of this war think of anything except the safety of the country. Republicanism would be of little use to a Roumania absorbed either into the Dual Monarchy or into the Tsardom of Russia or ravaged by the hellish Bulgarians. I tell you that we see precipices before our steps whichever way we turn for the path; but because we are young we dress ourselves up and gamble and sing and dance and swagger and boast; we are young, my dear girl, very very young, perhaps not old enough for our death to be anything but pathetic.

'You're in a very pessimistic mood tonight,' Sylvia said.

'Who could be anything but gloomy when he looks round a room like this? A crowd of French, Roumanian, and Austrian cocottes dancing to *Tipperary* in this infernal tinkling din – forgive my frankness, but you know I don't include *you* in the *galère* – while over there I see a cousin of my own, a member of one of our greatest families, haggling with a dirty German agent over the price of sending another six aeroplanes to Turkey disguised as agricultural implements; and over there I see a man, who I had always hoped was an honest editor, selling his pen to the fat little German baron that will substitute poison for ink and banknotes for honest opinions; and over there are three brother officers with three girls on the knees singing the words of *Tipperary* with as much intelligence as apes, while they brag to their companions of how in six weeks they will be marching to save France.'

'They don't miss much by not understanding the words,' Sylvia said with a smile.

'I don't understand how a woman like you can tolerate or endure this life,' Philidor exclaimed fanatically. 'Why don't you take that pretty little sister of yours out of it and back to England? I don't understand how you can stay here with your country at war.'

'That's too long a story to tell you now,' Sylvia said. 'But between ourselves she's not really my sister.'

'I never supposed she was,' Philidor answered. 'She's not English either is she?'

Sylvia looked at him sharply.

'Have you heard anyone else say that?' she asked.

'Nobody else here knows English as well as I do.'

The dance stopped, and Queenie leaving her partner came up to their table with a smile.

'You're happy anyway,' said Philidor.

'Oh, yes. I'm so happy. She is so sweet to me,' Queenie cried, embracing Sylvia impulsively.

A French girl sitting at the next table laughed and murmured an epithet in *argot*. Sylvia's cheeks flamed; she was about to spring up and make a quarrel, but Philidor restrained her.

'Do you wonder that I protest against your exposing yourself to that sort of thing?' he said. 'What are you going to do? It wouldn't be quite you, would it, to hit her over the head with a champagne bottle? Let the vile tongue say what it pleases.'

'Yes, but it's so outrageous, it's so – ah, I've no words for the beastliness of people,' Sylvia exclaimed.

'May I dance this dance?' Queenie interrupted timidly.

'Good heavens, why do you ask me, girl? What has it to do with me? Dance with the devil if you like.'

Queenie looked bewildered by Sylvia's emphasis and went off again in silence.

'And now you see the only person that's really hurt is your little friend,' Philidor observed. 'You're much too sure of yourself to care about a sneer like that, and she didn't hear what the woman called you or perhaps understand it if she heard.'

Sylvia was silent; she was thinking of once long ago when Lily had asked her if she could dance with Michael; now she blushed after nine years lest he might have thought for a moment what that woman had said.

'You're quite right,' she agreed with Philidor. 'This is a damnable life. Would you like to hear Queenie's story?'

'There's no need for you to defend yourself to me,' he laughed.

'Ah, don't laugh about it. You mustn't laugh about certain things. You'll make me think less of you.'

'I was only being *gauche*,' he apologised. 'Yes, tell me her story.'

So Sylvia told him the sad history, and when she had finished asked his advice about Queenie.

'You were talking just now about your country as if she were a child,' she said eagerly. 'You were imagining her individuality and independence destroyed. I feel the same about this girl. I want to make her really English. Do you think that I shall be able to get her a passport? We're saving up our money now to go to England.'

Philidor said he did not know much about English regulations, but that he could not imagine that any consul would refuse to help when he heard the story.

'And the sooner you leave Roumania the better. Look here. I'll send you the money to get home.'

Sylvia shook her head.

'No, because that would interfere with my part of the story. I've got to get back without help. I have a strong belief that if I accept help I shall miss my destiny. It's no good trying to argue me out of a superstition, for I've tried to argue myself out of it a dozen times and failed. No, if you want to help me, come and talk to me every night and open a bottle or two of champagne to keep the manager in a good temper; and stand by me, if there's ever a row. I won't answer for myself if I'm alone and I hear things said like what was said tonight.'

Philidor promised he would do that for her as long as he was quartered in Bucharest, and presently Queenie came back.

'Don't be so frightened. I'm sorry I was cross to you just now.'

'You were being so savage,' said Queenie with wide-open wondering eyes. 'What was happening?'

'Something stung me.'

'Where?'

'Over the heart,' Sylvia answered.

When they were back in their room Queenie returned to the subject of Sylvia's ill-temper.

'I could not be thinking it was you,' she murmured. 'I could not be thinking it.'

'It was something that passes as quickly as it came,' Sylvia said. 'Forget about it, child.'

'Were you angry because I was being too much with that boy? If you like I shall say to him tomorrow that I cannot dance with him longer.'

'Please, Queenie, forget about it. Somebody said something that made me angry, and I vented my anger on you. It was of no importance.'

Queenie looked only half convinced and when she was in bed she turned for consolation to the little chromolithographs that were always at hand. She had the custom of wearing a lace night-cap and, sitting up thus in bed while her rapt gaze sought in those fairy landscapes the reflection of her own visions, she was remote and impersonal as a painted figure in some adoring angelic company. Sylvia felt that the moment was come to raise the question of the spiritual mood with which Queenie's outward appearance seemed in harmony, and that it was her duty to suggest a way of positively capturing and for ever enshrining the half revealed wonders of which these pictures spoke to her. Sylvia fancied that Queenie's development had now only reached as far as her own at about fifteen and, looking back to herself at that age, she thought how much it might have meant to her if somebody could have given expression to her capacity for wonder then. Moreover, it was improbably that Queenie would grow much older mentally, and it was impossible for Queenie to reach her own present point of view by her own long process of rejecting every other point of view in turn. Queenie would never reject anything of her own accord, and it seemed urgent to fortify her with the simple and in some eyes childish externals of religion, which precisely on account of such souls have managed to endure.

'The great argument in favour of the Church seems to me,' Sylvia thought, 'that it measure humanity by the weakest and not by the strongest link, which of course means that it never overestimates its power and survives assaults that shatter more ambitious and progressive organisations of human belief. Well, Queenie is a weak enough link, and I shan't feel happy until I have secured her incorporation first into the Church and secondly – I suppose into the State. Yet why should I want to give her nationality? What is the aim of a state? Material comfort really – nothing else. I'm tempted to give her to the Church, but deny her to the State. Alas, it's a material world, and it's not going to be spiritualised by me. The devil was sick, etc. No doubt at present everything promises well for a spiritual revival after this orgy of insane destructiveness. But history with its mania for repetition isn't encouraging about the results of war. As a matter of fact I've got no right to talk about the war at present. I choked and spluttered for a while in some of its vile backwash, and Bucharest hasn't managed to get the taste out of my mouth. Queenie,' she said aloud, 'You know that during these last weeks I've been going to church regularly?'

Queenie extricated herself from whatever path she was following in her pictures and looked at Sylvia with blue eyes that were intensely willing to believe anything her friend told her.

'I knew you were always going out,' she said. 'But I thought it was to see a boy.'

'Great heavens, child, do you seriously think that I should so much object to men's getting hold of you if I were doing the same thing myself in secret? Haven't you yet grasped that I can't do things in secret?'

'Don't be cross with me again. I think you are cross, yes?' Sylvia shook her head.

'What I want to know is: did you ever go to church in your life, and if you did do you ever think about wanting to go again?'

'I was going to church with my mother when I was four; my stepmother was never going to church, and so I was never going myself until two years ago at Christmas. There was a girl who asked me to go with her, and it was so sweet. We looked at all the dolls, and there was a cow, but some woman said quite loudly: "Well, if this is the sort of women we was meeting on Christmas night, I'm glad Christmas only comes once in the year." My friend with me was very *maquilleé*. Too much paint she was having really, and she said to this woman such rude things, and a man came and was asking us to move along further. And then outside my friend sat down on the steps and cried and cried. *Ach,* it was dreadful. She was making a scene. So I was not going more to church, because I was always remembering this and being unhappy.'

On the next day Sylvia took Queenie to the mission-church and introduced her to the priest; afterwards they often went to Mass together. It was like taking a child; Queenie asked the reason of every ceremony, and Sylvia, who had never bothered her head with ceremonies, began to wish she had never exposed herself to so many unanswerable questions. It seemed to her that she had given Queenie nothing except another shadowy land in which her vague mind would wander without direction; but the priest was more hopeful and undertook to give her instruction so that she might be confirmed presently. When the question was gone into, there was no doubt that she had been baptised, for by some freak of memory she was able to show that she understood the reason of her being called Concetta from being born on the eighth of December. However, the revelation of her true name to the priest gave Queenie a horror of his company, and nothing would induce her to go near him again, or even to enter the church.

'This was going to bring me bad luck,' she told Sylvia. 'That

106

name! that name! How was you so unkind to tell him that name?'

Sylvia was distressed by the thought of the fear she had roused and explained the circumstances to the priest, who rather to her irritation seemed inclined to resort placidly to prayer.

'But I can only pray when I am in the mood to pray,' she protested; and though she was aware of the weakness of such a habit of mind, she was anxious to shake the priest out of what she considered his undue resignation to her failure with Queenie.

The fact was that the atmosphere of the Petit Maxim was getting on Sylvia's nerves. Apart from the physical revolt that it was impossible not to feel against the fumes of tobacco and wine, the scent of Eau de Chypre and Quelques Fleurs, the raucous chatter of conversation and the jangle of fidgety tunes, there was the perpetual inner resentment against the gossip about herself and Queenie. Sylvia did not lose any of her own joy at being able to rest in the high airs of Christian thought away from all this by reading the books of doctrine and ecclesiastical history that the priest lent her; but she was disappointed at her inability to provide any alternative for Queenie except absolute dependence upon herself. She was quite prepared to accept the final responsibility of guardianship, and she made it clear to the child that her ambition to have a permanent sister might be considered achieved. What she was not prepared to do was to invoke exterior aid to get them both back to England. She reproached herself sometimes with an unreasonable egotism; yet when it came to the point of accepting Philidor's offer to lend her enough money to return home, she always drew back. Life with Queenie at Mulberry Cottage shone steadily upon the horizon of her hopes, but she had no belief in the value of that life unless she could reach it unaided and offer its freedom as the fruit for her own perseverance and indomitableness. She was annoyed by Queenie's forebodings over the revelation of her name, and her annoyance was not any the less because she had to admit that her own behaviour in holding out against accepting the means of escape from Roumania was based on nothing more secure than a superstitious fancy.

The Petit Maxim closed at Easter; at the beginning of May the whole company was re-engaged for an open air theatre called the Petit Trianon. Sylvia and Queenie were still many francs short of their fares to England and were forced to re-engage themselves for the summer. The new place was an improvement on the cabaret, because at any rate during the first half of May it was too cold for the public to enjoy sitting about in a garden and drinking sweet champagne. After a month, however, all Sylvia's friends went away, some to Sinaia whither the court had moved; others, and amongst them Philidor, were sent to the Austrian frontier; the expedition to the Dardanelles and the intervention of Italy had brought Roumania much nearer to the prospect of entering the war. Meanwhile in Bucnarest the German agents worked more assiduously than ever to promote neutrality and secure the passage of arms and munitions to Turkey.

At the end of May the manager of the Petit Trianon, observing that Sylvia had for some time failed to take advantage of the warmer weather by gathering to her table a proper number of champagne drinkers and having received complaints from some of his clients that she made it impossible to cultivate Queenie's company to the extent they would have liked, announced to her that she was no longer wanted. Her songs at the beginning of the evening were no attraction to the thin audience scattered about under the trees, and he could get a cheaper first number. This happened to be Lottie, who was engaged to thump on the piano for half an hour at two hundred francs a month.

'I never knew that I was cutting you out,' Lottie explained. 'But I've been playing for nearly four months at a dancing-hall in a low part of the town and I only asked two hundred in desperation. He'll probably engage you again if you'll take less.'

Sylvia forced herself to ask the manager, if he would not change his mind. She hinted as a final threat that she would make Queenie leave if he did not, and he agreed at last to engage her again at three hundred francs instead of three hundred and fifty, which meant that she could not save a sou towards her going home. At the same time the manager dismissed Lottie, and everybody said that Sylvia had played a mean trick. She would not have minded so much if she had not felt really sad about the fat girl, who was driven back to play in a low dancing-saloon at less than she had earned before; but she felt that there was no time to be lost in getting Queenie away from this life, and if it were a question of sacrificing Queenie or Lottie, it was certainly the fat girl who must go under.

Since the manager's complaint of the way she kept admirers away from her friend, Sylvia had for both their sakes to relax some of her discouraging stiffness of demeanour. One young man was hopeful enough of ultimate success to send Queenie a bunch of carnations wrapped up in a thousand-franc note. Normally Sylvia would have compelled her to refuse such a large earnest of future liberality; but these months upon the verge of penury had hardened her, and she bade Queenie keep the money, or rather she kept it for her to prevent its being frittered away in petty extravagance. Queenie could not hold her tongue about the offering; and the young man, when he found that the thousand francs had brought him no nearer to his goal than a bottle of champagne would have done, was loud in his advertisement of the way Sylvia had let Queenie take the money and give nothing in return. Everybody at the Petit Trianon was positive that Sylvia was living upon her friend, and much unpleasant gossip was brought back to them by people who of course did not believe it themselves, but thought it right that they should know what all the world was saying.

This malicious talk had no effect upon Queenie's devotion, but it added greatly to Sylvia's disgust for the tawdry existence they were both leading, and she began to play with the idea of using the thousand francs to escape from it and get back to England. She was still some way from bringing herself to the point of such a surrender as would be involved by temporarily using this money, but each time that she argued out the point with herself the necessity of doing so presented itself more insistently. In the middle of July something occurred which swept on one side every consideration but immediate flight.

All day long a warm and melancholy fog had suffused the suburbs of Bucharest, from which occasional scarves of mist detached themselves to float through the high centre of the town dislustring the air as they went, like steam upon a shining metal. Sylvia had been intending for some time to visit Lottie and explain to her the circumstances in which she had been supplanted by herself; such a day as this accorded well with such an errand. As with all cities of its class a few minutes after one left the main streets of Bucharest to go downhill one was aware or the artificiality of its metropolitan claims. Within five hundred yards of the sumptuous Calea Victoriei the side turnings were full of children playing in the gutter, of untidy women gossiping to one another from untidy windows, and of small rubbish-heaps along the pavement: and a little farther on were signs of the unquiet newness of the city in the number of half-constructed streets and half-built houses.

Lottie lived in one of these unfinished streets in a tumbledown house that had survived the fields by which not long ago it had been surrounded. A creeper-covered doorway opened into a paved triangular courtyard shaded by an unwieldy tree, along one side of which at an elevation of about two feet ran Lottie's room. As Sylvia crossed the courtyard she could see indistinct forms moving about within; and she stopped for a moment listening to the drip of the fog above the murmur of human voices. She did not wish to talk to Lottie in front of strangers and turned to go back; but the fat girl had already observed her approach and was standing on the rotten threshold to receive her.

'You're busy,' Sylvia suggested.

'No, no. Come in. One of my friends is an English girl.'

'But I wanted to talk to you alone. I wanted to explain that I couldn't refuse to sing again at the Trianon; I've been worrying about you all this time.'

'Oh, that's all right,' Lottie said cheerfully. 'I never expected anything else.'

'But the other girls —'

'Oh, the other girls,' she repeated with a contemptuous laugh. 'Don't worry about the other girls. People can always afford to be generous in this world if it doesn't hurt themselves and does hurt somebody else. One or two of them came here to condole with me, and I'm sure they got more pleasure out of seeing my wretched lodging than I got out of their sympathy. Come in and forget all about them.'

Sylvia squeezed her pudgy hand gratefully; it was a relief to find that the object of so much commiseration had grasped the shallowness of it.

'Who are your friends?' she whispered.

'The man's a juggler who wants an engagement at the Trianon. He's a Swiss called Krebs. The girl's an English dancer and singer called Maud. You'll see them both up there to-night for certain. You may as well come in. What a dreary day, isn't it?'

Sylvia agreed and was aware of ascribing to the weather the faint malaise that she experienced on following Lottie into her room, which smelt of stale wallpaper and musty wood and which on account of the overhanging tree and the dirty French windows was dark and miserable enough.

'Excuse me getting up to shake hands,' said Krebs in excellent English. 'But this furniture is too luxurious.'

He was lying back smoking a cigarette in an armchair, all the legs of which were missing and the rest of it covered with exudations of flocculence that resembled dingy cauliflowers. Sylvia saw that he was a large man with a large undefined face of dark complexion. He offered a huge hand, brutal and clumsy in appearance an appropriate hand for a juggler, she thought vaguely. His companion, crudely coloured and shapeless as a quilt, sprawled on another chair. Everything about this woman was defiant; her harsh accent, the feathers in her hat, her loose mouth, her magenta cheeks, her white boa, and her white boots affronted the world like an angry housemaid.

'This is a fine hole, this Roumania,' she shrilled. 'Gawd! I went to the English consul at Galantza expecting to be treated with a little consideration, and the — pushed me out of his office. Yes, we read a great deal about England nowadays, but I've been better treated by everybody than what I have by the English. Stuck-up la-di-da set of — that's what they are, and anybody as likes can hear me say so.'

She raised her voice for the benefit of the listeners without that might be waiting anxiously upon her words.

'Don't kick up such a row,' Krebs commanded; but Maud paid no attention to him and went on.

'England! Yes, I left England ten years ago, and if it wasn't for my poor old mother I'd never go back. Treat you as dirt that's what the English do. That consul threw me out of his office the same as a commissionaire might throw any old two-and-four out of the Empire. Yes, they talk a lot about patriotism and all pulling one way, but when you ask a consul to lend you the price of your fare to Bucharest you don't hear no more about patriotism. As I said to him, "I suppose you don't think I'm English?" and he sat there grinning for answer. Yes, I reckon when they christened that talking chimpanzee at the Hippodrome "Consul", it was done by somebody who'd had a bit of consul in his time. What's a consul for? that's what I'm asking. As I said to him, "What are you for? Are you paid," I said, "to sit there smoking cigarettes for the good of your country?" "This ain't a workhouse," he answered very snotty. "You're right," I said. "No fear that anyone ever making that mistake. Why, I reckon it's a bloody sleeping-car, I do." And with that I slung my hook out of it. Yes, I could have been very rude to him; only it was beneath me, the uneducated la-di-da savage! Well, all he's done is to put me against my own country. That's *his* war work.'

The tirade exhausted itself, and Sylvia unwilling to be Maud's sponsor at the Petit Trianon that evening made some excuse to leave. While she was walking across the courtyard with Lottie, she heard:

'And who's she? I'll have to tell *her* off, that's very plain. Did you see the way she looked down her nose at me? Nice thing if anyone can't say what they think of a consul without being stared at like a mummy by *her*.'

Sylvia asked Lottie if she had known this couple long.

'I've known him a year or two, but she's new. I met them coming up from the railway-station this morning. The girl was stranded without any money at Galantza, and Krebs brought her on here. He's a fine juggler and conjurer. Zozo he calls himself on the stage.'

Sylvia's heart throbbed as she climbed the streets that led toward the high centre of the city away from the hot mists below; it was imperative to get Queenie out of Roumania at once, and while she walked along she began to wonder if she could not procure an English passport, the delight of possessing which would counter-balance for Queenie the shock of hearing that the dreaded Zozo was in Bucharest.

'It's such a ridiculous name for a bogey,' Sylvia thought. 'And the man himself was not a bit as I pictured him. I'd always imagined someone lithe and subtle. I wonder what his object was in helping that painted hussy he was with. Queer rather.'

She reached the British Consulate, but was told rather severely to direct herself to the special office that occupied itself with passports.

'Do you want a visa for England?' the clerk enquired.

'Yes, and I also want to enquire about a new passport for my sister who's lost hers.'

'Lost her passport?' the clerk echoed; he shuddered at the information.

'It seems to upset you,' Sylvia said.

'Well, it's a pretty serious matter in war time,' he explained. 'However, we have nothing to do with passports at the consulate.'

The clerk washed his hands of Sylvia's past and future; and she left the consulate to discover the other office. By the time she arrived it was nearly five o'clock, and the clerk looked hurt at receiving a visitor so late.

'Do you want a visa for England?' he asked.

She nodded, and he pointed to a printed notice that hung above his desk.

'The morning is the time to make such applications,' he told her fretfully.

'Then why are you open in the afternoon?' Sylvia asked.

'If the application is favourably entertained, the recommendation is granted in the afternoon. You must then take your passport to the consulate for the consular visa, which can only be done in the morning between twelve and one.'

It was like the eternal competition between the tube-lifts and the tube-trains, she thought.

'But they told me at the consulate that they have nothing to do with passports.'

'The consulate *has* nothing to do with passports until the applicant for a visa has been approved here.'

'Then I must come again tomorrow morning?' Sylvia asked.

'Tomorrow morning,' the clerk repeated, bending over with intrepid fervour to the responsible task upon which he was engaged. Sylvia wondered what it was: the whole traffic of Europe might hang upon these few minutes.

'I'm sorry to interrupt you again,' she said. 'But in addition to requiring a visa, my sister wants a new passport.'

She decided not to say anything about a lost passport, the revelation of which had so much shocked the man at the consulate.

'Miss Johnstone,' the clerk call in a weary voice to somebody in an inner office. 'Kindly bring Form AQ – application for renewal of expired passport.'

A vague looking young women, who seemed to have been collecting native jewellery since her arrival in Bucharest, tinkled into the office.

'There aren't any AQ forms left, Mr Mathers,' she said, plaiting as she spoke a necklace of coins into another of what looked like broken pieces of mosiac.

'It really is too bad that the forms are not given out more regularly,' Mr Mathers cried in exasperation. 'How am I to finish transferring these Greeks beginning with *C* to *K*? You know how anxious Mr Iredale is to get the index in order, and the *F*'s haven't been check with the *Ph*'s yet.'

'Well, it's Miss Henson's day off,' said Miss Johnstone, 'so it's not my fault is it? I'm sure I hate the forms! They're always a bother. Won't an AP one do for this lady? We've a lot of them left, and there's only a difference in one question.'

'Excuse me,' Sylvia asked. 'Did you mention a Mr Iredale?'

'Mr Iredale is the O.C.P.T.N.C. for Bucharest,' said Mr Mathers.

'Not Mr Philip Iredale by chance?' she went on.

That transposition of Greek initials had sounded uncommonly like Philip.

'That's right,' the clerk replied.

'Oh well, I know him. I should like to see him personally.'

'See Mr Iredale? But he's the O.C.P.T.N.C.'

'Does that confer invisibility?' she asked. 'I tell you I'm a friend of his. If you send up my card, I'm sure he'll see me.'

'But he never sees anybody,' Mr Mathers objected. 'I'm afraid you didn't understand that he's the Officer Controlling Passenger Traffic from Neutral Countries in Bucharest. If he was to see everybody that came to this office, he wouldn't be able to control *himself*, let alone passenger traffic. No really, joking apart, madam, Mr Iredale is very busy and by no means well.'

'He's worn out,' put in Miss Johnstone, who having by now plaited four necklaces into a single coil was swinging the result round and round like a skipping-rope. 'His nerves are worn out. But if you like I'll take up your card.'

'You might ask him at the same time if he wants all the Greek names entered under *Y* transferred to *G*, will you?' said Mr Mathers. 'Oh, and Miss Johnstone,' he called after her, 'there seems to be some confusion between *T ch* and *Ts*. Ask him if he's got any preference. Awful names the people in this part of Europe get hold of,' he added to Sylvia, 'Even Mr Iredale can't transpose the Russians, and of course the War Office likes accuracy. There was rather a strafe the other day because a man travelling from here to Spain got arrested three times on the way owing to his name being rather like a suspect spelt differently by us, the French, and the Italians. As a matter of fact, the original suspect's dead, but his name was spelt a fourth way in the notification that was sent round, and so it's not realised yet.'

'It must be rather like that whispering game,' Sylvia said. 'You know, where somebody at one end of the room starts a sentence and it comes out quite differently at the other.'

Sylvia could not make out why she did not feel more nervous when she was following Miss Johnstone upstairs to meet Philip for the first time since she had run away from him thirteen years ago. The fact was that her anxiety to escape from Roumania with Queenie outweighed everything else, and she was so glad to find somebody she knew in a position of authority who would be able to help her in the matter of Queenie's passport that any awkwardness was quenched in relief. The discovery of Philip was such an encouraging answer by destiny to the reappearance of Zozo.

He came forward to greet her from behind a large rolltop desk, and she saw that he looked tired and ill, yet except for his baldness not really much older.

'Would you have recognised me, Philip?' she asked.

He was far more nervous than she was, and he stumbled a good deal over Mr Mathers' questions.

'I'll tell him you're too busy now to answer,' said Miss Johnstone at last in a cheerful voice.

This was a happy solution of the problem of *Ts* and *Tch,* and Philip gratefully accepted it.

'And I daresay I might find time to help him with the transpositions, if you're very anxious to get them done.'

'Oh, will you? Yes, thank you, that would be excellent.'

Miss Johnstone turned to leave the room; one of her necklaces broke under the strain of continuous plaiting, and a number of tiny green shells peppered the floor.

'There, that's the third time it's done that today,' she exclaimed. 'I'm so sorry.'

Sylvia, Philip and she gathered up as many as were not trodden upon in the search, and at last Miss Johnstone managed to get out of the room.

'No wonder you're worn out,' said Sylvia with a smile. It seemed quite natural to comment rather intimately like this upon Philip's health. 'But you haven't answered my question. Would you have recognised me?'

'Oh yes, I should have recognised you. I saw you only last year at the Pierian Hall.'

'Did you go to see me there?' she exclaimed, touched by his having wanted to see her act without letting her know anything about his visit.

'Yes, I enjoyed the performance; it was excellent. I wonder why you're in Bucharest. Wouldn't you be better in England in war time?'

'I think it's much more surprising to find you here,' she said.

'Oh, I was sent out here to look after passports.'

'But, Philip, why were you chosen as an expert on human nature?'

She could not resist the little stab; and he smiled sadly.

'I knew the country,' he explained. 'I'd done some excavating here, so the War Office made me an honorary captain and sent me out.'

'Are you a captain? What fun! Do you remember when I wanted you to enlist for the South African war and you were so annoyed? But I suppose you're shocked by my reviving old memories like this. Are you shocked, Philip?'

'No, no, I'm not shocked. I'm still rather overcome by the suddenness of your visit. What are you doing here?'

'I'm singing at the Trianon. All the winter I was at the Petit Maxim.'

'Those places,' he said with a look of distaste.

'It would take too long to explain to you why,' she went on. 'But you can't disapprove of my being there more than I do myself; and it's for that very reason that I want a visa for England.'

'Of course you shall have one immediately. You're much better at home in these detestable times.'

'But I also want something else. I want a passport for a friend – an English girl.'

'Hasn't she got a passport? Does she want hers renewed?'

'I'd better tell you the whole story. I expect that since you've become the U.V.W.X.Y.Z. of Bucharest, you've listened to plenty of sad stories, but you must pay special attention to this one for my sake. I don't know why I say "for my sake" – it's rather an improper remark for a divorced wife. Philip, do you remember in my show at the Pierian an Improvisation about a girl who had been horribly ill-treated as a child and was supposed to be lost in a great city?'

'Yes, I think I do, in fact I'm sure I do. I remember that at the time I was reminded of our first meeting in Brompton Cemetery.' He blinked once or twice very quickly, and coughed in his old embarrassed way.

'Well, that's the girl for whom I want a passport.'

Sylvia told him Queenie's story in detail from the time she met her first in Granada to the present moment under the shadow of Zozo's return.

'But, My dear Sylvia, I can't possibly procure an English passport for her. She's not English.'

'I want her to be my sister,' Sylvia pursued. 'I'm prepared to adopt her and to be responsible for her. Any difference in the name she had been generally known by can easily be put down to the needs of the stage. I myself want to take once more my own name Sylvia Snow, and I thought you could issue two passports, one to Sylvia Snow professionaly known as Sylvia Scarlett, and the other to Queenie Snow known professionally as Queenie Walters. Surely you won't let mere pedantry interfere with a deed of charity?'

'It's not a question of pedantry. This is war time. I should render myself liable to – to – a court-martial for doing a thing like that. Besides, the principle of the thing is all wrong.'

'But you don't seem to understand.'

'Indeed I understand perfectly,' Philip interrupted. 'This girl was born in Germany.'

'Of an Italian father.'

'What papers has she?' he asked.

'None at all. That's the whole point. She couldn't get even a German passport if she wanted to. But she doesn't want one. She longs to be English. It's the solitary clear ambition that she has. She was living in England before war broke out, and she only came away to help this girl who was kind to her. Surely the most rigid rule can be unbent to fit a special case?'

'I could not possibly assume the responsibility,' Philip declared.

'Then you mean to say you'll condemn this child to damnation for that's what you're doing with your infernal rules and regulations? You're afraid of what will happen to you.'

'Excuse me, even if I were certain that nothing could possibly be known about the circumstances in which this passport was issued, I should still refuse the application. Everybody suffers in this war; I suffer myself in a minor degree by having to abandon my own work and masquerade in this country as what you well call an U.V.W.X.Y.Z.'

'But even if we grant that in some cases suffering is inevitable,' Sylvia urged eagerly, 'here's a case where it is not. Here's a case where by applying a touch of humanity you can save a soul. But I won't put it that way, because I know you have no use for souls. Here's a case where you can save a body for civilisation, for that fetish on whose account you find yourself in Bucharest and half Europe is slaughtering the other half. You are not appealing to any divine law when you refuse to grant this passport; you are appealing to a human law. Very well then. You are in your own way at this moment fighting for England; yet when somebody longs to be English you refuse her. If there is any reality behind your patriotism, if it is not merely the basest truckling to a name, a low and cowardly imitation of your next door neighbour whose opinion of yourself you fear as much as he fears your opinion of him, if your patriotism is not just this, you'll be glad to give this child the freedom of your country. Philip, you and I made a mess of things. I was to blame for half the mess; but when you married me, though you married me primarily to please yourself, there was another motive behind – the desire to give a lonely little girl a chance to deal with the life that was surging round her more and more dangerously every day. Now you have another opportunity of doing the same thing, and this time without any personal gratification. It isn't as if I were asking you to do something that could possibly hurt England. I tell you I will be responsible for her. If the worst came to the worst and anything were found out, I could always take the blame and you could never be even censured for accepting my word in such a case.'

Sylvia could see by Philip's face that her arguments were doing nothing to convince him, yet she went on desperately:

'And if you refuse this, you don't merely condemn her, you condemn me too. Nothing will induce me to abandon her to that man. By your bowing down to the letter of the regulation, you expose me for the second time to the life that you drove me to before.'

Philip made a gesture of protest.

'Very well, then I won't accuse you of being responsible on the first occasion, certainly not wantonly. But this time, if I'm driven to the same life, it *will* be your fault and your fault alone. I'm not going to bother about my body, if I think that by destroying it I can save a soul. I shall stick at nothing to preserve Queenie – at nothing, do you hear? You have the chance to send us both safely back to England. Philip, you won't refuse!'

'I'm sorry. It's terribly painful for me to say "no". But it's impossible. Only quite recently the Foreign Office sent round a warning that we were to be specially careful in this part of the world. No papers of naturalisation are issued in time of war. Why, I'm sent here to Bucharest for the express purpose of preventing people like your friend obtaining fraudulent passports.'

'The Foreign Office!' Sylvia scoffed. 'How can you expect people not to be Christians? It was just to redeem mankind from the sin that creates Foreign Offices and War Offices and bureaucrats and shoddy kings and lawyers and politicians that Christ died. Oh, you can sneer; but your unbelief is condemned out of your own mouth. You puny little U.V.W.X.Y.Z. with your nose buried in your own waste-paper basket, with a red tapeworm gnawing at your vitals, with some damned fool of a narrow-headed general for an idol, you have the impertinence to sneer at Christianity. Do you think that after this war people are going to be content with the kind of criminal state that you represent? Life is not a series of rules, but a set of exceptions. Philip, forgive me if I have been rude, and let this girl have a passport, please, please!'

'You must not think,' Philip answered, 'that because I plead the necessities of war in defence of what strikes you as mere bureaucratic obscurantism that therefore I am defending war itself; I loathe war from the bottom of my heart. But just as painful operations are often necessary in accidents which might easily have been avoided, yet which having happened must be cured in the swiftest way: so in war time for the good of the majority the wrongs of the nation must take precedence over the wrongs of the individual. I sympathise profoundly with the indignation that you feel on account of this girl, but the authorities in England after due consideration of the danger likely to accrue to the State from the abuse of British nationality by aliens have decided to enforce with the greatest strictness the rules about the granting of passports.'

'Oh, don't explain the reasons to me as if I were a baby,' Sylvia burst in. 'The proposition of the Foreign Office is self-evident in its general application. My point is with you personally. You are not a professional bureaucrat who depends for his living on his capacity for de-humanising himself. In this case you have a special reason to exercise your rights and your duties as an amateur. You are as positive as you can ever hope to be positive about anything, even your absurd positivist creed, that while no harm can result to your country, a great mercy will be conferred upon an individual as the result of enlightened action.'

'It is precisely this introduction of the personal element,' Philip said, 'that confirms me in refusing your request. You are taking advantage of – our – of knowing me to gain your point. As a stranger you would not stand the least chance of doing this, and you have no business to make the matter a personal one. You don't seem to realise what such a proceding would involve. It is not merely a question of issuing a passport as passports used to be issued before the war on the applicant's bare word. A whole set of searching questions has to be answered in writing, and you ask me to put my name to a tissue of lies. Go back to England yourself. You have done your best for this girl, and you must bow before circumstances. She has reached Roumania, and if she does not try to leave it, she will be perfectly all right.'

'But have you appreciated what I told you about this man who has just arrived? He's a German-Swiss, and if he's not a spy, he has all the makings of one. Suppose he gets hold of Queenie again? Can't you see that on the lowest ground of material advantage you are justified – more than justified, you owe it to your country to avoid the risk of creating another enemy?'

119

'My dear Sylvia,' said Philip more impatiently than he had spoken yet. 'It is none of my business to interfere with potential agents of the enemy. I have quite enough to do to keep pace with the complete article. If your little friend is in danger of being turned into a spy, it seems to me that you have started the final argument against granting your request.'

'If she were with me, she could never become a spy; but if I were to leave her helpless here, anything might happen. I am struggling for this child's soul, Philip, more bitterly than I ever struggled for my own. Your mind is occupied with the murder of human bodies: my mind is obsessed with the destruction of human souls.'

'Well, if I accept your own definition of your attitude,' Philip answered, 'perhaps you will admit that logically a passport occupies itself with the body, and that Christians do not consider nationality necessary to salvation. I can't make out your exalted frame of mind. You used to be rather sensible on this subject. But if, as I gather, you have taken refuge in that common weakness of humanity — religion, let me recommend you to find therein the remedy for your friend's future.'

'Yes, I suppose logically you've scored,' Sylvia said slowly.

'But please don't think I want to score,' Philip went on in a distressed voice. 'Please understand that for me to refuse is torture. I've often wondered about a judge's emotions when he puts on the black cap; but since I've faded out of real life into this paper world, I've worn myself out with worrying over private griefs and miseries. It's only because I feel that, if everyone on our side does not martyr himself for a year or so, the future of the world will be handed over to this sort of thing; and that is an unbearable thought.'

'You're very optimistic about the effect upon your own side,' Sylvia said. 'Have you such faith in humanity as to suppose that this war will cure it more radically than all the wars that have gone before? I doubt it. When I listened to our arguments this afternoon, I began to wonder if either side is fighting for anything but a sterile nominalism. I can't argue any more. It's not your fault, Philip. You lack the creative instinct. I'll fight out this Queenie business by myself without invoking state aid. I am rather ashamed of myself really. I feel as if I'd been compelled to ask a policeman the way. Perhaps I've got everything out of proportion. Women usually manage to do that somehow. There must be something very satisfying about personal conflict — bayonet to bayonet I mean: but even in the trenches

I suppose men get taken out and shot for cowardice. Even there you wouldn't escape from the grim abstract heartlessness that hangs like a fog over a generalised humanity – generalised is doubly appropriate in this connection. What a wretched thing man is in the mass and how rare and wonderful in the individual. The mass creates the arch-bureaucrat God, and the individual seeks the heart of Christ. Good-bye, Philip, I'm sorry you look so ill. I'm afraid I've tired you. No, no,' she added seeing that he was bracing himself up to talk about themselves. 'This wasn't really the personal intrusion you accuse me of making. We were never very near to one another, and we are more remote than ever now.'

'But what about your own visa?' he asked.

'It's no use to me at present. When I want it, I'll apply in the morning to Mr Mathers and come for it in the afternoon most correctly. I promise to attempt no more breaches in the formality of your office. By the way, one favour I would ask: please don't come to the Trianon. You wouldn't understand the *argot* in my songs, and if you did you wouldn't understand my being able to sing them. Get better.'

'Yes, I'm taking Sanatogen,' Philip said hopefully. At this moment Miss Johnstone entered with a cup on a small tray, which just escaping being lassoed by one of her chains was set down on his desk.

'I'm afraid I haven't got it quite so smooth as Miss Henson does,' said Miss Johnstone.

'Oh never mind, please. It was so kind of you to remember.'

'Well, I didn't think you ought to miss it on Miss Henson's day off.'

Sylvia waved her hand and left him with Miss Johnstone; he seemed to be hesitating between the injury to her feelings if he did not take the lumpy mixture and the harm to his digestion if he did.

'Even offices are subject to the clash of temperament on temperament,' said Sylvia to herself. 'A curious thing really that Philip should be prepared to choke himself over a cup of badly mixed Sanatogen rather than wound that young woman's feelings, and yet that he should be able to refuse me what I asked him to do this afternoon.'

She nodded to Mr Mathers, as she passed through the outer office, who jumped up and opened the door for her. He had evidently been impressed by the length of her interview with the O.C.P.T.N.C. in Bucharest.

'I believe I've had the pleasure of hearing you sing,' he murmured. 'Are you staying long at the Trianon?'

'I hope not,' she answered.

'Quite, quite,' he murmured, nodding his head with an air of deep comprehension, while he bowed her forth with marked courtesy.

The fog had cleared away when Sylvia started to walk back to her hotel, and though it was still very hot there was a sparkle in the air that made it seem fresher than it really was. The argument with Philip had braced her point of view to accord with the lightening of the weather; it had thrown her so entirely back upon her own resources that the notion of ever having supposed for an instance that he could help her in the fight for Queenie now appeared ludicrous. Although her arguments had been unavailing, and although at the end Philip had actually defeated her by the very logic on which she had prided herself, she nevertheless felt wonderfully elated at the prospect of a struggle with Zozo and no longer in the least sensible of that foreboding dejection which was lying so heavily upon her heart when she left Lottie's house three hours ago.

Poor Philip! he had spoken of his own sufferings in a minor degree from the war. Yet to be rooted up at his age – he was nearly fifty after all – and to be set down in Roumania to dig for human motives, he who had no instinct to dig for anything but dry bones and ancient pottery, it was surely for him suffering in a major degree. He had been so pathetically proud of being a captain, and at the same time so obviously conscious of the radical absurdity of himself in such a position; it was like a prematurely old child playing with soldiers to gratify his parents. And here in a neutral country he was even debarred from dressing up in uniform. When she first saw him she had been surprised to find that he did not appear much older than thirteen years ago; now looking back at him in his office he seemed to her a very old man. Poor Philip, he did not belong to that type that is rejuvenated in war time by a sense of his official importance. Sylvia had seen illustrations in English newspapers of beaming old gentlemen 'doing', as it was called, 'their bit', proud of the nuisance they must be making of themselves, incorrigible optimists about the tonic effects of war because they had succeeded in making their belts meet round their fat paunches, pantaloons that should have buried themselves out of sight instead of pirouetting while young men were being killed in a war for which they and their accursed Victorianism were responsible by licking the boots of Prussia for fifty years.

Sylvia found Queenie in a state of agitation at her long absence; she did not tell her anything about Zozo at once in the hope that he would not come to the Trianon on the first night of his arrival. She did think it advisable, however, to tell Queenie of her failure to secure the passport.

'Then we can't be going to England?' Queenie asked.

'Well, not directly from here,' Sylvia answered. 'But we'll move on as soon as we can into Bulgaria. We can get down to the Piraeus from Dedeagatch. I don't think these neutral countries are very strict about passports. We'll manage somehow to get away from here.'

'But if we cannot be going to England why must we be going from Bucharest? Better to stay, I think. Yes?'

'We might want to go,' Sylvia said. 'We might get tired of the Trianon. It wouldn't be difficult.'

'I shall never be going to England now,' said Queenie in a toneless voice. 'Never shall I be going! I shall learn a new song and a new dance, yes?'

Sylvia felt tired after her long afternoon and thought she would rest for an hour before getting ready for the evening's work. The mist gathered again at sunset, and the gardens of the theatre, though they were unusually full, lacked any kind of gaiety. When they were walking down the narrow laurel-bordered path that screened the actors from the people sitting at their tables under the trees, Sylvia was sure that Zozo would be standing by the stage door at the end of it; but he was nowhere to be seen. After the performance, however, when they came out, as the custom was, to take their seats in the audience, the juggler made a dramatic appearance from behind a tree; Queenie seemed to lose all her fairy charm and become a terrified little animal.

'I don't think there's room at our table for you,' Sylvia said.

'There are plenty of chairs,' Maud insisted stridently; she had followed the juggler into the lamplight round the table.

'I am quite sure there's no room for you,' said Sylvia sharply; and taking advantage of Queenie's complete limpness she dragged her away by the wrist and explained quickly to the manager who was walking up and down by the entrance gate that Queenie was ill and must go home at once.

'Ill!' he exclaimed sceptically. 'Well, I shall have to fine you both your evening's salary. Why, it's only half-past eleven!'

Sylvia did not wait to argue with him, but hurried Queenie

to a carriage, in which they drove back immediately to their hotel.

'I said to you that it was going to bring me bad luck when you said to that priest my real name. *Ach!* what shall I be doing? What shall I be doing now?' Queenie wailed.

'You must pay no attention to him,' Sylvia told her; but she found that Queenie did not recover herself as she usually did at the tone of command. 'What can he do to you while you're with me?' she continued.

'You don't know him,' Queenie moaned. 'He's very strong. Look at the mark on my leg where he was shooting at me. *Ach,* if we could be going to England, but we cannot. We are here and he is here. You are not strong like he was, Sylvia.'

'If you're going to give way like this before he has touched you and frighten yourself to death in advance, of course he'll do what he likes, because I can do nothing without support from you. But if you'll try to be a little bit brave and remember that I can protect you, everything will be all right and we'll get away from Roumania at the first opportunity.'

'*Ach,* you have papers. You are English. Nobody will protect me. Anyone was being able to do what they was liking to do with me.'

Sylvia tried to argue courage into her until early morning; but Queenie adopted an attitude of despair, and it was impossible to convince her that Zozo could not at whatever moment he chose take her away and, if he wished, murder her without anyone's interfering or being able to interfere. In the end Sylvia fell asleep exhausted, resolving that if Queenie was not in a more courageous frame of mind next day she should not move from the hotel. When Sylvia woke up she found that Queenie was already dressed to go out, and for an instant she feared that the juggler's power over her was strong enough to will her to go back to him by the mere sense of his being near at hand. She asked her almost angrily why she had dressed herself so quietly and where she was going.

'To the hairdresser's,' Queenie answered in a normal voice.

Sylvia was puzzled what to do. She did not like to put the idea into Queenie's head of the juggler's being able to mesmerise her into following him apparently of her own accord, and if she really intended to go to the hairdresser's, it might imply that the terror of the night before had burnt itself out. Certainly she did not seem very nervous this morning. It was taking a risk, but probably the only way out of the situation was by taking risks, and in the end she decided not to oppose her going out by herself.

Two hours passed; when Queenie had· not returned to the hotel Sylvia went out and made enquiries at the hairdresser's. Yes, she had been there earlier that morning and had bought several bottles of scent. Sylvia made a gesture of disapproval; scent was an extravagance of Queenie's, and she was strictly rationed in this regard on account of the urgency of saving all the money they could for their journey. She returned to the hotel; Queenie was still absent, and she opened her bag to look for the address of a girl whom Queenie occasionally visited; she found the card, but the thousand-franc note that she was guarding for her had vanished. Queenie must have joined that infernal Swiss after all, and the old instinct of propitiating him with money had been too strong for her.

'Fool that I was to let her go this morning,' Sylvia cried. As she spoke, Queenie came in, her cheeks flushed with excitement, her arms full of packages.

'Where have you been and what have you been doing?' she demanded.

'Oh, you must pardon me for taking the money from your bag,' Queenie cried. 'I was taking it to buy presents for all the girls.'

'Presents for the girls?' Sylvia echoed in amazement.

'Yes, yes, it was the only way to make them on my side against him. Tonight in the dressing-room I shall give these beautiful presents. I was spending all of my thousand francs. It was no use any longer, because we cannot be going to England. Better that I was buying these presents to make all the girls be on my side.'

Sylvia was between laughter and tears, but she could not bring herself to be angry with the child; at least her action showed that she was taking her own part against the juggler. Queenie spent the rest of the day quite happily, arranging how the presents were to be allotted. Those that were small enough she put into chocolate boxes that she had bought for this purpose; the larger ones were tied up with additional pink and blue silk ribbons to compensate for the lack of a box. To each present – there were fifteen of them – a picture postcard was tied, on which Sylvia had to write the name of the girl for whom it was intended *with heaps of love and kisses from Queenie:* it was like a child preparing for her Christmas party.

They went down to the Trianon earlier than usual in order

125

that Queenie might get ready in time to sit at the entrance of the dressing-room and hand each girl her present as she came in. Sylvia tried to look as cheerful as possible under the ordeal, for she did not want to confirm the tale that she was living on Queenie's earnings by seeming to grudge her display of generosity. The girls were naturally eager to know the reason of the unexpected entertainment. When Queenie took each of them aside in turn and whispered a long confidence in her ear, Sylvia supposed that she was explaining about the advent of Zozo; but it turned out Queenie was explaining that, having no longer any need for the money since she could not get a passport for England, she was doing now what she had wanted to do before, but had been unable to do on account of saving up for the journey. Sylvia remonstrated with her for this indiscretion, and she said:

'I think it was you that was being silly not me, yes? If I say to the girls "here is a silver brush, help me against Zozo," they was thinking that I was buying them to help me. But when he tries to take me, I shall call out to them and they will be loving me for these presents and will be fighting against him I think, yes?'

Sylvia had her doubts, but she had not the heart to discourage such trust in the grateful appreciation of her companions.

Neither Zozo nor Maud came to the Trianon that evening; nevertheless, outside on the playbill was an announcement that next Sunday would appear ZOZO: LE MEILLEUR PRESTIDIGITATEUR DU MONDE.

'It was always so that he was writing himself,' said Queenie, when Sylvia read her the announcement; she spoke in a voice of awe as if the playbill had been inscribed by a warning fate. In due course the juggler made a successful first appearance, dressed in green with a snake of shimmering tinsel wound round him. They watched the performance from the wings; when he came off he asked Queenie with a laugh if she would stand for his dagger act, as in the old days she had stood.

'You've got Maud for that,' Sylvia interposed quickly.

'Maud!' he scoffed.

Earlier in the evening she had thundered about the stage in what she described as the world famous step-dance of the world famous American cow-girl Maud Moffat to the authentic and original native melody, which happened this year to be *On the*

126

Missisippi and might just as easily have been *A Life on the Ocean Wave.*

Sylvia was puzzled by the relationship between Zozo and Maud, for there was evidently nothing even in the nature of affection between them, and as far as she could make out they had never met until the day he paid her fare from Galantza to Bucharest. Her first idea had been that he was a German agent and intended to use Maud in that capacity, her patriotism, judging by her loud denunciations of England and everything English, not being very deep. But Sylvia had already outlived the habit of explaining as a spy everyone in war time that is not immediately and blatantly obvious. She could imagine nobody less fitted to be a spy than Maud, who was attractive neither to her compatriots nor to foreigners and who even had she possessed attraction would have had no brains to take advantage of it. Yet she came back to the theory that Zozo was a German agent when she saw with whom he consorted in Bucharest, and she decided that when he had brought Maud here he had done so in the hope of having found a useful recruit, but that on discovering her dull coarseness he had come to the conclusion that her hostility to England was counter-balanced by England's hostility to her. Sylvia decided that if her surmises were at all near to being correct she must be particularly on her guard against any attempt on the part of the Swiss to corrupt Queenie. She had supposed at first that she should only have to contend with his lust or with his desire of personal domination; now it seemed that the argument she had used with Philip to procure Queenie a passport had really been a sound argument. Superficially Queenie might not strike anybody as a valuable agent; knowing her charm for men, her complete malleableness, and her almost painful simplicity, Sylvia could imagine that she might be a practical weapon in the hands of an unscrupulous adventurer like the Swiss, who was finding like so many other rascals of his type that in war natural dishonesty is a lucrative asset. She wondered to what extent her ideas about his intentions were based upon his behaviour at Granada and whether after all she was not attributing to him all sorts of schemes of which he was entirely innocent. Really he had always been for her a symbol of evil that she was inclined to turn into a crude personification. It was strange the way that one was apt in changing one's mode of life to abandon simultaneously the experience one had gathered formerly. Most probably she was giving this juggler with an absurd name an importance quite beyond his power,

127

simply because she herself was giving her present surroundings a permanence far more durable and extensive than they actually possessed. After all, could one but perceive it, the way from the Petit Trianon to Mulberry Cottage did exist as a material fact: there was no impassable gulf of space or time between them.

After Zozo had been juggling for about a fortnight in Bucharest without having given the least sign of wanting to interfere with Queenie, Sylvia began to think that she had worked herself up for nothing, though the problem of his relationship to Maud with whom he remained on terms of contemptuous intimacy still puzzled her. She thought of making a report on the queer association to Philip, but she was afraid he might think it was an excuse to meet him again; and since Philip himself had made no effort to follow up their interview, she gave up speculating upon Zozo and Maud and took to speculating instead upon Philip's want of curiosity, as she called it. Unreasonable as she admitted to herself that the emotion was, she could not help being piqued by his indifference, and she resented now the compassion she had felt for him when she left the office that afternoon. She could not understand any man, however badly a woman had treated him – and she had not treated Philip badly – being able to contemplate so calmly that woman's existence as a cabaret singer without wanting to know what had brought her to it so short a time after her success. No, certainly she should not trouble Philip with her suspicions of Zozo and Maud; it was inviting a rebuff.

Just when Sylvia was beginning to feel reassured about Queenie and not to worry about anything except the waste of that thousand francs and the continuous difficulties in the way of saving any money, the girls at the Trianon began to whisper among themselves. Queenie's presents had given her a brief popularity that began to fade when it was evident that no more presents were coming; her attempt to secure the friendship of her companions, inasmuch as it seemed a token of weakness, reacted against her and made her in the end less popular than before. The story about the refusal of a passport by the British authorities was soon magnified into a demand for her expulsion from Roumania as a German agent masquerading as an English girl. Hence the whispers. The French girls were naturally the most venomous; but the Austrian girls were nearly as bad, because having lived for months under the perpetual taunt of being spies they were anxious to re-establish their own virtue at Queenie's expense. Zozo commiserated with her on the unfairness of the whispers, and one evening to Sylvia's dismay Queenie told her that he had offered to secure her a passport and take her with him when he left Bucharest.

'He was really being very nice to me,' Queenie said. 'Oh, Sylvia, what shall I do? I cannot stay here with these girls who are so unkind to me.'

The following evening Sylvia asked Zozo straight out about the kind of passport he proposed to find for Queenie and where he proposed to take her.

The juggler sneered.

'That's my business I think. What can you do for her? If the kid's anything, she's German. What the hell's the good of you trying to make her English? Why don't you let her alone instead of stopping her from earning good money?'

Sylvia kept her temper with a great effort and contented herself with denying that Queenie was German and with asking who had first made the assertion. The juggler spat on the floor and walked away without replying.

After the performance that night, a hot thunderous night in August, Zozo with Maud and two well-known pro-German natives took the next table to Sylvia and Queenie. Maud was drinking heavily and presently she began to talk in a loud voice:

'Well, I may have spoken against England once or twice, but thank gawd, I'm not a bloody little yellow-haired German pretending to be English. I never went and tried to pass off a dirty little German as my sister the same as what some people who's proud of being English does. Yes, I earn my living honestly. I've never heard anyone call me a spy and any — as did wouldn't do it twice. My name's Maud Moffat, born and bred a cockney, and proud I am when I see some people who think theirselves superior and all the time is dirty German spies betraying their country. Does anyone presume to say I'm not English?' she shouted, rising unsteadily to her feet. 'And if he does, where is he so as I can show him he's a bloody liar by breaking his head open?'

Her companions made a pretence of restraining her, but it was plain that they were enjoying the scene, and Maud continued to hold forth.

'German! And calls herself English. Goes around giving presents to honest working girls so as she can carry on her dirty work of spying. Goes around trying to get a girl's boy away from her by low dirty mean tricks as she's learnt from the bloody Germans who she belongs to. Yes, it's you I'm talking to,' she shrieked at Queenie. White as paper she sprang up from her seat and began to answer Maud, notwithstanding Sylvia's efforts to silence her.

'You was being a bad wicked girl,' she panted. 'You dare to say I was being German! I hate the Germans! I *am* English. I *am* English. You dare to say I was being German!'

Upon this an Austrian girl at another table began to revile Queenie from her point of view for abusing the Germans; before ten seconds had passed the gardens were in an uproar.

A fat French Jewess stood on a table and shouted:

'*Oh, les sales boches! Oh, les sales boches!*'

Whereupon an Austrian girl pushed her from behind, and she crashed down into a party of Francophile young Roumanians who instantly began to throw everything within reach at a party of Germanophile young Roumanians. Glasses were shivered; fairy lamps were pulled out of the trees and hurtled through the air like Roman candles; somebody snatched a violin from the orchestra and broke it on the head of his assailant; somebody else climbed on the stage and made a speech in Roumanian calling upon the country to intervene on behalf of the Entente, until two pro-Germans seized him and flung him down on top of the melancholy dotard who played the doublebass; the manager and the waiters rushed into the street to find the police; everybody argued with everybody else.

'*Tu dis que je suis boche, moi? Merde pour toi!*'

'*La ferme! La ferme! Espionne! Type infecte!*'

'*Moi, je suis Roumaine. Si tu dis que je suis Hongroise, je dis que t'es une salope. Tu m'entends?*'

'*Oh, la vache! Elle m'a piquée!*'

'*Elle a bien fait! Elle a bien fait!*'

Some French girls began to sing –

> *Les voyez-vous?*
> *Les hussards! Les dragons! la gar-rrde!*
> *Glorieux fous. . . .*

and a very shrill little soprano who was probably a German, but declared she was a Dane, sang:

> *It's a larway to Tipperary,*
> *It's a larway to go,*
> *It's a larway to Tipperary,*
> *It's a la-a-way to go!*
> *Gooba, Piccadilli,*

Farwa lar-sa sca-aa!
It's a lar-lar-way to Tipperary
Ba-ma-ha's ra-tha.

After which somebody hit her on the nose with a vanilla ice: then the police came in and quieted the uproar by arresting several people on the outskirts of the riot.

The next evening, when Sylvia and Queenie presented themselves for the performance, the manager told them that they were dismissed: he could not afford to let the Petit Trianon gain a disorderly reputation. Sylvia was glad that the decision of taking a definite step had been settled over her head. As they were passing out, they met Lottie looking very happy.

'I've been engaged for three hundred francs to play the piano in the orchestra. The accompanist broke his wrist last night in the row,' she told them. 'So they sent for me in a hurry.'

'We've been sacked,' Sylvia said.

'Oh, I am sorry,' the fat girl exclaimed, trying to curb her own pleasure. 'What will you do?'

Sylvia shrugged her shoulders.

'Why don't you go to Galantaza and Bralatz and Avereshti? You ought to be able to get engagements there in the summertime – especially at Avereshti.'

Sylvia nodded thoughtfully.

'Yes, that's rather an idea. But Lottie, don't tell Zozo where we've gone. Goodbye, good luck. I'm glad you've got an engagement.'

'Yes, I shall leave that room now. It smells rather, as the summer gets on.'

The next morning Sylvia and Queenie left Bucharest for Galantza.

Chapter V

NEITHER IN Galantza nor in Bralatz did Sylvia and Queenie perceive any indication of a fortune. They performed for a week at the Varietés High Life in Bralatz; but the audience and the salary were equally low, the weather was hot and misty, and

131

the two hotels they tried were full of bugs. In Galantza they performed for two days at the Varietés Tiptop; but here both the audience and the salary were lower still, the weather was hotter and more misty, and there were as many bugs in the one hotel as in the two hotels at Bralatz put together. Sylvia thought she should like to visit the British vice-consul who had angered Maud so much by his indifference to her future. He was a pleasant young man, not recognisable from her description of him except by the fact that he certainly did smoke incessantly. He invited them both to dine and grumbled loudly at the fate which had planted him down in this god-forsaken corner of Roumania in war time. He was disappointed to hear that they could not stay in Galantza, but agreed with them about the audience and the salary.

'I can't think who advised you to come here,' he exclaimed. 'Though I'm glad you did come; it has cheered me up a bit.'

'It wasn't Maud,' Sylvia said with a smile.

'Maud?' he repeated. 'Who is she?'

'An English girl who took a great fancy to you. She wanted you to pay her fare to Bucharest.'

'Oh, my hat, a most fearful creature,' he laughed. 'A great pink blowsy woman with a voice like two trains shunting. I had a terrible time with her. Upon my word I had actually to push her out of the consulate. Oh, an altogether outrageous phenomenon! What became of her finally? In Bucharest, is she? Well, she's not a good advertisement of our country in these times. What part of England do you come from?' he added, turning to Queenie.

'London,' Sylvia said quickly. She always answered this kind of question before Queenie could blush and stammer something unintelligible. 'But she's been on the continent since she was a little girl, and can't speak any language except with the accent of the one she spoke last.' Then she changed the subject by asking him where he advised them to next.

'I should advise you to go back to England. These are no times for two girls to be roaming about Europe.'

'You'd hardly describe me as a girl,' Sylvia laughed. 'Even I can no longer describe myself as one. Passports have been fatal to some cherished secrets. No, we can't get back to England chiefly because we haven't saved enough money for the fare, and secondly because the passport-office in Bucharest didn't consider me a good enough voucher for Queenie's right to a British passport.'

'Wouldn't they recommend the consul to issue one?'

Sylvia shook her head.

'Too bad,' said the vice-consul in a cheerful voice. 'But that's one of the minor horrors of war, this accumulation of a new set of officials begotten by the military upon the martial enthusiasm of non-combatants. It's rather ridiculous, isn't it, to assume that all consuls are incapable of their own job? . . . but I suppose I've no business to be displaying professional jealousy at such a moment,' he broke off.

'Would you have given her a passport?' Sylvia asked.

The vice-consul looked at Queenie with a smile.

'I could hardly have refused, eh?'

But Sylvia knew that once inside his consulate he would probably be even more pedantic than Philip, and this affectation of gallantry over coffee annoyed her.

'But what *are* you going to do?' he went on.

'Oh, I don't know,' said Sylvia curtly. 'Leave things to arrange themselves, I suppose.'

'Yes, that's a very good attitude to take up when your desk is untidy, but seriously I shouldn't advise you to leave things to arrange themselves by touring round Roumania. These provincial towns are wretched holes.'

'What's Avereshti like?'

'I don't know. I've never been there. It's not likely to be any better than Galantza or Bralatz, except for being a good deal nearer to Bucharest. Oh dear, everything's very gloomy. That Suvla business will keep out the Roumanians for some time. In fact I don't think myself they'll ever come in now, unless they come in with the Germans. Why don't you take a week's holiday here?'

But the vice-consul, who had seemed agreeable at first, was getting on Sylvia's nerves with his admiration for Queenie, and she told him that they should leave next day.

'Too bad,' he exclaimed. 'But that's the way of the world. When a consul would like to be thoroughly bothered by somebody, nothing will induce that person to waste five minutes of his precious time. Your friend Maud on the contrary haunted me like a bluebottle.'

Avereshti turned out to be a much smaller place than Sylvia had expected. She had heard it spoken of in Bucharest as a favourite summer resort, and had pictured it somehow with a casino, gardens, good hotels, and pretty scenery: the very name had appealed to her with a suggestion of quietude. She had deliberately not gone there at once with Queenie when they left Bucharest, because being not more than sixty kilometres from the capital she had had an idea that Zozo might think it a likely place for them to visit and take it into his head to seek them out. Even in the train coming back from Galantza she had doubts of the wisdom of turning on their tracks so soon; but their taste of Galantza and Bralatz had been so displeasing that Avereshti with its prefigured charm of situation promised a haven with which the risk of being worried by their enemy could not interfere. They would take a week's holiday before engaging themselves to appear at the casino or whatever the home of amusement was called in Avereshti; then after a short engagement they might perhaps venture back to Bucharest and start saving up money again.

'For what good?' Queenie asked sadly.

'Oh, something will turn up,' Sylvia replied. 'Perhaps the war will come to a sudden end, and you'll be able to go to England without a passport.'

'You are always dreaming, Sylvia. Happy things cannot come to me so easily as you was thinking.'

Since the night of the row at the Trianon Queenie had settled down to a steady despair about the whole of her future, and it was partly Sylvia's powerlessness to restore her to the childish gaiety that was so attractive in one whom she was conscious of protecting which had made her conceive such a distaste for the two towns they had just left. She was beginning indeed to doubt if her intervention between Queenie and the life she had been leading was really worth while. She upbraided herself with a poor spirit, with a facile discouragement, with selfishness and want of faith; yet all the way in the train she was on the verge of proposing that they should go back at once to Bucharest and there definitely part company. The dreary country through which they were travelling and the moist heat of the September afternoon created such a desire for England that the thought of remaining five minutes longer in Roumania was becoming intolerable. Sylvia began to make plans to telegraph home for money, and while she pondered these she began to think about Jack and Olive and the twins. Jack of course would be a soldier by now; but Olive would be in Warwickshire. Perhaps at this moment she was walking through a leafy path in Arden and wondering what her lost friend was doing. Sylvia tried to conjure familiar English scents – the smell of bluebells and young leaves, the smell of earth in a London window-box after being

134

watered, and most wistfully of all the smell of the seaside on a breathless day of late summer when the sun was raining diamonds into the pale blue water – that so poignantly English seaside smell of salt sand and pears in paper bags, of muslin frocks and dusty shrubs and warm asphalt. It might be such a day in England now, such a day at Eastbourne or Hastings. The notion of enduring any longer these flat Roumanian fields, this restless and uncertain existence upon the fringe of reality, this pilgrimage in charge of a butterfly that must soon or late be caught, clouded her imagination.

'In seeking to direct Queenie's course I am doing something that is contrary to my dearest theory of behaviour. When I met her again at Jassy I was in an abnormal and hysterical condition. The sense of having failed myself led me to seize desperately upon her salvation to justify this long withdrawal from the activity of my own world. This world of gipsies is no longer my world. Why, I believe that the real reason I feel annoyed with Philip is because, having roused in me a sense of my unsuitableness to my present conditions and actions, he does not trouble to understand the effect that talking to him had upon me. Here I am at thirty-two thinking like an *exaltée* schoolgirl. Thirty-two! Just when I ought to be making the most tremendous efforts to anchor myself to some stable society that will carry me through the years to come, the years that without intellectual and spiritual pleasures will be nothing but a purgatory for my youth, I find myself more hopelessly adrift than ever before. It will end in my becoming a contemplative nun in one last desperate struggle to avoid futility. It is a tragedy for the man or woman who comprehends futility without being able to escape from it. That's where the Middle Ages were wiser than we. Futility was impossible then. That's where we suffer from that ponderous bog of Victorianism. When one pauses to meditate upon the crimes of the Victorian era! And it's impossible not to dread a revival of Victorianism after this war. It's obvious that unless we defeat the Teuton quickly – and there's no sign of it – we shall be Teutonised in order to do it. And then indeed, O grave where *is* thy victory? Will the Celtic blood in England be enough to save her in ten years' time from a base alliance with these infernal Germans in order that the two stupidest nations in the world may combine to overlay it? Will this war at last bring home to Europe the sin of handing herself over to lawyers? Better the Middle Ages priest-ridden than To-day lawyer-ridden. At least if we are going to pay these rascals who exploit their country, let us have it well exploited. Don't let us call in one political plumber after another whose only object is to muddle the State for his successor to muddle it still more that he may be called in again to muddle it again – and muddle – and muddle eternally! When one reads in the papers the speeches of politicians, of what can one be reminded but of children playing cat's cradle over the tortured body of their mother? Yet what business have I to be abusing lawyer and politician when I lack the strength of mind to persevere in a task which I set myself with my eyes open? Unless I suffer in achieving it, it will not be worth the achievement. Surely the human soul that has suffered deeply can never again acknowledge futility? O England, perhaps it is a poor little pain to be away from you now, a mean little egotistical ache at the best, but away from you I see your faults so much more clearly and love you for them all the more.'

The train entered the station, and Sylvia perceived that there was nothing beautiful about Avereshti in the way she had fancied. Yet she was ashamed now of the temptation to desert Queenie; therefore, though the train was going on to Bucharest, she hurried her out on the platform, and when they reached the Hotel Moldavia she took a room for two weeks, paying for it in advance lest she should be tempted by her disappointment with Avereshti to hurry back to Bucharest again, the inevitable result of which in her present mood would be to abandon her friend.

Avereshti instead of being situated amid the romantic scenery that one expected from a celebrated summer resort was surrounded by oilfields which disfigured still more the flat environment. It was too large for genuine rusticity, too small for its assumption of European civilisation, and too commercial for gaiety. Possibly during the season shareholders and owners of the oilfields came here to gloat for a week upon the sources of their prosperity; if they did, they had all of them left by the middle of September; The Varietés Alcazar was closed and the playbills were already beginning to peel off the walls. Whatever life there was in Avereshti displayed itself in the Piatza Carol I, the pavement of which was planted with trees clipped out of any capacity to cast a pleasant shade. The Hotel Moldavia flanked by cafés occupied one side of it, a row of respectable shops another, a large municipal hall of the crudest Germanic architecture fronted the hotel, and along the remaining side ran a row of market booths, the insult of which to the progress of

Avereshti was greatly resented by the inhabitants and always apologised for and explained in the first few minutes of conversation.

The appearance of Sylvia and Queenie in this square on the morning after their arrival created an interest that soon developed into a pertinacious and disconcerting curiosity. If they entered a shop to make some small purchases, a crowd gathered outside and followed them to the next shop, and finally became such a nuisance that they retired to the balcony outside their room – a long wooden balcony of a faded tint of green – and watched the populace gathering to stare at them from below. When the sun became too hot for this entertainment, they took refuge in the big bedroom which had the unusual merit of being free from bugs. Queenie dreamed away the morning with her lithographs; Sylvia read *War and Peace*. Late in the afternoon they went out again on the balcony and were amused to see that the frequenters of the cafés on either side of the hotel had moved their chairs hornwise far enough out into the square to obtain a view of their movements. Sylvia suggested to the waiter that they should give a musical performance from the balcony, but he replied quite seriously that it was not strong enough: otherwise, he left them to understand, there would have been no objection.

'Yet really after all it's not so bad here,' Sylvia declared. 'We'll stay a few days, and then I'll go into Bucharest and prospect. Perhaps Zozo will be gone by now.'

Avereshti possessed at any rate the charm of making one feel lazy; to feel lazy and to be able to gratify one's laziness was after nearly a year of ceaseless work pleasant enough. On the third afternoon the waiter came up with six visiting-cards from local gentlemen who desired their acquaintance. Sylvia told him that they were not anxious to make any friends; he smiled and indicated two names as those that would best repay their choice.

'We wish to be left quite alone,' Sylvia repeated irritably.

'Then why do you walk about on the balcony?' the waiter asked.

'We walk about on the balcony because it's the only place where we can walk without being annoyed by a crowd. You don't expect us to remain in our room day and night, do you?'

The waiter smiled and again called attention to the desirable qualifications of the two visiting-cards he had first thrust into prominence. He added that both the gentlemen, M. Stefan Florilor and M. Toma Enescu, were particularly anxious to

137

make the acquaintance of the fair young lady; that M. Florilor was young, handsome, and the son of the richest man in Avereshti; and that though M. Enescu was not young he was very rich. Perhaps the ladies would invite them to take coffee? It would be easy to get rid of the other four visiting-cards.

Sylvia told the waiter to get rid of all six and never again to have the impudence to refer to the subject; but he continued to extol his clients, until at last Sylvia in a rage knocked the card-tray out of his hand with the volume of *War and Peace* that he was interrupting, upon which he retired muttering abuse.

About ten minutes afterwards the waiter came back and told Sylvia that all the gentlemen were gone away except M. Florilor who insisted upon being received.

'Insists?' cried Sylvia. 'But is he the crown-prince of Avereshti?'

The waiter shrugged his shoulders.

'His father has a mortgage on the hotel,' he explained. 'And the proprietor would be very much upset to think that any discourtesy had been shown to the son.'

'Have we paid for this room?' Sylvia demanded.

The waiter agreed with her that they had paid for it.

'Very well, when we asked for free board and lodging it will be time enough to talk about the proprietor's annoyance at our refusal to receive his creditors.'

She indicated the direction of the door with a contemptuous inclination of the head, and the waiter retired.

'I don't know how you can be so strong to talk like that,' Queenie marvelled. 'If I was being alone here I should be too frightened to speak so to the waiter. Suppose they was all to murder us tonight?'

When Queenie spoke like this, Sylvia's old sense of guardianship flowed again as fast as ever, and any impulse to abandon her was drowned in a flood of rage against the arrogance of money with its sale and purchase of human lives. There was something less distasteful about the domination of Zozo than about the attempted domination of this young Roumanian puppy yelping in his backyard of a town. If the juggler were to arrive in Avereshti tonight and in a frenzy of baulked passion were to murder both herself and Queenie, there would be a kind of completeness about the action that made the presentiment of it a sane and feasible terror; but that Queenie should have been reduced to a condition of semi-idiocy merely by the fact that the accidents of her childhood had put her for sale on the market of

138

life did seem to Sylvia inexpressibly revolting.

'And we credit ourselves with the abolition of slavery! I am not sure that the frank slavery of the past was not more moral than the unadmitted slavery of the present. At any rate it carried with it its own penalty in the demoralisation and decay of the owners; but I perceive no prospective penalty for this sort of thing. A young barbarian whose father has grown rich and fat upon petroleum sees a girl that takes his fancy and sends up his card; the proprietor of the hotel threatens us through that pimping waiter with the enmity of his father's debtor. This happens to be a crude case because we are living temporarily in a crude country; but less crudely the same thing goes on in England. It is true that we shrink there from the licensed brothel, and that we are still able to shrink from that is something to be grateful for; yet though we refrain from inflicting an open shame upon womanhood, we pay very little attention to the rights of the individual woman and child, or for the matter of that to the rights of the individual man. We no longer allow the bodies of children to be slowly murdered in factories, but we offer not the least objection to their employment in nice healthy amusing occupations such as selling newspapers for great monopolies or dancing in the theatres. There *can* be no defence of employing child-labour, and the man who defends it is the equal of the most brutalised and hardened *souteneur*. I still think that the greater part of humanity is so naturally inclined to be enslaved that the bestowal of freedom will in a short time land the world in the same state as before; but what I don't understand is the necessity for a reformer or the philanthropist to be anything except profoundly cynical. It always seems to be assumed that a desire to help other people implies a belief that other people will benefit from the help. I should like to meet an unadvertising philanthropist who was willing to admit that his philanthropy was a vice like secret drinking. One occasionally perceives signs of a sick conscience in some large anonymous contribution to charity. I always suspect the donor of expiating a monstrous crime. I can imagine being haunted by the fear of a peerage in return for the expenditure upon a Lord Mayor's fund of the superfluous savings of a wicked life.'

'Of what are you thinking?' Queenie asked.

'I'm thinking, my dear, that visits from the *jeunesse dorée* of Avereshti tend to infect me with an odious feeling of self-righteousness. The result of reading Tolstoy and arguing with a waiter about the sale of your body to M. Florilor has reduced me to a state of morbid indignation with the human race. But the problem that's bothering me is my ultimate ineffectiveness. I'm like a chained-up dog, and I am realising that noise to be a real weapon of defence requires listeners. I'm a little afraid, Queenie, that unless I can do more than bark, I shall lose you.'

'When shall you lose me?'

'When the web of my theory in which I'm sitting like a spider gets swept away by something more powerful than you, my butterfly, whom even without interference I can scarcely retain. You'll escape me then and be caught finally in a net, and I shall scuttle off and hide myself in a dark corner until I die of inanition and chagrin.'

'I was not understanding one word of what you were saying,' said Queenie. 'First you were being a dog. After you were being a spider. Who was ever to understand you?'

'Who indeed?' Sylvia murmured with half a sigh, as she went out on the balcony and looked down upon the frequenters of the cafés, whose heads when she appeared were simultaneously lifted to regard her with a curiosity that her elevated position made impersonal as the slow glances of cattle at pasture.

That evening after dinner the first sign of the proprietor's displeasure at the snub administered to the heir of his chief creditor was visible in a bill for their board of three days. The sum was not large, but by using up their small cash it involved breaking into the five-hundred-franc note that represented the last of the money they had saved since February. Sylvia had always kept this note in a pocket of her valise; now when she went up to their room to fetch it it was gone. The discovery of the loss was such a blow at this moment that she could not speak of it to Queenie when she came downstairs again; she paid what was owing with the last halfpenny they had, and sat back revolving internally in her mind how, when, and where that five-hundred franc note could possibly have been lost. Suddenly she had an idea that she might have moved it to another pocket and, leaving a half-smoked cigarette balanced against the saucer of her coffee-cup, she ran upstairs again to verify the conjecture. Alas, it was the emptiest of conjectures, and in a fever of exasperation she searched wildly in all sorts of unlikely places for the missing money. When the bedroom was scattered with her clothes to no purpose, she went back to the dining-room, where she found that the waiter had taken the half-smoked cigarette in clearing away the coffee-cups.

'Didn't you keep that cigarette?' she demanded.

Queenie looked at her in surprise.

'Why to keep a cigarette?' she asked.

'Because I haven't another.'

'Well, ring for the waiter. He shall bring one for you.'

'No, no, it doesn't matter,' Sylvia muttered; but the waste of the last precious cigarette brought home to her more than anything else that there was absolutely not even a halfpenny left in her purse after paying for the food they had had, and abruptly with the transmutation of that insignificant object to something of immense value arrived a corresponding change in Sylvia's attitude to the whole of life.

In the first case the larger share of the money she had lost so carelessly – with an effort she drove from her brain the revolving problem of how, when, and where – belonged to Queenie. Hence her responsibility toward Queenie was doubled, because if in certain moods of disillusionment she had been able to set aside her former responsibility as nothing but a whim, there was now a positive and material obligation that no change of sentiment could obliterate. Any harm that threatened Queenie now must be averted by herself, no matter at what cost to herself; somehow money must be obtained. It was plain that they could expect no consideration from the proprietor of the hotel; the way in which he had demanded payment for their day's board proved as much. Having accepted the money in advance for this room, he could not eject them into the street; but unless it suited him he was under no obligation to feed them. What a precipitate fool she had been to pay for a fortnight's lodging in advance! Seventy francs flung away! She might ask him for them back, or at any rate for the fifty francs' worth of lodging of which they would not have availed themselves if they left tomorrow. With fifty francs they would reach Bucharest, where something might turn up. But supposing nothing did turn up? Suppose that damned juggler found Queenie and herself without a halfpenny? Even that was better than starving here or surrendering to M. Stefan Florilor.

Sylvia went out to ask the proprietor if he would give her back the money she had paid in advance for a room she and her friend found themselves unable any longer to occupy. The proprietor shrugged his shoulders, informed her in his vile French that he had never demanded the sum in advance, assured her that he had refused the room twice to important clients who had wanted it for next week, and altogether showed by his attitude that he had been too much embittered by the reception of M. Florilor to stand upon anything except his strict rights. It was clear that these rights would include refusal of any food that was not paid for at the time. Such behaviour might be unjust and unreasonable, she thought, but after all it was not to be expected than an empty pocket was going to tempt the finer side of human nature. Sylvia went back to Queenie, who was looking in bewilderment at the clothes strewn about the bedroom. She explained what had happened, and Queenie ejaculated:

'There, fancy! We have no money now. Never mind, I can be friends with that gentleman who was asking to know me. He will give me the money, because if he wants me very much he will have to give much money. Yes, I think?'

Sylvia could have screamed aloud her rejection of such a course.

'What, after keeping you away from men for six months to let you go back to them on account of my carelessness? Child, you must be mad to think of it.'

'Yes, but I have been thinking, Sylvia. I have been thinking very much. When I was going to be English and you wer: saying to me that I should have a passport and be going to England and be English myself, it was good for me to care nothing at all for men; but now what does it matter? I am nothing. I am just being somebody lost, and if I am going with men or not going with men I am still nothing. Why to be worried for money? I shall show you how easy it is for me to have money. It is true what I am speaking. You could be having no idea how much money I can have. And if I am nothing, always nothing, why must I be worrying any more about money? You are so sweet to me, Sylvia, so kind. No one was ever being so kind to me before. So I must be kind to you now. Yes, I think? Are you crying about that money? I think you are stupid to cry for such a little thing as money.'

'There are things, my rose, that must not, that shall not happen,' Sylvia cried, clasping the child in her arms. 'And that you should ever again sell yourself to a man is one of them.'

'But I am nothing.'

'Ah,' thought Sylvia, 'here is the moment when I should be able to say that everyone to God is everything; but if I say it she will not understand. What hope is there for this child?' Then aloud she added. 'Are you nothing to me?'

'No, to you I am something, and if my brother was here I would be something to him.'

'Very well then, you must not think of selling yourself. I lost

142

the money. I shall find a way of getting more money. I have a friend in Bucharest. I will telegraph to him tomorrow and he will send us money.' And to herself she thought: 'This is indeed the ultimate irony, that I should ask a favour of Philip. Yet perhaps I am glad, for if I did him the least injury years ago, no priest could have imagined a more appropriate penance. Yes, perhaps I deserve this.'

The next morning, when Sylvia ordered coffee, the waiter presented the bill for it at the same time, and when she tore it up he seemed inclined to take away the coffee; he retreated finally with a threat that in future nothing should be served to them that was not paid for in advance.

'They are being nasty with us,' Queenie solemnly enunciated.

'Never mind. We shall have some money tonight, or at any rate tomorrow morning. We must put up with fasting today. It's Friday appropriately enough. Good heavens,' Sylvia exclaimed, 'I haven't even got the money to send a telegram. We must raise a few francs. Perhaps I could borrow some money with a trinket. Good gracious, I never realised until this moment that I haven't a single piece of jewellery! It takes the sudden affliction of extreme poverty to discover one's abnormality and to prove how essential it is to be different from everybody else. Come, Queenie, you must lend me your two brooches.'

Sylvia took the daisy of brilliants set around a topaz, and the swallow of sapphires – all that Queenie had kept after her disastrous expulsion from Russia – and visited the chief local jeweller, who shrugged his shoulders and refused to buy them.

'But at least you can lend me twenty francs upon them until tomorrow,' Sylvia urged.

He shrugged his shoulders again and bent over to pick at the inside of a watch with that maddening indifference of the unwilling purchaser. Sylvia could not bring herself to believe in his refusal and suggested a loan of fifteen francs. Nothing answered her except the ticking of a dozen clocks and the scraping of a small file. There was a smell of drought in the shop that seemed to symbolise the personality of its owner.

'Ten francs?' Sylvia begged.

The jeweller looked up slowly from his work and regarded her with a fishy eye, the fishiness of which was many times magnified by the glass that occupied it. He raised his chin in a cold negative and bent over his work more intently. Every clock in the shop told a different time and ticked away more loudly than ever. Sylvia gathered up the trinkets and went away. She tried two other jewellers without success, and she even proposed the loan to a chemist who had a pleasant exterior; finally she had to go back to the hotel without obtaining the money. The day dragged itself along; not even *War and Peace* could outlast it, and Sylvia wondered why she had ever grasped before how much of life radiated from lunch, the absence of which dislocated time itself. Toward six o'clock she came to a sudden resolution, and going out into the square she began to sing outside the café. Four lean dogs came and barked; a waiter told her that the singing was not required. Somebody threw a stone at one of the dogs and cut open its leg; whereupon the other three set upon it, until it broke away and fled howling across the square, leaving a trail of blood in its wake. The drinkers outside the café looked at Sylvia over the tops of their newspapers, until she went back to the hotel. Such a retirement would ordinarily have made her hot with shame; but she was already hardened by the first pangs of hunger and had only a savage contempt for the people who had thought to humiliate her; she had not been hungry long enough to feel the pathos of a broken spirit; after all, she had only missed her lunch.

Dinner consisted of two stale chocolate creams that were found in a pocket of one of Queenie's jackets; even the bits of silver paper adhering to them seemed to possess a nutritive value.

'But we cannot be going on like this,' Queenie protested.

'There must be some way of raising money enough to get to Bucharest,' Sylvia insisted. 'There must be. There must be. If we really starve, the police will send us there to avoid a death in this cursed hole of a town.'

'We must ask that gentleman to tea with us tomorrow,' Queenie declared, as she put out the light.

Want of food prevented Sylvia from sleeping, and in her overwrought spirit those good-night words of Queenie seemed to presage the collapse of everything.

'It shall not be. It shall not be,' she vowed to herself. 'I will not be defeated by squalid circumstances in this dreary little Roumanian town. If thirteen years ago I could sell my body to save my soul, now I can sell my body to save the soul of another. Surely that sacrifice will defeat futility. I had a presentiment of this situation when I was arguing with Philip that afternoon. I warned him that nothing should stand in my way over this girl. And nothing shall! Tomorrow I will invite this youth who is the son of the richest man in Avereshti. He will not refuse me twenty francs for my body. If I cannot do this I am worth no more than those trinkets that the jeweller refused to buy for ten francs. I will do this, and accept its accomplishment as the sign that I have fought long enough. Then I will go to Philip and tell him what his refusal has brought about. I will *make* him give me the passport. But suppose that he is no longer capable of being horrified? Suppose that my behaviour of thirteen years ago has rendered him proof against such an emotion? Oh well, we shall see. Am I light-headed? No, no, no. On the contrary, hunger makes one clear-sighted. It must be. It shall be. The duty of the human soul lies in such a complete, such a reckless, such a relentless, such a victorious self-will as can only be assuaged by self-sacrifice. This is the great paradox of life. This is the Divine egotism.'

Toward dawn Sylvia slept, and woke at sunrise from dreams that were strangely serene in contrast with the tormenting fevers of the night to find that Queenie was still fast asleep. The beauty of her lying there in this lucid and golden morn was like the beauty of a flower that blooms at daybreak in a remote garden. It was a beauty that caught at Sylvia's heart, a beauty that could only be expressed with tears; which were silent as the dew and which like the dew sparkled in the daybreak of the soul.

'It is through such tears that people have seen the fairies,' she murmured.

Sylvia half raised herself in bed, and leaning upon her elbow she watched the sleeping girl so intently that it seemed as if some of herself was passing away to Queenie. This still and virginal hour was indeed time transmuted to the timelessness of dreams, in which absolute love like a note of music rose quivering upon its own shed sweetness to such an ecstasy of sustained emotion that the barest memory of it would secure the wakeful one for ever against disillusionment.

'Call it hunger or the Divine vision, the result is the same,' she murmured. 'I was lifted out of myself, and I take it that is the way martyrs died for their faith. From an outsider's point of view I may be only worthy of a footnote in a manual of psychology; but I "on honeydew have fed and drunk the milk of paradise". Another queer thought: the fasting saint and the drunken sinner both achieve ecstasy by subduing the body, the one with mortification, the other with indulgence. Those whom the gods love die young – they drink too deep and too often of honeydew and become intoxicated even unto death. Wine must serve the man who would live long. Perhaps I am one of those less rare spirits that depends too much on purely material beauty;

yet even in defence of so little I can act. Some nightingales love roses: the rest of them love other nightingales. Which do I love? Ah, whether Queenie be rose or nightingale what does it matter? Nobody that would not stoop to save a woodlouse in his path can claim to love. And I will stoop as low as hell to save this rosebud that has already been gathered and wired and worn in a buttonhole and dropped by the roadside, but surely not yet trodden underfoot.'

Queenie woke with a bad headache, and Sylvia went downstairs to see if she could persuade the waiter to let her have some coffee. He was going to refuse, but when she asked him if he would tell M. Florilor that a visit would be welcomed that afternoon, his manner changed, and presently he came back from an interview with the proprietor to say that he would serve coffee at once. At the same time he brought the bill of fare for lunch, and seemed anxious that they should choose some special delicacy to fortify themselves against the ill effects of the day before. There was no talk of paying for the meal, and the best wine was indicated with that assumption of subservient greed which is common to all good waiters.

After lunch Sylvia told Queenie that she was going out to send off the delayed telegram to Bucharest and left her lying down with her pictures. Then she consulted the waiter about a room. The waiter agreed that it would be inconvenient to receive M. Florilor in their own, and informed her that the best room in the hotel was ready, adding that he had ordered plenty of cakes and put flowers in the vases.

'I'll go there now,' Sylvia announced. 'When he comes, bring him straight up.'

The brightness of the early morning had been dimmed by a wet mist, and the room allotted for the reception of M. Florilor which was on the other side of the hotel looked out over houses covered with sodden creepers and down into gardens of dishevelled sunflowers; it was a view that suited the mood Sylvia was in, and for a long time she stood gazing out of the window, trying to detect beyond the immediate surroundings of the hotel some definition of a landscape in the distance. In the light of the morning her resolution had not presented itself as morbidly as now; then it had appeared essentially poetic – a demonstration really of the creative power of the human will; now like the dejected flowers in the gardens below it hung limp and colourless. She turned away from the window and sat down in a tight new armchair, the back of which seemed to be enclosed

146

in corsets. Everything in this room was new, and like all hotel rooms it depressed one with that indeterminate bleakness which is the property of never having been touched by the warmth of personality. It was bleak as an abandoned shell on the beach and stirred by nothing save the end of the tide's ebb and flow. The waiter's attempt to give it the significance of human life by cramming bunches of dahlias into a pair of fluted vases only added to the desolate effect. For want of something to do Sylvia began to arrange the flowers with a little consideration for their native ugliness, as one tries to smarten an untidy woman with a bad figure; but when she poured some water into a china bowl and saw floating upon its surface the ends of burnt-out matches and cigarettes, she gave up the task. These burnt-out relics of transitory occupants seemed typical of the room's effect upon the pensive observer. A confused procession of personalities made up its history, and as these had cast away their burnt-out cigarettes and matches, so had they cast behind them the room where they had lodged, preserving no memory of its existence and leaving behind not a single emotion to vitalise the bleak impersonal shell they had thankfully forsaken.

Yet Sylvia, waiting here for the beginning of the heartless drama that would be wrought of her heart's blood pulsing to reinforce her will, rejoiced in this sterility of the setting; it helped her to achieve a similar effect in her own attitude. Just as this room had succeeded in preserving itself from any impression of having ever been lived in by human beings, so she when the drama was played through should retain of it no trace. That in it which was real – the lust of man – should be left behind, an ignominious burnt-out thing less than a cigarette-stump at the bottom of a china bowl.

The waiter came in with a basket of cakes, the cold and sugary forms of which were no more capable than the dahlias of imparting life to the merciful deadness. And how dead it all was! Those red plush curtains eternally tied back in symmetrical hideousness – they had never lived since the time when some starved and withered soul had sewn those pompons along their edges one after another, pompons as numerous and monotonous as the days of their maker. Indeed, there was not a single piece of furniture, not an ornament nor a drapery that was not stamped with the hatred of its maker. There was no trace of the craftsman's joy in his handiwork either in thread or tile or knob. There was nothing except the insolence of profit and the dreary labour of slaves. Yet a world stifled by such ugliness

147

talked with distasteful surprise of men who profited by war. With the exploitation of the herd and the sacrifice of the individual that was called civilisation what else could be expected? Nowadays even man's lust had to be guaranteed pure and unadulterated like his beer. Better that the whole human race should rot on dunghills with the diseases they merited than that they should profit from an added shame imposed upon the meanest and most miserable tinker's drab. People were shocked at making a hundred per cent upon a shell to blow a German to pieces; but they regarded with equaniminity the same profit at the expense of a child's future. Wherever one looked, there was nothing but material comfort set as the highest aim of life at the cost of beauty, religion, love, childhood, womanhood, virtue, everything. Then two herds met in opposition, and there was war; the result had made everybody uncomfortable, and everybody had declared there must never again be war. But so long as the individual submitted to the herd, war would go on; and the most efficient herd with the greatest will for war would succeed because it would be able to offer greater comfort at the time and higher profits afterwards. Yet the individual had nearly always much that was admirable; the most sordid profiteer possessed a marvellous energy and perception that might be turned to good, if he could but grasp that virtue is the true egotism and that vice is only a distorted altruism.

'I've always hated ants and loathed bees,' Sylvia cried. 'And in certain aspects the human race makes one shudder with that sense of co-operative effort running over one which I believe is called formication.'

The waiter came to announce M. Florilor's arrival.

'Now we get the individual at his worst just when I've been backing him against the herd. This is formication spelt with an "n".'

Stefan Florilor resembled a figure in a picture by Guido Reni. A superficial glance would have established him as a singularly handsome, well-built, robust, and attractive young man; a closer regard showed that his good looks owed too much to soft and feminine contours, that the robustness of his frame was only the outward form of strength with all the curves but nothing of the hardness of muscle, and that his eyes flashed not as the mirrors of an inward fire but with liquid gleams of sensuous impressions caught from outside. He really was extremely like one of Guido Reni's triumphant and ladylike archangels.

They talked in French, a language that Florilor spoke without distinction but with a pothouse fluency – no doubt much as one of Guido Reni's archangels might have picked it up fron one of Guido Reni's devils.

'What a fatally seductive language it is,' Sylvia exclaimed at last, when she had complimented him as he evidently expected to be complimented upon his ease. 'Whenever I hear a tea-table conversation in French I suspect everyone of being a poet or a philosopher: whenever I read a French poet I want to ask him if he likes his tea strong or weak.'

'Your friend is English also?' Florilor enquired.

He took advantage of the ethnical turn in the conversation to express his own interest in a problem of nationality.

'Yes, she is English.'

'And no doubt she will be coming down soon?'

'She's not coming down. She has a headache.'

'But perhaps she will be well enough to dine this evening with me?'

'No, I don't think she will be well enough,' said Sylvia.

The young man's face clouded with the disappointment; his features seemed to thicken, so much did their fineness owe to the vitality of sensual anticipation.

'Perhaps tomorrow, then?'

'No, I don't think she will ever be well enough,' Sylvia continued. Then abruptly she put her will to the jump and cleared it breathlessly. 'You'll have to make the best of me as a substitute.'

Afterwards when the reality that stood at the back of this scene had died away Sylvia used to laugh at the remembrance of the alarm in Florilor's expression when she made this announcement. She must have made it in a way so utterly different from any solicitation that he had ever known. At the moment she was absurdly positive that she had offered herself to him with as much freedom and as much allurement as his experience was able to conjecture in a woman. When therefore he showed by his temper that he had no wish to accept the offer, it never struck her that, even had he felt the least desire, her manner of encouragement would have frozen it. A secondary emotion was one of swift pride in the detachment of her position, which was brought home to her by the complete absence of any chagrin – such as almost every woman would have felt – at the obvious dismay caused by her proposal to substitute herself for her friend.

'I'm afraid I must go. I'm busy,' he muttered.

'But you haven't had any cake,' Sylvia protested.

'*Vous vous fichez de moi,*' he growled. '*Vous m'avez posé un sale lapin.*'

He looked like a greedy boy, a plump spoilt child that has been deprived of a promised treat.

'What did she come here for,' he demanded, 'if she's not prepared to behave like any other girl? You can tell her from me that finer girls – girls in Paris – have been glad enough to be friends with me.'

'Caprice and mystery are the prerogatives of woman,' Sylvia said.

'I'm glad she can afford to be capricious when she has not enough money to pay for her food.'

'I'm not going to argue with you about your behaviour, though I could say a good deal about it. At present I can't be as rude as I should like. You see, you've just paid me the compliment of declining to accept the offer of myself. The fact that either I am sufficiently inhuman or that you are too bestial for the notion of any intercourse between us leaves me with a real hope in my heart that there is a difference between you and me. You've no idea of the lowering effect, nay more, of the absolute despair it would cast over my view of life, had I to regard you as belonging to the same natural order as myself. It would involve belief in the universal depravity of man.'

'*Ah, vous m'emmerdez,*' he shouted, as he ran from the room. Sylvia cried after him to remember the fate of the Gadarene swine and to avoid going downstairs too fast. Then to herself she added:

'Ecstasies and dreams of self-abnegation! What are they beside the pleasure of conflict face to face? The pleasure would have been keener though, if I could have hurt him physically.'

In the first elation of escaping from the fulfilment of her intention Sylvia overlooked all the consequences involved in Florilor's withdrawal. Soon in the stillness shed by this bleak room, in the sight of the frozen cakes upon the table, in the creeping obscurity of the afternoon, she was more sharply aware than before of the future, aware of it not as a vague and faintly disturbing horizon too far away still to affect anything except her moods of depression, but as the immediate future in the shape of a chasm at her feet, a future so impassable that she could scarcely think of it in other terms than those of space. It had positively lost the nebulous outlines of time and acquired in their stead the sharp materialism of hostile space. The future! Calculations of how to bridge or leap this gap went whirling through Sylvia's brain, calculations that even included projects of fantastic violence, but never one that envisaged the surrender of a single scruple about Queenie. The resolve she had made that morning, however its practical effect seemed to have been nullified by Florilor's rejection of her sacrifice, had woven each separate strand of her thought and emotion so tightly round the steel wire of her will that nothing could have snapped the result. There was not a bone in her body, not a nerve nor a corpuscle that did not thrill to the command of her will, and wait upon its fresh intention with a loyalty that must endow it with an invincible tenacity of purpose.

The sense of an omnipotent force existing in herself was so strong that when Sylvia saw a golden ten-franc piece lying in the very middle of the fiddle-backed armchair on which Florilor had been sitting, she had for a moment the illusion of having created the coin out of air by the alchemy of her own will.

'Many miracles have deserved the name less than this,' she murmured, picking up the piece of gold. For the second time in her life she was able to enjoy the sensation of illimitable wealth; by a curious coincidence the sum had been the same on both occasions. She preened her nail along the figured edge, taking a delight in the faint luxurious vibration.

'Misers may get very near to paradise by fingering their gold,' she thought. 'But the fingering of gold preparatory to spending it is paradise indeed.'

She went back to Queenie, clasping the coin so tightly that even when she had put it in her purse it seemed to be resting in her palm.

'Will you be leaving me here?' Queenie exclaimed in dismay, when she heard of Sylvia's plan for going to Bucharest tomorrow morning and interviewing Philip.

'There's not enough money to take us both there, but I shall come back tomorrow evening; and then we'll flaunt our wealth in the faces of these brutes here.'

'But I shall be so hungry tomorrow,' Queenie complained.

'Fool that I am,' Sylvia cried. 'The cakes!'

She rushed away and reached the other room a moment before the waiter arrived with his tray.

'These cakes belong to me,' she proclaimed, snatching up the china basket and hugging it to her breast.

The waiter protested that they had not been paid for; but she swept him and his remonstrances aside, and passed out triumphantly into the corridor, where the proprietor of the hotel, a short greasy man, began to abuse her for the way she had treated Florilor.

'*Va-t-en,*' she said scornfully.

'*Quoi? Quoi ditez? Moi bâton? Non! Vous bâton! Comprenez?*'
He was in such a rage at the idea of Sylvia's threatening him with a stick, which was the way he understood her French, that he began to dribble; all his words were drowned in a foam of saliva, and the only way he could express his opinion of her behaviour was by rapid expectoration. Again Sylvia tried to pass him in the narrow corridor, instinctively holding up the cakes beyond his reach. The proprietor evidently thought she was going to bring down the basket upon his head, and in an access of fear and fury he managed to knock it out of her hands.

'Those cakes are mine,' Sylvia really screamed. She felt like a cat defending her kittens when she plunged down upon the floor to pick them up. The proprietor jumped right over her, stamping upon the cakes and the pieces of broken china and grinding them underfoot into the carpet until it looked like a pavement of broken mosaics. Sylvia completely lost her temper at the sight of the destruction of her dinner; and when the proprietor trod upon her hand in the course of his violence she picked up the broken handle of the basket and jabbed his instep, which made him yell so loudly that all the hidden population of the kitchens came out like disturbed animals, holding in their hands the implements of the tasks upon which they had been engaged.

'*Vouz payez! Vous payez tout! Oui, oui, vous payez,*' the proprietor shouted.

The intensity of his anger made his veins swell and his nose bleed, and not being able to find a handkerchief he began to bellow for the attentions of his staff. This seemed an appropriate moment for the waiter to get himself back into his master's good graces, and with a towel in one hand and a chamber-pot in the other he came running out of the room where he had been hiding. At the sight of more china the proprietor uttered a stupendous Roumanian oath and kicked the pot out of the waiter's hand with such force that a piece of it flew up and cut his cheek. Sylvia left a momentarily increasing concourse of servants chatering round their master and the man, each of whom was stanching blood with his own end of the towel they held between them: they were all shovelling aside bits of china while they talked, so that they seemed like noisy hens scratching in a garden.

152

Queenie was standing with big frightened eyes when Sylvia got back to their room.

'Whatever was happening?'

'An argument over our dinner,' Sylvia laughed.

Then suddenly she began to cry, because at such a moment the loss of the cakes was truly a disaster and the thought of Queenie alone without food waiting here for her return from Bucharest was too much after the strain of the afternoon. She caught the child to her heart and told the story of what had happened with Florilor.

'Now do you understand?' she asked fiercely. 'Now do you understand how much I want you never – but never never again – even so much as to think of the possibility of selling yourself to a man? You must always remember when the temptation comes what I was ready to do to prevent such a horror. You must always believe that I am your friend and that if the war goes on for twenty years I will never leave you. You *shall* come back to England with me. With the money that I'm going to borrow in Bucharest we'll get as far as Greece anyway. But whatever happens I will never leave you, child, because I bear on my heart the stigmata of what I was ready to do for you.'

'I was not understanding much of what you are talking,' Queenie sighed.

'There is only one thing to understand – that I love you. You see this golden bag? The man who gave it to me left inside it a part of his soul; and if he has been killed, if he is lying at this moment a dreadful and disfigured corpse, what does it matter? He lives for ever with me here. He walks beside me always, because he obeyed the instinct of pure love. For you I was ready to do an action to account for which when I search deep down into myself I can find no motive but love. You must remember that and let the memory of that walk beside you always. Let me go on talking to you. You need not understand anything except that I love you and I must not lose you. I shall be thinking of you tomorrow when I'm in Bucharest, and I shall eat nothing all day, because I could not eat while you are waiting here hungry. It won't be for long. I shall be back tomorrow night with money. You don't mind my leaving you? And promise me, promise me that you won't unlock your door for a moment. Don't let that horrible youth have his way when I'm gone for the sake of a lunch. You won't, will you? Promise me, promise me.'

'Of course I would never do anything with him,' Queenie said.

Sylvia held up the ten-franc piece.

'Isn't it a wonderful little coin?' she laughed. 'It will take us so far from here. Once when I was a very small girl I found just such another.'

'You were being a small girl long ago,' Queenie exclaimed. 'Fancy! I was always forgetting that anybody else except me was ever being small.'

'What a lonely world she lives in,' Sylvia thought. 'She is conscious of nothing but herself, which is what makes her desire to be English such a tragedy, because she is feeling all the time that she has no real existence. She is like a ghost haunting the earth with incommunicable desires.'

Sylvia passed away the supperless evening for Queenie by telling her stories about her own childhood, trying to instil into her some apprehension of the continuity of existence, trying to populate the great voids stretching between her thoughts that so terrified her with the idea of being lost. Queenie really had no conception of her own actuality, so that at times she became positively a doll dependent upon the imagination of another for her very life. In the present stage of her development she might be the plaything of men without suffering; but Sylvia was afraid that if she again exposed her to the liability by deserting her at this point, Queenie might one day suddenly wake up to a sense of identity and find herself at the moment in a brothel. People always urged in defence of caging birds that if they were caged from the nest they did not suffer. Yet it was hard to imagine anything more lamentable than the celestial dreams of a lark that never had flown. Sylvia knew that at last she had been able to frame clearly the fear she had for Queenie; it lent new strength to her purpose. The horror of the brothel had become an obsession ever since earlier in the year she had passed by a vast and gloomy building which seemed a prison, but which she had been told was the recognised pleasure-house of soldiers. In this building behind high walls were two hundred women, most of whom in a Catholic country would have been cherished as penitents by nuns. Instead of that they were doomed to expiate their first fault by serving the State and slaking the lust of soldiers at the rate of a franc or a franc and a half. These women were fed by the State; they were examined daily by State doctors; everybody agreed that such forethought by the State was laudable. People who protested against such a debasement of womanhood were regarded as sentimentalists: so were people who believed in hell.

154

'This Promethean morality that enchains the world and sets its bureaucratic eagle to gnaw the vitals of humanity,' Sylvia cried 'Prometheus himself was surely only another personification of Satan, and this is his infernal revenge for what he suffered in the Caucasus. The future of the race! Or is my point of view distorted and am I wrong in mocking at the future of the majority? No, no, it cannot be right to secure the many by debasing the few. Am I being Promethean myself in trying to keep hold of you, Queenie? You came back into my life at such a moment that I feel as if you were a part of myself. Yet I can't help divining that there's a weakness in my logic somewhere.'

The next morning Sylvia went to Bucharest. She did not remember until she was in the train that it was Sunday; but the passport-office was open and Mr Mathers was at work as usual. She asked if Mr Iredale was too busy to see her.

'Mr Iredale?' the clerk repeated. 'I'm sorry to say that Mr Iredale's dead.'

Sylvia stared at him; for a moment the words had no more meaning than a conventional excuse to unwelcome visitors.

'But how can he be dead?' she exclaimed.

'I'm sorry to say that he died very suddenly. In fact he was taken ill almost immediately after you were here last. It was a stroke. He never recovered consciousness. Mr Abernethy is in charge temporarily. If you're anxious about your visa, I'm sure Mr Abernethy will do everything in his power – subject of course to the regulations. Oh certainly yes, everything in his power.'

Mr Mathers tried by the tone of his voice to convey that, though his late chief was dead, he could not forget the length of the interview he had granted to Sylvia and that the present rulers of the office would pay a tribute to the dead by treating her with equal condescension.

'No, I wanted to see Mr Iredale privately.'

The clerk sighed his sympathy with her position in face of the unattainable.

'Perhaps I shall be wanting a visa presently,' she added.

The clerk brightened. Sylvia fancied that in the remote and happy days before the war he must have had experience of the counter. He had offered her the prospect of obtaining a visa instead of seeing Philip again much as a shop assistant might offer one shade of ribbon in the place of another no longer in stock.

Sylvia left the passport-office and without paying any heed in

155

what direction she walked she came to the Cimisgiu Gardens and sat down upon a seat beside the ornamental lake. It was a hot morning, and there was enough mist in the atmosphere to blur the outlines of material objects and to set upon the buildings of the city a charm of distance that was as near as Bucharest ever approximated to the mellowing of time. The shock of the news that she had just heard, coming on top of the fatigue caused by her journey without even a cup of coffee to sustain her body, blurred the outlines of her mental attitude and made her glad of the fainting landscape that accorded with her mood and did not jar upon her with the turmoil of a world insistently, almost wantonly alive.

So Philip was dead. Sylvia tried to imagine how the news of his death would have affected her, if he had not lately re-entered her life. Poor Philip! Death out here seemed to crown the pathos of his position, had she wished that she had not parted from him so abruptly, that she had not tried so hard to make him aware of his incongruity in Bucharest, and now most of all that she had let him talk, as he had wanted to talk, about their life together. If she had only known that he was near to death she should have told him of her gratitude for much that he had done for her; had he lived to hear the request that she had been going to make him this morning, she was sure that he would have taken pleasure in his ability to be of use once more. She had been wrong to blame him for his attitude toward Queenie. After all, his experiment with herself had not encouraged him to make other experiments in the direction of obeying impulses that took him off the lines he had laid down for his progress through life. She was really the last person who should have asked him to forgo another convention in favour of a child like Queenie. How had he been paid for marrying a child whom he had met casually in a London cemetery? Very ill, he might consider. Poor Philip! Early next month it would be the fifteenth anniversary of their marriage. He had never known how to manage her; yet how preposterous it should have been to expect anything else. The more Sylvia meditated upon their marriage, the more she felt inclined to blame herself for its collapse; and in her present state of weakness the thought that it was now for ever too late to tell Philip how sorry she was fretted her with the poignancy of missed opportunity. Beneath that weight of pedagogic ashes there had always been the glow of humanity; if only she could have fanned it to a flame before she left Bucharest by giving him the chance of feeling that he

156

was helping her! Yet she had regarded the favour she was about to ask as such an humiliation that almost she had been inclined to put it on the same level of self-sacrifice as the offer of herself to that Roumanian youth. Now that she had failed with both her self-imposed resolves, how easy it was to see the difference in their degree! Her appeal to Philip would have been the just payment she owed him for that letter she wrote when she ran away; it would have washed out that callow piece of cruelty. But Philip was dead, and the relation between them must remain eternally unadjusted.

In meditating upon her married life and in conjuring scenes that had long been tossed aside into the lumber room of imagination, Sylvia's spirit wandered again in the green English country and forgot its exile. The warmth and mystery of the autumnal air drowsed all urgency with dreams of the past; for a minute or two she actually slept. She was disturbed by the voices of passing children, and she woke up with a shiver to the imperative and tormenting facts of the present – to the complete lack of money, to the thought of Queenie waiting hungry in Avereshti, and to Roumania clouding with the fog of war.

'What on earth am I going to do?' she murmured. 'I must sell my bag.'

The decision seemed to be made from without; it was like the voice of a wraith that had long been waiting incapable of speech, and involuntarily she turned round as if she could catch the spirit in the act of interfering with her affairs.

'Were I a natural liar, I should vow it was a ghost and frame the episode of Philip's death with a supernatural decoration. How many people who have penetrated to the ultimate confines of themselves have preferred to perceive the supernatural and in doing so destroyed the whole value of their discovery! Yet lying is the first qualification of every explorer.'

But setting aside considerations of the subconscious self, Sylvia was for a while horrified at the damnable clarity with which her course of action presented itself. There was no possible argument against selling the bag, and yet to sell it would demand a greater sacrifice than borrowing money from Philip or selling herself to Florilor. The fact that during all this time of strain the idea had never suggested itself before showed to what depths of her being it had been necessary to pierce before she could contemplate the action. Her feeling for the bag far transcended anything in the nature of sentiment; without blasphemy she could affirm that she would as soon have attributed her

157

sense of God in the sacrifice of the Mass to sentiment. But without incurring an imputation of idolatry by such a comparison she could at least award the bag as much value as devout women awarded a wedding-ring; for this golden bag positively was the outward sign that she had affirmed her belief in human love. In whatever tirades she might indulge against the natural depravity of man when confronted by the evidence of it so repeatedly as lately she had been, this bag was a continual reminder of his potential nobility. Certainly a critic of her extravagant reverence might urge that the value of the bag was created by the man who gave it and that any transference of such an emotion to a natural object was nothing but a surrender to sentiment which involved her in the common fault of seeking to express the eternal in terms of the temporal. But certain acts of worship lay outside the destructive logic of an unmoved critic; the circumstances in which the gift had been made were exceptional and her attitude towards it must remain equally exceptional. And now it must go; its talismanic and sacramental power must rest unappreciated in the hands of another. Yet in selling the bag was she not giving final and practical expression to the impulse of the donor? He had told her when she had protested against his generosity that before he was lost in the war his money would be better spent in giving someone something that was desired than in gambling it all away. Equally now would he not say to her that the money was better spent in helping a Queenie than in serving as a symbol rather than as an instrument of love? Or was the intrusion of Queenie into this intimacy of personal communion a kind of sacrilege? The soldier had never intended the bag to acquire any redemptive signification; he had merely chosen Sylvia by chance as the vehicle of one of those acts of sacred egotism which illuminate the Divine purpose. It was not to be supposed that the woman with the cruse of ointment was actuated by anything except self-expression, which was precisely what gave her impulse value as an act of worship. The commonplace utilitarian point of view on that occasion was perfectly expressed by Judas.

'And my own point of view about Queenie is not in the least altruistic. I want to give her something of which I have more than my fair share. I am burdened with an overflowing sense of existence. I have attached Queenie to myself and assumed a responsibility for her in exactly the same way as if I had brought a child into the world. There is no false redemptionism about the mother's relation to her child: there is merely a passion to bequeath to the child the sum of her own experience. My feeling about Queenie partakes of the passionate guardianship with which a loose woman so often shields her child. Certainly I must sell the bag. Who knows what chain of good may not weave itself from that soldier's action? To me he gave an imperishable store of love at the very moment when without the assurance of love my faith must have withered. I in turn give all that I can give to balance Queenie's life in the way I think it should be balanced. The next purchaser of the bag may, I should like to think without superstition, inherit with it a sacramental of love that will carry on the influence. And the one who first gave it to me? That almond-eyed soldier swept like a grain of chaff before the winnowing-fan of war? At this very moment perhaps the bullet has struck him. He has fallen. His company presses forward or is pressed back. He will lie rotting for days between earth and sky, and when at last they come to bury him they will laugh at the poor scarecrow that was a man. They will speculate neither whence he came nor who may weep for him; but his reward will be in his handiwork, for he will have shown love to a woman and he will have died for his country; such men like stars may light a very little of the world's darkness, but they proclaim the mysteries of God.'

With all her conviction that she was right in selling the bag, it was with a heavy heart that Sylvia left the Cimisgiu Gardens to seek a jeweller's shop; when she found that all the shops were shut except those open for the incidental amusements of the Sunday holiday, she nearly abandoned in relief the idea of selling the bag in order to go back to Avereshti and trust to fate for a way out of her difficulties. On reflection, however, she admitted the levity of such behaviour, if she wished to regard her struggle as worth anything at all, and she sharply brought herself back to the gravity of the position by reminding herself that it was she who had lost the five hundred francs, a piece of carelessness that was the occasion if not the cause of what had happened afterwards. If anything was to be left to hazard, it must be Queenie tonight alone in that hotel; besides, if further argument were necessary, there was not enough change from the ten francs to get back. Sylvia had promised Queenie that she would not eat until she saw her again, but she had not counted upon the effect of this long day to be followed by another long day tomorrow. How much money had she? Three francs twenty-five. Oh, she must eat; and she must also send a telegram to Queenie. Otherwise the child might do anything.

But she *must* eat; and suddenly she found herself sitting at a table outside a café with a waiter standing by on tiptoe for her commands. The coffee tasted incredibly delicious, but the moment she had finished she was overcome by a sensation of nausea and pierced by remorse for her weakness in giving way. She left the café and went to the post-office, where she spent all that was left of her money in a long telegram of exhortation and encouragement to Queenie.

The problem of how to pass the rest of the day weighed upon her. She did not want to meet any of the girls at the Trianon; she did not want to meet anybody she knew until she could meet them with money in her pocket. Tonight she would stay at their old hotel in Bucharest; she would say that she had missed the train back to Avereshti, if they wondered at the absence of luggage. Oh, but what did it matter if they did wonder? It was her sensitiveness to such trifles as these that brought home to Sylvia how much the strain of the last week had told upon her. Walking aimlessly along, she found herself near the little mission church and turned aside to enter it. At such an early hour of the afternoon the church was empty, and the incense of the morning mass was still pungent. There was the same sort of atmosphere that exists in a theatre between a matinée and an evening performance; the emotion of the departed worshippers was mingled with the expectation of more worshippers to come. Sylvia sat contemplating the images and wondering about the appeal they could make. She tried to put herself in the position of the humble and faithful soul that could derive consolation and help from praying before that tawdry image of the Sacred Heart. She wished that she could be given the mentality of a poor Italian girl whose sense of awe was so easily satisfied and could behold those flames of cheap gold paint round the Heart burning like the eyes of Seraphim.

'Yet after all,' she thought, 'are we superior people, who suppose that such representations hurt the majesty of God, any nearer to Him without equally pretentious theories of His manifestation? What in the ultimate sum of this world's history, when the world itself hangs in the sky like a poor burnt-out moon, will mark the difference between the greatest philosopher with his words and the most degraded savage with his idols? And am I with my perception of God's love in a golden bag less hopelessly material than the poor Italian girl who bows before that painted heart?'

The influence of the church began to penetrate Sylvia's mind with a tranquillising assurance of continuity, or rather with the assurance of silent and universal forces undisturbed by war. The sense of the individual's extinction in the strife of herd with herd had been bound to affect her very deeply, coming as it did at a time when she had once again challenged life as an individual by refusing any co-operation with the past.

'The worst of feeling regenerated,' she thought, 'is that such an emotion or condition of mind implies the destruction of all former experience. Of course, former experience must still produce its effect unconsciously; but one is too sensible of trying to bring the past into positively the same purified state as the present. When I was thinking about Philip this morning and reliving bygone moments, I was all the time applying to them standards which I have only possessed for about a year. Certainly I perceive that what I call my regeneration must be the fruit of past experience − otherwise the description would be meaningless − but it is the fruit of individual experience ripening at the very moment when individual experience counts for less than it has ever counted since the beginning of the world. Had I always been a social and political animal the idea of the war would not have preyed on my mind as it does; I should have been educated up to the point of expecting it. I remember when I was first told in the Petrograd hospital that a war had broken out what a trifling impression the news made compared with my own discovery of the change in myself. Gradually during this past year I have found at every turn my new progress barred by the war. My individual efforts perpetually shrink into insignificance before the war, and I am beginning to perceive, unless I can in some way fall into step with the rest of mankind, that what I considered progress is really the retreat of my personality along a disused bypath where I am expending all my energy in cutting away briers that were better left alone, at any rate at such a moment in history. Certainly one of the effects of an ordered religion is to restore the individual to the broad paths along which mankind is marching. An ordered religion is equally opposed either to short cuts or to cul-de-sacs, or to what by their impenetrability to the individual are equivalent to cul-de-sacs. My first instinct about Queenie was certainly right when I was anxious to entrust her to religion rather than to rely upon my personal influence. I think I must have lacked conviction in the way I approached the subject. I must have been timid and self-conscious; and the sceptical side of me that has just been wondering about the appeal of that image of the Sacred Heart may have defeated my purpose without my noticing its intrusion. I was all the time like a grown-up person who plays with children in order to get pleasure from their enjoyment rather than from his own.

'Yes, sitting here in this tawdry little church, I am beginning to make a few discoveries. I must positively lose the slightest consciousness of being superior to Queenie in any way whatsoever. Equally I must get over the slightest consciousness of being superior to any of the worshippers in this church. I must get over the habit of being injured by the monstrousness of this war until I have been personally injured by it in the course of sharing its woes with the rest of mankind. I have got to find an individualism that while it abates nothing of its unwillingness to be injured by the State is simultaneously always careful in its turn never to injure or impede the State, which from the individual's point of view must be regarded not as a state but as another individual. Presumably the chief function of an ordered religion is by acting through the individual to apply the sum of mankind's faith, hope, and love under the guidance of the Holy Ghost to the fulfilment of the Divine purpose. In such a way the self-perfection of the individual will create the self-perfection of the State, and oh, what a long time it will take! God is a great conservative; yet when He was incarnate He was a great radical. I wonder if I had ever had a real logical training or indeed any formal education at all whether I should be tossed about as I am from one paradox to another. The Church was significantly enough built upon Peter, not upon John nor upon Thomas; it was founded upon the most human of the apostles. If one might admit in God what in men would be called an afterthought, it might be permissable to look upon Paul as an afterthought to leaven some of the ponderousness of Peter's humanity. Anyway the point is that the paradoxes began in the very beginning, and it's quite obvious that I'm not going to help myself or anybody else by exposing myself to them rather than to the mighty moral, intellectual, and spiritual fabric into which they have all been absorbed or by which they have all been rejected.'

During Sylvia's meditation the church had gradually filled with worshippers to receive the Benediction of the Blessed Sacrament. Generally, that strangely wistful concession to the pathetic side of human nature had not made a deep appeal to Sylvia's instinct for worship; but this afternoon the bravery

162

of self had fallen from her. For the first time she felt in all its force – not merely apprehending it as a vague discomfort – the utter desolation of the soul without God. In such a state of mind faith shrank to infatuate speculation, hope swelled to arrogance, and even love shivered in a chill and viewless futility, until the mystical sympathy of other souls, the humblest of whom was a secret only known to God, led her to identify herself with them and to cry with them:

> *O salutaris Hostia,*
> *Quæ cœli pandis ostium:*
> *Bella premunt hostilia,*
> *Da robur, fer, auxilium.*

They were very poor people, these Albanians and Italians who knelt round her in this church; and Sylvia bowed before the thought that all over the world in all the warring nations somewhere about this hour poor people were crying out to God the same words in the same grave Latin. The helplessness of humanity raged through her like a strong wind, and her self-reliance became as the dust that was scattered before it. When the priest held the monstrance aloft, and gave the Benediction, it seemed that the wind died away; upon her soul the company of God was shed like a gentle rain, which left behind it faith blossoming like a flower, and hope singing like a bird, and above them both love shining like a sun.

Sylvia went out of the church that afternoon with a sense of having been personally comforted; she was intensely aware of having made more spiritual progress in the last hour than in all the year that had gone by since the first revelation of God.

'Without Him I am nothing, I am nothing, I am nothing,' she murmured.

That evening – an evening that she had dreaded indescribably – she sat by the window of her bedroom, happier than she could remember that she had ever been; when the chambermaid on her way to bed came to ask her if she wanted anything, Sylvia nearly kissed her in order that perhaps so she might express a little of her love towards all those who in this world serve.

'For such a girl with the eyes of a nymph to be serving you and for you to have presumed to consider yourself above all service that did not gratify your egotism,' she exclaimed aloud to her reflection in the glass.

The next morning Sylvia sold her golden bag for fifteen hundred francs. On the way to the station she felt very faint, and finding when she arrived that she would have to wait an hour for the train to Avereshti she drank some coffee. She told herself that it was only the weakness caused by fasting which made her regard so seriously this second breach of her promise to Queenie; nevertheless nothing could put out of her head the superstitious dread that the surrender caused her. The drinking of coffee while her friend was still hungry took on a significance quite out of proportion to what it actually possessed; she felt like the heroine of a fairy story who disobeys the warnings of her fairy godmother. While she was waiting in the *salle d'attente* and reproaching herself for what she had done, she heard a familiar voice behind her and looking round saw Philidor in uniform. He was travelling to Bralatz on military duty, and she was glad of his company as far as Avereshti, for all sorts of fears about what might have happened to Queenie during her absence were assailing her fancy. Philidor was surprised to find her still in Roumania and spoke seriously to her about the necessity of leaving at once if she did not want to travel home by Russia.

'You must get away. No one knows what may happen in the Balkans presently. You must get within sight of the sea. You English are lost away from the sea. I assure you that Bulgaria will come in soon. There is no doubt of it. I cannot understand the madness of your English politicians in making speeches to deceive everybody that the mobilisation is in self-defence. It is in self-defence, but not on the side of the Entente. You have been poisoned in England by the criminal stupidity of the Englishmen who come out here and see reflected in the eyes of the Bulgarian peasant their own liberal ideals. It is a tradition inherited from your Gladstone. To us out here such density of vision is incomprehensible. The Bulgarian is the Prussian of the Balkans: he is a product of uncompromising materialism. One of your chief Bulgarian propagandists was shot in the jaw the other day; it was a good place to wound him, but it's a pity he wasn't hit there before he did so much harm with his activities. We in Roumania were blamed by idealistic politicians for the way we stabbed Bulgaria in the back in 1913 you might as well blame a man for shooting at a slightly injured wild beast. You have always been too sporting in England, as you say; and not even war with Germany seems to have cured you of it. The Austrians are preparing to invade Serbia, and this time there will be no mistake. Get out of Roumania and get through Bulgaria before the carnage begins.'

164

The conviction with which he spoke gave Sylvia a thrill; for the first time the active side of the war seemed to be approaching her.

'And what is Roumania going to do?' she asked.

The young officer made a gesture of bewilderment.

'Who knows? Who knows? It will be a struggle between sentiment and expediency. I wish that the cry of the rights of small nations was not being so loudly shouted by the big nations. Battle cries are apt to die down when the battle is over. An idea that presents itself chiefly as a weapon of offence has little vitality; ideas, which are abstractions of liberty, do not like to be the slaves of other ideas. There is one idea in the world at this moment which overshadows all the rest – the idea of victory: the idea of the rights of small nations does not stand much chance against that. God fights on the side of the big battalions. Perhaps I'm too pessimistic. We shall see what happens in Serbia. But to put aside ideas for the moment, don't waste time in following my advice. You must leave Roumania now, if you want to leave at all. And I do not recommend you to stay. A woman like you following your profession should be in her own country in times of war. You are too much exposed to the malice of any private person, and in war justice like everything else is only regarded as a contribution to military efficiency.'

'You mean I might be denounced as a spy?'

'Anybody without protection may be denounced as a spy. Probably nothing would follow from it except expulsion, but expulsion would be unpleasant.'

'I wonder what is the fundamental reason for spymania,' said Sylvia. 'Is it due to cheap romanticism or a universal sense of guilt? Or is it the opportunity for the first time to give effect to vulgar gossip? I think it's the last probably. It must be very pleasant to glorify the meanest vice with the inspiration of a patriotic impulse.'

'I said that justice was subordinated to military efficiency.'

'Yes, and even slander has a temporary commission and is dressed up in a romantic uniform and armed with anonymous letters. Bullets are not the only things with long noses.'

'I suppose you can get away? You have money?' Philidor asked.

'Oh, I'm rich,' she declared.

'And your little friend, how is she?'

'She's waiting for me at Avereshti.'

165

Sylvia gave an account of her adventures, and Philidor shook his head.

'But it has all ended satisfactorily,' he said.

'I hope so.'

'It only shows how right I was to warn you of the spy danger – the double danger of being made the victim of a genuine agent and the risk of a frivolous accusation. You may be sure that now when you go back to the hotel with money, you will be accused everywhere of being a spy. If you have any trouble telegraph to me at Bralatz. Here's my address.'

'And here's Avereshti,' Sylvia said. 'Goodbye and good luck. *Et vive la Roumaine!*'

She waved her hand to him and walked quickly from the station to the hotel. It was good to see the waiter on the threshold and to be conscious of being able to rule him with the prospect of a tip. How second-rate the hotel seemed, with money in one's pocket! How obsequiously it seemed to beg one's patronage! There was not a single window that did not have the air of cringing to the new arrival.

'Lunch for two at once,' Sylvia cried, flinging him a twenty-franc note.

'For two?' the waiter repeated.

'For myself and Mademoiselle Walters – my friend upstairs,' she added, when the waiter stared first at her and then at the money. 'What's the matter? Is she ill? *Cretin,* if she's ill you and your master shall pay.'

'The lady who was staying here with madame left this morning with a gentleman.'

'*Crapule, tu mens!*'

'Madame may look for herself. The room is empty.'

Sylvia caught the waiter by the throat and shook him.

'You lie! You lie! Confess that you are lying. She was starved by you. She has died, and you are pretending that she has gone away.'

She threw the waiter from her, and ran upstairs. Her own luggage was still in the room; of Queenie's nothing remained except a few pieces of pink tissue-paper trembling faintly in the draught. Sylvia rang the bell, but before anyone could answer her summons she had fainted.

When she came to herself her first action – an action that seemed when afterwards she thought about it to mark well the depths of her disillusionment – was to feel for her money lest she might have been robbed during her unconsciousness. The wad of notes had not shrunk; the waiter was looking at her with all the sympathy that could be bought for twenty francs; a blowsy chambermaid dragged for the operation from a coal-cellar to judge by her appearance was sprinkling water over her.

'What was the man like?' she murmured.

The waiter bustled forward.

'A tall gentleman. He left no name. He said he brought a message. He paid a few little items on the bill that were not paid by madame. They took the train for Bucharest. Mademoiselle was looking ill.'

Sylvia mustered all that will of hers, which lately had been tried hardly enough to obliterate Queenie and everything that concerned Queenie from her consciousness. She fought down each superstitious reproach for not having kept her word by drinking the coffee in Bucharest: she drove forth from her mind every speculation about Queenie's future: she dried up every regret for any carelessness in the past.

'Clear away all this paper, please,' she told the chambermaid; then she asked the waiter for the menu.

He dusted the grimy card and handed it to her.

'*J'ai tellement faim,*' said Sylvia. '*Que je saurais manger même toi sans beurre.*'

The waiter inclined his head respectfully as if he would intimate his willingness to be eaten; but he tempered his assent with a smile to show that he was sensible that the sacrifice would not be exacted.

'And the wine?' he asked.

She chose half-a-bottle of the best native wine; and the waiter hurried away like a lame rook.

After lunch Sylvia carefully packed her things and put all her professional dresses away at the bottom of her large trunk. In the course of packing, the golden shawl that contained the records of her ancestry was left out of the trunk by accident, and she put it in the valise, which so far on her journeys she had always managed to keep with her. Philidor's solemn warning about the political situation in the Balkans had made an impression, and thinking it was possible that she might have to abandon her trunk at any moment she was glad of the oversight that had led her to making this change; though if she had been asked to give a reason for paying any heed to the shawl now she would have found it difficult. When she had finished her packing she sat down and wrote a letter to Olive.

My darling Olive,

This is not a communication from the other world as you might very well think. It's Sylvia herself writing to you from Roumania with a good deal of penitence, but still very much the same Sylvia. I'm not going to ask you for your news, because by the time you get this you may quite easily have got me with it. At any rate you can expect me almost on top. I shall telegraph when I reach France, if telegrams haven't been made a capital offence by that time. I've wondered dreadfully about you and Jack. I've a feeling the dear old boy is in Flanders or likely soon to go there. Dearest thing, I need not tell you that though I've not written I've thought terribly about you both during all this ghastly time. And the dear babies! I'm longing to see them. If I started to tell you my adventures I shouldn't know where to stop, so I won't begin. But I'm very well. Give my love to anybody you see who remembers your long long lost Sylvia.

How colourless the letter was, she thought, on reading it through. It gave as little indication of herself as an electric bell gives of the character of a guest when he is waiting on the doorstep. But it would serve its purpose like the bell to secure attention.

Sylvia intended to leave Avereshti that evening, but feeling tired she lay down upon her bed and fell fast asleep. She was woken up three hours later by the waiter, who announced with an air of excitement that Mr Porter had arrived at the hotel and was intending to spend the night.

'What of it?' she said coldly. 'I'm leaving by the nine o'clock train for Bucharest.'

'Oh, but Mr Porter will invite you to dinner.'

'Who is Mr Porter?'

'He's one of the richest men in Roumania. He is the head of many big petroleum companies. I told him that there was an English lady staying with us, and he was delighted. You can't leave tonight. Mr Porter will never forgive us.'

'Look here. Is this Florilor the Second?'

The waiter help up his hands in protest.

'Ah, no, madame! This is an Englishman. He could buy up M. Florilor ten times over. Shall I say that madame will be delighted to drink a cockataila with him?'

168

'Get out,' said Sylvia, pointing to the door.

But afterwards she felt disinclined to make a journey that night, and notwithstanding Philidor's urgency she decided to waste one night more in Avereshti. Moreover, the notion of meeting an Englishman was not so dull after all. Ten minutes later, she strolled downstairs to have a look at him.

Mr Porter was a stout man of about sixty, who was sometimes rather like Mr Pickwick in appearance, but generally bore a greater resemblance to Tweedledum. He was dressed in a well-cut suit of pepper and salt check and wore a glossy collar with a full black cravat, in which a fine diamond twinkled modestly; a clear somewhat florid face with that priestly glimmer of a very close shave, well-brushed boots, white spats, and a positive impression of having clean cuffs completed a figure that exhaled all the more prosperity and cheerfulness because the background of the hotel was so unsuitable.

'Going to introduce myself. Ha-ha! Apsley Porter's my name. Well known hereabouts. Ha-ha! Didn't expect to meet a compatriot in these times at Avereshti. Ugly little hole. Business before pleasure, though, by George, I don't see why pleasure should be left out in the cold altogether. What are you going to have? Ordered a Martini here the other day. "What's that?" I said to the scoundrel who served it. "Martini? Pah! Almost as dangerous as a Martini-Henry," I said. Ha-ha-ha-ha! But of course the blackguard didn't understand me. Going to have dinner with me, I hope? I've ordered a few special dishes. Always bring my own champagne with me in case of accidents. I forced them to get ice here though. Ha-ha! By George I did. I said that if there wasn't ice whenever I came I should close down one of the principal wells I control. Did I tell you my name? Ah, glad I did. I've got a deuced bad habit of talking away without introducing myself. Here comes the villain with your cocktail. You must gin and bear it. What? Ha-ha-ha-ha-ha-ha-ha!'

Sylvia liked Mr Porter and accepted his invitation to dinner. He was distressed to hear that a friend had been staying with her in the hotel so recently as this morning and that he had had the bad luck to miss entertaining her.

'What, another little Englishwoman in Avereshti? By George, what a pity I didn't turn up yesterday! I shan't forgive myself. Come along, waiter. Hurry up with that champagne. Fancy! Another jolly little Englishwoman and I missed her. Too bad!'

There was irony in meeting upon the vigil of her return to England this Englishman redolent of the Monico. Sylvia had spent so much of her time intimately with people at the other pole of pleasure that she had forgotten how to talk to this type and could only respond with monosyllables to his boisterous assaults upon the present. He was so much like a fine afternoon in London that she sunned herself as it were in his effluence and let her senses occupy themselves with the noise of the traffic, as if she had suddenly been transplanted to the Strand and was finding the experience immediately on top of Avereshti pleasant, but rather bewildering. And now he was talking about the war.

'Nothing to worry about. Nothing to worry about at all. Pity about the Dardanelles. Great pity, but we had no luck. They are making a great fuss here over this coming Austrian attack upon Serbia. Don't believe in it. Shan't believe in it until it happens. But it won't happen, and if it does happen – waiter, where's that champagne? – if it does happen, it won't alter the course of the war. Not a bit of it. I'm an optimist. And in times like these I consider that optimism is of as much use to my country at my age as a rifle would have been if I were a younger man. Pessimism in times like these is a poison.'

'But isn't optimism apt to be an intoxicant?' Sylvia suggested.

She felt inclined to impress upon Mr Porter the difference between facing misfortune with money and without it, and she told him a few of her adventures in the past year, winding up with an account of the behaviour of the proprietor of this very hotel.

'You don't mean to say old Andrescu refused to serve you with anything to eat?'

The notion seemed to shake Mr Porter to the depths of his being.

'Why, I never heard anything like it. Waiter, go and tell M. Andrescu to come and speak to me at once. I shall give him a piece of my mind.'

The jovial curves of his face had all hardened: his bright little eyes were like steel: even the dimple in his chin had disappeared in the contraction of his mouth. When Andrescu came in, he began to abuse him in rapid Roumanian, while his complexion turned from pink to crimson, and from crimson in waves of colour to a uniform purple. In the end he stopped talking for a moment, and the proprietor begged Sylvia's intercession.

'That's the way to deal with rascally hotel-keepers,' said Mr Porter, fanning himself with a red and yellow bandana handkerchief and drinking two glasses of champagne.

'What annoyed me most of all,' he added, 'was that his

170

behaviour should have made me miss the chance of asking another jolly little English girl to dinner. Too bad!'

Sylvia had not told him more than the bare outlines of the story; she had not confided in him about Florilor or the sale of her bag or the fact that she had lost Queenie for ever. Her tale could have seemed not much more than a tale of temporary inconvenience, and she was therefore only amused when Mr Porter deduced from it as the most important result his own failure to entertain Queenie.

After dinner she and her host sat talking for awhile, or rather she sat listening to his narratives of holidays spent in England, which evidently appealed to him as a much more vital part of his career than his success in the Roumanian oilfields. When about eleven o'clock she got up to take her leave and go to bed, he expressed his profound dismay at the notion of thus breaking up a jolly evening.

'Tell you what we'll do,' he announced. 'We'll make a night of it. We will, by George we will. A night of it. We'll have half-a-dozen bottles put on ice and take them up to my room. I can talk all night on champagne. Now don't say no. It's a patriotic duty, but George it's a patriotic duty when two English people meet in a god-forsaken place like this, it's a patriotic duty to make a night of it. Eat and drink today, for tomorrow we die.'

Sylvia was feeling weary enough, but the fatuous talk had cheered her by its sheer inanity, and the thought of going to bed in that haunted room – her will was strong, but the memory of what she had endured for Queenie was not entirely quenched – and of perhaps not being able to sleep was too dismal. She might just as well help this amiable old buffoon's illusion that champagne was the elixir of eternal life and that pleasure was nothing but laughing loudly enough.

'All right,' said Sylvia, 'But I'd rather we made the night of it in my room. I'll get into a wrapper and make myself comfortable, and when dawn breaks I can tumble into bed.'

Mr Porter hesitated a moment.

'Right you are, my dear girl. Of course. Waiter! Where's the ruffian hidden himself?'

'I'll leave you to make the arrangements. I shall be ready in about a quarter of an hour,' Sylvia said.

She left him and went upstairs.

'I believe the silly old fool thought I was making overtures to him when I suggested we should make merry in my room,' she

171

laughed to herself. 'Oh dear, it shows how much one can tell and how little of oneself need be revealed in the telling of it. Stupid old ass! But rather pleasant in a way. He's like finding an old Christmas number of the *Graphic* – coloured heartiness, conventional mirth, reality mercifully absent, and *O mihi præteritos* printed in Gothic capitals on the cover. I suppose these pre-war figures still abound in England. And I'm not sure he isn't right in believing that his outlook on life is worth preserving as long as possible. Timbered houses, crusted port, and Dickens are nearer to fairyland than anything else that's left nowadays. To what old age will this blackened, mutilated, and agonised generation grow? Efficiency and progress have not spared the monuments of bygone art except to imprison them in libraries, museums, and iron-railings. Will it spare the Englishman? Or will the generations of a century hence read of him only, and murmur "This was a man". Will they praise him as the last and noblest individual, turning with repulsion and remorse from the sight of themselves and their fellows, the product of the triumphant herd eternally sowing where it does not reap? Night thoughts of the young on perceiving a relic of insular grandeur in an exceptionally fine state of preservation – preserved in oil! And here he comes to interrupt my sad soliloquy.'

The night passed away just as the evening had passed away. Mr Porter sustained his joviality in a fashion that would have astounded Sylvia, if all capacity for being astounded had not been exhausted in watching him drink champagne. It was incredible not so much that his head could withstand the fumes as that his body, fat though it was, should be expansive enough to contain the cubic quantity of liquor. It was four o'clock before he had finished the last drop, and was shaking Sylvia's hand in cordial farewell.

'Haven't enjoyed an evening so much for months. By George, I haven't. Ha-ha-ha! Well, you'll forgive an old man – always accuse myself of being old when the wine is low, but I shall be as young as a chicken again after three hours' sleep – you'll excuse an old man. Little present probably damned useful in these hard times. Ha-ha-ha! Under your pillow. Good girl. Never made me feel an old man by expecting me to make love. I've often set out to make a night of it, and only succeded in making a damned fool of myself. Sixty-four next month. Youth's the time! Ha-ha-ha. Good-bye. God bless you. Shan't see you in the morning. By George! I *shall* have a busy day.'

He shook her warmly by the hand, avoided the ice-stand with a grave bow, and left her with a smell of cigar-smoke. Under the pillow she found four five-hundred franc notes.

'Really,' Sylvia exclaimed. 'I might be excused for thinking myself a leading character in a farce by fate. I fail to make a halfpenny by offering myself when the necessity is urgent and make two thousand francs by not embarrassing an old gentleman's impotence. Meanwhile, it's too late – it's just too late. But I shall be able to buy back my golden bag. I suppose fate thinks that's as good a curtain as I'm entitled to in a farce.'

Sylvia left Avereshti next morning with a profound conviction that whatever the future held nothing should induce her to put foot in that town again. There was some satisfaction in achieving even so much sense of finality, negative though the achievement might be.

'I don't advise you to go to Dedeagatch,' said Mr Mathers when Sylvia presented herself at the passport-office for the recommendation for a visa. 'I may tell you in confidence that the situation in Bulgaria is very grave – very grave indeed. Anything may happen this week. The feeling here is very tense too. If you are determined to take the risk of being held up in Bulgaria, I counsel you to travel by Rustchuk, Gorna Orechovitza, and Sofia to Nish. From Nish you'll get down to Salonika, and from there to the Piræus. At the same time I strongly advise you to keep away from Bulgaria. With the mobilisation, passenger traffic is liable to be very uncertain.'

'But if I go back through Russia I may find it just as hard to get back to England. No, no. I'll risk Bulgaria. Today's Tuesday the 28th. When can I have my visa?'

'Well, strictly speaking it's already too late today to entertain applications, but as you were a friend of Mr Iredale, I'll ask Mr Abernathy to put it through for you. It you come in tomorrow morning at ten, I will give you a letter for the Consulate. There will be the usual fee to pay there. Oh dear me, you haven't brought the four photographs that are necessary. I must have them, I'm afraid. Two for us, one for the Consulate, and one for the French authorities. The Italians don't insist upon a photograph at present. I'm afraid I shan't be able to put it through for you today. The French are very strict and insist on a minimum of four days. But in view of the Bulgarian crisis I'll get them to relax the rule. Luckily one of the French officers is a friend of mine – a very nice fellow.'

Three days elapsed before Sylvia was finally equipped with her passport *visé* for Bulgaria, Serbia, Greece, Italy, France, and England. The representatives of the first two nations, who seemed most immediately concerned with her journey, made the least bother; the representative of Italy, the nation that seemed least concerned with it, made the most.

While she was waiting for the result of the accumulated contemplation upon her age, her sex, her lineaments, and her past history, Sylvia bought back her gold bag for eighteen hundred francs, which left her with just over fifteen hundred francs for the journey – none too much, but she should no longer have any scruples in telegraphing to England for help if she found herself stranded.

On Friday afternoon she called for the last time at the passport-office to get a letter of introduction that Mr Mathers had insisted on writing for her to a friend of his in the American Tobacco Company at Cavalla.

'You're not likely to go there,' he said, 'But if you do, it may be useful.'

The clerk handed her the letter, and there was something magnificently protective in the accompanying gesture; he might have been handing her a personal letter to the Prime Minister and giving her an assurance that the Foreign Secretary would personally meet her at Waterloo and see that she did not get into the wrong tube.

When Sylvia was leaving the office, Maud Moffat came in, at the sight of whom Mr Mathers' spectacled benevolence turned to an aspect of hate for the whole of humanity.

'It's too late, madam, today. Nothing can be done until further enquiries have been made,' he said sharply.

'Too late be damned,' Maud shouted. 'I'm not going to be —— about any longer. My passport's been stolen and I want another. I'm an honest English girl who's been earning her living on the continent and I want to go home and see my poor old mother. Perhaps you'll say next that I'm not English?'

'Nobody says that you're not English,' Mr Mathers replied through set teeth. 'And please control your language.'

At this moment Maud recognised Sylvia.

'Oh, you've come back, have you? I suppose *you* didn't have any difficulty with *your* passport. Oh, no, people as frequents the company of German spies can get passports for nothing, but me who's travelled for seven years on the continent without ever having anyone give me so much as a funny look, me I repeat gets cross-examined and messed about as if I was a murderer

174

instead of an artiste. Yes, war's a fine thing for some people,' she went on. 'Young fellows that ought to be fighting for their country instead of bullying poor girls from the other side of a table thoroughly enjoys *their*selves. Nice thing when an honest English girl – and not a German spy – can't mislay her passport without being —— '

'I must repeat, madam,' Mr Mathers interrupted, 'that the circumstances have to be gone into.'

'Circumstances? I'm in very good circumstances, thank you. But I shan't be if you keep me mucking about in Bucharest so as I forfeit my engagement at the White Tower, Saloniker. You'll look very funny, Mr Nosey Parker, when my friend the Major who I know in Egypt and still writes to me lodges a complaint about your conduct. Why don't you ask this young lady about me? She knows I'm English.'

'I keep telling you that nobody questions your nationality.'

'Well, you've asked me enough questions. You know the size of my corsets and the colour of my chemise and how many moles I've got, and whether my grandmother was married and if it's true my uncle Bill ran away to Africa because he couldn't stand my aunt Jane's voice. Nationality! I reckon you couldn't think of any more questions, unless you became a medical student and started on my inside. Why don't you tell him you know all about me?' she added, turning to Sylvia.

'Because I don't,' Sylvia replied coldly.

'Well, there's a brazen-faced bitch!' Miss Moffat gasped.

Sylvia said goodbye hurriedly to Mr Mathers and left him to Maud. When she was in the train on the way to Rustchuk, it suddenly struck her that Zozo might be able to explain the missing passport.

Chapter VI

THE MORE Sylvia pondered the coincidence of Queenie's flight with the loss of Maud's passport, the more positive she became that Zozo had committed the theft. And with what object? It seemed unlikely that the passport could be altered plausibly enough to be accepted as Queenie's own property in these days when so much attention was being given to passports and their reputed owners. Probably he had only used it as a bait with which to lure her in the first instance; he would have known that she could not read and might have counted upon the lion and the unicorn to impress her with his ability to do something for her that Sylvia had failed to do. Queenie must have been in a state of discouragement through her not having come back to Avereshti on the Sunday evening, as she had promised. The telegram she sent had really been a mistake, because Queenie would never have asked anyone in the hotel to read it for her, and Zozo would assuredly have pretended whatever suited his purpose if by chance it had been shown to him.

At first Sylvia had been regretting that she had not divined sooner the explanation of Maud's missing passport, so that she could have warned Mr Mathers; but now she was glad, because whatever Queenie did the blame must be shared by herself and the British regulations. She reproached herself for the attitude she had taken toward Queenie's disappearance; she had done nothing in these days at Bucharest to help the poor child, not even as much as to find out where she had gone. If Zozo were indeed a German agent, what might not be the result of that callousness? Yet after all he might not be anything of the kind; he might merely have been roused by her own opposition to regain possession of Queenie. Really it was difficult to say which explanation was more galling to her own conscience. However, it was useless to do anything now; there was as little probability of Queenie's being still in Bucharest as of her being anywhere else. If Zozo were in German pay he would find it easy enough to secure Queenie's entrance into a neutral country; and if he were once more enamoured of his power over her, he would certainly have taken precautions against any new intervention by herself.

Late in the afternoon of Saturday the third of October Sylvia arrived at Giurgiu, the last station in Roumania before crossing the Danube to enter Bulgaria. It had been a slow journey owing to the congestion of traffic caused by the concentration of Roumanian troops upon the frontier. When she was leaving the station to take the ferry she caught sight of Philidor upon the platform.

'You here? I thought you were at Bralatz,' she cried.

She was thinking that Philidor's presence was of good omen to her journey; and as they walked together down to the quay she was glad that her last memory of Roumania should be of this tall figure in his light blue cloak appearing indeed of heroic mould in the transmuting fog of the Danube that enmeshed them.

'You've left it very late,' he said. 'We expect every hour the Bulgarian declaration of war upon the Entente. Ah, this disastrous summer! The failure at the Dardanelles! The failure of the Russians! And now I doubt if we shall do anything but cluster here upon the frontier like birds gathering to go south.'

'I am going south,' Sylvia murmured.

'I wish that I were,' he sighed. 'Now is the moment to strike. When I think of the Bulgarians on the other side of the river, and of my troop – such splendid fellows – waiting and waiting! Sylvia, I am filled with intuitions of my country's fate. Wherever I look the clouds are black. If when you are back in England you read one day that Roumania is fighting with you, do not remember the tawdry side of her, but think of us waiting where in the fog, waiting and waiting. If – and God forbid that you should read this – if you read that Roumania is fighting against you, think that one insignificant lieutenant of cavalry will hope to fall very early upon a Russian bayonet.'

He held her for a moment in the folds of his bedewed cloak, while they listened to the slow lapping of the river; then she mounted the gangway, and the ferry glided into the fog.

There was a very long wait at Rustchuk; but Sylvia did not find the Bulgarian officials discourteous; in fact for the representatives of a country upon the verge of going to war with her own they were pleasant and obliging. It was after midnight before the train left Rustchuk, and some time before dawn that it reached Gorna Orechovitza where it seemed likely to wait for ever. A chill wind was blowing down from the Balkans, which had swept the junction clear of everybody except a squat Bulgarian soldier who marched up and down in his dark-green overcoat, stamping his feet; so little prospect was there of the train starting again that all the station officials were dozing round a stove in the buffet and the passengers had gone back to their *couchettes*. To Sylvia the desolation was exhilarating with a sense of adventure. Roumania had already receded far away – at any rate the tawdry side of it – and the only picture that remained was of Philidor upon the bank of the misty river. It seemed to her now that the whole of the past eighteen months had been a morbid night, such a new and biting sense of reality was blown down from the mountains upon this windy October dawn, such magical horizons were being written across this crimson sky.

The train did not reach Sofia until the afternoon; the station was murmurous with excitement on account of the rumour of an ultimatum presented that morning by the Russian Minister; Sylvia as an Englishwoman became the object of a contemplative stare of curiosity in which was nothing insolent or hostile, but which gave her the sensation of being just a material aid to dim unskilful meditations, like a rosary in the hands of a converted savage. There was not such a long wait at Sofia as she had expected, and toward dusk after changing trains they reached Slivnitsa; but at Zaribrod, the last station before crossing the Serbian frontier, the train pulled up and showed no sign of proceeding. The platform was thronged with Bulgarian troops, the sound of whom all talking excitedly was like a prolonged sneeze.

At Slivnitsa a tall fair man had got into Sylvia's compartment. In excellent French he told her that his name was Rakoff and that he was a rose-grower. Sylvia expressed her astonishment that a Bulgarian rose-grower should travel to Serbia at such a time, but he laughed at the notion of war between Bulgaria and the Entente, avowed that the agrarian party to which he belonged was unanimously against such a disastrous step, and spoke cheerfully of doing good business in Salonika. At Zaribrod he went off to make enquiries about the chance of getting on that night, but he could obtain no information, and invited Sylvia to dine with him at the station buffet. He also helped her to change her *lei* and *lewa* into Serbian money and generally made himself useful in matters of detail such as putting her clock back an hour to mid-European time. Upon these slight courtesies Sylvia and he built up, as travellers are wont, one of those brief and violent friendships that colour the memory of a voyage like brilliant fugacious blooms. Rakoff expressed loudly his disgust at seeing the soldiers swarming upon the frontier; they had had quite enough war in Bulgaria two years ago, and it was madness to think of losing the advantages of neutrality, especially on behalf of the Germans. He talked of his acres of roses, of the scent of them in the early morning, of the colour of them at noon, and gave Sylvia a small bottle of attar that drenched with its stored up sweetness even the smell of the massed soldiery. Sylvia in her turn talked to him of her life on the stage, described her success in London, and even confided in him her reason for abandoning it all.

'One has these impulses,' he agreed. 'But it is better not to give way to them. That is the advantage of my life as a rose-grower. There is always something to do. It is a tranquil and beautiful existence. One becomes almost a rose oneself. I hate to leave my fields, but my brother was killed in the last war, and I have to travel occasionally since his death. Ah, war! It is the sport of kings; yet our King Ferdinand is a great gardener. He is only happy with his plants. It is terrible that a small group of *arrivistes* should deflect the whole course of our national life, for I'm sure that a gardener must loathe war.'

Sylvia thought of Philidor's denunciations of Englishmen who had found that the Bulgarians were idealists, and sympathised with their partiality when she listened to this gentle rose-grower.

At last about two o'clock in the morning the train was allowed to proceed to Serbia. As it left the station the Bulgarian soldiers shouted 'Hourrah! Hourrah! Hourrah! in accents between menace and triumph. She turned to her companion with lifted eyebrows.

'They don't sound very pastoral,' she said.

'Some Serbians in the train must have annoyed them,' Rakoff explained.

'Well, I hope for the sake of the Serbians that we're not merely shunting,' Sylvia laughed.

The train went more slowly than ever after they left Pirot, the first station in Serbia, where there had been an endless searching of half the passengers, of which apparently everybody had suddenly got tired, because the passengers in their portion of the train were not examined at all.

'I doubt if this train will go beyond Nish,' said Rakoff. 'The Austrians are advancing more rapidly than was expected. There is a great feeling in Serbia against us. I shall travel back by sea from Salonika.'

They reached Nish about seven o'clock in the morning. When Rakoff was standing outside the window of the compartment to help Sylvia with her luggage he was touched on the shoulder by a Serbian officer, who said something to him at which he started perceptibly. A moment later, however, he called out to Sylvia that he should be back in a moment and would see her to the hotel. He waved his hand and passed on with the officer.

Sylvia turned round to go out by the corridor, but was met in the entrance by another Serbian officer who asked her to keep her seat.

'*Mais je suis Anglaise*,' she protested.

'No doubt there's some mistake,' he answered politely in excellent English. 'But I must request you to stay in the compartment.'

179

He seated himself and asked her permission to smoke. The passengers had all alighted, and the train seemed very still. Presently another officer came and demanded her papers, which he took away with him. Half an hour went by, and Sylvia began to feel hungry. She asked the officer in the compartment if it would be possible to get some coffee.

'Of course,' he answered with a smile, calling to someone in the corridor. A soldier with fixed bayonet came along and took his commands; presently two cups of black coffee and a packet of cigarettes arrived.

The officer was young and had a pleasant face, but he declined to be drawn into conversation beyond offering Sylvia her coffee and the cigarettes. An hour passed in this way.

'How long am I likely to be kept here?' she asked irritably.

The young officer looked uncomfortable, and invited her to have another cup of coffee, but he did not answer her question. At last, when Sylvia was beginning to feel thoroughly miserable, there was a sound of voices in the corridor, and an English captain in much-stained khaki appeared in the entrance to the compartment.

'Good morning,' he said. 'Sorry you've been kept waiting like this. My fault, I'm afraid. Fact is I won a bath at piquet last night, and not even the detention of a compatriot would make me forgo one exquisite moment of it.'

He was a tall thin man in the early thirties with a languid manner of speech and movement that, though it seemed at first out of keeping with the substance of his conversation, nevertheless oddly enhanced it somehow. Sylvia had an impression that his point of view about everything was worn and stained like his uniform, but that like his uniform it preserved a fundamentally good quality of cloth and cut. His arrival smoothed away much of her annoyance, because she discerned in him a capacity for approaching a case upon its own merits and a complete indifference to any professionalism real or assumed for the duration of the war. In a word she found his personality sympathetic, and long experience had given her the assurance that wherever this was so she could count upon rousing a reciprocal confidence.

'Good morning, Antitch,' he was saying to the young Serbian officer who had been keeping guard over her. And to Sylvia he added: 'Antitch was at Oxford and speaks English like an Englishman.'

'I've had very little chance of knowing if he could even speak his own language,' she said sharply.

Her pleasure in finding an English officer at Nish was now being marred, as so many pleasures are marred for women by consciousness of the sight she must present at this moderately early hour of the morning after thirty-six hours in the train.

The Englishman laughed.

'Antitch takes an occasion like this very seriously,' he said.

'It's the only way to treat half-past eight in the morning,' Sylvia answered. 'Even after a bath.'

'I know. I must apologise for my effervescence at such an hour. We try to assume this kind of attitude toward life when we assume temporary commissions. I'm a parvenu to such an hour and don't really know how to behave myself. Now at dawn you would have found my manner as easy as a doctor's by a bedside. Well, what have you been doing?'

'Really, I think that's for you to tell me' Sylvia replied.

'Where did you meet your fellow-traveller – the Bulgarian?'

'The rose-grower?'

'Oh, you think he *is* a rose-grower?'

'I didn't speculate upon the problem. He got into the train at Slivnitsa and did all he could to make himself useful and agreeable,' Sylvia said.

'That's one for you, Antitch,' the Englishman laughed. 'Another Bulgarophile. We're hopeless, aren't we? Upon my soul, people like Prussians and Bulgarians are justified in thinking that we're traitors to our convictions when they witness the affinity between most of them and most of us. I say, you must forgive me for being so full of voluble buck this morning,' he went on to Sylvia. 'It really is the effect of the bath. I feel like a general who's been made a knight commander of that most honourable order for losing an impregnable position and keeping his temper. Well, I'm sorry to bother you, but I think you'd better be confronted by your accomplice. We have reason to doubt his bona fides, and Colonel Michailovitch, our criminal expert, would like to have your testimony. You'll entrust this lady to me?' he asked Antitch, who saluted ceremoniously. 'All right, old thing, you'll bark your knuckles if you try to be too polite in a railway-carriage. Come along then, and we'll tackle the Colonel.'

'I think I will come as well,' said Antitch.

'Of course, of course. I don't know if it's etiquette to introduce a suspected spy to her temporary gaoler, but this is Lieutenant Antitch, and my name's Hazlewood. You've come from Roumania, haven't you? Here, let me carry your valise.

Even if you are condemned by the court, you won't be condemned to travel any more in this train. What an atrocious sentence! *Voyages forcés* for twenty years!'

'Roumania was very well,' said Sylvia, as they passed along the corridor to the platform.

'Still flirting with intervention, I suppose?' Hazlewood went on. 'Odd effect this war has of making one think of countries as acquaintances. All Europe has been reduced to a suburb. I was sent up here from Gallipoli, and I find Nish – which with deep respect to Antitch, I had always regarded as an unknown town consisting of mud and pigs, or as one of the stations where it was possible to eat between Vienna and Constantinople – as crowded and cosmopolitan as Monte Carlo. The whole world and his future wife is here.'

Sylvia was trying to remember how the name Hazlewood was faintly familiar to her, but the recollection was elusive, and she asked about her big trunk.

'If you're going on to Salonika,' he advised. 'You'd better get on as soon as possible after the stain of suspicion has been erased from your passport. Nish is full up now, but presently – ' he broke off, and looked across at Antitch with an expression of tenderness.

The young Serbian shrugged his shoulders; and they passed into the office of Colonel Michailovitch, who was examining Sylvia's passport with the rapt concentration of gaze that could only be achieved by someone who was incapable of understanding a single word of what he was apparently reading. The colonel bowed to Sylvia when she entered and invited her to sit down. Hazlewood asked him if he might look at the passport.

'It's quite in order, I think, *mon colonel*,' he said in French. The Colonel agreed with him.

'You have no objection to its being returned?'

'*Pas du tout, pas du tout! Plaisir, plaisir*,' exclaimed the Colonel.

'And I think you would like to hear from – ' Hazlewood glanced at the passport – 'from Miss Scarlett? Sylvia Scarlett?' he repeated, looking at her. 'Why, I believe we have a friend in common. Aren't you a friend of Michael Fane?'

Sylvia realised how familiar his name should be to her; and she felt that her eyes brightened in assent.

'He's in Serbia, you know,' said Hazlewood.

'Now?' she asked.

'Yes. I'll tell you about him. *Je demande pardon, mon colonel,*

182

mais je connais cette dame.'

'*Enchanté, enchanté,*' said the Colonel getting up and shaking hands cordially. '*Le Capitaine Antonivitch. Le Lieutenant Lazarevitch,*' he added, indicating the other officers, who saluted and shook hands with her.

'They're awful dears, aren't they?' murmured Hazlewood. Then he went on in French: 'But, *mon colonel,* I beg you will ask Miss Scarlett any questions you want to ask about this man Rakoff.'

'*Vous me permettez, madame?*' the Colonel enquired. '*Desolé, mais vous comprenez, la guerre c'est comme ça, n'est-ce pas? Ah oui, la guerre.*'

Everybody in the office sighed in echo: '*Ah oui, la guerre!*'

'Where did this man get into the train?'

'At Slivnitsa, I believe.'

'Did he talk about anything in particular?'

'About roses mostly. He said he did not believe there could be war with Serbia. He spoke very bitterly against Germany.'

Sylvia answered many more questions in favour of her fellow traveller. The Colonel talked for a few moments in Serbian to his assistants; presently a grubby looking peasant was brought in, at whom the Colonel shouted a number of questions, the answers to which seemed to reduce him to a state of nervous despair. One of the officers retired and came back with the Bulgarian rosegrower; after a great deal of talking the peasant was sent away, and Rakoff's passport was handed back to him.

'*Je suis libre?*' asked the Bulgarian, looking round him.

The Colonel bowed stiffly.

'This lady has spoken of your horticultural passion,' said Hazlewood, looking at Rakoff straight in the eyes.

'*Je suis infiniment reconnaissant,*' the Bulgarian murmured with a bow. Then he saluted the company and went out .

'I daren't precipitate the situation,' the Colonel told Hazlewood. 'He must leave Nish at once, but if he tries to alight before the Greek frontier, he can always be arrested.'

Renewed apologies from the Colonel and much cordial saluting from his staff ushered Sylvia out of the office, whence she was followed by Hazlewood and Antitch, the latter of whom begged her to show her forgiveness by dining with him that night.

'My dear fellow,' Hazlewood protested. 'Miss Scarlett has promised to dine with me.'

In the end she agreed to dine with both, and begged them not to bother about her any more, lest work should suffer.

'No, I'll see you into town,' Hazlewood said. 'Because I don't know if there's a room in any hotel. You ought really to go on to Salonika at once, but I suppose you want to see Nish on the eve if its calvary.'

She looked at him in surprise: there was such a depth of bitterness in his tone.

'I should hate to be a mere sightseer.'

'No, forgive me for talking like that. I'm sure you're not, and to show my penitence for the imputation let me help you about your room.'

Sylvia and Hazlewood bowed to Antitch and walked out of the station.

'They've started to commandeer every vehicle and every animal,' Hazlewood explained. 'So we shall have to walk. It's not far. This youth will carry your bag. Your heavy luggage had better remain in the *consigne*. I suppose you more or less guessed what was Michailovitch's difficulty about your friend the Bulgarian rose-grower?'

'No, I don't think I did really.'

Sylvia did not care anything about the Bulgarian or the Colonel; she was only anxious to hear something about Michael Fane; but because she was so anxious she could not bring herself to start the topic and must wait for Hazlewood.

'Well, this fellow Rakoff was identified by that peasant chap who was brought in – or at any rate so almost certainly recognised as to amount to identification – as one of the most bloodthirsty comitadji leaders.'

'What do they do?'

She felt that she must appear to take some interest in what Hazlewood was telling her, after the way he had helped and was helping her and perhaps would help her.

'Their chief mission in life,' he explained, 'is the Bulgarisation of Macedonia, which they effect in the simplest way possible by murdering everybody who is not Bulgarian. They're also rather fond of Bulgarising towns and churches by means of dynamite. Altogether the most unpleasant ruffians left in Europe, and in yielding them the superlative I'm not forgetting Orangemen and Junkers. The Colonel did not believe that he was a rose-grower, but he was afraid to arrest him, because at this moment it is essential not to give the least excuse for precipitating the situation. We expect to hear at any moment that Bulgaria has declared war on Serbia; but all sorts of negotiations are still in progress. One of the characteristics of our policy during this war is to give a frenzied attention to the moulding of a situation after it has hopelessly hardened. This Austrian advance is bad enough, but there's probably worse to follow, and we don't want the worst yet. The people here are counting on French and English help and they are frightened to death of doing anything that will upset us. As a matter of fact your evidence was a godsend to the Colonel, because it gave him an excuse to let Rakoff go without losing his dignity. And of course there's always a chance that the fellow is what he claims to be – a peaceful rose-grower, though I doubt it: I can't imagine anyone of that trade travelling through Serbia at such a moment. I believe myself that the Germans furnish condemned criminals with sufficiently suspicious accessories to occupy the Allied Intelligence, while they get away with the real goods. Do you ever read spy-novels? Our spy-novels and spy-plays must have been of priceless assistance to the Germans in letting them know how to coach their condemned criminals for the part. There's only one thing on earth that bears less resemblance to its original than the English novelist's spy and that is his detective.'

'Where is Michael Fane?' Sylvia asked; she could bear it no longer.

'He's out here with Lady What's-Her-Name's Red Cross unit. I don't really know where he is at the moment – probably being jolted by a mule on a track leading south from Belgrade. His sister's out here too. Her husband – an awfully jolly fellow – was killed at Ypres. When did you see Michael last?'

'Oh, not for – not for nearly nine years,' she answered.

There was a silence; Sylvia wished now that she had let Hazlewood lead up to the subject of Michael; he must be thinking of the time when his friend was engaged to Lily; he must be wondering about herself, for that he had remembered her name after so many years showed that Michael's account of her had impressed itself upon him.

'If he's on his way south, he'll be in Nish soon,' Hazlewood said, breaking the silence abruptly. 'You'd better wait and see him. Nine years last month: September 1906.'

'No, it was June,' Sylvia said. 'Early June.'

'Sorry,' he said, 'I was thinking of Michael in relation to myself.'

He sighed, and at that moment coming down the squalid street appeared a band of children shepherded by a fussy schoolmaster and carrying bouquets of flowers, who at the sight of Hazlewood cheered shrilly.

'You seem to be very popular here already.' Sylvia observed.

'Do you know what those flowers are for?' he asked gravely.

She shook her head.

'They're for the British and French troops that these poor dears are expecting to arrive by every train to help them against the Austrians. I tell you it makes me feel the greatest humbug on earth. They are going to decorate the station tomorrow. It's like putting flowers on their country's tomb. Ah, don't let's talk about it – don't let's think about it,' he broke out passionately. 'Serbia has been one of my refuges during the last nine years, and I stand here now like a mute at a funeral.'

He walked on, tugging savagely at his moustache, until he could turn round to Sylvia with a laugh again.

'My moustache represents the badge of my servitude. I tug at it as in the old Greek days slaves must have tugged at their leaden collars. The day I shave it off I shall be free again. Here's the hotel where I hang out – almost literally, for my room is so small and so dirty that I generally put my pillow on the window-sill. The hotel is full of bugs and diplomats, but the coffee is good. However, it's no good raising your hopes, because I know that there isn't a spare room. Never mind,' he added. 'I've got another room at another hotel which is equally full of bugs, but unfrequented by diplomats. It is being reserved for my lady-secretary, but she hasn't turned up yet, and so I make you a present of it till she does.'

'Why are you being so kind?' Sylvia asked.

'I don't know,' Hazlewood replied. 'You amused me. I think, sitting there in that railway-carriage with Antitch. It's such a relief to arrest somebody who doesn't instantly begin to shriek "Consul! Consul!" Most women regard consuls as Gieve waistcoats, that is to say something which is easily inflated by a woman's breath, has a flask of brandy in one pocket, and affords endless support. No, seriously, it happens that Michael Fane talked a great deal about you on a memorable occasion in my life, and since he's a friend of mine I'd like to do all I can for you. For the moment – here's the other hotel, nothing is far apart in Nish, not even life and death – for the moment I must leave you, or rather for the whole day, I'm afraid, because I've got the dickens of a lot to do. However, it's just as well the lady-secretary hasn't turned up, because it's really impossible to feel very securely established in Nish. I expect as a matter of fact, she's been kidnapped by some white slavery of the Staff en route. Miss Potberry is her name. It's a depressing name for a secretary, but true romance knows no laws of nomenclature, so I still have hope. Poor lady;

> Miss Potberry muttered, "Oh, squish!
> I don't want to go on to Nish.
> I like Malta better!"
> The General said, "Let her
> Remain here, if that is her wish,

and send a telegram to London to say that she has been taken ill and is unable to proceed further, but that her services can be usefully employed here." I say, I must run! I'll come and fetch you for dinner about half-past seven.'

He handed her over to the care of the hotel-porter and vanished.

The room that Hazlewood had lent to Sylvia possessed a basin, a bed, five hooks, a chair, the remains of a table, an oleograph of a battle between Serbians and Bulgarians that resembled a fire, a circus, and a balcony. At such a time in Nish a balcony made up for any absence of comfort, so much was there to look at in the square full of stunted trees and mud, surrounded by stunted houses, and crammed with carts, bullocks, donkeys, horses, diplomats, soldiers, princes, refugees, peasants, poultry, news-paper correspondents, and children, the whole mass flushed by a spray of English nurses as a pigsty by a Dorothy Perkins rambler.

Sylvia searched the crowd for a glimpse of Michael Fane, though she knew that he was almost certainly not yet arrived. Yet if the Serbians were evacuating Belgrade and if Michael had been in Belgrade, he was bound to arrive ultimately in Nish. She wondered how long she could keep this room and prayed that Miss Potberry would not appear. The notion of travelling all the way here from Petrograd, only to miss him at the end was not to be contemplated; his sister was in Serbia too, that charming sister who had flashed through her dressing-room at the Pierian like a lovely view seen from a train. After the last eighteen months she was surely justified in leaving nothing undone that might bring about another meeting. Hazlewood had spoken of being overworked. Could she not offer her services in place of Miss Potberry? Anything, anything to have an excuse to linger in Nish, an excuse that would absolve her from the charge of a frivolous egotism in occupying space that would soon be more than every badly needed. She had thought that destiny had driven her south from Petrograd to Kieff, from Kieff to Odessa, from Odessa to Bucharest, from Bucharest

187

to Nish for Queenie and for Philip, but surely it was for more than was represented by either of them.

'Incredible ass that I am,' she thought. 'What is Michael to me and what am I to Michael? Not so easily is time's slow ruin repaired. If we meet, we shall meet for perhaps a dinner together: that will be all. What romances must this war have woven and what romances must it not have shattered as swiftly! Romances! Yet how dare I use such a word about myself? Nine years, nine remorseless deadening years lie on top of what was never more than a stillborn fancy, and I am expecting to see it burst forth to bloom in Nish. It's the effect of isolation. Time goes by more slowly when one only looks at oneself, and one forgets the countless influences in other people's lives. But I should like to see him again. Oh yes, quite ordinarily and unemotionally I should like to shake hands with him and perhaps talk for a little while. There is nothing extravagently sentimental in thinking so much.'

Sylvia had often enough been conscious of her isolation from the world and often enough she had tried to assuage this sense of loneliness by indulging it to the utmost – to such an extent indeed that she had reached the point of hating not merely anything that interfered with her own isolation, but even anything that interfered with the isolation of other people. She had turned the armour of self-defence into a means of aggression, although by doing so she had destroyed the strength of her position. Her loneliness that during these last months seemed to have acquired the more positive qualities of independence was now only too miserably evident as loneliness; and unless she could apply the vital suffering she had undergone recently so that the years of her prime might bear manifest fruit, she knew that the sense of futility in another nine years would be irreparable indeed. At present the treasure of eighteen months of continuous and deliberate effort to avoid futility was still rich with potentiality; but the human heart was a deceptive treasure-house never very strong against the corruption of time, which when unlocked might at any moment display nothing except coffers filled with dust.

'But why do I invite disillusionment by counting upon this meeting with Michael Fane? Why should he cure this loneliness and how will he cure it? Why in two words do I want to meet him again? Partly, I think, it's due to the haunting incompleteness of our first intercourse, to which is added the knowledge that now I am qualified to complete that intercourse, at any rate so far as my attitude towards him is concerned. And the way I want to show my comprehension of him is to explain about myself. I am really desperately anxious that he should hear what happened to me after we parted. For one thing he is bound to be sympathetic with this craving for an assurance of the value of faith. I want to find how far he has travelled in the same direction as myself by a different road. I divine somehow that his experience will be the complement to my own, that it will illumine the wretched cross-country path which I've taken through life. If I find that he, relying almost entirely upon the adventures of thought, has arrived at a point of which I am also in sight, notwithstanding that I have taken the worst and roughest road, a road moreover that was almost all the time trespassing upon forbidden territory, then I shall be able to throw off this oppression of loneliness. But why should I rely more upon his judgement than anybody else's?'

Sylvia shrugged her shoulders.

'What is attraction?' she asked herself. 'It exists, and there's an end of it. I had the same sense of intimacy with his sister in a conversation of five minutes. Then am I in love with him? But isn't being in love a condition that is brought about by circumstances out of attraction? Being in love is merely the best way of illustrating affinity. Ah, that word! When a woman of thirty-two begins to talk about affinities, she has performed half her emotional voyage; the sunken rocks and eddies of the dangerous age may no longer be disregarded. Thirty-two, and yet I feel younger than I did at twenty-three. At twenty-three experience most bitter was weighing me down; at thirty-two I know that experience must not be regarded as anything more important than food or drink or travelling in a train or any of the incidental aids to material existence. Then what is important? I should be rash to hazard a statement while I am looking at this heterogeneous mob below. One cannot help supposing that the war will bring about a readjustment of values.'

The feeling of unrest and insecurity in the square at Nish on that Monday morning was almost frightful in its emotional actuality; it gave Sylvia an envy to fling herself into the middle of it, as when one sits upon a rock lashed by angry seas and longs to glut an insane curiosity about the extent of one's helplessness. This squalid Serbian town gave her the illusion of having for the moment concentrated upon itself the great forces that were agitating the world.

'I don't believe anybody realises yet how much was let slip with the dogs of war,' she said to herself. 'People are always

189

talking about the vastness of this war, but they are always thinking in terms of avoirdupois; they have never doubted that the decimal system will express their most grandoise calculations. The biggest casualty-list that was ever known, the longest battle, the heaviest gun, all these flatter poor humanity with a sense of its importance: but when all the records have been broken and when all the congratulations upon outdoing the past have been worn thin, to what will humanity turn from the new chaos it has created? And this is one of the fruits of the great nineteenth century, this miserable square packed with the evidence of civilisation. Perhaps I'm too parochial: at the other end of the universe planets may be warring upon planets. If that be so, we lose even the consolation of a universal record and must fall back upon a mere world-record; in eternity our greatest war will have sunk to a brawl in a slum. How can mankind believe in man? How can mankind reject God?' She demanded passionately.

Sylvia did not dine with Hazlewood or Antitch that evening, because they were both too busy. Hazlewood begged her to stay on in the room and promised that he would try to make use of her; though he was too busy at present to find time to explain how she could be useful. Sylvia did not like to worry him with enquiries about Michael, and she spent the next few days watching from her balcony the concourse of distracted human beings in the square. On Saturday when news had arrived that the Austrians had entered Belgrade and when every hour was bringing convoys of refugees from the north, a rumour suddenly sprung up that thousands of British and French troops were on their way from Salonika, that the Greeks had invaded Bulgaria and that Turkey had made peace. Such an accumulation of good news meant that the miseries of Serbia would soon be over. The railway station was hung with more flags and scattered with more flowers than ever; and an enterprising coffee-house keeper anticipated the arrival of British troops by hanging out a sign inscribed GUD BIIR IS FOR SEL PLIS TO COM OLD ENGLAND BIRHOUS.

Sylvia was reading this notice, when Hazlewood came up and asked her to dine with him that evening.

'I'm so sorry I've had to leave you entirely to yourself, but I've not had a moment, and I hate dining when I can't talk. Tonight there seems a lull in the stream of telegraphic questions to which I've been subjected all this week.'

'But please don't apologise. I feel guilty in staying here at all, especially when I'm doing nothing but stare.'

190

'Well, I was going to talk to you about that. You ought to leave tomorrow or the next day. The Bulgarians are sure to move, now that the Austrians have got Belgrade, and that means fresh swarms of fugitives from the east; it may also mean that communications with Greece will be cut.'

'But the British advance?'

Hazlewood looked at her.

'Ah yes, the British advance,' he murmured.

'And you promised that you'd find me some work,' Sylvia said.

'Frankly it's no good your beginning to learn now.'

She must have shown as much disappointment as she felt, for he added:

'Well, after dinner tonight you shall take down the figures of one or two long telegrams.'

'Anything,' offered Sylvia eagerly.

'It's all that Miss Potberry could have done at present. I'm not writing any reports; so her expert shorthand of which I was assured would have been wasted. Reports! One of the revelations of this war to me was the extraordinary value that professional soldiers attach to the typewritten word. I suppose it's a minor manifestation of the impulse that made Wolfe say he would rather have written Gray's *Elegy* than taken Quebec. If typewriters had been invented in his time he might have said, 'I would rather be in the War Office and be able to read my report of the capture of Quebec than take it. I'm sure that the chief reason of a knowledge of Latin being still demanded for admission to Sandhurst is the hope universally cherished in the Army that every cadet's haversack contains a new long Latin intransitive verb which can be used transitively to supplant one of the short Saxon verbs that still disfigure military correspondence. I can imagine such a cadet saying, "Sir, I would sooner have been the first man that wrote of evacuating wounded than take Berlin." The trouble with men of action is that something written means for them something done. The labour of writing is so tremendous and the consequent mental fatigue so overwhelming that they cannot bring themselves to believe otherwise. The general public, even after fifteen months of war, has the same kind of respect for the printed word. How long does it take you to read a letter? I imagine that two readings would give you the gist of it? Well, it takes a British general at least five readings, and even then he only understands a word here and there, unless it's written in his own barbaric departmental

191

English. If I had a general over me here – which thank heaven I've not – and I were to make a simple suggestion, he would invite me to put it on paper. This he would do because he would presume that life would be too short for me to succeed and that therefore he should be for ever spared having to make up his mind in response to any prompting on my side. If on the other hand I did by chance embody my suggestion in typescript, he would be amazed at the result, and by some alchemy of thought, if he could write on the top "Concur", he would feel that he had created the suggestion himself. The effort even to write "Concur" represents for the average British general the amount of labour involved by a woman in producing a child, and . . . but look here – tonight at half-past seven. So long!'

Hazlewood hurried away; at dinner that night he went on with his discourse.

'You know that among savages certain words are taboo and that in the middle ages certain words possessed magic properties? The same thing applies to the Army and to the Navy. For instance the Navy has a word of power that will open anything. That word is "submit". If you wrote "submitted" at the top of a communication I believe you could ,ell an admiral that he was a damn fool, but if you wrote "suggested" you'd be shot at dawn. In the same way a naval officer endorses your "submission" by writing "approved", whereas a soldier writes "concur". I've often wondered what would happen to a general who wrote "agree". Certainly any junior officer who wrote "begin" for "commence" or "allow" for "permit" would be cashiered. I was rather lucky because, after being suspected for the simplicity of my reports, I managed to use the word "connote" once. My dear woman, my reputation was made. Generals came up and congratulated me personally, and I'm credibly informed that all the new military cyphers will include the word, which was just what was wanted to supplant "mean", a monosyllable that had been a blot on military correspondence for years.'

'Are you talking seriously? Sylvia asked. 'You can't really connote what you say.'

Hazlewood indicated the room where they were dining.

'Which are the English diplomats?' he demanded.

'That's perfectly easy to tell,' she replied.

'And why?' he went on. 'Simply because they've made no concession to being in Nish at a moment of crisis. I invite you to regard my friend Harry Vereker. See how he defies any Horatian regret for lapsed years. Positively he is still at Oxford. Can't you hear above all this clatter of cosmopolitanism in a pigsty the suave insistency of his voice impressing upon you by its quality of immutable self-assurance that whatever happens to the rest of the world nothing vitally deformative ever happens to England?'

'But what has the voice of a Secretary to do with the military abuse of Latin derivations?'

'Not much, I admit, except in its serene ruthlessness. An English officer compels a Latin verb to fit in with his notion of what a Latin verb ought to do just in the same way as he expects a Spaniard to regard with pleasure his occupation of Gibraltar: any protest by a grammarian or an idealistic politician would strike him as impertinent. Harry Vereker's voice is a still more ineradicable manifestation of the spirit. Listen! He is asking the waiter in Serbian for salt, but he does do so in a way that reminds one of mankind's concession to animals in using forms of communication that the latter can understand. It is not be be supposed that the dog invented patting: Harry's Serbian is his way of patting the waiter: it is *his* language, not the waiter's. Personally I can't help confessing that I admire this attitude to the world, and I only wish that it could be eternally preserved. The great historical tragedy of this war – I'm putting on one side for the moment the countless personal tragedies that are included in it, and trying to regard the war as Mr Buckle regarded civilisation – the great historical tragedy will be the Englishman's loss of his personality. When we look back at the historical tragedy of the fall of the Roman Empire, we think less of the *civis Romanus sum* than of the monuments of architecture, law, political craft, and the rest that remain imperishably part of human progress. In the same way a thousand years hence I assume that the British Empire will be considered to have played a part only second to the Roman Empire in the manifest results of its domination. But what has been lost and what will be lost is the individual Roman's attitude and the individual Englishman's. Not all the remains of the Roman Empire have been enough really to preserve for us the indefinable flavour of being a Roman, and with much more material at his disposal I defy the perfect cosmopolitan of mixed Aryan, Mongol, and Semitic blood to realise a thousand years from now Harry Vereker's tone of voice in asking that waiter for the salt. No, no, the cosmopolitan of the future will turn aside from the records of the past and in Esperanto murmur sadly to himself that something is missing from his appreciation. Perhaps I can illustrate my meaning better if I compare the Athenians with the French. I feel that the Art of both enduring through time to come will be enough. I have no regret for the personal attitude of the Athenian, and in the same way I don't feel that the cosmopolitan of a thousand years hence will lose anything by not meeting the Frenchman of today. It is Athens and France rather than the Athenian or the Frenchman of which the world is enamoured. How often have I heard a foreigner say 'The politics of England do not please me: I find it a brigand policy, but the individual Englishman is always a gentleman.' An individual Englishman like Byron is worth more to England than twenty Chamberlains or Greys, who yet have more right to represent their country: he comes as such a romantic surprise. A Frenchman like Lafayette is taken for granted. The word of an Englishman is proverbial; the perfidy of Albion equally so.'

'And the Germans?' Sylvia asked.

'Oh, they have never been thought worthy of a generalisation. We have apprehended them vaguely as one apprehends pigs – as a nation of gross feeders and badly dressed women drinking a mixture of treacle and onions they call beer, with a reputation for guttural peregrination and philosophy.'

'Their music,' Sylvia protested.

'Yes, that is difficult to explain. Yes, I think we must give them that; but when we remember Bach and Schumann, we must not forget Wagner and the German band.'

'I think your characterisation is rather crude,' Sylvia said.

'It is crude. But there is no bygone civilisation with which Germanic *Kultur* can be compared. So as with any novelty one depends upon a sneer to hide one's own ignorance.'

'The Italians interest me more,' Sylvia said.

'The Italians seem to me rather to resemble the English, and naturally, because they are the most direct heirs of Rome. I'm bound to say that I don't believe in an imperial future for them now. It's surely impossible to revive Rome. They still preserve an immense capacity for political craft, but it is an egotism that lacks the sublime unconsciousness of English egotism. The Italians have never recovered from *Il Principe* of Machiavelli. It's an eclectic statecraft; like their painting from Raphael onwards it's too *soigné*. Moreover, Italy suffers from the perpetual sacrifice of the Southern Italian to the Northern. The real Italians belong to the South, and for me the *risorgimento* has always been a phoenix rising from the ashes of the South: the bird is most efficient, but I distrust its aquiline appearance. One of the most remarkable surprises of this war has been the superior fighting quality – the more quickly beating heart – of the Neapolitans and Sicilians. I found the same surprising quality in the Greeks during the last Balkan war. To me who regard the Mediterranean as still *the* civilised sea of the world the triumph of Naples has been a delight.'

'And the Russians?' Sylvia went on.

'Ah, the future of Russia is as much an unknown quantity as the future of womanhood. Personally I am convinced that the next great civilisation will be Slavonic, and my chief grudge against mortality is that I must die long before it even begins to draw near, for it is still as far away as Johannine Christianity will be from the Petrine Christianity to which we have been too long devoted. But when it does come, I am sure that it will easily surpass all previous civilisations, because I believe it will resolve the eternal dualism in humanity that hitherto we have expressed roughly by Empire and Papacy or by Church and State. I envisage Russia as containing the civilisation of the soul, though God knows through what agony of blood and tears it may have to pass before it can express what it contains. In Russia there still exists a genuine worship of the Czar as a superior being, and a nation that respects the divinity about a king is still as deep in the mire of fetichism as the most debased Melanesians. We worship kings in England, I admit, but only snobbishly; we significantly call the pound a sovereign. Not even our most exalted snobs dream of paying divine honours to kingship; we are too much heirs of Imperial Rome for that. I always attribute Magna Carta to an inherited consciousness of Ceasarian excesses.'

'And now you've only Austria left,' said Sylvia.

'Austria,' Hazlewood exclaimed. 'A battered cocotte who sustains herself by devoting to pietism the settlements of her numerous lovers – a cocotte with a love of finery, a profound cynicism, and an acquired deportment. Austria! rouged and raddled, plumped and corseted, a suitable mistress for that licentious but still tragic old buffoon who rules her.'

'What a wonderful sermon on so slight a text as a friend's asking a Serbian waiter for salt,' Sylvia said.

'Ah, you led me away from the main thread by asking me direct questions. I meant to confine myself to England.'

'*On peut toujours revenir à ses moutons,*' Sylvia said.

'New Zealand mutton, eh?' Hazlewood laughed. 'Wasn't it a New Zealander who was to meditate upon the British Empire a thousand years hence amid the ruins of St. Paul's?'

'Well, go on,' she urged.

'You're one of those listening sirens so much more fatal than the singing variety,' he laughed.

'Oh, but I'm very rarely a good listener,' she protested. Hazlewood bowed.

'And don't forget that sirens have always an *arrière pensée*,' she went on. 'However well you talk, you'll find that I shall demand something in return for my attention. Don't look alarmed; it won't involve you personally.'

Sylvia was getting a good deal of pleasure out of his monologue; it was just what her nerves needed, this sense of being entertained while all the time she preserved, so far as any reality of personal intercourse was concerned, a complete detachment. She was quite definitely aware of wanting Hazlewood to exhaust himself that she might either bring her part of the conversation round to Michael or at any rate extract from him an excuse for lingering in Nish until Michael should come here. Now her host was off again:

'Have you ever thought,' he was asking her, 'about the appropriateness of our national animal – the British lion? We are rather apt to regard the lion as a bluff, hearty sort of beast with a loud roar and a consciousness of being the finest beast anywhere about. But after all, the lion *is* one of the great cats. He's something much finer than the British bulldog, which with most unnecessary self-depreciation we have elected as our secondary pattern or prototype among the animals. There are few animals so profoundly, so densely, so hopelessly stupid as the bulldog. Its chief virtue is alleged to be its never knowing when it is beaten, but this is only an incidental ignorance merged in its ignorance of everything. Why a dog that approximates in character to a mule and in appearance to an hippopotamus should be accepted as the representative of English character I don't know. The attribution takes its place with some of the great fundamental mysteries of human conduct; it is comparable with those other riddles of why a chauffeur always waits till you get into the car again before he turns round, or why kidneys are so rare in beefsteak-and-kidney pudding, or why every man in the course of this life has either wanted to buy or has bought a rustic summerhouse. The lion, however, really is typical of the Englishman: somewhat blonde and very agile, physically courageous, morally timid, fierce, full of domestic virtues, tolerant of jackals, generous, cunning, graceful, arrogant, and acquisitive: he seems to me a perfect symbol of the British race.'

'Is your friend at the diplomats' table so very leonine?' Sylvia asked.

'Oh no, Harry is the individual Englishman; the lion represents the race.'

'But the race is an accumulation of individuals.'

'I say, don't listen too intelligently,' Hazlewood begged. 'It's not fair either to my babbling or to your dinner.'

'Well, I want to bring you back to the point you made when you talked about the historical tragedy of this war.'

Hazlewood looked serious.

'I meant what I said. I've just come down from the grave of what was England, and already the deeds of Gallipoli have taken on the aspect of an heroic frieze. We might have repeated Gallipoli here in Serbia, but we shan't; we've learnt our lesson; I do not think that on such a scale such a decorative heroism can ever happen again. Gallipoli saw the death of the amateur; and a conservative like myself feels the historical tragedy of such a death. I suppose there are few people who would be prepared to argue that such a spirit ought to be purchased at such a price, and yet I don't know – I believe I would. I wasn't in Flanders at the beginning; but I imagine the same spirit existed there. Don't you remember the childlike amateurish pleasure that all the soldiers took in being ferried across the Channel without anybody's knowing they had gone? The successful secrecy compensated them for all that hell of Mons. You'll never again hear of that childlike enjoyment. Very soon we shall have conscription, and from that moment the amateur in a position of responsibility who sacrifices any man's life to his own sense of exterior form will become a criminal. Surely it is an appalling tragedy that we shan't be able to carry on such a war as this without conscription? England, our England, disappears with conscription: nothing will ever be the same again. They accused us of decadence, had you seen the landing last April – had you seen the immortal division of Englishmen, Scotsmen, Irishmen, and Welshmen literally dyeing the sea with their blood, you could never have thought of decadence again. And yet, mark my words, so much of England was lost upon that day that already the unthinking herd led by the newspapers, which are always waiting to hail the new king, talks of the landing as famous chiefly for the Australian share in it. My God, it enrages me to read about the Australians when I think of that deathless dead division. Whatever else may happen in this, whatever our fate at the hands of intriguing politicians and

197

backbiting generals, England was herself upon that day: it stands with Trafalgar and Agincourt in a trinity of imperishable glory.'

'But why do you say that so much of England was lost? You don't think we shall disgrace ourselves henceforth in this war?'

'We have already done so morally in failing to come to the help of the Serbians. Gallipoli turned us into professionals, and though I'm not saying that there is a single good professional argument in favour of helping Serbia, I still believe against all professionals that we shall pay for our failure in bitter years of prolonged war. The Dardanelles could have been forced. What stopped it? Professional jealousy at home.'

'It's a hard thing of which to accuse the people at home.'

'It was a hard thing to land that day at Sedd-el-bahr, but it was done. No, we've fallen a prey to the glamour of Teutonism, and of being expedient and Hunnish. By the time the war is over I don't doubt we shall be a very pretty imitation of the real article that we're setting out to destroy. But, thank heaven, we shall always be able to point to Mons and to Antwerp and to Gallipoli: though we are fast forgetting to be gentlemen, we've already forgotten more than the Germans ever dreamed of in that direction. Mind you, I'm not attempting to say that we haven't got to hit below the belt: we have, because we are fighting with foul fighters; but that is what I conceive to be the historical tragedy of this war – the debasement of our ideals in order that we may compete with the Germans, and with the old men in morocco-chairs at home, and with the guttural press. I remember how the waning moon of dawn came up out of Asia while we were still waiting for news of the Suvla landing. There was a tattoo of musketry over the sea, a lisp of wind in the sandy grass; and in a moment of apprehensive chill I divined that with a failure at Suvla this waning moon was the last moon that would rise upon the old way of thinking, the rare old way of acting, the old, old merry England built in a thousand years.'

'But a greater England may arise from that failure.'

'Yes, but it won't be our England. The grave of our England was dug by the Victorians; this generation has planted the flowers upon it; the monument will be raised by the new generation. Oh yes, I know, it's an egotistical regret, a superficial and sentimental regret if you will, but you must allow some of us to cherish it; otherwise we could not go on. And in the end I believe history will endorse the school of thought I follow. In the end I'm convinced that it will blame the men who failed to see that England was great by the measure of her greatness, and that the real way to win this war was by what were sneeringly called side-shows. All our history has been the alternate failure and triumph of our side-shows; we made ourselves what we are by side-shows.'

Hazlewood swept aside from the table the pile of crumbs he had been building while he was talking, and smiled at Sylvia.

'It's your turn now,' he said.

'You've deprived me of any capacity for generalisation. I think perhaps you may have got things out of focus. I know it's a platitude, but isn't one always inevitably out of focus nowadays? When I was still at a distance from the war the whole perspective was blurred to my vision by the intrusion of individual humiliations and sufferings. Now I'm nearer to it I feel that my vision is equally faulty from an indifference to them,' Sylvia said earnestly.

Then she told Hazlewood the story of Queenie and the passport, and asked for his opinion.

'Well, of course, there's an instance to hand of sterile professionalism. Naturally, had I been the official in Bucharest, I should have given the girl her passport. At such a moment I should have been too much moved by her desire of England to have done otherwise. Moreover, if her desire of England was not mere lust, I should have been right to do so.'

Sylvia finished her story by telling him of Queenie's escape with the juggler after the probable theft of Maud's passport.

'By Jove,' he exclaimed. 'I'll bet they've gone to Salonika. We'll send a telegram to our people there and warn them to keep a look out.'

'What a paradox human sympathy is,' Sylvia murmured. 'Ever since I got to Nish it's been on my conscience that I didn't tell you about this girl before, and yet in Bucharest the notion of doing anything like that was positively disgusting to my sense of decency. And look at you! A moment ago you were abusing the official in Bucharest for his red tape, and now your eyes are flashing with the prospect of hunting her down.'

'Not even Heraclitus divined quite the rapidity with which everything dissolves in flux,' said Hazlewood. 'That's another thing that will be brought home to people before the war's over – the intensity and rapidity of change, of course considerably strengthened and accelerated by the impulse that war has given to pure destruction. You can see it even in broad ideas. We began by fighting for a scrap of paper; we shall go on fighting for different ideas until we realise we are fighting for our existence. Then suddenly we shall think we are fighting about nothing, and the war will be over.'

Hazlewood sat silent; most of the diners had finished and left the room, which accentuated his silence with an answering stillness.

'Well, what is to be your reward for listening?' he asked at length.

'To stay on in Nish for the present,' she answered firmly.

'No, no,' he objected, with a sudden fretfulness that was the more conspicuous after his late exuberance. 'No, no, we don't want more women than are necessary. You'd better get down to Salonika on Monday. Look here, I must send a telegram about that friend of yours. Come round to my office and give me the details.'

Sylvia accompanied him in a state of considerable depression; she could not bear the idea of revealing so much of herself as to ask him directly to give her an excuse to remain in Nish because she wanted to see Michael; it was seeming impossible to introduce the personal element in this war-cursed town, and particularly now when she was quenching so utterly the personal element by thus allying herself with Hazlewood against Queenie. She waited while he deciphered a short telegram which had arrived during his absence and while he occupied himself with writing another.

'How will this do for their description?' he read. '*A certain Krebs known professionally as Zozo, acrobatic juggler and conjurer, alleged Swiss nationality, tall, large face, clean shaven, very large hands, speaking English well, accompanied by Queenie Walters of German origin possibly carrying stolen passport of Maud Moffat, English variety artiste. Description, slim, very fair, blue eyes, pale, delicate, speaks German, Italian, French and English, left Bucharest at end of September. Probably travelled via Dedeagatch and Salonika, Nothing definite known against them, but man frequented company of notorious enemy agents in Bucharest and is known to be bad character. Suggest he is likely to use woman to get in touch with British officers.*'

'But what will they do to her?' Sylvia asked, dismayed by this metamorphosis of Queenie into a police-court case.

'Oh, they won't do anything,' Hazlewood replied irritably. 'She'll be added to the great army of suspects whose histories in all their discrepancies are building up the Golden Legend of this war. She'll exist in card-indexes for the rest of her life; and her reputation will circulate only a little more freely than herself.

In fact really I'm doing her a favour by putting her down for the observation of our military psychologists and criminologists; her life will become much easier henceforth. The war has not cured human nature of a passion for bric-à-brac, and as a catalogued article *de vertu* – or should I say *de vice?* – she will be well looked after.'

'Then if that's all, why do you send the telegram?' Sylvia asked.

'I really don't know – probably because I've joined in the may-pole dance for ribbons with the rest of the departmental warriors. Card-indexes are the casualty-lists of officers commanding *embusqués*: the longer the list of names, the longer the row of ribbons.'

'You've become very bitter,' Sylvia said. 'It's like a sudden change of wind. I feel quite chilled.'

'Well, you shall warm yourself by taking down a few hundred groups. Come along.'

Sylvia listened for an hour to the endless groups of five figures that Hazlewood dictated to her, during which time his voice that began calmly and murmurously reached a level of rasping and lacerating boredom before he had done.

'Thank heaven, that's over, and we can go to bed,' he said.

He seemed to be anxious to be rid of her, and she went away in some disconsolation at his abrupt change of manner. Nothing that she could think of occurred to cause it, and ultimately she could only ascribe it to nerves.

'And after all why not nerves?' she said to herself. 'Who will ever again be able to blame people for having nerves?'

The next morning a note came from Hazlewood apologising for his rudeness and thanking her for her help.

'*I was in a vile humour,*' he wrote, '*because when I got back to my room I found a refusal to let me leave Nish and join the Serbian headquarters on the Serbian frontier. This morning they've changed their minds and I'm off at once. Keep the room, if you insist upon staying in Nish. If Miss Potberry by any unlucky chance turns up, say I've been killed and that she had better report in Salonika as soon as possible. If I see Michael Fane, which is very unlikely, I'll tell him you want to see him.*'

With all his talk Hazlewood had plumbed her desire; with all his talk about nations he had not lost his capacity for divining the individual. Sylvia wished now that he was not upon his way to the Bulgarian frontier; she should like to watch herself precipitated by his acid. Did acids precipitate? It did not matter; there was no second person's comprehension to be considered at the moment. Sylvia stayed on in the room, watching from the balcony the now unceasing press of refugees.

Three days after she had dined with Hazlewood, there was a murmur in the square, a heightened agitation that made a positive impact upon the atmosphere; Bulgaria had declared war. She had the sense of a curtain's rising upon the last and crucial act, the sense of an audience strung to such a pitch of expectancy, dread and woe, that it was become a part of the drama. During the next three days the influx of pale fugitives was like a scene upon the banks of Styx. The odour of persecuted humanity hung upon the air in a positively visible miasma; white exhausted women suckled their babies in the mud; withered crones dragged from bed sat nursing their ulcers; broken-hearted old men bowed their heads between their knees, seeming actually to have been trampled underfoot in the confused terror that had brought them here; the wailing of tired and hungry children never ceased for a single instant. The only thing that seemed to keep this dejected multitude from rotting in death where they lay was the assurance that everyone gave his neighbour of the British and French advance to save them. Two French officers sent up on some business from Salonika walked through the square in their celestial uniforms like angels of God, for the people fell down before them and gave thanks; faded flowers were flung in their path, and women caught at their hands to kiss them as they went by. Once there was a sound of cavalry's approach, and the despairing mob shouted for joy and pressed forward to greet the vanguard of rescue; but it was a Serbian patrol covered with blood and dust which had been ordered back to guard the railway line. The troopers rode through sullenly and the people did not even whisper about them, so deep was their disillusion, so bitter their resentment. And through all this fetid and pitiful mob the English nurses wound their way like a Dorothy Perkins rambler.

A week after Hazlewood had left Nish, Sylvia saw from her balcony a fair young Englishwoman followed by a ragged boy carrying a typewriter in a tin case. It struck her as the largest typewriter that she had ever seen, and she was thinking vaguely what a ridiculous weapon it was to carry about at such a moment when it suddenly flashed upon her that this might be the long expected Miss Potberry. She hurried downstairs and heard her asking in the hall if anyone knew where

Captain Hazlewood could be found. Sylvia came forward and explained his absence.

'He did not really expect you, but he told me to tell you that if you did come you ought to go back immediately to Salonika.'

'I don't think I can go back to Salonika,' said Miss Potberry. 'Somebody was firing at the train as I came in, and they told me at the station that there would be no more trains to Salonika, because the line had been cut.'

The boy had put her typewriter upon a table in the hall; she stood by, embracing it with a kind of serene determination that reminded Sylvia of the images of patron saints that hold in their arms the cathedrals they protect.

'I'm surprised that they let you come from Salonika,' Sylvia said. 'Didn't they know the line was likely to be cut?'

'I had to report to Captain Hazlewood,' Miss Potberry replied firmly. 'And as I had already been rather delayed upon my journey I was anxious to get on as soon as possible.'

The consciousness of being needed by England radiated from her eyes; it was evident that nothing would make her budge from Nish until she had reported herself to her unknown chief.

'You'd better share my room,' Sylvia said. She nearly blushed at her own impudence when Miss Potberry gratefully accepted the offer. However, she could no longer reproach herself for staying in Nish without justification, for now it was impossible to go away in ordinary fashion.

'It seems funny that Captain Hazlewood shouldn't have left any written instructions for me,' said Miss Potberry, when she had waited three days in Nish without any news except the rumoured fall of Veles. 'I'm not sure if I oughtn't to try and join him wherever he is.'

'But he's at the front,' Sylvia objected.

'I had instructions to report to him,' said Miss Potberry seriously. 'I think I'm wasting time and drawing my salary for nothing here. *That* isn't patriotism. If he'd left something for me to type – but to wait here like this doing nothing seems almost wicked at such a time.'

Two more days went by; Uskub had fallen; everybody gave up the idea of Anglo-French troops arriving to relieve Nish, and everybody began to talk about evacuation. About six o'clock of a stormy dusk, four days after the fall of Uskub, a Serbian soldier came to the hotel to ask Sylvia to come at once to a hospital. She wondered if something had happened to Michael, if somehow he had heard she was in Nish, and that he had sent for her. But when she reached the schoolroom that was serving as an improvised ward she found Hazlewood lying back upon a heap of straw that was called a bed.

'Done a damned stupid thing,' he murmured. 'Got hit, and they insisted on my being sent back to Nish. Think I'm rather bad. Why haven't you left?'

'The line is cut.'

'I know. You ought to have been gone by now. You can take my horse. Everyone will evacuate Nish. No chance. The Austrians have joined up with the Bulgarians. Bound to fall. I want you to take the keys of my safe and burn all my papers. Don't forget the cypher. Go and do it now and let me know it's done. Quick, it's worrying me. Nothing important, but it's worrying me.'

Sylvia decided to say nothing to him about Miss Potberry's arrival in order not to worry him any more. Miss Potberry should have his horse: Nish might be empty as a tomb, but she herself should stay on for news of Michael Fane.

'What are you waiting for?' he asked fretfully. 'Damn it, I shan't last for ever. That's Antitch you're staring at in the next bed.'

Sylvia looked at the figure muffled in bandages. Apparently all the lower part of his face had been shot away, and she could see nothing but a pair of dark and troubled eyes wandering restlessly in the candlelight.

'We took our finals together,' said Hazlewood.

Sylvia went away quickly; if she had paused to compare this meeting with the first meeting in the railway-carriage not yet three weeks ago, she should have broken down.

When Miss Potberry heard of her chief's arrival in Nish she insited upon going to see him.

'But, my dear woman, he may be dying. What's the good of bothering him now? I'll find out whatever he can tell me. You must get ready to leave Nish. Pack up your things.'

'He may be glad to dictate something,' Miss Potberry argued. 'Please let me come. I am anxious to report to Captain Hazlewood. I'm sure if you had told him that I was here he would have wished to meet me.'

Sylvia did not feel that she could contest anything; with Miss Potberry's help she burnt the few papers that remained in the safe together with the cypher, which glowed and smouldered in the basin for what seemed an interminable time. When not a single record of Hazlewood's presence in Serbia remained, Sylvia and Miss Potberry went back to the hospital.

'You've burnt everything?' he asked.

Sylvia nodded.

'Is that a nurse? I can't see in this infernal candlelight and I'm chockful of morphia, which makes my eyelids twitch.'

'It's I, Captain Hazlewood – Miss Potberry. I had instructions from the War Office to report to you. I was unfortunately delayed upon my journey, and when I arrived from Salonika you had left. Is there anything you would like done?'

'Oh, my god,' he half groaned, half laughed. 'I see that even my deathbed is going to be haunted by departmental imbecility. Who on earth sent you to Nish from Salonika?'

'Colonel Bullingham-Jones to whom I reported in Salonika knew nothing about me and advised me to come on here as soon as possible.'

'Officious ass!' Hazlewood muttered. 'Why didn't you go back, when you found I wasn't there?' he added to his secretary.

'There was no way of getting back, Captain Hazlewood. I believe that the enemy has cut the line.'

'I'm sorry you've had all this trouble for nothing,' he said. 'However, you and Miss Scarlett must settle between you how to get away. You'd better hang on to one of the Red Cross units.'

'I'm afraid I may have to leave my typewriter behind,' said Miss Potberry. 'Have I your permission?'

'You have,' he said, smiling with his eyes through the glaze of the drug.

'You couldn't give me a written authorisation?' asked Miss Potberry. 'Being government property – '

'No, I can only give you verbal instructions. Both my arms have been shot away, or as nearly shot away as doesn't make it possible to write.'

'Oh, I beg your pardon. Then to whom should I report next?'

'I don't know. It might be St Peter, with winter coming on and Albania to be crossed. No, no, don't you bother about reporting. Just follow the crowd and you'll be all right. Goodbye, Miss Potberry. Sorry you've had such a long journey for nothing. Sorry about everything.'

He beckoned Sylvia close to him with his eyes.

'For heaven's sake get rid of her or I shall have another hemorrhage.'

Sylvia asked Miss Potberry to go back to the hotel and get packed. When the secretary had gone, she knelt by Hazlewood.

'Michael Fane arrived yet?' he asked.

She shook her head.

'I had something to give him.'

The wounded man's face became more definitely lined with pain in the new worry of Fane's non-appearance.

'I want you to give him a letter. It's under my pillow. If by chance he doesn't come, perhaps you'd be good enough to post it when you get an opportunity. Miss Pauline Grey, Wychford Rectory, Oxfordshire.'

Sylvia found the letter which was still unaddressed.

'If Michael comes, I'd like him to take it to her himself when he gets to England. Thanks awfully. Give him my love. He was a great friend of mine. Yes, a great friend. Thanks awfully for helping me. I don't like to worry the poor devils here. They've got such a lot to worry them. Antitch died while you were burning my papers.'

Sylvia looked at the muffled figure whose eyes no longer stared with troubled imperception.

'Of course I may last for two or three days,' he went on. 'And in that case I may see Michael. Mind you bring him if he comes in time. Great friend of mine, and I'd like him to explain something to somebody. By the way, don't take all my talk the other night too seriously. I often talk like that. I don't mean half I say. England's all right really. Perhaps you'll look me up in the morning, if I'm still here? Goodbye. Thanks very much. I'm sorry I can't shake hands.'

'Would you like a priest?' Sylvia asked.

'A priest?' he repeated in a puzzled voice. 'Oh no, thanks very much, priests have always bored me. I'm going to lie here and think. The annoying thing is, you know, that I've not the slightest desire to die. Some people say that you have at the end, but I feel as if I was missing a train. Perhaps I'll see you in the morning. So long.'

But she did not see him in the morning, because he died in the night, and his bed was wanted immediately for another wounded man.

'What a dreadful thing war is,' sighed Miss Potberry. 'I've lost two first cousins and four second cousins, and my brother is soon going to France.'

The evacuation of Nish was desperately hastened by the news of the swift advance of the enemy on three sides. Sylvia with the help of Colonel Michailovitch managed to establish her rights over Hazlewood's horse, and Miss Potberry fired with the urgency of reporting to somebody else and of explaining why she had abandoned her typewriter was persuaded to attach herself to a particularly efflorescent branch of Dorothy Perkins that had wound itself round Harry Vereker to be trained into safety on the other side of the mountains. The last that Sylvia saw of her was when she drove out of Nish in a bullock-cart, still pink and prim, because the jolting had not yet really begun. The last Sylvia heard of Harry Vereker was his unruffled voice leaving instructions that if some white corduroy riding-breeches which he had been expecting by special courier from Athens should by chance arrive before the Bulgarians they were to follow him. One had the impression of his messenger and his breeches as equally important entities marching arm in arm toward the Black Drin in obedience to his instructions. The next day came news of the fall of Kragujevatz following upon that of Pirot, and the fever of flight was aggravated to panic.

In the evening when Sylvia was watching the tormented square, listening to the abuse and blasphemy that was roused by the scarcity of transport and trying to accept in spite of the disappointment the irremediable fact of Michael's failure to arrive, she suddenly caught sight of his sister pushing her way through the mob below. Her appearance alone like this could only mean that Michael had been killed; Sylvia cursed the flattering lamp of fortune, which had lighted her to Nish only to extinguish itself in this moment of confusion and horror. How pale that sister looked, how deeply ringed her eyes, how torn and splashed her dress: she must have heard the news of her brother and fled in despair before the memory. All Sylvia's late indifference to suffering in the actual presence of war was kindled to a fury of resentment against the unreasonable forces that the world had let loose upon itself; even the envelope that Hazlewood had given to her now burnt her heart with what it enclosed of eternally unquenched regret, of eternal unfulfilment. She hurried downstairs and out into the mad, screaming, weeping mob and bathed herself in the stench of wet and filthy rags and in the miasma of sick, starved, and verminous bodies. A child was sucking the raw head of a hen; it happened that Sylvia knocked against it in her hurry, whereupon the child grabbed the morsel of blood and mud, snarling at her like a famished hound. Wherever she looked there were children searching on all fours among the filth lodged in the cracks of the rough paving-stones; it was an existence where nothing counted except the ability to trample over one's neighbour to reach food or safety; and she herself was searching for Michael's sister in the fetid swarm, just as these children were shrieking and scratching for the cabbage-stalks they found among the dung. At last the two women met, and Sylvia caught hold of Mrs Merivale's arm.

'What do you want? What do you want?' she cried. 'Can I help you?'

The other turned and looked at Sylvia without recognising her.

'You're Mrs Merivale – Michael's sister,' Sylvia went on.

'Don't you remember me? Sylvia Scarlett. What has happened to him?'

'Can't we get out of this crowd?' Mrs. Merivale replied. 'I'm trying to find an English officer – Captain Hazlewood.'

Before Sylvia could tell her what had happened a cart drawn by a donkey covered with sores interposed between them; it was impossible for either woman to ask or answer anything in this abomination of humanity that oozed and writhed like a bunch of earthworms on a spade. Somehow they emerged from it all, and Sylvia brought her upstairs to her room.

'Is Michael dead?' she asked.

'No, but he's practically dying. I've got him into a deserted house. He fell ill with typhus in Kragujevatz. The enemy was advancing terribly fast, and I got him here, heaven knows how, in a bullock-cart – I've probably killed him in doing so; he certainly can't be moved again. I must find this friend of ours – Guy Hazlewood. He'll be able to tell me how long we can stay in Nish.'

Sylvia broke the news of Hazlewood's death and was momentarily astonished to see how casually she took it. Then she remembered that she had already lost her husband, that her brother was dying, and that probably she had heard such tidings of many friends. This was a woman who was beholding the society in which she had lived falling to pieces round her every day; she was not like herself cloistered in vagrancy, one for whom life and death had waved at each other from every platform and every quay in partings that were not less final. There occurred to Sylvia the last utterance of Hazlewood about missing a train; he perhaps had found existence to be a destructive business; but even so she could not think that he had loved it more charily.

'Everybody is dying,' said Mrs Merivale. 'Those who survive this war will really have been granted a second life and will have to begin all over again like children – or lunatics,' she added to herself.

'Could I come with you to see him?' Sylvia asked. 'I had typhus myself last year in Petrograd and I could nurse him.'

'I don't think it's any longer a matter for nursing,' the other answered hopelessly. 'It's just leaving him alone and not worrying him any more. Oh, I wonder how long we can count on Nish not being attacked.'

'Not very long, I'm afraid,' said Sylvia. 'Hardly any time at all in fact.'

They left the hotel with that sense of mechanical action which sometimes relieves a strain of accumulated emotion. Sylvia had the notion of finding a Serbian doctor whom she knew slightly, and was successful in bringing him along to the house where Michael was lying. It was dark when they arrived in the deserted side-street now strewn with the rubbish of many families' flight.

Michael was lying on a camp bed in the middle of the room. On the floor a Serbian peasant wearing a Red Cross brassard was squatting by his head and from time to time moistening his forehead with a damp sponge. In a corner two other Serbians armed with fantastic weapons sat cross-legged upon the floor, a winking candle and strewn playing-cards between them. Sylvia felt a sudden awe of looking at him directly, and she waited in the doorway while the doctor went forward with his sister to make his examination. After a short time the doctor turned away with a shrug; he and Mrs Merivale rejoined Sylvia in the doorway and together they went in another room, where the doctor in sibilant French confirmed the impossibility of moving him if his life was to be saved. He added that the Bulgarians would be in Nish within a few days and that the town would be empty long before that. Then after giving a few conventional directions for the care of the patient he saluted the two women and went away.

Sylvia and Mrs Merivale looked at each other across a bare table on which was set a lantern covered with cobwebs; it was the only piece of furniture left, and Sylvia had a sense of dramatic unreality about their conversation; standing up in this dim room, she was conscious of a make-believe intensity that tore the emotions more completely into rags than any normal procedure or expression of passionate feeling. Yet it was only because she divined an approach to the climax of her life that she felt thus; it was so important that she should have her way in what she intended to do that it was impossible for her to avoid regarding Michael's sister not merely as a partner in the scene, but also as the audience on whose approval success ultimately depended. The bareness of the room was like a stage, and the standing up like this was like a scene; it seemed right to exaggerate the gestures to keep pace with the emotional will to achieve her desire.

'Mrs Merivale,' she began, 'I beg you to let me stay behind in Nish and look after Michael so far as anything can be done – and of course it will be better for him that a woman should oversee the devotion of his orderly. Nothing will induce me to leave Nish. Nothing. You must understand that now. There is nothing to prevent me from staying here; you must take Captain Hazlewood's horse and go tomorrow.'

'Leave my brother? Why, the idea is absurd. I tell you I almost dragged that cart through the mud from Kragujevatz. Besides, I'm a more or less qualified nurse. You're not.'

'I'm qualified to nurse him through his fever because I know exactly what is wanted. If any new complication arose, you could do no more than I could do until the Bulgarian doctors arrived. If you stay here, you will be taken to Bulgaria.'

'And why not?' demanded the other. 'I'd much rather be taken prisoner with Michael than go riding off on my own and leave him here. No, no, the idea's impossible.'

'You have your mother – his mother to think of. You have your son,' Sylvia argued.

'Neither mother nor son could be any excuse for leaving Michael at such a moment.'

'Certainly not, if you could not find a substitute. But I shall stay here in any case, and you've no right to desert other obligations,' Sylvia affirmed.

'You're talking to me in a ridiculous way. There is only one obligation, which is to him.'

'Do you think you can do more for him than I can do?' Sylvia challenged. 'You can do less. You have already had the fearful strain of getting him here from the north. You are worn out. You are not fit to nurse him as he must be nursed. You are not fit to deal with the Bulgarians when they come. You are already breaking down. Why – there is no force in your arguments! They are as tame and conventional as if you were inventing an excuse to break a social engagement.'

'But by what right do you make this – this violent demand?' asked the other.

There suddenly came over Sylvia the futility of discussing the question in this fashion: this flickering room echoing faintly to the shouts of the affrighted fugitives in the distance lacked any atmosphere to hide the truth, for which in its bareness and misery it seemed to cry aloud. The question that his sister had put demanded an answer that would evade nothing in the explanation of her request; and if that answer should leave her soul stripped and desolate for the contemptuous regard of a woman who could not comprehend, why then thus was her destiny written and she should stand humiliated while the life that she had not been great enough to seize passed out of her reach.

'If my demand is violent, my need is violent,' she cried. 'Once in my dressing-room – the only time we met – you told me that you half regretted your rejection of art; you envied me my happiness in success. Your envy seemed to me then the bitterest irony, for I could not find in art that which I demanded. I have never found it until now in the chance to save your brother's life. That is exaggerating, you'll say. Yet I do believe – and if you could know my history you would believe it too – I do believe that my will can save him now not merely from death, but from the captivity that will follow. I know what it feels like to recover from this fever; and I know that he will not wish to see you and himself prisoners. He will fret himself ill again about your position. I am nothing to him. He will never know that we changed places deliberately. He will accept me as a companion in misfortune, and I will give all that love can give, love that feeds upon and inflames itself without demanding fuel except from the heart of the one who loves. You cannot refuse me now, my dear – so dear to me because you are his sister. You cannot refuse me when I ask you to let me stay because I love him.'

'Do you love Michael?' asked the other wonderingly.

'I love him, I love him, and one does not speak lightly of love at a moment like this. Do you remember when you asked me to come and stay with you in the country to meet him? It was eighteen months ago. Your letter arrived when I had just been jilted by a man I was going to marry in a desperate effort to persuade myself that domesticity was the cure for my discontent. My discontent was love for your brother. It has never been anything else since the moment we met, though I cried out "Never" when I read your invitation. I abandoned everything. I have lived ever since as a mountebank, driven always by a single instinct that sustained me. That instinct was merely a superstition to travel south. Whenever I travelled on, I had always the sense of an object. I have found that object at last, and I know absolutely that fate stood at your elbow and dragged with you at those weary bullocks in the mud to bring Michael here in time. I know that fate chained me to my balcony at Nish, where for nearly a month I have been watching for your arrival. You are wise; you have suffered; you have loved: I beseech you that just for the sake of your pride you will not rob me of this moment to which my whole life has been the mad overture.'

'What you say about my being a worry to him when he recovers consciousness is true,' said the sister. 'It's the only good argument you've brought forward. Ah, but I won't be so ungenerous. Stay then. Tonight I will wait here and tomorrow you shall take my place.'

The flickering bareness of the room flashed upon Sylvia with unimaginable glory; the dark night of her soul was become day.

'I think you can hear the joy in my heart,' she whispered. 'I can't say any more.'

Sylvia fell upon her knees; bowing her head upon the table she wept tears that seemed to gush like melodious fountains in a new world.

'You have made me believe that he will not die,' the sister murmured. 'I did not think that I should be able to believe that; but I do now, Sylvia.'

An assurance that positively seemed to contain life came over both of them. Sylvia rose from her knees, and abruptly they began to talk practically of what should be done that night and of what it would be wise to provide tomorrow. Presently Sylvia left the house, and slept in her hotel one of those rare sleeps whence waking is a descent upon airy plumes from heights where action and aspiration are fused in a ravishing unutterable affirmative, of which somehow a remembered consciousness is accorded to the favoured soul.

The next morning, Michael's sister mounted her horse. The guns of the desperate army of Stephanovitch confronting the Bulgarian advance were now audible; their booming gave power of flight to the weakest that remained in Nish; and the coil of fugitives writhed over the muddy plain toward the mountains.

'I think he seemed a little better this morning,' she said wistfully.

'Don't be jealous of leaving me,' Sylvia begged. 'You shall never regret that impulse. Will you take this golden bag with you? I don't want it to adorn a Bulgarian; it was a token to me

of love, and it has been a true token. At the end of your journey
sell it and give the money to poor Serbians. Will you? And this
letter for Captain Hazlewood. Please post it in England. Good-
bye, my dear, my dear.'

Michael's sister took the bag and the letter. In the light of
this grey morning her grey eyes were profound lakes of grief.

'I am envying you for the second time,' she said. Then she
waved her crop and rode quickly away. Sylvia watched her out
of sight, thinking what it must have cost that proud sister to make
this sacrifice. Her heart ached with a weight of unexpressed
gratitude, and yet she could not keep it from beating with a fierce
and triumphant gladness when she went up to where Michael
was lying and found him alone. The orderly and servants had
fled from the fear that clung to Nish like the clouds of this heavy
day, and Sylvia taking his hand bathed his forehead with a
tenderness that she half dreaded to use, so much did it seem a
flame that would fan the fever in whose embrace he tossed
unconscious of all but a world of shadows.

For a week she stayed beside him, sleeping sometimes with her
head against his arm, listening to the sombre colloquies of
delirium, striving to keep the soul that often in the long trances
seemed to flutter disconsolately away from the exhausted body.
There was no longer any sound of people in Nish: there was
nothing but the guns coming nearer and nearer every hour.
Then suddenly the firing ceased: there was a clatter and splash
of cavalry upon the muddy paving-stones. The noise passed.
Michael sat up and said:

'Listen!'

She thought he was away upon some adventure of delirium
and told him not to worry, but to lie still. He was so emaciated
that she asked herself if he could really be living: it was like
brushing a cobweb from one's path to make him lie down again.
A woman's scream, the thin scream of an old woman, shuddered
upon the silence outside; But the noise did not disturb him, and
he lay perfectly still with his eyes fixed upon the ceiling. A few
minutes later he again sat up in bed.

'Am I mad, or is it Sylvia Scarlett?' he asked.

'Yes, it's Sylvia. You're very ill. You must keep still.'

'What an extraordinary thing,' he murmured seriously to himself. 'I suppose I shall hear all about it tomorrow.'

He lay back again without seeming to worry about the problem
of her presence; nor did he ask where his sister was. Sylvia
remembered her own divine content in the hospital when the

fever left her, and she wanted him to lie as long as possible thus. Presently, however, he sat up again and said:

'Listen, Sylvia, I thought I wasn't wrong. Do you hear a kind of whisper in the air?'

She listened to please him, and then upon the silence she heard the sound. From a whisper it grew to a sigh, from a sigh it rose to a rustling of many leaves: it was the Bulgarian army marching into Nish, a procession of silent-footed devils, mysterious, remorseless, innumerable.

Chapter VII

TO SYLVIA'S surprise and relief, the conquerors paid no attention to the house that night. Michael, after he had listened for awhile to the dampered progress of that soft-shod army, fell back upon his pillow without comment and slept very tranquilly. Sylvia who had now not the least doubt of his recovery busied herself with choosing what she conceived to be absolute necessities for the immediate future and packing them into her valise. In the course of her preparations she put on one side for destruction or abandonment the contents of the golden shawl. Daguerrotypes and photographs; a rambling declaration of the circumstances in which her alleged grandfather had married that ghostly Adèle her grandmother; and a variety of letters that illustrated her mother's early life: all these might as well be burnt. She lay down upon her bed of overcoats and skirts piled upon the floor and found the shawl a pleasant addition to the rubber hot-water bottle she had been using as a pillow. Michael was still sleeping; it seemed wise to blow out the candle and, although it was scarcely seven o'clock, to try to sleep herself. It was the first time for a week that she had been able to feel the delicious and inviting freedom of untrammelled sleep. What did the occupation of a Bulgarian army signify in comparison with the assurance she felt of her patient's convalescence? The brazier glowed before her path towards a divine oblivion.

When Sylvia woke up and heard Michael's voice calling to her, it was six o'clock in the morning. She blew up the dull brazier to renewed warmth, set water to boil, and in a real exultation lighted four candles to celebrate with as much gaiety as possible the new atmosphere of joy and hope in the stark room.

'It's all very mysterious,' Michael was saying. 'It's all so delightfully mysterious that I can hardly bear to ask any questions lest I destroy the mystery. I've been lying awake, exquisitely and self-admiringly awake for an hour, trying to work out where I am, why I'm where I am, why you're where you are, and where Stella is.'

Sylvia told him of the immediate occasion of his sister's departure, and when she had done so had a moment of dismay lest his affection or his pride should be hurt by her willingness to leave him in the care of one who was practically a stranger.

'How very kind of you,' he said. 'My mother would have been distracted by having to look after her grandson in the whirlpool of war-work upon which she is engaged. So you had typhus too? It's a rotten business, isn't it? Did you feel very weak after it?'

'Of course.'

'And we're prisoners?'

'I suppose so.'

The water did not seem to be getting on, and Sylvia picked up her family papers to throw into the brazier.

'Oh, I say, don't destroy without due consideration,' Michael protested. 'The war has developed in me a passionate conservatism for little things.'

'I am destroying nothing of any importance,' Sylvia said.

'Love-letters?' he murmured with a smile.

She flushed angrily and discovered in herself a ridiculous readiness to prove his speculation beside the mark.

'If I ever had any love-letters I certainly never kept them,' she avowed. 'These are only musty records of a past, the influence of which has already exhausted itself.'

'But photographs?' he persisted. 'Let me look. Old photographs always thrill me.'

She showed him one or two of her mother.

'Odd,' he commented. 'She reminds me of my sister. Something about the way the eyes are set.'

'You're worrying about her?' Sylvia put in quickly.

'No, no. Of course I shall be glad to hear she's safely by the sea on the other side, but I'm not worrying about her to the extent of fancying a non-existent likeness. There really is one; and if it comes to that, you're not unlike her yourself.'

215

'My father and my grandfather were both English,' Sylvia said. 'My mother was French and my grandmother was Polish. My grandfather's name was Cunningham.'

'What?' Michael asked sharply. 'That's odd.'

'Quite a distinguished person according to the old Frenchman whom the world regarded as my grandfather.'

She handed him Bassompierre's rambling statement about the circumstances of her mother's birth, which he read and put down with an exclamation.

'Well, this is really extraordinary! Do you know that we're second cousins? This Charles Cunningham became the twelfth Lord Saxby. My father was the thirteenth and last earl. What a trick for fate to play upon us both! No wonder there's a like-ness between you and Stella. How strange it makes that time at Mulberry Cottage seem. But you know, I always felt that under-neath our open and violent hostility there was a radical sympathy quite inexplicable. This explains it.'

Sylvia was not at all sure that she felt grateful toward the explanation; mere kinship had never stood for much in her life.

'You must try to sleep again now,' she said sternly.

'But you don't seem at all amazed at this coincidence,' Michael protested. 'You accept it as if it was a perfectly ordinary occurrence.'

'I want you to sleep. Take this milk. We are sure to have a nerve-racking day with these Bulgarians.'

'Sylvia, what's the matter?' he persisted. 'Why should my dis-covery of our relationship annoy you?'

'It doesn't annoy me, but I want you to sleep. Do remember that you've only just returned to yourself and that you'll soon want all your strength.'

'You've not lost your battling quality in all these years,' he said, and lay silent when he had drunk the warm milk she gave and while she tidied the floor of the coats that served for a bed. The letters and the photographs she threw into the brazier and drove them deep into the coke with a stick, looking round defiantly at Michael when they were ashes. He shook his head with a smile, but he did not say anything.

Sylvia was really glad when the sound of loud knocking upon the door downstairs prevented any further discussion of the accident of their relationship; nevertheless she found a pleasure in announcing to the Bulgarian officer her right to be found here with the sick Englishman, her cousin: it seemed to launch her once more upon the flow of ordinary existence, this kinship with one who without doubt belonged to the world actively at war. The interview with the Bulgarian officer took place in the stark and dusty room where she had argued with Stella for the right to stay behind with her brother. Now in the light of early morning it still preserved its scenic quality, and Sylvia was absurdly aware of her resemblance to the pleading heroine of a melodrama, when she begged this grimy, shaggy creature whose slate-grey overcoat was marbled by time and weather to let her patient stay here for the present, and furthermore to accord her facilities to procure for him whatever was necessary and obtainable. In the end the officer went away without giving a more decisive answer than was implied by the soldier he left behind. Sylvia did not think he could have understood much of her French, so little had she understood of his, and the presence of this soldier with fixed bayonet and squashed Mongolian countenance oppressed her. She wondered what opinion of them the officer had reached and ached at the thought of how perhaps in a few minutes she and Michael should be separated, intolerably separated for ever. She made a sign to the guard for leave to go upstairs again; but he forbade her with a gesture, and she stood leaning against the table, while she stared before him with an expression of such unutterable nothingness as by sheer nebulosity acquired a sinister and menacing force. He was as incomprehensible as a savage beast encountered in a forest, and the fancy that he had ever existed with his own little ambitions in a human society refused to state itself. Sylvia could make of him nothing but a symbol of the blind mad forces that were in opposition throughout the old familiar world, the blindness and madness of which were fitly expressed by such an instrument.

Half an hour of strained indifference passed, and then the officer came back with another who spoke English. Perhaps the consciousness of speaking English well and fluently made the newcomer anxious to be pleasant; one felt that he would have regarded it as a slight upon his own proficiency to be rude or intransigent. Apart from his English there was nothing remarkable in his appearance or his personality. He went upstairs and saw for himself Michael's condition, came down again with Sylvia, and promised her that, if she would observe the rules imposed upon the captured city, nothing within the extent of his influence should be done to imperil the sick man's convalescence. Then after signing a number of forms that would enable her to move about in certain areas to obtain provisions and to call upon medical help, he asked her if she knew Sunbury-on-

Thames. She replied in the negative, which seemed to disappoint him. Whereupon she asked him if he knew Maidenhead, and he brightened up again.

'I have had good days in the Thames,' he said, and departed in a bright cloud of riverside memories.

The next fortnight passed in a seclusion that was very dear to Sylvia. The hours rolled along on the easy wheels of reminiscent conversations, and Michael was gradually made aware of all her history. Yet at the end of it, she told herself that he was aware of nothing except the voyages of the body; of her soul's pilgrimage he was as ignorant as if they had never met. She reproached herself for this and wanted to begin over again the real history; but her own feelings towards him stood in the way of frankness and she feared to betray herself by the emotion that any deliberate sincerity must have revealed. Yet, as she assured herself rather bitterly, he was so obviously blind to anything but the coincidence of their relationship that she might with impunity have stripped her soul bare. It was unreasonable for her to resent his showing himself more moved by the news of Hazlewood's death than by anything in her own history, because anything in her own history that might have moved him she had omitted, and his impression of her now must be what his impression of her had been nine years ago – that of a hard and cynical woman with a baffling capacity for practical kindliness. She had often before been dismayed by a sense of life slipping out of her reach, but she had never before been dismayed by the urgent escape of hours and minutes. She had never before said *ruit hora* with her will to snatch the opportunity palsied, as if she stood panting in the stifling impotence of a dream. Already he was able to walk about the room, and like all those who are recovering from a serious illness was performing little feats of agility with the objective self-absorption of a child.

'Do people – or rather,' she corrected herself quickly, 'does existence seem something utterly different from what it was before you saw it fade out from your consciousness at Kragujevatz?'

'Well, the only person I've really seen is yourself,' he answered. 'And I can't help staring at you in some bewilderment, due less to fever than to the concatenations of fortune. What seems to me so amusing and odd is that, if you had known we were cousins, you couldn't have behaved in a more cousinly way than you did over Lily.'

'When I found myself in that hospital at Petrograd,' Sylvia

declared, 'I felt like the Sleeping Beauty being waked by the magic kiss – ' she broke off, blushing hotly and cursing inwardly her damned self-consciousness; and then blushed again because she had stopped to wonder if he had noticed her blush.

'I don't think anything that happened during this war to me personally,' Michael said, 'could ever make any impression now. The war itself always presents itself to me as a mighty fever, caught, if you will, by taking foolish risks or ignoring simple precautions, but ultimately and profoundly inevitable in the way that one feels all illness to be inevitable. Anything particular that happens to the individual must lose its significance in the change that he must suffer from the general calamity. I think perhaps that as a Catholic I am tempted to be less hopeful of men and more hopeful of God, but yet I firmly believe that I am more hopeful of men than the average – shall we call him humanitarian, who perceives in this war nothing but a crime against human brotherhood committed by a few ambitious knaves helped by a crowd of ambitious fools. I'm perfectly sure for instance that there is no one alive and no one dead that does not partake of the responsibility. However little it may be apprehended in the case of individuals, nothing will ever persuade me that one of the chief motive forces that maintain this state of destruction to which the world is being devoted is not a sense of guilt and a determination to expiate it. Mark you, I'm not trying to urge that God has judicially sentenced the world to war, dealing out horror to Belgium for the horror of the Congo, horror to Serbia for the horror of the royal assassination, horror to France, England, Germany, Austria, Italy, and Russia for their national lapses from grace – I should be very sorry to implicate Almighty God in any conception based upon our primitive notions of justice. The only time I feel that God ever interfered with humanity was when He was incarnate amongst us, and the story of that seems to forbid us our attribution to Him of anything in the nature of fretful castigation. The most presumptuous attitude in this war seems to me the German idea of Good in a *pickelhaube,* of Christ bound to an Iron Cross, and of the Dove as a bloody-minded Eagle; but the Allies' notion of the Pope as a kind of diplomat with a licence to excommunicate seems to me only less presumptuous.'

'Then you think the war is in every human heart?' Sylvia asked.

'When I look at my own I'm positive it is.'

'But do you think it was inevitable because it was salutary?'

219

'I think blood-letting is old-fashioned surgery: aren't you confusing the disease with the remedy? Surely no disease is salutary, and I think it's morally dangerous to confuse effect with cause. At the same time I'm not going to lay down positively that this war may not be extremely salutary. I think it will be, but I acquite God of any hand in its deliberate ordering. Free will must apply to nations. I don't believe that war which, while it brings out often the best of people, brings out much more often the worst is to be regarded as anything but a vile exhibition of human sin. The selflessness of those who have died is terribly stained by the selfishness of those who have let them die. Yet the younger generation, or such of it as survives, will have the compensation when it is all over of such amazing opportunities for living as were never known, and the older generation that made the war will die less lamented than any men that have ever died since the world began. And I believe that their purgatory will be the greyest and the longest of all purgatories. But as soon as I have said that I regret my words, because I think it will be fatal for the younger generation to become precocious Pharisees; and so I reiterate that the war is in every human heart, and you're not to tempt me any more into making harsh judgements about anyone.'

'Not even the great Victorians?' said Sylvia.

'Well, that will be a difficult and very penitential piece of self-denial, I admit. And it is hard not to hope that Carlyle is in hell. However, I can just avoid doing so, because I shall certainly go to hell myself if I do, where his Teutonic borborygmi would be an added woe, gigantic genius though he was. But don't let's joke about hell. It's – infernally credible since August, 1914. What were we talking about before we began to talk about the war? Oh, I remember, the new world that one gets up to face after a bad illness.'

'Perhaps my experience was peculiar,' Sylvia said.

But what did it matter how he regarded the world, she thought, unless he regarded her? Already the topic was exhausted; he was tired by his vehemence; once more the ruthless and precipitate hour had gone by.

During this period of seclusion Sylvia often had to encounter in its various capacities the army of occupation, by which generally she was treated with consideration, and even with positive kindness. Nish had been so completely evacuated that after the medley which had thronged the streets and squares it now seemed strangely empty. The uniformity of the Bulgarian characteristics added to the impression of violent change; there was never a moment in which one could delude oneself with the continuation of normal existence. At the end of the fortnight, the English-speaking officer came to make a visit of inspection in order to give his advice at headquarters about the future of the prisoners. Michael was still very weak and looked a skeleton, so much so indeed that the officer went off and fetched a squat little doctor to help his deliberation; the latter recommended another week, and the prisoners were once more left to themselves. Sylvia was half sorry for such considerate action; the company of Michael which had seemed to promise so much and had in fact yielded so little was beginning to fret her with the ultimate futility of such an association. She resented the emotion she had given to it in the prospect of a more definitely empty future that was now opening before her, and she gave way to the reaction against her exaggerated devotion by criticising herself severely. The supervention of such an attitude made irksome what had been so dear a seclusion, and going beyond self-criticism she began to tell herself that Michael was cold, inhuman and remote, that she felt ill at ease with him and unable to talk, and that the sooner their separation came about, the better. Perhaps she should be released, in which case she should make her way back to England and become a nurse.

At the end of the third week Sylvia desperately tried to arrest the precipitate hour.

'I think I suffer from a too rapid digestion,' she announced.

He looked at her with a question in his eyes.

'You were talking to me the other day,' she went on, 'about your comtemplative experiences, and you were saying how entirely your purely intellectual and spiritual progress conformed to the well-trodden mystical way. You added, of course, that you did not wish to suggest any comparison with the path of greater men, but allowing for conventional self-depreciation you left me to suppose that you were content with your achievement. At the moment war broke out you felt that you were ripe for action, and instead of becoming a priest after those nine years of contemplative preparation, you joined an hospital unit for Serbia. You feel quite secure about the war; you accept your fever, your possible internment for years in Bulgaria, and indeed anything that affects you personally without the least regret. In fact you're what an American might call in tune with the infinite. I'm not! And it's all a matter of digestion.'

'My illness has clouded my brain,' Michael murmured. 'I'm a

long way from understanding what you're driving at.'

'Well, keep quiet and listen to my problems. We're on the verge of separation, but you're still my patient and you owe me your attention.'

'I owe you more than that,' he put in.

'How feeble,' she scoffed. 'You might have spared me such a pretty-pretty sentence.'

'I surrender unconditionally,' he protested. 'Your fierceness is superfluous.'

'I suppose you've often labelled humanity in bulk? I mean for instance – you must have often said and certainly thought that all men are either knaves or fools?'

'I must have thought so at some time or another,' Michael agreed.

'Well, I've got a new division. I think that all men have either normal digestions, slow digestions, rapid digestions, or no digestions at all. Extend the physical fact into a metaphor and apply it to the human mind.'

'Dear Sylvia, I feel as if I were being poulticed. How admirably you maintain the nursing manner. I've made the application. What do I do now?'

'Listen without interrupting, or I shall lose the thread of my argument. I suppose you'll admit that the optimists outnumber the pessimists? Obviously they must, or the world would come to an end. Very well then, we'll say that the pessimists are the people with no digestions at all: on top of them will be the people with slow digestions, the great unthinking herd that is optimistic because the optimists shout most loudly. The people with good normal digestions are of course the shouting optimists. Finally come the people whose digestions are too rapid. I belong to that class.'

'Are they optimists?'

'They're optimists until they've finished digesting, but between meals they're outrageously pessimistic. The only way to illustrate my theory is to talk about myself. Imagine you're a lady-palmist and prepare for a debauch of egotism from one of your clients. All through my life, Michael, I have been a martyr to quick digestion. Your friend Guy Hazlewood suffered from that complaint, judging by the way he talked about the war. I can imagine that his life has been made of brief exquisite illusions followed by long vacuums. Am I right?'

Michael nodded.

'Cassandra, to take a more remote instance, suffered from

rapid digestion – in fact all prophets have the malady. Isn't it physiologically true to say that the unborn child performs in its mother's womb the drama of man's evolution? I'm sure it's equally true that the life of the individual after birth and until death is a microcosm of man's later history, or rather I ought to say that it might be, for only exceptional individuals reproduce the history of humanity up to contemporary development. A genius – a great creative genius seems to me a man whose active absorption can keep pace with the rapidity of his digestion. How often do we hear of people who were in advance of their time! This figure of speech is literally true, but only great creative geniuses have the consolation of projecting themselves beyond their ambient in time. There remain a number of sterile geniuses, whom nature with her usual prodigality has put on the market in reserve, but for whom later on she finds she has no use on account of the economy that always succeeds extravagance. These sterile geniuses are left to fend for themselves and some- how to extract from a hostile and suspicious environment food to maintain them during the long dreary emptiness that suc- ceeds their too optimistic absorption. Do you agree with me? '

'At one end of the pole you would put Shakespeare, at the other the Jubilee Juggins?' Michael suggested.

'That's it,' she agreed. 'Although a less conspicuous wastrel would serve for the other end.'

'And I suppose if you're searching for the eternal rhythm of the universe, you'd have to apply to nations the same classifica- tion as to individuals?' he went on.

'Of course.'

'So that England would have a good normal digestion and Ireland a too rapid digestion? Or better, let us say that all Teutons eat heartily and digest slowly, and that all Celts are too rapid. But come back to yourself.'

Sylvia paused for a moment, and then continued with swift gestures of self-agreement:

'I certainly ascribe every mistake in my own life to a rapid digestion. Why I've even digested this war that, if we think on a large scale, was evidently designed to stir up the sluggish liver of the world. I'm sick to death of the damned war already, and it hasn't begun yet really. And to come down to my own little particular woes, I've laboured toward religion, digested it with horrible rapidity, and see nothing in it now but a half truth for myself. In art the same, in human associations the same, in every- thing the same. Ah, don't let's talk any more about anything.'

In the silence that followed she thought to herself about the inspiration of her late theories; and looking at Michael, pale and hollow-eyed in the grim November dusk, she railed at herself because with all her will to make use of the quality she had attributed to herself she could not shake off this love that was growing every day.

'Why, in God's name,' she almost groaned aloud, 'can't it go the way of everything else? But it won't. It won't. It never will. And I shall never be happy again.'

A rainy nightfall symbolised for her the darkness of the future, and when in the middle of the evening meal, while they were hacking at a tin of sardines, a message came from headquarters that tomorrow they must be ready to leave Nish, she was glad. However, the sympathy of the English-speaking officer had exercised itself so much on behalf of the two prisoners that the separation which Sylvia had regarded as immediate was likely to be postponed for some time. The officer explained that it was inconvenient for them to remain any longer in Nish, but that arrangements had been made by which they were to be moved to Sofia and therefore that Michael's convalescence would be safe against any premature strain. They would realise that Bulgaria was not unmindful of the many links, now unfortunately broken, which had formerly bound her to England, and they would admit in the face of their courteous treatment how far advanced his country was upon the road of civilisation.

'Splendid,' Michael exclaimed. 'So we shan't be separated yet for a while and we shall be able to prosecute our philosophical discoveries. The riddle of life finally solved in 1915 by two prisoners of the Bulgarian Army! It would almost make the war worth while. Sylvia, I'm so excited at our journey.'

'You're tired of being cooped up here,' she said sharply. And then to mask whatever emotion might have escaped, she added: 'I'm certainly sick to death of it myself.'

'I know,' he agreed, 'It must have been a great bore for you. The invalid is always blissfully unconscious of time, and forgets that the pleasant little services which encourage him to go on being ill are not natural events like sunrise and sunset. You do well to keep me up to the mark; I'm not really forgetful.'

'You seem to have forgotten that we may have months, even years of imprisonment in Bulgaria,' Sylvia said.

He looked so frail in his khaki overcoat that she was seized with penitence for the harsh thoughts of him she had indulged, and with a fondling gesture tried to atone:

'You really feel that you can make this journey? If you don't, I'll go and rout out our officer and beg him for another week.'

Michael shook his head.

'I'm rather a fraud. Really, you know, I feel perfectly well. Quite excited about this journey, as I told you.'

She was chilled by his so impersonally cordial manner and looked at him regretfully.

'Every day he gets farther away,' she thought. 'In nine years he has been doing nothing but place layer after layer over his sensitiveness. He's a kind of mental coral-island. I know that there must still exist a capacity for suffering, but he'll never again let me see it. He wants to convince me of his eternal serenity.'

She was looking at him with an unusual intentness, and he turned away in embarrassment, which made her jeer at him to cover her own shyness.

'It was just the reverse of embarrassment really,' he said. 'But I don't want to spoil things.'

'By doing what?' she demanded.

'Well, if I told you –' he stopped abruptly.

'I have a horror of incomplete or ambiguous conditionals. Now you've begun, you must finish.'

'Nothing will induce me to. I'll say what I thought of saying before we separate. I promise that.'

'Perhaps we never shall separate.'

'Then I shall have no need to finish my sentence.'

Sylvia lay awake for a long time that last night in Nish, wondering, with supreme futility as she continually reminded herself, what Michael could have nearly said. Somewhere about two o'clock she decided that he had been going to suggest adopting her into his family.

'Damned fool,' she muttered, pulling and shaking her improvised bed as if it were a naughty child. 'Nevertheless he had the wit to understand how much it would annoy me. It shows the lagoon is not quite encircled yet.'

The soldiers who arrived to escort them to the railway station were like grotesques of hotel-porters; they were so ready to help with the baggage that it seemed absurd for their movements to be hampered by rifles with fixed bayonets. The English-speaking officer accompanied them to the station and expressed his regrets that he could not travel to Sofia; he had no doubt that later on he should see them again and in any case when the war was over he hoped to revisit England. Sylvia suddenly remembered her big trunk, which she had left in the *consigne* when she first reached Nish nearly two months ago. The English-speaking officer shrugged his shoulders at her proposal to take it with her to Sofia.

'The station was looted by the Serbs before we arrived,' he explained. 'They are a barbarous nation, many years behind us in civilisation. We never plunder. And of course you understand that Nish is really Bulgarian? That makes us particularly gentle here. You heard, perhaps, that when the Entente Legations left we gave them a champagne lunch for the farewell at Dedeagatch? We are far in front of the Germans, who are a very strong but primitive nation. They are not much liked in Bulgaria: we prefer the English. But, alas, poor England!' he sighed.

'Why poor?' Sylvia demanded indignantly.

He smiled compassionately for answer, and soon afterwards in a first-class compartment to themselves Michael and she left Nish.

'Really,' Michael observed, 'when the conditions are favourable, travelling as a prisoner-of-war is the most luxurious travelling of all. I've never experienced the servility of a private courier, but it's wonderful to feel that other people are under an obligation to look after you. However, at present we have the advantages of being new toys. Our friend from Sunbury-on-Thames may be as compassionate as he likes about England, but there's no doubt it confers on the possessor a quite peculiar thrill to own English people – even two such non-combatant creatures as ourselves. It's typical of the Germans' newness to European society that they should have thought the right way to treat English prisoners was to spit at them. I remember once seeing a grandee of Spain who'd been hired as secretary by a Barcelona Jew, and by Jove! he wasn't allowed to forget it. The Bulgarians on the other hand have a superficial air of breeding, which they've either copied from the Turks or inherited from the Chinese. Didn't you love the touch about the champagne lunch at Dedeagatch? There's a luxurious hospitality about that, which you won't find outside the *Arabian Nights* or Chicago. Really the English nation should give thanks every Sunday, murmuring with all eyes on the East window and Germany: "There but for the grace of God blowing in the west wind goes John Bull." Yet I wonder if the hearts would be humble enough to keep the Pharisee out of the thanksgiving.'

The train went slowly with frequent stoppages, often in wild country far from any railway-station, where in such surroundings its existence seemed utterly improbable. Occasionally small bands of comitadjis would ride up and menace theatrically the dejected Serbian prisoners who were being moved into Bulgaria. There was a cold wind, and snow was lying thinly on the hills.

In the rapid dusk Michael fell asleep; soon after, the train seemed to have stopped for the night. Sylvia did not wake him up, but sat for two hours by the light of one candle stuck upon her valise and pored upon the moonless night that pressed against the window-panes of the compartment with a scarcely endurable desolation. There was no sound of those murmurous voices that make mysterious even suburban tunnels when trains wait in them on foggy nights. The windows were screwed up; the door into the corridor was locked; in the darkness and silence Sylvia felt for the first time in all its force the meaning of imprisonment. Suddenly a flaring torch carried swiftly along the permanent way threw shadowy grotesques upon the ceiling of the compartment, and Michael waking up with a start asked their whereabouts.

'Somewhere near Zaribrod as far as I can make out, but it's impossible to tell for certain. I can't think what they're doing. We've been here for two hours without moving, and I can't hear a sound except the wind. It was somebody's carrying a torch past the window that woke you up.'

They speculated idly for a while on the cause of the delay, and then gradually under the depression of the silence their voices died away into occasional sighs of impatience.

'What about eating?' Sylvia suggested at last. 'I'm not hungry, but it will give us something to do.'

So they struggled with tinned foods, glad of the life that the fussy movement gave to the compartment.

'One feels that moments such as these should be devoted to the most intimate confidences,' Michael said, when they had finished their dinner and were once more enmeshed by the silence.

'There's a sort of portentousness about them, you mean?'

'Yes, but as a matter of fact one can't even talk about commonplace things, because one is all the time fidgeting with the silence.'

'I know,' Sylvia agreed. 'One gets a hint of madness in the way one's personality seems to shrink to nothing. I suppose there really is somebody left alive in the world? I'm beginning to feel as if it was just you and I against the universe.'

'Death must come like that sometimes,' he murmured.

'Like what?'

'Like that thick darkness outside and oneself against the universe.'

'I'd give anything for a guitar,' Sylvia exclaimed.

'What would you play first?' he enquired gravely.

She sang gently:

> '*La donna è mobile qual piuma al vento,*
> *Muta d'accento e di pensiero,*
> *Sempre un amabile leggiadro viso,*
> *In pianto o in riso, è menzognero –*

and that's all I can remember of it,' she said, breaking off.

'I wonder why you chose to sing that.'

'It reminds me of my father,' she answered. 'When he was drunk, fair cousin, he always used to sing that. What a charming son-in-law he would have made for our grandfather! Oh, are we ever going to move again?' she cried, jumping up and pressing her face against the viewless pane. 'Hark! I hear horses.'

Michael rose and joined her. Presently flames leapt up into the darkness, and armed men were visible in silhouette against the bonfire they had kindled, so large a bonfire indeed that, in the shadows beyond, the stony outcrop of a rough steep country seemed in contrast to be the threshold of titanic chasms. A noise of shouting reached the train, and presently Bulgarian regulars, the escort of the prisoners, joined the merry-makers round the fire. Slow music rumbled upon the air, and a circle of men shoulder to shoulder with interwoven arms performed a stately swaying dance.

'Or are they just holding one another up because they're drunk?' Sylvia asked.

'No, it's really a dance, though they may be drunk too. I wish we could get this window open. It looks as if all the soldiers had joined the party.'

The dance came to an end with shouts of applause, and one or two rifles were fired at the stars. Then the company squatted round the fire, and the wine circulated again.

'But where are the officers in charge?' Michael asked.

'Playing cards probably. Or perhaps dining with the rest. Anyway, if we're going to stay here all night, it's just as well to have the entertainment of this al fresco supper-party. Anything is better than that intolerable silence.'

Sylvia blew out the stump of candle, and they sat in darkness watching the fire-flecked revel. The shouting grew louder with the frequent passing of the wineskins; after an hour groups of comitadjis and regulars left the bonfire and wandered along the permanent way, singing drunken choruses. What happened presently at the far end of the train they could not see, but there was a sound of smashed glass followed by a man's scream. Those who were still sitting round the fire snatched up their weapons and stumbled in loud excitement toward the centre of the disturbance. There were about a dozen shots, the rasp of torn woodwork, and a continuous crash of broken glass with curses, cries, and all the sounds of quarrelsome confusion.

'The drunken brutes are breaking up the train,' Michael exclaimed. 'We'd better sit back from the window for a while.'

Sylvia cried out to him that it was worse and that they were dragging along by the heels the bodies of men and kicking them as they went.

'Good God!' he declared, standing up now in horror. 'They're murdering the wretched Serbian prisoners. Here, we must get out and protest.'

'Sit down, fool,' Sylvia commanded. 'What good will your protesting do?'

But as she spoke she gave a shuddering shriek and held her hands up to her eyes: they had thrown a writhing, mutilated shape into the fire.

'The brutes, the filthy brutes,' Michael shouted, and jumping upon the seat of the compartment he kicked at the window-panes until there was not a fragment of glass left. 'Shout, Sylvia, shout. Oh, hell, I can't remember a word of their bloody language. We must stop them. Stop, I tell you. Stop!'

One of the prisoners had broken away from his tormentors and was running along the permanent way, but the blood from a gash in the forehead blinded him and he fell on his face just outside the compartment. Two comitadjis banged out his brains on the railway line; with clasp-knives they hacked the head from the corpse and merrily tossed it in at the window, where it fell on the floor between Sylvia and Michael.

'My God,' Michael muttered. 'It's better to be killed ourselves than to stay here and endure this.'

He began to scramble out of the window, and she seeing that he was nearly mad with horror at his powerlessness followed him in the hope of deflecting any rash action. Strangely enough, nobody interfered with their antics, and they had run nearly the whole length of the train, in order to find the officers in charge, before a tall man descending from one of the carriages barred their progress.

'Why, it's you,' Sylvia laughed hysterically. 'It's my rose-grower! Michael, do you hear? My rose-grower.'

It really was Rakoff, decked out with barbaric trappings of silver and bristling with weapons, but his manners had not changed with his profession and as soon as he recognised her, he bowed politely and asked if he could be of any help.

'Can't you stop this massacre?' she begged. 'Keep quiet, Michael, it's no good talking about the Red Cross.'

'It was the fault of the Serbians,' Rakoff explained. 'They insulted my men. But what are you doing here?'

The violence of the drunken soldiers and comitadjis had soon worn itself out, and most of them were back again round the fire, drinking and singing as if nothing had happened. Sylvia perceived that Rakoff was sincerely anxious to make himself agreeable and treading on Michael's foot (he was in a fume of threats) she explained their position.

Rakoff leaned up at the carriage from which he had just descended.

'The officers in command are drunk and insensible,' he murmured. 'I'm under an obligation to you. Do you want to stay in Bulgaria? Have you given your parole?' he asked Michael.

'Give my parole to murderers and torturers?' shouted Michael. 'Certainly not, and I never will.'

'My cousin has only just recovered from typhus,' Sylvia reminded Rakoff. 'The slaughter has upset him.'

In her anxiety to take advantage of the meeting she had cast aside her own horror and forgotten her own inclination to be hysterical.

'He must understand that in the Balkans we do not regard violence as you do in Europe. He should remember that the Serbians would do the same and worse to Bulgarians.'

Rakoff spoke in a tone of injured sensibility, which would have been comic to Sylvia without the smell of burnt flesh upon the wind, and without the foul bloodstains upon her own skirt.

'Quite so. *A la guerre comme à la guerre*,' she agreed. 'What will you do for us?'

'I'm really anxious to return your kindness at Nish,' Rakoff said gravely. 'If you come with me and my men, we shall be riding southward, and you could perhaps find an opportunity to get over the Greek frontier. The officer commanding this train deserves to be punished for getting drunk. I'm not drunk, though

I captured a French outpost a week ago and have some reason to celebrate my success. It was I who cut the line at Vrania. *Alors, c'est entendu? Vous venez avec moi?*'

'*Vous êtes trop gentil, monsieur.*'

'*Rien du tout. Plaisir! Plaisir!* Go back to your carriage now, and I'll send two of my men presently to show you the way out. What's that? The door is locked on the outside? Come with me then.'

They walked back along the train, and entered their compartment from the other side on which the door had been broken in.

'You can't bring much luggage. Wrap up well. *Il fait très froid.* Is your cousin strong enough to ride?'

At this point Rakoff stumbled over the severed head on the floor, and struck a match.

'What babies my men are,' he exclaimed with a smile.

He picked up the head and threw it out on the track. Then he told Sylvia and Michael to prepare for their escape and left them.

'What do you think of my aesthetic Bulgarian?' she asked.

'It's extraordinary how certain personalities have the power to twist one's standards,' Michael answered emphatically. 'A few minutes ago I was sick with horror – the whole world seemed to be tumbling to pieces before human bestiality – and now before the blood is dry on the railway-sleepers I've accepted it as a fact and – Sylvia – do you know what I was thinking the last minute or two – I'm in a way appalled by my own callousness in being able to smile – but I really was thinking with amusement what a pity it was we couldn't hand over a few noisy stay-at-home Englishmen to the sensitive Rakoff.'

'Michael,' Sylvia demanded anxiously, 'do you think you *are* strong enough to ride? I'm not sure how far we are from the Greek frontier, but it's sure to mean at least a week in the saddle. It seems madness for you to attempt it.'

'My dear, I'm not going to stay in this accursed train.'

'I've a letter of introduction for a clerk in Cavalla,' Sylvia reminded him with a smile.

'Let's hope he invites us to lunch when we present it,' Michael laughed.

The tension of waiting for the escape required this kind of feeble joking; and break in the conversation gave them time to think of the corpses scattered about in the darkness, which with the slow death of the fire was reconquering its territory. They followed Rakoff's advice and heaped extra clothes upon themselves, filling the pockets with victuals. Sylvia borrowed a cap from Michael and tied the golden shawl round her head; Michael did the same with an old college scarf. Then he tore the red cross brassard from his sleeve:

'I haven't the impudence to wear that during our pilgrimage with this gang of murderers. I've tucked away what paper money I have in my boots, and I've got twenty sovereigns sewn in my cholera belt.'

Two smiling comitadjis appeared from the corridor and beckoned the prisoners to follow them to where on the other side of the train ponies were waiting; within five minutes the wind blowing icy cold upon their cheeks, the smell of damp earth and saddles and vinous breath, the ragged starshine high overhead, the willing motion of the horses, all combined to obliterate everything except drowsy intimations of adventure. Rakoff was not visible in the cavalcade, but Sylvia supposed that he was somewhere in front. After riding for three hours, a halt was called at a deserted farmhouse, and in the big living-room he was there to receive his guests with pointed courtesy.

'You are at home here,' he observed with a laugh. 'This farm belonged to an Englishman before the war with Greece and Serbia. He was a great friend of Bulgaria; the Serbians knew it and left very little when their army passed through. We shall sleep here tonight. Are you hungry?'

The comitadjis had already wrapped themselves in their sheepskins and were lying in the dark corners of the room, exhausted by the long ride on top of the wine. A couple of men, however, prepared a rough meal to which Rakoff invited Sylvia and Michael. They had scarcely sat down, when to their surprise a young woman dressed in a very short tweed skirt and Norfolk jacket and wearing a Tyrolese hat over two long plaits of flaxen hair came and joined them. She nodded curtly to Rakoff and began to eat without a word.

'Ziska disapproves of the English,' Rakoff explained. 'In fact the only thing she really cares for is dynamite. But she is one of the great comitadji leaders and acts as my second in command. She understands French, but declines to speak it on patriotic grounds, being half a Prussian.'

The young woman looked coldly at the two strangers; then she went on eating. Her silent presence was not favourable to conversation; and a sudden jealousy of this self-satisfied and comtemptuous creature overcame Sylvia. She remembered how she had told Michael's sister the secret of her love for him, and the thought of meeting her again in England became intolerable. She had a mad fancy to kill the other woman and to take her place in this wild band beside Rakoff, to seize her by those tight flaxen plaits and hold her face downwards on the table, while she stabbed her and stabbed her again. Only by such a duel could she assert her own personality, rescuing it from the ignominy of the present and the greater ignominy of the future. She had actually grasped a long knife that lay in front of her, and she might have given expression to the mad notion if at that moment Michael had not collapsed.

In a moment her fantastic passions died away; even Ziska's sidelong glance of scorn at the prostrate figure was incapable of rousing the least resentment.

'He should sleep,' said Rakoff. 'Tomorrow he will have a long and tiring day.'

Soon in the shadowy room of the deserted farmhouse they were all asleep except Sylvia, who watched for a long time the dusty lanternlight flickering upon Ziska's motionless form; as her thoughts wavered in the twilight between wakefulness and dreams, she once more had a longing to grip that smooth pink neck and crack it like the neck of a wax doll. Then it was morning; the room was full of smoke and the smell of coffee.

Sylvia's forecast of a week's journeying with the comitadjis was too optimistic; as a matter of fact they were in the saddle for a month, and it was only a day or two before Christmas new style when they pitched their camp on the slopes of a valley sheltered from the fierce winds of Rhodope about twenty kilometres from the Bulgarian outposts beyond Xanthi.

'We are not far from the sea here,' Rakoff said significantly.

Whatever wind reached this slope had dropped at nightfall, and in the darkness Sylvia felt like a kiss upon her cheek the salt breath of the mighty mother to which her heart responded in awe as to the breath of liberty.

It had been a strange experience, this month with Rakoff and his band, and seemed already, though the sound of the riding had scarcely died away from her senses, the least credible episode of a varied life. Yet looking back at the incidents of each day, Sylvia could not remember that her wild companions had ever been conscious of Michael and herself as intruders upon their monotonously violent behaviour. Even Ziska, that riddle of flaxen womanhood, had gradually reached a kind of remote cordiality toward their company. To be sure, she had not invited Sylvia to grasp, or even faintly to guess, the reasons that might have induced her to adopt such a mode of life; she had never afforded the least hint of her relationship to Rakoff; she had never attempted to justify her cold, almost it might have been called her prim mercilessness. Yet she had sometimes advised Sylvia to withdraw from a prospective exhibition of atrocity, and this not from any motive of shame, but always obviously because she had been considering the emotions of her guest. It was in this spirit, when once a desperate Serbian peasant had flung a stone at the departing troop, that she had advised Sylvia to ride on and avoid the fall of mangled limbs that was likely to occur after shutting twenty villagers in a barn and blowing them up with a charge of dynamite. She had spoken of the unpleasant sequel as simply as a meteorologist might have spoken of the weather's breaking up. Michael and Sylvia used to wonder to each other what prevented them from turning their ponies' heads and galloping off anywhere to escape this daily exposure to the sight of unchecked barbarity; but they could never bring themselves to pass the limits of expediency and lose themselves in the uncertainties of an ideal morality; ultimately they always came back to the fundamental paradox of war and agreed that in a state of war the life of the individual increased in value in the same proportion as it deteriorated. Rakoff had taken pleasure in commenting upon their attitude, and once or twice he had been at pains to convince them of the advantages they now enjoyed of an intellectual honesty from which in England, so far as he had been able to appreciate criticism of that country, they would have been eternally debarred. But perhaps no amount of intellectual honesty would have enabled them to remain quiescent before the rapine and slaughter of which they were compelled to be cognisant if not actually to see, had not the journey itself healed their wounded conscience with a charm against which they were powerless. The air of the mountains swept away the taint of death that would otherwise have reeked in the very accoutrements of the equipage. The light of their bivouac fires stained such an infinitesimal fragment of the vaulted night above that the day's violence used to shrink into an insignificance which effected in its way their purification. However rude and savage their companions, it was impossible to eliminate the gift they offered of human companionship in these desolate tracts of mountainous country. In the stormy darkness they would listen with a kind of affection to the breathing of the ponies and to the broken murmurs of conversation between rider and rider all round them. There was always something of sympathy in the touch of a sheepskin coat, something of a wistful consolation in the flicker of a lighted cigarette, something of tenderness in the offer of a water-flask; and when the moon shone frostily overhead so that all the company was visible, there was never far away an emotion of wonder at their very selves being a part of this hurrying silver cavalcade, a wonder that easily was merged in gratitude for so much beauty after so much horror.

For Sylvia there was above everything the joy of seeing Michael growing stronger from day to day, and upon this joy her mind fed itself and forgot that she had ever imagined a greater joy beyond. Her contentment may have been of a piece with her indifference to the sacked villages and murdered Serbs; but she put away from her the certainty of the journey's end and surrendered to the entrancing motion through these winds of Thrace rattling and battling southward to the sea.

And now the journey was over. Sylvia knew by the tone of Rakoff's voice that she and Michael must soon shift for themselves. She wondered if he meant to hint his surprise at their not having made an attempt to do so already, and she tried to recall any previous occasion when they would have been justified in supposing that they were intended to escape from the escort. She could not remember that Rakoff had ever before given an impression of expecting to be rid of them, and fancy came into her head that perhaps he did not mean them to escape at all, that he had merely taken them along with him to wile away his time until he was bored with them. So insistent was the fancy that she looked up to see if any comitadjis were being despatched toward the Bulgarian lines, and when at that moment Rakoff did give some order to four of his men she decided that her instinct had not been at fault. Some of her apprehension must have betrayed itself in her face, for she saw Rakoff looking at her curiously, and to her first fancy succeeded another more instantly alarming that he would give orders for Michael and herself to be killed now. He might have chosen this way to gratify Ziska: no doubt it would be a very gratifying spectacle, and possibly something less passively diverting than a spectacle for that fierce doll. Sylvia was not really terrified by the prospect in her imagination; in a way she was rather attracted to it. Her dramatic sense took hold of the scene, and she found herself composing a last duologue between Michael and herself. Presumably Rakoff would be gentleman enough to have them killed decently by a firing party; he would not go farther toward gratifying Ziska than by allowing her to take a rifle with the rest. She decided that she should decline to let her eyes be bandaged; though she paused for a moment before the ironical pleasure of using her golden shawl to veil the approach of death. She should turn to Michael when they stood against a rock in the dawn, and when the rifles were levelled she should tell him that she had loved him since they had met at the masquerade in Redcliffe Hall and walked home through the fog of the Fulham Road to Mulberry Cottage. But had Mulberry Cottage ever existed?

At this moment Michael whispered to her a question so absurdly redolent of the problems of real life and yet so ridiculous somehow in present surroundings that all gloomy fancies floated away on laughter.

'Sylvia, it's quite obvious that he expects us to make a bolt for the Greek frontier as soon as possible. How much do you think I ought to tip each of these fellows?'

'I'm not very well versed in country-house manners,' Sylvia laughed, 'but I was always under the impression that one tipped the head gamekeeper and did not bother oneself about the local poachers.'

'But it does seem wrong somehow to slip away in the darkness without a word of thanks,' Michael said with a smile. 'I really can't help liking these ruffians.'

At that moment Rakoff stepped forward into their conversation.

'I'm going to ride over to our lines presently,' he announced. 'You'd better come with me, and you'll not be much more than a few hundred metres from the Greek outposts. The Greek soldiers wear khaki. You won't be called upon to give any explanations.'

Michael began to thank him, but the Bulgarian waved aside his words.

'You are included in the fulfilment of an obligation, *monsieur*, and being still in debt to *mademoiselle* I should be embarrassed by any expression from her of gratitude. Come, it is time for supper.'

Throughout the meal, which was eaten in a ruined chapel, Rakoff talked of his rose-gardens, and Sylvia fancied that he was trying to reproduce in her mind her first impression of him in order to make this last meal seem but the real conclusion of their long railway journey together. She wondered if Ziska knew that this was the last meal and if she approved her leader's action in helping two enemies to escape. However, it was waste of time to speculate about Ziska's feelings: she had no feelings: she was nothing but a finely perfected instrument of destruction; and Sylvia nodded a casual good-night to her when supper was over, turning round to take a final glance at her bending over her rifle in the dim tumbledown chapel, as she might have looked back at some inanimate object which had momentarily caught her attention in a museum.

They rode downhill most of the way toward the Bulgarian lines, and about two hours after midnight saw the tents like mushrooms under the light of a hazy and decrescent moon.

'Here we bid one another farewell,' said Rakoff reining up.

In the humid stillness they sat pensive for a little while listening to the ponies nuzzling for grass, tasting in the night the nearness of the sea and straining for the shimmer of it upon the southern horizon.

'*Merci, monsieur, adieu,*' Michael said.

'*Merci, monsieur, vous avez été plus que gentil pour nous. Adieu,*' Sylvia continued.

'*Enchanté,*' the Bulgarian murmured: Michael and Sylvia dismounted 'Keep well south of those tents and the moon over your right shoulders. You are about three kilometres from the shore. The sentries should be easy enough to avoid. We are not yet at war with Greece.'

He laughed, and spurred away in the direction of the Bulgarian tents; Michael and Sylvia walked silently toward freedom across a broken country where the dwarfed trees like the dwarfed Bulgarians themselves seemed fit only for savage hours and pathetically out of keeping with this tranquil night. They had walked for about half-an-hour, when from the cover of a belt of squat pines they saw ahead of them two figures easily recognisable as Greek soldiers.

'Shall we hail them?' Sylvia whispered.

'No, we'll keep them in view. I'm sure we haven't crossed the frontier yet. We'll slip across in their wake. They'd be worse than useless to us if we're not on the right side of the frontier.'

The Greeks disappeared over the brow of a small hill; when Sylvia and Michael reached the top they saw that they had entered what looked like a guard-house at the foot of the slope at the farther side.

'Perhaps we've crossed the frontier without knowing it,' Michael suggested.

Sylvia thought it was imprudent to make any attempt to find out for certain; but he was obstinately determined to explore and

237

she had to wait in a torment of anxiety while he worked his way downhill and took the risk of peeping through a loophole at the back of the building. Presently he came back crawling up the hill on all fours until he was beside her again.

'Most extraordinary thing,' he declared. 'Our friend Rakoff is in there with two or three Bulgarian officers. The fellows we saw *were* Greeks – one is an officer, the other is a corporal. The officer is pointing out various spots on a large map. Of course one says "traitor" at first, but traitors don't go attended by corporals. I can't make it out. However, it's clear that we're still in Bulgaria.'

'Oh, do let's go on and leave it behind us,' Sylvia pleaded nervously.

But Michael argued the advisableness of waiting until the Greeks came out and of using them as guides to their own territory.

'But if they're traitors, they won't welcome us,' she objected.

'Oh, they can't be traitors. It must be some military business that they're transacting.'

In the end they decided to wait; after about an hour the Greeks emerged, passing once more the belt of pines where Sylvia and Michael were waiting in concealment. They allowed the visitors to get a long enough lead, and then followed them, hurrying up inclines while they were covered and lying down on the summits to watch their guides' direction. They had been moving like this for some time and were waiting above the steep bank of a ravine, the stony bed of which the Greeks were crossing, when suddenly the corporal leaped on the back of the officer, who fell in a heap. The corporal rose, looked down at the prostrate form for a moment, then knelt beside him and began to perform some laborious operation, which was invisible to the watchers. At last he stood upright and with outstretched fingers flung a malediction at the body, kicking it contemptuously; then with a gesture of despair to the sky he collapsed against a boulder and began to weep loudly.

Sylvia had seen enough violence in the last month to accept the murder of one Greek officer as a mere incident on such a night; but somehow she was conscious of a force of passion behind the corporal's action that lifted it far above her recent experience of bloodshed. She paused to see if Michael was going to think the same, unwilling to let her emotion run away with her now in such a way as to deprive them of making use of the deed for their own purpose. Michael lay on the brow of the cliff, gazing in perplexity

at the man below whose form shook with sobs in the grey moonlight and whose victim seemed already nothing more important
than one of the stones in the rocky bed of the ravine.

'I'm hanged if I know what to do,' Michael whispered at last.

'Personally,' Sylvia whispered back, 'it's almost worth while to
spend the rest of our life in a Bulgarian prison-camp, if we can
only find out the meaning of this murder.'

'Yes, I was rather coming to that conclusion,' he agreed.

'Don't think me absurd,' she went on hurriedly. 'But I've got
a quite definite fancy that he's going to play an important part
in our escape. Would you mind if I went down and spoke to
him?'

'No, I'll go,' Michael said. 'You don't know Greek.'

'Do you?' she retorted.

'No. But he might be alarmed and attack you.'

'He'll be less likely to attack a gentle female voice,' Sylvia
argued; and before Michael could say another word, she began
to slide down the side of the gully, repeating very quickly 'Don't
make a noise, we're English,' laughing at herself for the probable
uselessness of the explanation, and yet all the time laughing with
an inward conviction that there was nothing to fear from the
encounter.

The corporal jumped up and held high his bayonet, which was
gleaming black with moonlit blood.

'English?' he repeated doubtfully in a nasal voice.

'Yes, English prisoners escaped from the Bulgarians,' she
panted as she reached him.

'That's all right,' said the corporal. 'You got nothing to be
frightened of. I'm an American citizen from New York City.'

Sylvia called to Michael to come down, whereupon the
corporal took hold of her wrist and reminded her that they were
still in Bulgaria.

'Don't you start hollering so loud,' he said severely.

She apologised, and presently Michael reached them.

'Wal, mister,' said the Greek. 'I guess you saw me kill that
dog. Come and look at him.'

He turned the dead man's face to the moon. On the forehead,
on the chin, and on each cheek the flesh had been sliced away to
from Π'.

'Προδότης,' explained the corporal. 'Traitor in American. I'm
an American citizen, but I'm a Greek man too. I fought in the
last war and was in Thessaloniki. I killed four Toiks and nine

239

Voulgars in the last war. See here?' He pointed to the pale blue ribbons on his chest. 'I went to New York and was in a shoe-shine parlour. Then I learnt the barber-shop. I was doing well. Then I come home and fought the Toiks. Then I fought the Voulgars. Then I went back to New York. Then last September come the mobilising to fight them again. Yes, mister, I put my razor in my pocket and come over to Piræus. I didn't care for submarines. Hundreds of Greek mens come with me to fight the Voulgars. The Greek mens hate the Voulgars. But things is differ-ent this time. They was telling tales how our officers was chummy with the Voulgar officers. I didn't believe it. Not me. But it was true. With my own eyes I see this dog showing the plans of Rupel and other forts. With my own ears I heard this sunnavabitch telling the Voulgars the Greek mens wouldn't fight. My heart swelled up like a water-melon. My eyes was bursting and I cursed him inside of me saying, "I wish your brains for to become beans in your head." But when he was alone I thought of what big mens the Greeks was in old times, and I said to him " κύριε λόχαγε," which is Mister Captain in American, "what means this what we have done tonight?" And he says to me, "It means the Greek mens ain't going to fight for Venizelo who is a Senegalese and προδότης of his country. And he cursed the French and cursed the British and he said that the Voulgars must be let drive them into the sea. But I said nothing. I just spit. Then after a bit I said " κύριε λόχαγε ", does the other officers think like you was?" And he says all Greek mens what is not traitors think like him, and if I tell him who is for Venizelo in our regiment I will be a sergeant good and quick. But I didn't say nothing: I am only spitting to myself. Then we come to this place, and my heart was busting out of my body, and I killed him. Then I took my razor and marked his face for a προδότης.'

The corporal threw up his arms to heaven in denunciation of the dead man. They asked him what he would do, and he told them that he should hide on his own native island of Samothrace until he could be an interpreter to an English ship at Mudros or until Greece should turn upon the Bulgarians and free his soul from the stain of the captain's treachery.

'Can you help us to get to Samothrace?' they asked.

'Yes, I can help you. But what you have seen tonight swear not to tell, for I am crying like a woman for my country; and other peoples and mens must not laugh at Hellas, because tonight this σκυλάκι this dog, has had the moon for eats.'

'And how shall we get to Samothrace?' they asked, when they had promised their silence.

'I will find a caique and you will hide by the sea where I show you. We cannot go back over the river to Greece. But how much can you pay for the caique? Fifty dollars? There are Greek fishmens, sure, who was going to take us.'

Michael at once agreed to the price.

'Then it will be easy,' said the corporal, after he had calculated his own profit under the transaction.

'And ten dollars for yourself,' Michael added.

'I don't want nothing out of it myself,' the corporal declared indignantly; but after a minute's hesitation he told them that he did not think it would be possible to hire the caique for less than sixty dollars, and looked sad when Michael did not try to contest the higher figure.

They had started to walk seaward along the bed of the ravine, when the corporal ran back with an exclamation of contempt to where the dead officer was lying.

'If I ain't dippy,' he laughed. 'Gee! I 'most forgot to see what was in his pockets.'

He made up for the oversight by a thorough search and came back presently, smiling and slipping the holster of the officer's revolver on his own belt. Then he patted his own pockets, which were bulging with what he had found, and they walked forward in silence. The end of the ravine brought them to an exposed upland, which they crossed warily, flitting from stunted tree to stunted tree, because the moonlight was seeming too bright here for safety. The upland gave place to sandy dunes, the hollows of which were marshy and made the going difficult; but the night was breathless and not a leaf stirred in the oleander thickets to alarm their progress.

'Not much wind for sailing,' Michael murmured.

'That's all right,' said the corporal, whose name was Yanni Psaradelis. 'If we find a caique, we can wait for the wind.'

Sylvia was puzzled by Rakoff's not having said a word about any river to cross at the frontier. She wondered if he had salved his loyalty thereby, counting upon their recapture, or if by chance they were to get away throwing the blame on providence. Yet had he time for such subtleties? It was hard to think he had, but by Yanni's account of the river it seemed improbable that they would ever have escaped without his help, and it was certainly strange that Rakoff if his benevolence had been genuine should not have warned them. And now actually the dunes were dipping to the sea; on a simultaneous impulse they ran down the last sandy slope and knelt upon the beach by the edge of the tide, scooping up the water as though it were of gold.

'Say, that's not the way to go escaping from the Voulgars,' Yanni told them reproachfully. 'We've got to go slow and keep out of sight.'

The beach was very narrow and sloped rapidly up to low cliffs of sand continually broken by wide drifts and water-courses; but they were high enough to mask the moonlight if one kept close under their lea, and one's footsteps were muffled by the sand. They must have walked in this fashion for a couple of miles when Yanni stopped them with a gesture and bending down picked up the cork of a fishing-net and an old shoe.

'Guess there's folk around here,' he whispered. 'I'm going to see. You sit down and rest yourselves.'

He walked on cautiously; the sandy cliffs apparently tumbled away to a flat country almost at once, for Yanni's figure lost the protection of their shadow and came into view like a grey ghost in the now completely clouded moonlight. Presumably they were standing near the edge of the marshy estuary of the river between Bulgaria and Greece.

'How will he explain himself to any of the enemy on guard?' Sylvia whispered.

'He must have had the countersign to get across earlier tonight,' Michael replied.

'It's nearly five o'clock,' she said. 'We haven't got so very much longer before dawn.'

They waited for ages, it seemed, before Yanni came back and told them that there was no likelihood of getting a caïque on this side of the river, but that he should cross over in a boat and take the chance of finding one on the farther beach before his captain's absence was remarked. He should have to be careful because the Greek sentries would be men from his own regiment and his presence so far down the line might arouse suspicion.

'But if you find a caïque, how are we going to get across the river to join you?' Michael asked.

'Say, give me twenty dollars,' Yanni answered after a minute's thought. 'The fish-mens won't do nothing for me unless I show them the money first. I'll say two British peoples want to go Thaso. We can give them more when we're on the sea to go Samothraki. They'd be afraid to go Samothraki at first. You must go back to where we come down to the sea. Got me? Hide in the bushes all day and before the φεγγάρι, what is it, before the moon is beginning tomorrow night, come right down to the beach and strike one match; then wait till you see me, but not till after the moon is beginning. If I don't come tomorrow, go back and hide and come right down the next night till the moon is beginning. And if I don't come the next night –' he stopped. 'Sure, Yanni will be dead.'

Michael gave him five sovereigns; he walked quickly away, and the fugitives turned on their traces in the sand.

'Do you feel any doubt about him?' Sylvia whispered after a spell of silence.

'About his honesty? Not in the least. If he can come, he will come.'

'That's what I think.'

They found by their old footprints the gap in the cliffs through which they had first descended and took the precaution of scrambling farther along so that there should remain only the marks of their descent. In the first oleander thicket they hid themselves by lying flat on the marshy ground; so tired were they that they both fell asleep until they were awakened by morning and a drench of rain.

'One feels more secluded and safe somehow in such weather,' said Sylvia with an attempt at optimism.

'Yes, and we've got a box of Turkish-delight,' said Michael.

'Turkish-delight?' she repeated in astonishment.

'Yes, one of Rakoff's men gave it to me about a week ago, and I kept it with a vague notion of its bringing us luck or something. Besides, another thing in the rain's favour is that it serves as a kind of bath.'

'A very complete bath, I should say,' laughed Sylvia.

They ate Turkish-delight at intervals during that long day when not for a single moment did the rain cease to fall. Sylvia told Michael about the Earl's Court Exhibition and Mabel Bannerman.

'I remember a girl called Mabel who used to sell Turkish-delight there, but she had a stall of her own.'

'So did my Mabel the year afterwards,' she said.

Soon they decided it must be the same Mabel. Sylvia thought what a good opening this was to tell Michael some of her more intimate experiences, but she dreaded that he would in spite of himself show his distaste for that early life of hers, and she could not bear the idea of creating such an atmosphere now – or in the future, she thought with a sigh. Nevertheless, she did begin an apostrophe against the past, but he cut her short.

'The past? What does the past matter? Without a past, my dear Sylvia, you would have no present.'

'And after all,' she thought, 'he knows already I have a past.'

Once their hands met by accident, and Michael withdrew his with a quickness that mortified her, so that she simulated a deep preoccupation in order to hide her chagrin, for she had outgrown her capacity to sting back with bitter words, and could only await the slow return of her composure before she could talk naturally again.

'But never mind, the adventure is drawing to a close,' she told herself, 'and he'll soon be rid of me.'

Then he began to talk again about their damned relationship and to speculate upon the extent of Stella's surprise when she should hear about it.

'I think, you know, when I was young,' Michael said presently, 'that I must have been rather like your husband. I'm sure I should have fallen in love with you and married you.'

'You couldn't have been in the least like him,' she contradicted angrily.

For a moment, so poignant in its revelation of a divine possibility as to stop her heart while it lasted, Sylvia fancied that he seemed disappointed at her abrupt disposal of the notion that he might have loved her. But even as the thought was born, it died upon his offer of another piece of Turkish-delight and of his saying:

'I *think* it's time for the eighth piece each.'

So that was the calculation he had been making, unless indeed their proximity and solitude through this long day in the face of danger had induced in him a sentimental desire to express an affection born of a conventional instinct to accord with favouring circumstance, bred of a kind of pity for a wasted situation. If that were so, she must be more than ever careful of her pride; and for the rest of the day she kept the conversation to politics, forcing it away from any topic that in the least concerned them personally.

A night of intense blackness and heavy rain succeeded that long day in the oleander thicket. Moonrise could not be expected by their reckoning much before three in the morning. The wet hours dragged so interminably that prudence was sacrificed to a longing for action; feeling that it was impossible to lie here any longer, sodden, hungry, and apprehensive, they decided to go down to the beach and strike the first match at midnight and notwithstanding the risk to strike matches every half-hour. The first match evoked no response; but the splash of the little waves broke the monotony of the rain, and the sand, wet though it was, came as a relief after the slime in which they had been lying for eighteen hours. The second match gained no answering signal, neither did the third nor the fourth. They consoled themselves by whispering that Yannie had arranged his rescue for the hour before moonrise. The fifth and sixth matches flamed and went out in dreary ineffectiveness; so thick was the darkness over the sea it began to seem unimaginable for anything to happen out there. Suddenly Michael whispered that he could hear the clumping of oars and struck the seventh match. There was silence; then the oars definitely grew louder; a faint whistle came over the water: the darkness before them became tremulous with a hint of life, and their straining eyes tried to fancy the outline of a boat standing off from the shore. Presently low voices were audible; then the noise of a falling plank and a hurried oath for someone's clumsiness; a little boat grounded, and Yanni jumped out.

'Quick,' he breathed. 'I believe I heard footsteps coming right down to the shore.'

They pushed off the boat; and when they were about twenty strokes from the beach, what seemed after so much whispering and stillness a demoniac shout rent the darkness inland. Yanni and the fishermen beside him pulled now without regard for the noise of the oars; they could hear the sound of people's sliding down the cliff; there were more shouts, and a rifle flashed.

'Those Voulgars,' Yanni panted, 'won't do nothing except holler. They can't see us.'

Another rifle banged, and Sylvia was thrilled by the way their escape was conforming to the rules of the game; she revelled in the confused sounds of anger and pursuit on land.

'They don't know where we are,' laughed Yanni.

But the noise of the fugitives scrambling on board the caique and the hoisting of the little boat brought round them a shower of bullets, the splash of which was heard above the rain. One of these broke a jar of wine, and every man aboard bent to the long oars, driving the perfumed caique deeper into the darkness.

'I had a funny time getting this caique,' Yanni explained, when with some difficulty he had been dissuaded from firing his late captain's revolver at the country of Bulgaria, by this time at least two miles away. 'I didn't have no difficulty to get across, but I had to walk half-way to Cavalla before I found the old fish-man who owns this caique. I told him two British people

wanted him and he says "are them Mr B's fellows for Cavalla?"
I didn't know who Mr B was anyway, so I says "Sure, they're
Mr B's fellows," but when we got off at dusk, he says his orders
was for Porto Lagos and to let go the little boat when he could
hear a bird calling. He didn't give a dern for no matches. Wal,
Mr B's fellows didn't answer from round about Lagos, and he
said bad words and how it was three days too soon and who in
hell did I think I was anyway telling him Mr B's fellows was
waiting. So I told him there was a mistake somewheres and
asked him what about taking you Thaso for twenty dollars. We
talked for a bit and he said "Yes". Now we got to make him go
Samothraki.'

At this point the captain of the caique, a brown and shrivelled
old man seeming all the more shrivelled in the full-seated
breeches of the Greek islander, joined them below for an
argument with Yanni that sounded more than usually acrimoni-
ous and voluble. When it was finished, the captain had agreed,
subject to a windy moonrise, to land them at Samothraki on
payment of another ten pounds in gold. They went on deck and
sat astern, for the rain was over now. A slim rusty moon was
creeping out of the sea and conjuring from the darkness forward
the shadowy bulk of Thasos; presently with isolated puffs that
frilled the surface of the water like the wings of alighting birds
the wind began to blow; the long oars were shipped, and the
crew set the curved mainsail that crouched in a defiant bow
against whatever onslaught might prepare itself; from every
mountain gorge in Thrace the northern blasts rushed down with
life for the stagnant sea, and life for the dull decrescent moon,
which in a spray of stars they drove glittering up the sky.

'How gloriously everything hums and gurgles,' Sylvia shouted
in Michael's ear. 'When shall we get to Samothrace?'

He shrugged his shoulders and leant over to Yanni, who told
them that it might be about midday if the wind held like this.

For all Sylvia's exultation, the vision of enchanted space that
seemed to forbid sleep on such a night soon faded from her
consciousness, and she did not rouse herself from dreams until
dawn was scattering its roses and violets to the wind.

'I simply can't shave,' Michael declared, 'but Samothrace is in
sight.'

The sun was rising in a fume of spindrift and fine gold, when
Sylvia scrambled forward into the bows. Huddled upon a coil
of wet rope, she first saw Samothrace faintly relucent like an
uncut sapphire, where already it towered upon the horizon,

though there might be thirty thundering miles between.

'I'm glad we ended our adventure with this glorious sea race,' shouted Michael, who had joined her in the bows. 'Are you feeling quite all right?'

She nodded indignantly.

'See how grey the sky is now,' he went on. 'It's going to blow even harder, and they're shortening sail.'

They looked aft to where the crew, whose imprecations were only visible so loud was the drumming of the wind, were getting down the mainsail; and presently they were running east-south-east under a small jib, with the wind roaring upon the port quarter and the waves champing at the taffrail. It did not strike either of them that there was any reason to be anxious until Yanni came forward with a frightened yellow face and said that the captain was praying to St Nicholas in the cabin below.

'Samothraki bad place to go,' Yanni told them dismally. 'Many fish-mens drowned there.'

A particularly violent squall shrieked assent to his forebodings, and the helmsman looking over his shoulder crossed himself as the squall left them and tore ahead, decapitating the waves in its course so that the surface of the water blown into an appearance of smoothness resembled the powdery damascene of ice in a skater's track.

'It's terrible, ain't it?' Yanni moaned.

'Cheer up,' Michael said. 'I'm looking forward to your shaving me before lunch in your native island.'

'We shan't never come Samothraki,' Yanni said. 'And I can't pray no more somehows since I went away to America. Else I'd go and pray along with the captain. Supposing I was to give a silver ship to the παναγία in Teno, would you lend me the money for the workmens to do it?'

'I'll pay half,' Michael volunteered. 'A silver ship to Our Lady of Tenos,' he explained to Sylvia.

'Gee!' Yanni shouted more cheerfully .'I'm going to pray some right now. I guess when I get kneeling the trick'll come back to me. I did so much kneeling in New York to shine boots that I used to lie in bed on a Sunday. But this goddam storm's regular making my knees itch.'

He hurried aft in a panic of religious devotion, whither Michael and Sylvia presently followed him in the hope of coffee. Everyone on board except the helmsman was praying, and there was no sign of fire; even the sacred flame before St Nicholas had gone out. The cabin was in a confusion of supplicating mariners prostrate amid onions, oranges, and cheese; the very cockroaches seemed to listen anxiously in the wild motion. The helmsman was not steering too well or else the sea was growing wilder, for once or twice a stream of water poured down the companion and drenched the occupants, until at last the captain rushed on deck to curse the offender, calling down upon his head the pains of hell should they sink and he be drowned.

Michael and Sylvia found the most sheltered spot in the caique and ate some cheese. The terror of the crew had reacted upon their spirits; the groaning of the wind in the shrouds, the seething of the waves, and the frightened litany below quenched their exultation and silenced their laughter.

Yanni, more yellow than ever, came up and asked Michael if he would mind paying the captain now.

'He says he don't believe he can get into port, but if he can't, he's going to try and get around on the south side of Samothraki, only he'd like to have his money in case anything should happen.'

Three hours tossed themselves free from time; and now in all its majesty and in all its menace the island rose dark before them, girdled with foam and crowned with snow above six thousand feet of chasms, gorges, cliffs, and forests.

'What a fearful leeshore,' Michael exclaimed with a shudder.

'Yes, but with a sublime form,' Sylvia cried. 'At any rate to be wrecked on such a coast is not a mean death.'

Yanni explained that the only port of the island lay on this side of the low-lying promontory that ran out to sea on their starboard bow. In order to make this the captain would have to beat up to windward first, which with the present fury of the gale and so lofty a coast was impossible. The captain evidently came to the same conclusion, though at first it looked as if he had changed his mind too late to avoid running the caique ashore before he could gain the southerly lee of the island. Sylvia held her breath when the mast lost itself against the darkness of land and breathed again when anon it stood out clear against the sky. Yet so frail seemed the caique in relation to the vast bulk before them that it was incredible this haunt of Titans should not exact another sacrifice.

'I think, as we get nearer, the mast shows itself less often against the sky,' Sylvia shouted to Michael.

'About equal, I think,' he shouted back.

Certainly the caique still laboured on, and it might be that after all they would clear the promontory and gain shelter.

'Do you know what I'm thinking of?' Michael yelled.

She shook her head, blinking in the spray.

'The Round Pond!' he yelled again.

'I can't imagine that even the Round Pond's really calm at present,' she shouted back.

Suddenly astern there was a cry of despair that rose high above the howling of the wind; the tiller had broken, and immediately the prow of the caique swerving away from the sky drove straight for the shore. Two men leapt forward to cut the ropes of the jib, which flapped madly aloft; then it gave itself to the wind and danced before them till it was no more than a gull's wing against dark and mighty Samothrace.

The caique rocked alarmingly until the oars steadied her; the strength of the rowers endured long enough to clear the promontory, but unfortunately the expected shelter on the other side proved to be an illusion, and though a new tiller had been provided by this time, it was impossible for the exhausted men to do their part. The caique began to ship water, so heavily indeed that the captain gave orders to run her ashore where the sand of a narrow cove glimmered between huge towers of rock. The beaching would have been effected safely, had it not been for a sunken reef that ripped out the bottom of the caique, which crumpled up and shrieked her horror like a live sentient thing. Sylvia found herself, after she had rolled in a dizzy switchback from the summit of one wave to another, clinging head downward to a slippery ledge of rock, her fingers in a mush of sea-anemones, her feet wedged in a crevice; then another wave lifted her off and she was swept over and over in green somersaults of foam, until there came a blow as from a hammer, a loud roaring, and silence.

When Sylvia recovered consciousness, she was lying on a sandy slope with Michael's arms round her.

'Was I drowned?' she asked; then commonsense added itself to mere consciousness and she began to laugh. 'I don't mean actually, but nearly?'

'No, I think you hit your head rather a thump on the beach. You've only been lying here about twenty minutes.'

'And Yanni and the captain and the crew?'

'They all got safely ashore. Rather cut about of course, but nothing serious. Yanni and the captain are arguing whether Our Lady of Tenos or St Nicholas is responsible for saving our lives. The others are making a fire.

She tried to sit up; but her head was going round, and she fell back.

'Keep quiet,' Michael told her. 'We're in a narrow sandy cove from which a gorge runs up into the heart of the mountains. There's a convenient cave higher up full of dried grass – a goatherd's I suppose, and when the fire's alight the others are going to scramble across somehow to the village and send a guide for us tomorrow. There won't be time before dark tonight. Do you mind being left for a few minutes?'

She smiled her contentment, and closing her eyes listened to the echoes of human speech among the rocks above, and to the beating of the surf below.

Presently Yanni and Michael appeared in order to carry her up to the cave; but she found herself easily able to walk with the help of an arm, and Michael told Yanni to hurry off to the village.

Sylvia and he were soon left alone on the parapet of smoke-blackened earth in front of the cave, whence they watched the sailors toiling up the gorge in search of a track over the mountain. Then they took off nearly all their clothes and wandered about in overcoats, breaking off boughs of juniper to feed the fire for their drying.

'Nothing to eat but cheese,' Michael laughed. 'Our diet since we left Rakoff has always run to excess of one article. Still, cheese is more nutritious than Turkish-delight, and there's plenty of water in that theatrical cascade. The wind is dropping; though in any case we shouldn't feel it here.'

Shortly before sunset the gorge echoed with liquid tinklings, and an aged goatherd appeared with his flock of brown sheep and tawny goats, which with the help of a wild-eyed boy he penned in another big cave on the opposite side. Then he joined Sylvia and Michael at their fire and gave them an unintelligible, but obviously cordial salutation; after which he entered what was evidently his dwelling place and came out with bottles of wine and fresh cheese. He did not seem in any way surprised by their presence in his solitude, and when darkness fell he and the boy piped ancient tunes in the firelight until they all lay down on heaps of dry grass. Sylvia remained awake for a long while in a harmony of distant waves and falling water and of sudden restless tinklings from the penned flock. In the morning the old man gave them milk and made them a stately farewell; he and his goats and his boy disappeared up the gorge for the day's pasturage in a jangling tintinnabulation that became fainter and fainter,

250

until the last and most melodious bells tinkled at rare intervals far away in the dim heart of the mountain.

The cove and the gorge were still in deep shadow; but on the slopes above toward the east bright sunlight was hanging the trees with emeralds beneath a blue sky, and seaward the halcyon had lulled the waves for her azure nesting.

'Can't we get up into the sunlight?' Michael proposed.

For all the sparkling airs above them, it was chilly enough down here, and they were glad to scramble up through thickets of holm-oak, arbutus, and aromatic scrub to a grassy peak in the sun's eye. Here not even the buzzing of an insect broke the warm wintry peace of the South, and it was hard to think that the restless continent of Asia was lapped by that tender and placid sea below. The dark blue wavy line of Imbros and the dove-grey bulk of Lemnos were the only islands in sight, though like lines of cloud upon the horizon they could fancy the cliffs of Gallipilo and hear, so breathless was the calm, the faint grumbling of the guns.

'It was in Samothrace they set up the Winged Victory,' Michael said. Then suddenly he turned to Sylvia and took her hand. 'My dear, when I dragged you up the beach yesterday I thought you were dead, and I cursed myself for a coward because I had let you die without telling you. Sylvia, this adventure of ours, need it ever stop?'

'Everything comes to an end,' she sighed.

'Except one thing – and that sets all the rest going again.'

'What is your magic key?'

'Sylvia, I'm afraid to ask you to marry me, but will you?'

She stared at him; then she saw his eyes, and for a long while she was crying in his arms with happiness.

'My dear, my dear, you've lost your yellow shawl in the wreck.'

'The mermaids can have it,' she murmured. 'I shall wrap up the rest of my memories in you.'

Then she stopped in sudden affright.

'But, Michael, how can I marry you? I haven't told you anything really about myself.'

'Foolish one, you've told me everything that matters in these two months of the most perfect companionship possible for human beings.'

'Companionship?' she echoed, looking at him fiercely. 'And cousinship, eh?'

'No, no, my dear, you can't frighten me any longer,' he laughed. 'Surely telling things belongs to the companionship of

251

a life together – love has no words except when one is still very young and eloquent.'

'But, Michael,' she went on, 'all these nine years of mystical speculation, are they going to end in the commonplace of marriage?'

'It won't be commonplace, and besides the war isn't over yet, and after the war there will be an empty world to fill with all we have learnt. Ah, how poor old Guy would have loved to fill it with his Spanish castles.'

'It seems wrong for us two up here to be so happy', Sylvia sighed.

'This is just a halcyon day, but there will soon be stormy days again.'

'You mean you'll go back now to –' she stopped in a desperate apprehension. 'But of course, we can't live for ever in these days of war between a blue sky and a blue sea. Yet somehow, oh, my dearest and dearest, I don't believe I shall lose *you*.'

Like birds calling to one another, in the green thickets far away two bells tinkled their monotone; and a small grey craft flying the white ensign glided over the charmed sea toward Samothrace.

THE INHERITORS
by Harold Robbins

They are a new breed of world conquerors – jet-soaring
buccaneers who have carved the youngest and wealthiest
empire in the world today: the communications industry.
Though their imperial domain is still in its infancy, it
already wields influence so vast and commands riches so
staggering that it has come to dominate a proud and
powerful nation.

   Only Harold Robbins could have written the towering
trilogy that began with THE DREAM MERCHANTS,
continued with THE CARPETBAGGERS and now reaches
a magnificent climax with THE INHERITORS.

NEW ENGLISH LIBRARY   60p

THE KAYWANA TRILOGY

by Edgar Mittelholzer

The bloody and horrifying saga of a slave empire

Edgar Mittelholzer has created three sensational and magnificent novels set in the West Indies slave plantations during the seventeenth century. CHILDREN OF KAYWANA, KAYWANA STOCK and KAYWANA BLOOD tell the panoramic story of a kingdom built on the backs of slaves, in all its cruelty, violent passion and tyranny. The KAYWANA TRILOGY teems with unforgettable characters and incidents, leaving out no aspect of the lives of men and women trapped amid the heat, the terrors and the smouldering frenzy of brutalised slaves.

'Mittelholzer is a writer with a frightening power of description and a mature sense of character.'
—**Daily Telegraph**

'Carries the reader along from horror to horror at a breath-taking gallop, and the resulting pictures of colonists fighting against primitive conditions and becoming degenerate is unforgettable.'
—**Time and Tide**

CHILDREN OF KAYWANA   37½p
KAYWANA STOCK   37½p
KAYWANA BLOOD   37½p

NEW ENGLISH LIBRARY

NEL BESTSELLERS

Science Fiction

W002 839	SPACE FAMILY STONE	*Robert Heinlein*	30p
W002 844	STRANGER IN A STRANGE LAND	*Robert Heinlein*	60p
W002 630	THE MAN WHO SOLD THE MOON	*Robert Heinlein*	30p
W002 386	PODKAYNE OF MARS	*Robert Heinlein*	30p
W002 449	THE MOON IS A HARSH MISTRESS	*Robert Heinlein*	40p
W002 754	DUNE	*Frank Herbert*	60p
W002 911	SANTAROGA BARRIER	*Frank Herbert*	30p
W002 641	NIGHT WALK	*Bob Shaw*	25p
W002 716	SHADOW OF HEAVEN	*Bob Shaw*	25p

War

W002 686	DEATH OF A REGIMENT	*John Foley*	30p
W002 484	THE FLEET THAT HAD TO DIE	*Richard Hough*	25p
W002 805	HUNTING OF FORCE Z	*Richard Hough*	30p
W002 494	P.Q. 17—CONVOY TO HELL	*Lund Ludlam*	25p
W002 423	STRIKE FROM THE SKY—THE BATTLE OF BRITAIN		
	STORY	*Alexandra McKee*	30p
W002 768	THE WAR RUNNERS	*Wilfred McNeilly*	25p
W002 471	THE STEEL COCOON	*Bentz Plagemann*	25p
W002 831	NIGHT	*Francis Pollini*	40p

Western
Walt Slade—Bestsellers

W002 634	THE SKY RIDERS	*Bradford Scott*	20p
W002 648	OUTLAW ROUNDUP	*Bradford Scott*	20p
W002 649	RED ROAD OF VENGEANCE	*Bradford Scott*	20p
W002 669	BOOM TOWN	*Bradford Scott*	20p
W002 687	THE RIVER RAIDERS	*Bradford Scott*	20p

General

W002 420	THE SECOND SEX	*Simone De Beauvoir*	42½p
W002 234	SEX MANNERS FOR MEN	*Robert Chartham*	25p
W002 531	SEX MANNERS FOR ADVANCED LOVERS	*Robert Chartham*	25p
W002 766	SEX MANNERS FOR THE YOUNG GENERATION		
		Robert Chartham	25p
W002 835	SEX AND THE OVER FORTIES	*Robert Chartham*	30p
W002 367	AN ABZ OF LOVE	*Inge and Sten Hegeler*	60p
W002 369	A HAPPIER SEX LIFE (Illustrated)	*Dr. Sha Kokken*	60p
W002 136	WOMEN	*John Philip Lundin*	25p
W002 333	MISTRESSES	*John Philip Lundin*	25p
W002 299	PENTHOUSE SEXICON	*Frederick Mullaly*	25p
W002 859	SMOKEWATCHERS HOW-TO-QUIT BOOK		
		Smokewatchers Group	25p
W002 511	SEXUALIS '95	*Jacques Sternberg*	25p
W002 584	SEX MANNERS FOR SINGLE GIRLS	*Dr. G. Valensin*	25p
W002 592	THE FRENCH ART OF SEX MANNERS	*Dr. G. Valensin*	25p

Mad

S003 702	A MAD LOOK AT OLD MOVIES	25p
S003 523	BOILING MAD	25p
S003 496	THE MAD ADVENTURES OF CAPTAIN KLUTZ	25p
S003 719	THE QUESTIONABLE MAD	25p
S003 714	FIGHTING MAD	25p
S003 613	HOWLING MAD	25p
S003 477	INDIGESTIBLE MAD	25p
S004 163	THE MAD BOOK OF MAGIC	25p
S004 304	MAD ABOUT MAD	25p

NEL P.O. BOX 11, FALMOUTH, CORNWALL

Please send cheque or postal order. Allow 5p per book to cover
postage and packing (Overseas 6p per book).

Name...

Address ....

....

Title ....
(MARCH)